THE SEAT BESIDE ME

"Nancy Moser delivers a fast-paced, absorbing ~~story~~ ~~Seat Beside~~ Me. I didn't want to put it down!

ROBIN LEE HATCHER,

Ribbon of Years

"A powerfully dramatic story that ~~asks~~, *How many times have I been spared?* After re~~ading The~~ Seat Beside Me, you will never sit by a stranger without the realization that every encounter is God appointed."

VONETTE ZACHARY BRIGHT, cofounder Campus Crusade for Christ

"Her characters leap off the pages and into your heart. Hear me well…you will love this book."

LISA SAMSON, author of *The Church Ladies*

"Nancy Moser is a wonderful storyteller whose novels plumb the depths of spiritual issues. *The Seat Beside Me* is no exception. It will keep you reading—and stay with you long after the last page."

JAMES SCOTT BELL, author of *The Nephilim Seed*

"Vividly written, heart-wrenching drama that brings haunting TV footage to life. A powerful story of how lives are changed by a hero's heart."

DEBORAH BEDFORD, author of *A Rose by the Door* and *The Story Jar*

"A thought-provoking page-turner guaranteed to make you reevaluate your next 'chance encounter' along life's way."

MELODY CARLSON, award-winning author of
Diary of a Teenage Girl and *Blood Sisters*

"Delving deeply into the intricacies of the human heart, she shows us our own desperation—then illuminates us with the brilliance of God's beauty, which is visible only when we allow Him complete control."

HANNAH ALEXANDER, author of The Healing Touch series

"Intense. Intricate. Inspired…. Nancy Moser's *The Seat Beside Me.*"

LYN COTE, author of *Winter's Secret*

"A riveting, poignant page-turner that will not soon be forgotten. The next time I soar on silver wings, my eyes will be on the stranger in the seat beside me. And soaring into the clouds, I will remember that miracles still happen to ordinary people…miracles that give a fresh glimpse of God's glory."

DORIS ELAINE FELL, author of *Blue Mist on the Danube*

"*The Seat Beside Me* is skillfully and grippingly written. Nancy Moser forces her characters and, ultimately, her readers to face the fundamental question, Why am I here?"

DeAnna Julie Dodson, author of *By Love Redeemed* and *To Grace Surrendered*

"Nancy Moser is in top form with *The Seat Beside Me*.... An absolute winner!"

Deborah Raney, author of *Beneath a Southern Sky* and *A Vow to Cherish*

THE INVITATION

"The plot moves quickly and the literary style makes this book difficult to put down."

CHRISTIAN LIBRARY JOURNAL

"A fascinating tale of four different people who are called together for a mysterious purpose. Through their intriguing story and the suspenseful ending, Nancy Moser sends her own invitation to the reader, asking us to consider how God can use us—and all ordinary people—in the most extraordinary ways."

Florence Littauer, speaker and author of *Personality Plus* and *Silver Boxes*

THE QUEST

"*The Quest* mirrors a bit of Frank Peretti's books as we see the battle for good and evil come to the forefront."

CHRISTIAN LIBRARY JOURNAL

"Nancy weaves a fascinating story showing how God uses ordinary people in extraordinary ways. Get ready for a page-turner!"

Karen Kingsbury, bestselling author of
Halfway to Forever and *On Every Side*

THE TEMPTATION

"Nancy Moser deftly melds page-turning suspense with engaging characters and solid biblical truth. Along with the two prequels, *The Temptation* deserves shelf space with spiritual warfare classics like those of Frank Peretti!"

Cindy Swanson, producer/host of *Weekend Magazine* radio show, Rockford, IL

THE SEAT BESIDE ME

A NOVEL BY

NANCY MOSER

Multnomah® Publishers *Sisters, Oregon*

THE SEAT BESIDE ME
Published by Multnomah Publishers, Inc.
Published in association with the literary agency of Alive Communications, Inc.
7680 Goddard Street, Suite 200, Colorado Springs, CO 80920
© 2002 by Nancy Moser

International Standard Book Number: 1-57673-884-1

Cover image of airplane by Getty Images/Mark Wagner
Background cover image by Getty Images/Terje Rakke

Scripture quotations are from:
The Holy Bible, New International Version © 1973, 1984 by International
Bible Society, used by permission of Zondervan Publishing House.

Also quoted:
The Holy Bible, King James Version

Multnomah is a trademark of Multnomah Publishers, Inc.,
and is registered in the U.S. Patent and Trademark Office.
The colophon is a trademark of Multnomah Publishers, Inc.

Printed in the United States of America

For information:
MULTNOMAH PUBLISHERS, INC.•Post Office Box 1720•Sisters, Oregon 97759

Library of Congress Cataloging-in-Publication Data
Moser, Nancy.
    The seat beside me / by Nancy Moser.
       p. cm.
    ISBN 1-57673-884-1 (pbk.)
    1. Survival after airplane accidents, shipwrecks, etc.--Fiction.
      2. Aircraft accidents--Fiction. I. Title.
    PS3563.O88417 S43 2002
    813'.54--dc21   2001006363

02 03 04 05 06—10 9 8 7 6 5 4 3 2 1 0

For Elaine Neumeyer:
a reader with flair,
friend beyond compare,
and child of God extraordinaire.

∞

Where can I go from your Spirit?
Where can I flee from your presence?
If I go up to the heavens, you are there;
if I make my bed in the depths, you are there.
If I rise on the wings of the dawn,
if I settle on the far side of the
sea, even there your hand will guide me,
your right hand will hold me fast.
PSALM 139:7–10

ACKNOWLEDGMENTS

Many people have been with me along the way, sitting in the seat beside me in all its forms.…

Thank you to my husband, Mark, for letting me do what I love (and need) to do. And thanks to Emily and Carson, for their constant support, and especially to my little Laurel (who isn't so little anymore), for reading through the entire manuscript and making wise suggestions at the ripe old age of sixteen. You make—and would make—a great editor, sweetie. The literary world would applaud your career choice.

Thanks to all my extended family, but especially Mom and Dad, Bev, Crystie, Lois, and Nikki, for always being there and for showing interest in my work.

And Elaine Neumeyer…we were friends way before we met—and always sisters in Christ. Thank you for reading through the entire book and making comments in your usual honest (but loving) way. You are a friend sent by God.

A thank you to the women of my octet, Seeds of Faith. Every Wednesday, in between singing, you ladies (and Dallas too) listened to the progress of this book. Liz Chandler, thanks for your special help with teacher Tina; Debbie Field, with Sonja's math career advice; Nancy Smithyman, for your help with the hero; and the rest of you: Kathryn Sparks, Linda McCray, Marilyn Lake, Jill Pearson, Sue Wall, and director Dallas Hainline, for your patient ears and encouraging words.

Thanks go to Mel and Cheryl Hodde and Harry Kraus, fine authors all, for their medical wisdom with regard to Anthony. Any errors are my own.

Thanks to fellow author Deb Raney, for literally sitting in the seat beside me on a plane to New Orleans where she endured my enthusiastic bubbling about the idea for a plane crash book. Hey, the fact we had to turn back because the landing gear wouldn't go up (better than the other way around, I'd say) was *not* my fault. I will never forget your comment: "If you wanted to do research, I wish you would have done it without me." Chicken.

And thanks to my agent Chip MacGregor, author buddies Doris Elaine Fell, Stephanie Whitson, James Scott Bell, and Lisa Samson, who sat in the seat of friendship and prayer. May the Lord enlarge your territories. And to the rest of the Chi Libris group… you're family, and I cherish you.

A special thanks to my editor, Julee Schwarzburg, whose enthusiasm, honesty, and skill made this book better. And your insight…thanks for being open to God's promptings, subtle though they may have been. Many would ignore such hard-to-express *feelings* about a scene or a character, but you didn't. I hope I did your insight justice.

And a special thanks to the many readers who send me letters or e-mails. Your kind words, prayers, and encouragement are priceless. And those special ones who often e-mail and say they've felt a nudge to pray for me…Anita Flenz, Pauline Bond, and Richelle Cope (my Aussie friend, and her grandma). Thank you all. You are the payment for my work.

Most of all, thanks be to God, for it is He who has called me to do this thing and arranged my life so it can be accomplished. Above all, I long to make Him proud of me—in all things. Thank you, Abba.

One

JANUARY 29
12:30 A.M.

I don't want to go.
Dora Roberts tossed her keys on the kitchen counter and flipped through her mail, quickly setting it aside. She was too tired to deal with bills and solicitations now. She'd do it when she got back.

I really *don't want to go.*

It wasn't that she didn't like visiting her mother in Phoenix, but Dora had just been home for Christmas the month before, and her bank account was strained by two plane flights spaced so closely together—especially this latest flight that had been booked at the spur of the moment, costing her a bundle.

And yet, how could she not be there when her mother went in for gallbladder surgery?

A painful flare-up had sent her mother to the doctor for tests and a quickly scheduled surgery. *If only it had happened while I was down at Christmas...*

Dora closed her eyes against the selfish thought and shucked off her shoes. Her mother was all alone in the world except for her.

9

Daddy gone. Dora, an only child. It was her responsibility to be there whenever she was needed, even if it was financially draining. Even if it had made her stay at the office of the *Chronicle* until nearly midnight, getting her work done so she could—

The phone rang, sending her heart to her toes. She glanced at the clock on her microwave. It was nearly twelve-thirty. No call at this time of night could be good news.

"Yes?"

"Dora, you don't have to come! You don't have to come!"

"Mom? What are you talking about?"

"I've been trying to call you and call you. Didn't you get my messages?"

Dora glanced at the answering machine. The message light was blinking. "I just got home from the office. I didn't think to listen." She'd gotten off track. "What's your message?"

"I don't have to have the surgery! It all started yesterday when I did a no-no and ate pizza. You know how hard it is for me to resist pizza, and so I had it for lunch knowing the pain would come. But then it didn't. And that was so remarkable, and I felt so good that I got my doctor to do another ultrasound. And am I ever glad I did. The ultrasound revealed there was nothing there. No blockage. No problem."

"But the previous ultrasound—?"

"The doctor doesn't have an explanation for it. One day it was there and I needed surgery, the next day it wasn't and I didn't. He didn't have an explanation, but I do. We do."

Dora's thoughts had taken the same path as her mother's. "You think it's a God-thing, Mom? You think God healed you?"

"What other explanation is there?"

"Perhaps they merely made a mistake."

"It was my innards in both those ultrasounds, Dora."

"Perhaps the doctor read them wrong?"

"Even I could see the difference."

"Or maybe—"

"Dora. Dear child, I'm ashamed of you. Quit trying to explain away a miracle. You've been praying for me, haven't you?"

"Of course."

"And I've been praying, and I know a lot of people at church have been praying. It's a miracle, and nothing you say can prove it otherwise. But the bottom-line blessing is that you don't have to rush back down here."

"I really don't mind," Dora said, hoping it was at least partially true.

"I know you don't. You're a good daughter. But I also know money is tight and you're swamped at the paper. Didn't you say so at Christmas?"

"Yes, but—"

"Well, now you don't have to come. Save your money and come down later in the spring, like we'd planned."

A wave of relief flooded over her. "Are you positive?"

"Absolutely. Now get to bed. You've got to get up to go to work in a few hours."

"Thanks, Mom. You know I love you."

"And I love you too. But the thanks? I didn't do anything. God did. So thank Him, all right?"

Dora hung up the phone and did exactly that.

11:30 A.M.

"It's good you're leaving."

Merry Cavanaugh coughed at her husband's statement. "It is?"

Lou turned the van into the terminal entrance leading to Sun Fun Airlines. Snow pummeled the windshield. "Sure. I know how close you were to Teresa in college. How long has it been since you've seen her?"

Merry was disappointed Lou was oblivious to her real reason for leaving. "She was here after Justin was first born."

"She's still single, right?"

"She's a vice president in her company." Merry said it as if one fact had something to do with the other.

"That's too bad—the single part, that is. I bet she's jealous of you."

Merry lifted an eyebrow. "I don't think—"

"She sees you living the ideal life with a husband who adores you and a fantastic little boy who likes nothing better than to climb on your lap and give you a hug. What does she have?" Merry took a breath to answer, but Lou continued. "She has a stressful job and a lonely house. Thanks, but no thanks."

No thanks? Are you crazy?

Merry looked to the Sun Fun entrance coming up on their right. She only had a few moments before she was free. And yet she longed to let him have it, make him understand how she really felt. Lou was so clueless sometimes.

Her chest heaved; her hands gripped and regripped the handles of the carry-on bag in her lap. The awful truth threatened.

Lou looked over at her and smiled. "You are so beautiful. Did you know that?"

She hugged the door to get as far away from the words as she could. The fight left her—as it usually did when he said nice things. Maybe it was better he was ignorant to reality. After the trip...after she'd had time to think things through and get Teresa's advice... The truth was, if she brought it all up now, he might not let her go.

"Here we are." Lou pulled up front, the tires slipping on the snow-covered street. He got out of the van to get her suitcase. Merry put her hood up, got out, opened the side door, and gave Justin a hug. "I'm going to miss you, sweetie." In spite of everything, it was the truth.

"I'll miss you too, Mommy. Daddy says he has a surprise for me."

"He does?"

"I hope he's taking me to McDonald's for breakfast. Do you think that's it?"

"Sure. I bet that's it." Merry gave her son a kiss and closed the door against the snow. She waved good-bye through the window.

Lou appeared at her side, suitcase in tow. The weather would prevent a lengthy good-bye. Just as well.

"Have a good trip, Mer. Love you."

She accepted his hug and kiss. "Love you too." It was the truth. But not all the truth.

Merry hurried inside the terminal and removed her coat, brushing away the flakes that melted in the heated building. She rolled her suitcase to the check-in line and allowed herself a deep breath. *I'm alone. Finally alone.* No husband. No son. No plan except to have fun and remember what life was like before a family had tied her down with responsibilities. Twenty-nine was too young to feel so old.

She felt absolutely decadent, even though part of the thrill had been dampened by the fact that Lou *wanted* her to go, urged her to go. When her old college chum had invited her, Merry was afraid to even mention the idea to her husband, and yet, when she did, he jumped on the plan, even offering to dip into their meager savings to fund the trip.

At first she was suspicious. *Why does he want me gone?* But she soon tossed such ridiculous notions away. Above all else, Lou could be trusted. Lou was true-blue, honest, hardworking, kind, generous, loyal...

Everything she was not.

But maybe a little time away would change all that. Maybe she was so down about her life because it was so disgustingly normal and routine. Maybe she was simply having a case of thirtyitis. Had her twenties been all she'd wanted them to be?

Although she'd always wanted to be a mother, Merry thought it would be more…rewarding. Like in the TV commercials with the ever patient mother, ruffling the naughty son's hair while she gave him a forgiving smile. Always under control, always smiling, always fulfilled.

Life didn't work that way. Although she loved her family, she often found herself on the verge of strangling them—at least in theory. When Justin had gotten into Merry's brand-new eye shadow, putting water in it, using it like watercolor paints, or when he had scribbled on the walls with red crayons, Merry never considered ruffling his hair and smiling. Not once.

And those women who pined for their man to come home, whose hearts beat a little faster at the sound of their husband's car? As often as not, Merry was relieved when Lou left in the morning, and her stomach grabbed ever so slightly when he returned. Not because she didn't love him, but because he thought so much of her—was constantly telling her what a wonderful wife and mother she was—she felt obligated to try to live up to his opinion. When he was home she couldn't let down her guard and be herself. She was way too flawed.

Lou deserved better. And she deserved…

She thought of Teresa and Phoenix and four days of fun, sun, and free—

An announcement came over the loudspeakers. "We're sorry, folks, but the airport has been temporarily shut down due to the blizzard. Please continue to check in and remain at your gates until further notice. Hopefully we'll begin boarding soon, and your delay will be as short as possible. Thank you for your patience."

Merry joined the groans of those around her. Apparently the fun and sun would have to wait.

11:45 A.M.

Suzy lifted her father's suitcase from the trunk of the car. "This is heavy. I thought you were only going for a few days."

George stifled a laugh. If only Suzy knew what was in the suitcase. The only reason it had any weight at all was so she wouldn't be suspicious. At the last minute George had scooped up two drawerfuls of Irma's things and dumped them in the suitcase for weight, adding as an afterthought his favorite framed picture of her. Of the women's clothing, a picture, and the pills, the pills were the only things that were a necessity.

Suzy closed the trunk and hurried to her father's side. She kissed him on the cheek. "Have a good trip, Dad. Stan and I think it's wonderful you're going. You and Mom loved to travel. It's good you're back at it again. Seven months is a long time."

Seven months, two days, and seven hours to be exact. And he wasn't getting *back* to anything. His life was winding down and he had no intention of grabbing any key to wind it up again. George hugged her longer than usual. *This will be my last hug.* He didn't let the thought linger but, with a final wave, hurried into the terminal and took a place at the check-in line.

He'd check in, get to Phoenix, then check out. Literally.

George had big plans. Once he was settled into their favorite condo in Sun City, he would visit some of his and Irma's old haunts—to say good-bye. Then he would take matters into his own hands. Fun, sun, and suicide. *Bon voyage, adios, auf Wiedersehen, arrivederci, sayonara.*

Soon, Irma, soon.

But then what? What happened after death? Would there be an angelic chorus to greet him for the good things he'd done in his life? Or the devil's jury to condemn him for his last act of desperation?

Was it desperation? He didn't feel desperate. Only weary, as if the air itself was too heavy to deal with. How could he be expected to go on living when breathing had become a burden?

Planning his suicide hadn't been easy; he tried to think of everything, but why did every moron on earth have to come into his presence these last few days? First it was the stupid travel agent who booked him in coach when he specifically asked for first class. Then his cleaning lady got all suspicious about why George had canceled her services. Then his lawyer made a huge to-do about his wanting to update his will. So what if George wanted to cut the church out of the bequests? Things had changed. It was his money, and he could toss it to the wind if he wanted to. People needed to mind their own business.

The final straw was the fiasco at the bank where he'd gone to withdraw all his money—all $68,392 of it. They acted as flustered as firemen forced to start a fire. Withdraw money? *Oh no, no, no, no, no.* He wondered if they even knew the difference between a Czech and a check. They were such a pain about it that he considered asking for it in ones, but he relented, not wanting to give the poor teller a heart attack.

But no matter. The money was now sitting in a desk drawer with a note to their daughter. Now that Suzy and her husband were taken care of, George could take this one last trip—in Irma's honor.

12:10 P.M.

As Sonja stood in line for coffee, she was flying—literally and emotionally. Allen, Dale, and Sonja. Off to Phoenix. The new chosen three from Sanford Industries.

The fact that Sonja had taken the place of another employee, Geraldine, through a little hook and crook was inconsequential. *All's fair in the business world.*

Or perhaps another truism was more appropriate here: Loose lips sink ships. If Geraldine hadn't been so careless as to tell a coworker that she really shouldn't be going to the convention because there were big problems with the numbers she put together for the Barston merger, Sonja would never have overheard, checked the numbers herself, and brought them to the attention of their boss. *"I really hate to do this, Allen, but I think you should know…"*

Sure Geraldine had been furious when she was pulled from the convention and Sonja was assigned in her place. Sure Geraldine had called Sonja vicious and had even threatened, *"Just wait, Sonja…some day…"*

So be it.

Sonja paid for her coffee and pulled her suitcase toward the gate, juggling her laptop bag over the other shoulder. *Some day what? I'll get what I deserve?* She shook the negative thought away and focused on another voice that was friendlier. *What you deserve is to be given a chance. Now you've got one. If your bosses were more savvy and fair in the first place, they would have seen your potential long ago instead of forcing you into this position. It's their fault.*

Sure it is.

Back and forth. Up and down. Guilt could be so annoying. This was not how she wanted to feel just minutes before her flight left for the convention. She needed to recapture the feeling of victory that had been hers just moments before. She needed…to call her parents.

Sonja got to her gate and nodded to Allen and Dale before taking a seat that offered a modicum of privacy. She dialed her parents' number. This trip would make them proud of her. This trip would make them stand up and notice that she was a success in her own right, that she wasn't the same underachiever who never worked to her full potential no matter what wonderful opportunities they'd given her. *After all we've done for you, Sonja…*

The inner voice from her memories matched the voice that answered the phone. "Hello?"

"Hi, Mom."

"Sonja? Is that you? Why are you calling?"

Sonja felt herself retreating. "No reason."

"There's always a reason. Now, your brother…he'll call for no reason whatsoever. He's such a good boy."

That *boy* was thirty-five, the cherished only son, Sheffield D. Grafton III. Sonja had long ago realized that being the only daughter did not carry the same level of adoration. Did it have something to do with the Roman numeral after her brother's name, his gender, or was it just her?

"Is Dad there?"

"So there *is* a reason."

"No, not really. I just wanted—"

"To talk to him more than me."

"Mom! I'm off to Phoenix, and I just wanted to tell you. Both of you."

"Playing hooky from work, are you?"

"Of course not. I was chosen to go to a convention. I'm one of only three people going—in the entire company."

Her mother laughed. "And there's four in the company, right?"

Sonja's breathing quickened. Her mother knew very well how many people worked at Sanford Industries. She'd even given her mother a tour of the office once.

"Shef went to Atlantic City for his last convention. He stayed in a room that had a marble tub right there in the middle of it. And two phones. One in the bathroom."

"We're going to be staying in a hotel at a desert resort." Did one painted desert beat a bathtub and two phones?

"I despise that dry air. Makes my skin feel like it's going to crack off."

Sonja massaged the space between her eyes.

"Did you know Shef just got a bonus? He said he'd buy us something nice with it. Last year he bought your father and me new watches. Expensive watches with the day and date on them. Did you know that?"

Sonja's finger pushed harder. "Yes, Mother, you told me." *And Shef told me. And Daddy told me. And Aunt Dottie told me.* Sonja wouldn't have been surprised if Shef had taken out a full-page ad to announce his good deed. Sonja thought of the last present she'd given her parents: a fancy food processor with five speeds. Last visit home she looked for it and asked where it was. Her mother had put it in the closet, saying it was too complicated to figure out.

Not any more complicated than a watch that showed the date and day.

"Oh! Here's more news. Did you know Shef is going to—?"

"Will you be quiet!"

"What?"

Sonja sucked in a breath and looked around the gate. A few waiting passengers glanced up, then down again.

"Sonja? Did you just tell me to—?"

She leaned into the phone. "Mother, I'm sorry, so sorry…"

"I can't believe you told—"

"I didn't mean it. I'm…I'm just nervous about the convention." *And how I got there.*

"I'm surprised they chose you to go anywhere with an attitude like that. If it were my choice you wouldn't—"

"I know. I was out of line. It's just that when you kept mentioning everything Shef was doing and didn't pay any attention to what I—"

"Can I help it if we're proud of your brother? He's done wonderful things with his life."

"And I'm doing wonderful things with my life too."

Silence. "Don't go getting into any contest with your brother, Sonja. You know that wouldn't be right. Comparisons are always wrong."

Exactly! A flurry of words escaped. "But you and Daddy are the ones who compare us, who pit us one against the other."

An intake of breath. "We…we do not."

"Mother…"

"Can I help it if we're proud parents?"

A question hovered near the surface. *Uh-uh, Sonja. Don't push it.*

"Proud of whom, Mother?"

Another moment of hesitation. Why was it so hard for her parents to say something nice? "I'm proud of all my family."

"Shef?"

"Of course Shef."

"And…?"

"And…you."

Sonja thought the compliment would mean more; she thought she would feel relief, or a surge of pride. Maybe the compliment was impotent because she had to drag it out of her mother.

Sonja looked at the cold snow outside. "Gotta go, Mother. I'll call you when I get back. Say hi to Daddy for me." She pushed the button on the phone, disconnecting herself from her parents. But she didn't really need to go to the trouble. They'd disconnected years ago.

12:29 P.M.

All airline people were idiots. Anthony Thorgood was sure of it. He stood in the first-class check-in line while his own personal airline idiot checked her computer…again.

Her fingers stopped tapping. She looked up at him and smiled a condescending smile he was sure she'd mastered her first day on the job. But if she thought he was going to merely accept the smile and move along, she was in for a surprise.

"I'm sorry, Mr. Thor—"

"*Doctor* Thorgood."

"Doctor Thorgood. The computer shows your reservation is in coach, not first class." She set his confirming printout on the counter between them. "See? It even states on your e-ticket that you're in coach."

She was right.

He scanned his mind for someone else to blame. Candy. His

receptionist. She was the one who made the reservation. He had trusted her and she'd blown it. He'd deal with her when he got back.

He read the clerk's name tag. "Fine. But, Sandy…certainly you can change—"

Their attention was diverted to the check-in line for regular passengers a few feet away. A dowdy woman was near tears, a young girl glued to her side. The woman slapped her hand on the counter, which was at her chin level. "Don't tell me to calm down. You're not listening to me! We *can't* go on that flight."

"Ma'am, the airport is closed, but I'm sure it's temporary. They just need some time to plow the runways. Everything will be running normally soon."

"No, it won't. Don't you get it? Something's going to happen to that flight."

The airline employee raised an eyebrow. "And how do you know this, ma'am?"

The woman put a fist to her gut and looked into the face of the girl at her side. "I just know it. I feel it. From the time I got up this morning I've felt a burden of impending disaster and now with the airport being shut down because of—"

The employee looked bored. "Does this feeling happen often?"

The woman set her jaw and stood the full extent of her five-foot frame. "Listen, miss, frankly, I don't care if you believe me or not. If you don't want me turning around and announcing my bad feelings to the rest of your passengers, I suggest you give us our money back."

"But you and your daughter have nonrefundable tickets, ma'am. See here? In the fine print?"

The woman snatched the tickets away from the employee, grabbed the hand of the little girl, and stomped away, the wheels of their suitcases whirring against the floor.

"Dr. Thorgood?"

He remembered the goal at hand: a first-class seat. He turned back to Sandy. She smiled at him nervously. "You get many of those?" he asked.

"Some people aren't as good at flying as others." She paused and smiled. "As good as people like yourself."

He knew he was being manipulated, but instead of jumping her for it, he let himself admire her tact. "So, what's the verdict?"

"There are no more first-class seats. Period. I'm sorry. But I have found you a first-class seat on your return flight. Of course, there will be an increase in price."

Anthony pulled out a Visa.

1:00 P.M.

Henry Smith sat at the gate, his eyes closed, praying. He hated to fly and thought it was ironic that God had placed him in a job that required him to continually face that which he feared the most.

It's not that he was afraid of dying. When the time came, he would be ready. The difficult thing about flying was that it required such a leap of faith, such a surrender of control. Even if he weren't a God-fearing man, it would require such a leap. Henry could think of no reason why this heavy, bulky plane should be able to fly. None. It defied logic. And so, once airborne, Henry had to trust that the pilots, the mechanics, the engineers, and the Wright Brothers knew what they were doing.

Beyond that, he also had to trust God. If a crash fit into God's plan, Henry realized that he had absolutely, positively no control over its outcome. Cruising at thirty thousand feet, traveling at hundreds of miles per hour, he understood how small and inconsequential he was. Not that God wouldn't listen to his prayers…He would. But there was always the bigger picture to consider. And during the large moments of life, Henry knew God had a lot to think about. One man's prayers were like a single piece of a jigsaw puzzle, and God had the unenviable job of putting all those pieces together into a finished work. Henry had no say whether he was an exasperating piece of the sky, a favored edge piece, or the beloved last piece in the puzzle.

But ever since last night, Henry felt as if he'd been handed a new piece of the puzzle—and he had no idea where it went.

It had all started with the temptation—the kind that was always there for a salesman on the road. The kind that was intent on chipping away at his good-man facade, trying to uncover the real Henry Smith.

Who was the real Henry Smith?

Last night had been an ample test. He ate in the hotel bar and grill, feeling the need for a celebratory steak with all the fixings after a great sales day. *If only Ellen were here.*

But his wife wasn't here, and the redhead was, all smiles and curves, with the flattering words he wanted to hear. "I just love a man with a beard." When she suggested a nightcap in his room...

He got so far as to have the door open before he came to his senses and told her thanks, but no thanks. He quickly closed it, locked it, and leaned against it, the smell of her perfume lingering like a tantalizing lure. He needed a distraction and ran to the bed, switched on the TV, flipped channels, and tried to think of anything but the woman.

And then, without planning it, he took the Bible from the drawer of the bedside table, opened it, and bowed his head, reintroducing himself to a God he'd previously put on a back burner.

His prayer was simple: *Help me through this.*

Before he opened his eyes, he felt a sudden wave of peace. He found he could even think about the redhead without wanting to go to her.

He was so thankful for God's instant response that he dared to ask another ever present question: *Show me what You want me to do with my life.* Then—for the second time in one night—he received an instant answer as his eyes were drawn to a set of verses someone had highlighted with a yellow marker. Isaiah 30:19–21.

The verses stayed with him even now…

Henry ran a hand over his beard, glanced around the airport, then closed his eyes and recited to himself. "You will weep no more. How gracious he will be when you cry for help! As soon as he hears, he will answer you. Although the Lord gives you the bread of adversity and the water of affliction, your teachers will be hidden no more; with your own eyes you will see them. Whether you turn to the right or to the left, your ears will hear a voice behind you, saying, 'This is the way; walk in it.'"

The last line was the clincher. *This is the way; walk in it.* Henry grabbed on to those seven words like a lifeline. They became his mantra, his hope for the future. And the cause of his confusion.

What was "the way"?

He opened his eyes and looked outside to the raging blizzard. At the moment he just wanted to finish his work and get home. Maybe Ellen would understand what it all meant. She was good at life issues and Bible verses. Much better than he was.

He'd hoped that the morning light would make everything clear. But it hadn't. He was pleased that he still remembered the verse, but as far as the rest? He traveled the road between thinking his life was in shambles to a kind of fearful anticipation. As if "the way" loomed in the near future, and no matter what it was, it would be better than what he had now.

In fact, what he had now…

He reached for his phone and dialed.

"Hey, Elly."

"Hiya, hon. What's up?"

He sat back, taking comfort from her voice. She was the constant in his life. The *"way"*? "The airport's closed for a while. I'm bored."

"Then I'll do my best to entertain you. Where you headed next?"

"Phoenix."

"Since when do you go to Phoenix? Isn't that Bill's territory?"

"Bill's son is getting married. He covered for me last year when Joey graduated from high school. Now it's my turn."

"You take too many turns," Ellen said. "You need to learn to say no."

"Except to you, right?"

"Now that's a good husband."

He considered telling her about the verse but decided he'd rather do it in person. "What are you doing?"

"I just made myself an omelette for lunch."

"You make the best omelettes."

"I do?"

She seemed so grateful. Why didn't he say nice things more often? He vowed to do better.

"Be careful, Henry. Get home safe to me. When you do, I promise we'll share an omelette. With the works."

"It's a date."

Henry's eyes were once again drawn to the window. He felt a wave of dread.

"Bye, Henry. See you—"

"Elly?"

"Yes?"

"I love you. You know that, don't you?"

"I do. And I love you too."

He hung up and let thoughts of home warm him.

"Ladies and gentlemen, we are confident the airport will be reopened soon. To be ready when that time comes, we have decided to start boarding the flight immediately. Now boarding from the rear of the plane…"

Henry stood. Home. He'd be there soon.

1:10 P.M.

Tina McKutcheon looked up from her book. Since her assigned seat was near the rear of the plane, her row had been called long ago, but she held back, having no intention of getting in first and sitting all cramped during the chaos of boarding. Calm, comfortable, and controlled. Those were the key words of the day. Especially after the bombshell David had tossed this morning. Marriage? She didn't want to think about it. Not now. Not yet. And the way he'd done it…so casually after stopping by on his way to work. Not that a romantic dinner at Lazlo's would have made her decision any easier.

Tina shut her book and scanned the remaining passengers, wondering what kind of person would be her seatmate. She saw old people and business travelers. Those she could tolerate. There was only one category of person she did not want seated beside her: the dreaded teenager. As a high school English teacher, this trip was an escape from them. If God was a good God, He would have mercy and keep them far, far away. The luggage hold would be good.

Tina spotted one lone teenager entering the jet way. Her hair was black and braided in cornrows. Her skin had an olive tone, though her facial features hinted of some oriental link. Headphones draped around her neck, a backpack over her shoulder. Her pants were too big; her shirt too tight. The *pièce de résistance* was the earring—in her nose.

Anyone but her…please, God. Anyone but her.

The only people left at the gate were a father and a young boy who'd run in at the last minute. In their hurry, the boy spilled the contents of his red-and-blue backpack. As they scrambled to collect the toys, Tina knew she couldn't put it off any longer. It was time.

She walked through the jet way, boarded, and eased her way down the aisle toward the back of the plane. She nearly gasped as the cornrowed teenager in front of her kept going down the aisle.

When the girl stopped near two empty seats, Tina's stomach knotted with a sick certainty.

The girl tossed her backpack in the overhead bin and slid into the middle seat—the middle seat next to Tina's aisle seat.

Tina couldn't believe it. God certainly had a sick sense of humor.

1:12 P.M.

Merry flipped through the in-flight magazine, thrilled the rest of her row was empty. Now *that* was luxury. Not only was she going on a trip alone, she had space to spread out and enjoy—

"Mommy!"

Merry's head hit the back of the seat. There in the aisle was Justin! And Lou!

Her husband beamed down at her. "Are you surprised?"

That wasn't the word.

Two

Find rest, O my soul, in God alone; my hope comes from him.
He alone is my rock and my salvation; he is my fortress,
I will not be shaken.

PSALM 62:5–6

1:15 P.M.
SCHEDULED TAKEOFF TIME

Merry let Lou get Justin settled between them. She let him buckle the seat belt, put the Scooby-Doo backpack under the seat, and show Justin how the tray table worked. She let their chatter about the light, the vent, and the drinks and snack that would be served pinch her nerves until she thought she would scream.

She stared outside. At the snow. At the cold, awful, horrible snow that reflected the state of her heart. How could Lou do this to her? And worse, why did she feel this way?

"There," Lou finally said, taking a breath. "All set."

She refused to look at him.

"Mer?"

She didn't move.

"What's wrong, Mommy?"

She still didn't move.

"Daddy, what's wrong with Mommy?"

"Nothing's wrong with Mommy, bud. We're going to have so much fun in—"

Merry swung toward him. *"We* were not supposed to have fun in Phoenix. *I* was supposed to have fun in Phoenix."

Justin looked at her face, then tugged at his father's arm. "Daddy…"

Lou put a calming hand on his leg. "We just surprised Mommy so much she hasn't had time to let it sink in."

Merry laughed and was amazed at how wicked it sounded. She angled her body toward him. "Mommy is not surprised. Mommy is shocked and appalled."

"Hey, Mer…that can't—"

"That can't be true?" She lowered her voice when her eyes met with those of the man across the aisle. "You can't handle the truth."

Justin drew his legs to his chest and started whimpering. Merry felt a twinge of regret but let it die. It was Lou's fault that their son was here, seated between them, a captive to their argument. Actually, they were all captives, buckled in their seats, unable to move or leave the situation. Unable to run away—as she'd tried to run away to Phoenix?

Lou unbuckled Justin's seat belt. The boy was in his lap within seconds, clinging to his neck. "Shh, shh, buddy. It'll be all—"

A flight attendant came by and touched Lou's shoulder. "Sir? Your son needs to get buckled into his seat."

"I know. Just a few minutes."

"Can I get you anything?"

"No. He'll be fine."

She nodded and moved on. Merry looked at her family, huddled together in one seat, with one empty seat separating them from her. What an apt picture of her life. Them against her.

Justin calmed down and cuddled against Lou's chest. Lou spoke softly, "So what's this truth you need to tell me?"

Faced with Lou's attention and his request to pinpoint her discontent, Merry's mind suddenly went blank. What *was* the truth anyway? That she hated them? That wasn't the truth. That she hated her life with them? That wasn't the truth, either.

"I know you're not happy, Mer."

She stared at him, incredulously. "Since when?"

"I may not have a college degree, but I'm not dumb."

"Then why haven't you said anything? Done anything?"

He thought a moment, stroking Justin's hair. "I was afraid—afraid I was losing you."

Obviously she was less subtle, and Lou more intuitive, than she thought.

"I don't know if you're losing me…"

"Then why is our surprise appalling?"

Merry rubbed her hands fiercely over her face. "Ohhh. I'm so confused."

"I can see that." Lou nudged Justin away from his chest. "Time to get in your own seat, bud."

Reluctantly, Justin sat down and fumbled with his seat belt.

"Here, let me do that," Merry said.

Justin looked up with hopeful eyes. "So it's okay we're here, Mommy?"

Merry looked at Lou, then at her son. She felt her fight evaporate like steam from a kettle of soup.

Yet maybe her resignation wasn't losing the war. Maybe the battle had changed. Maybe this trip was a chance for her and Lou to spell out the terms of mutual surrender. Maybe good could come out of bad.

Justin took her hand. Merry pulled it to her lips and kissed the tiny fingers.

And the anger left her. For now.

Sonja had expected to sit next to Allen and Dale on the plane. When her seat was rows behind them, she was disappointed—at first. But her disappointment soon turned to relief when she realized how much more relaxing the flight would be if she didn't have to keep up the pretense of being the great career woman. Plus, there was the advantage of not having to answer too many questions. Dale had already insinuated he knew how she'd gotten on the trip. And Allen had been the man she'd gone to with her information about Geraldine. So who cared if her seat was at the rear of the plane? What better place to hide?

Sonja felt an absurd freedom putting her laptop in the overhead bin. She felt no need to work without the eyes of her coworkers on her. She took her seat by the window and watched the snow that had started on their ride to the airport. The flurry had turned into a blizzard. Could planes fly in snow? She tossed the worry away. She had enough to think about.

She closed her eyes. The last few days had wrung the life from her cells, and each one screamed to be renewed, rejuvenated. These few hours on the plane would be her only chance to rest and regroup. Once they got to the convention, she would have to be "on" every waking moment.

She opened her eyes when she felt the person shift in the seat beside her. She looked in his direction for the first time. He was an African-American sporting a trim mustache and wearing a navy suit. He looked in her direction. "Afternoon."

"Afternoon." Sonja closed her eyes again, hoping to cut off further conversation.

"You look worried."

Sonja opened her eyes. "Why do you say that?"

He pointed to the space between her eyes. "Even with your eyes closed, you've got a worry line digging deep." He yanked at his suit coat, adjusting it under the seat belt. "I take it your trip to Phoenix is not for pleasure?"

"Work. A convention."

He nodded. "I used to go that route." He shook his head as if the memories disturbed him.

"You don't approve of conventions?"

"Not for me to approve or disapprove. All I know is every convention I ever attended was full of people trying too hard to be something they weren't, selling stuff they only pretended to believe in."

Bingo. Yet she couldn't let him know how on target he was. She pointed to his attire. "You're hardly dressed for a golf outing."

He adjusted his tie. "I'm heading home."

"Dressed like that?"

"My wife's picking me up at the airport. She likes me in suits."

Sonja shook her head. "You dressed up for her?"

"I like to please her."

Sonja laughed. "Sorry, but you're too good to be true. Care for a second wife?"

"No thanks. I've got my one and only, and she's plenty much for me."

Sonja clapped. "Wow. Loyal too. I am impressed." He nodded a bow. She glanced out the window as she felt the bump of luggage being placed in the storage compartment beneath them.

"So, miss…since I've done such a good job of impressing you, I might as well introduce myself." He held out a hand. "Roscoe Moore."

"Sonja Grafton."

"Nice to meet you, Ms. Grafton. Now suppose you tell me about that worry line you're etching into your forehead, and I, in turn, will tell you how to get rid of it for good."

"This I've got to hear."

"Gladly. But you first."

Sonja took a deep breath. Being tempted to confide in this stranger was disconcerting, yet everything about him oozed trust…

"Want to think about it?" Roscoe asked.

"That sounds good." If only she had her laptop.

At least I got the aisle.

That was Anthony Thorgood's only consolation when he didn't

get his first-class seat. He found that the back of the plane had a closed-in feel, and the fact his entire row was full and three wide instead of two didn't help matters. Add to that the type of person who inhabited the seat beside him.

He decided his wool blazer was too warm and stood to take it off. As he carefully folded it and put it in the overhead bin, he had a chance to look at her. He did not like what he saw.

She took up every inch of the seat, armrest to armrest. The fact that she sat with her hands clasped across her lap only accentuated her weight. The rest of her was no more impressive. Stringy straight hair, parted in the middle. No makeup, and clothes that probably cost the same amount as Anthony spent on one lunch. The obnoxious magenta of her sweater was totally wrong for her ruddy complexion. He hadn't heard her speak yet, but he assumed if she did so, her sentences would be punctuated with *ain't, gotta,* and offensive pairings such as *it don't* and *I got.*

White trash.

"I got snot on my nose, mister?"

Anthony smiled with satisfaction. He took his seat, trying hard not to nudge her as he put on the seat belt. He never had this problem in first class.

He felt the woman's eyes and glanced at her. She did not look away.

"What?" he asked.

"You're a rich la-di-da, aren't you?" She waved a pudgy finger at his watch and rings, then let it wave across his clothes.

He looked away, feeling himself flush. "I—"

"You a lawyer? Or maybe the CEO of some dot-com?"

He pulled the laminated instruction card from the pocket. "I'm a doctor."

When she didn't react, he risked another look. She was shaking her head, her jowl set.

"What's wrong?"

"Just my luck."

"What's that supposed to mean?"

Her nose wrinkled. "I hate doctors." She looked at him, her eyes narrowed. "All doctors."

"Don't you think that's unfair?"

She gave a small laugh. "Just like a doctor. Ready to defend the profession without even knowing why I feel the way I do."

Touché. But in truth, he didn't want to know. And he knew she wanted him to ask.

"Since you'll never have guts enough to ask, I'll tell you why I hate all doctors: because my father died of cancer."

"It happens. But why hate the doctors?"

"When Dad first went to them, they flipped him off. Told him it was nothing. When we finally found out, it was too late."

Anthony opened his mouth to speak, then closed it. What could he say?

"Cat got your tongue, Doc?"

"That's too bad."

"No kidding."

"I'm not that kind of doctor."

"You're not an arrogant—?"

"I'm not an oncologist. I don't treat cancer. I'm a plastic surgeon."

"Well, zipadee-do-da. Isn't that a cushy job? You don't have to deal with death at all, do you?"

"There is risk in any surgery."

She rolled her eyes. "Oh, pa-leaze."

She was right. It sounded lame.

"Bet you'd have a field day with me, wouldn't you, Doc?"

"Excuse me?"

"A little liposuction here, a tummy tuck there. Maybe a face-lift and a nose job. And bob my ears while you're at it."

He shoved the laminated card in the pocket and removed the

magazine, flipping it open. "I don't need to listen to—"

"Oh yes you do, Doc Doo-Da. For the next few hours you and I are joined at the hip. Aren't you thrilled?"

As soon as Tina was seated she opened her book, hoping to quell any possibility that this…this teenager seated beside her would have the nerve to talk to her. Hopefully she was like most teens, totally absorbed in her own little world, not caring who or what existed beyond her immediate boundary of sight, smell, and sound.

Sound.

Tina could hear the rasp of music playing through the girl's headphones. She despised secondhand music. It reminded her of her first apartment where the two guys upstairs had insisted on playing their stereos deep into the night, the boom, boom, boom of the bass driving into Tina's nerves like Chinese water torture. She'd broken her lease two months early because of them, absorbing the monetary penalty for doing so as her toll for leaving hell.

But more than her dislike of secondhand music was her dislike of the current trend for kids to constantly have noise in their lives. Kids mowing lawns, kids shoveling snow, kids walking down the hall at school—from the first thing in the morning to the last thing at night, kids had noise piped directly into their minds, brainwashing them into thinking silence was a thing to be feared instead of cherished. How could they ever hope to have an original thought if they never allowed a moment of silence? Headphones were a modern pacifier, sucking dry the brains of all who used them.

Tina glanced at the girl and the girl glanced back. Then, to Tina's surprise, she removed the headphones and shut them off.

"Sorry. My mom hates hearing my leftovers. I can see you do too."

Tina blinked, amazed this girl had been able to read her thoughts so adeptly. "Thanks."

The girl tucked the headphones into the seat pocket. With an exaggerated sigh she plopped her hands in her lap. "So, what shall we talk about?"

Tina nearly choked. "I…"

"Whatcha reading?"

Tina turned the book over, revealing the cover: *Pride and Prejudice*.

"Is it good?"

Tina nodded.

"I like to read too, but I read slow. Found out I was dyslexic a few years ago. It's no fun, but I was glad to find out. I was beginning to think I was as dumb as everyone said."

Great. Another student who was quick to find something—anything—to blame for their—

The girl continued as if Tina had shown interest. "But I can't blame my parents for calling me that. They didn't know about stuff like that, like dyslexia."

Tina turned a page of her book.

"My name's Mallory. What's yours?"

Tina closed her book, realizing once they exchanged names there was no going back. "Tina."

"What do you do, Tina?"

The girl's manners were impeccable. They did not match the slapdash stereotype of her clothes. Tina braced herself for Mallory's reaction to her answer. Certainly she wouldn't be any more thrilled about sitting next to a teacher than Tina was sitting next to a student. "I'm a teacher."

"Really? Cool. What do you teach?"

"Communication arts."

Mallory laughed. "No wonder you like to read."

Tina stroked the book, wishing she hadn't been so quick to close it. The book seemed to be the only way for her *not* to focus on the girl in the seat beside her.

"I live in Phoenix," Mallory said. "I'm going back to school Monday. I've been visiting my grandpa. He has a lot more rules than I'm used to, but I can handle that." She grinned. "For a little while anyway."

I wish my students would have some of your attitude.

"I like Grandpa Carpelli's stories. He was overseas in World War II for two years. He didn't see my dad until he was seventeen months old." She shook her head. "Can you imagine? Just getting married and then having to be shipped off for so long? I heard in Vietnam they didn't let soldiers stay more than a year. That's better, isn't it?"

Tina shrugged. She'd never thought of it.

Mallory turned in her chair slightly, as if she and Tina were having a heart-to-heart. "But if you're fighting for something you believe in, then it's okay, isn't it? To fight, I mean. To kill. To die."

Whoa. What a question.

"Aren't we supposed to take a stand? Fight for what's right?"

I do not want to talk about this. It's way too heavy, and I'm not in the mood.

"I mean, if we truly believe something with our whole hearts, shouldn't we be able to fight for it—whether or not we're a guy?"

She wants to join the military. Tina closed her eyes and inwardly sighed.

"I'm bothering you. I'm sorry." Mallory angled her body back to the front again. "I talk too much. My dad tells me that all the time. And lately, I'm worse, as if I've got all these thoughts that need to be said out loud."

The statement was begging for a follow-up question. To ignore the girl's lead-in would be the epitome of rudeness. Tina put her book in the seat pocket. "And why is that?"

Mallory grinned, obviously thrilled by Tina's attention. "I'm completely confused about my life."

Join the club. "You want to join the military?"

Mallory straightened in her chair and tugged the jeans across her thighs. "My parents are against it. They think college is the only way and anyone who doesn't go will amount to nothing." She looked at Tina. "I don't believe people have to get a degree in order for their life to count, do you?"

"I think it helps."

Mallory looked stricken. "But I'll learn in the service. I'll learn about service. Isn't that what life is all about? Serving people the best we can?"

How could she argue? "Yes, that's true," Tina said, "but a college degree will get you a much better job, more money."

"But I don't care about money!" Mallory lifted her hands and dropped them in her lap. She lowered her voice. "That's all my parents talk about. Money, money, money. There's more to life than having a whirlpool tub and driving a fancy car."

Tina agreed completely but wasn't about to say so.

"Why would they push me toward something I don't want? I know I'm the oddball. No one understands, not even my friends. Some of them are going to take a year off and bum around. All the military means to them is a shouting sergeant and obstacle courses like you see on TV." Her face lit up. "But when Grandpa talks about the war, you can understand why people were fighting. Fighting for their country…making a difference. I feel the tug of that."

"So you want to wave the American flag? Defend mom and apple pie?"

Mallory's face was serious. The stud in her nose heaved with emotion. "Don't make fun of me."

Tina backed down. She hadn't meant to be flip. "It's unusual to find such passion in one so young." She fingered the edge of her book in the pocket. "I used to have that kind of passion."

A moment of silence. "For what?"

Tina was taken aback. How had they gotten on this subject anyway?

"Come on. Tell me your passion."

Tina's mind flooded with memories. Getting good grades, honor roll, awards—and taunts from the other kids for being smart, fat, and different. *Fatty Tina isn't lean-a...*

"I hate them."

"Hate who?"

Tina sucked in a breath, ashamed at her admission. "Forget I said that."

"Somebody didn't appreciate your passion? Is that it?"

Tina had to laugh. "You are one smart girl."

"It wasn't hard to figure out." She twisted a braid around a finger. "It still bugs you?"

Tina shook her head in shame. "I should be over it."

"Not if it's your passion." Mallory's shoulders heaved with an exasperated sigh. "And the passion is...?"

What do I have to lose? "I'm passionate about books."

Mallory's shoulders dropped. "That's it?"

"You were expecting belly dancing maybe?"

"No, but..."

Tina could see Mallory file her more exotic expectations away. "When I was in school, it wasn't cool to like to read, especially if you were homely and overweight, and your face was covered with zits, and..."

"Not much has changed."

Tina nodded. "Exactly. And that's what makes me so frustrated. I see it around me every day: cruelty, intolerance, ignorance. The uncool kids getting ripped and—"

"And every time you see it happen, you feel like it was you, all over again."

Tina's mouth dropped open.

"That's it, isn't it?"

Tina pulled her purse from the floor and used her ChapStick. She didn't need to, but she did anyway.

"Hey, I didn't mean to upset you."

Tina tossed her purse on the floor and nudged it under the seat with a toe.

"Don't be mad."

Tina shook her head and managed a laugh. "I'm not mad. I'm just surprised…at myself. Why have I just revealed my insecurities and inadequacies? Nothing like making a fool of myself to a student."

"A seatmate."

Tina accepted Mallory's smile—and didn't even mind the nose ring. Much. "Right. A seatmate."

Mallory nodded approval.

"You're a good listener, Mallory. For a—" She clamped her mouth closed on the word.

"For a seatmate."

"Exactly."

They both watched the blizzard taking place a few feet away. It was almost surreal, set apart from their present by a distance no greater than the thin skin of metal and fiberglass.

Mallory turned away from the snow. "Grandpa says I'm a good listener too. He says no one wants to listen to his stories anymore except me. What he went through makes me proud to be his granddaughter."

Tina felt sudden tears push behind her eyes. Tears for the girl? Or tears for the girl who was Fatty Tina, the girl who had desperately wanted to hear such words of approval herself? Or tears for the adult Tina who was suffering through her own search for purpose and acceptance? She looked at her lap until the tears retreated. "You're quite a girl, Mallory. I'm sure your family is very proud."

Mallory looked toward the icy glass of the window. "I hope so."

George wanted to die. Now. Forget about killing himself once he got to Phoenix. He wondered if the stewardess had a few dozen barbiturates on her.

He was in the middle seat of three, with a widowed woman who just loved talking to eligible widowed men seated next to him by the window. There was no God.

If the woman had been a rambler, George could have tolerated it. All he would've been expected to do was nod occasionally while she gave a monologue. But this woman was a questioner. In the five minutes they'd been seated, she'd already asked where he lived, where he was staying in Phoenix, whether he was married, and whether he had children or grandchildren.

She was in the process of showing him pictures of her grand-child Willy (or was it Milly or Tilly?) when the man seated to George's left intervened.

"Excuse me? Don't I know you from somewhere?"

George studied the fortyish man with black hair and a beard. "I don't think so. You don't look familiar."

The man nodded toward the woman and winked. "Why, sure I do. Didn't you belong to Lincoln Country Club?"

It only took George a moment to catch on. "Yes! Yes, I did!" George angled his body toward the man, leaving the woman holding the family photos in her lap. Once his face was turned away from her, he whispered, "Thanks. You saved me."

The man laughed and whispered back, "I've needed saving a few times myself."

George couldn't risk even a glance at the woman beside him. "I've determined all widows have widower radar. Either that or someone stuck a Single Old Fool sign on my back without me knowing it."

The man laughed and held out his hand for George to shake, keeping it close to his chest so the woman wouldn't see. "Henry Smith, at your service."

"George Davanos. I owe you one." He looked the man over and noticed him wringing his hands. "You nervous about something?"

"I don't like to fly. I *have* to fly all the time for my job—I'm a salesman—but I hate it."

George leaned back in his chair as much as he dared without opening himself up to the old hot-to-trot beside him. "It doesn't bother me. The wife and I traveled a lot before…" He shrugged.

"When did she die?"

He decided to give the shortened version. "Seven months ago. Cancer."

"I'm sure she'd be pleased to see you moving on, traveling without her."

George slapped the armrest between them. "But I'm not moving on!"

Henry edged away from him, and George reined in his anger. "Sorry. But what you said…that's what our daughter has been trying to get me to do, and it galls me big time. I don't want to move on without Irma. We were married fifty-seven years and knew each other a dozen before that. She was my life. And without her I've got no reason for living another—" *What am I saying? Shut up, you old fool! Don't give yourself away.*

Henry's voice was soft. "You shouldn't talk like that."

"Yeah? Who says?"

Henry studied the man's eyes. They were hard and determined. *Lord, give me the right words.*

George jabbed a finger into Henry's arm. "Answer my question. Who says I don't have a right to talk about dying? About moving on in the ultimate way so I can be with my wife? I've had a long life. A good life, though I have to admit there are a few things I'd do differently. Nobody but me has a right to tell me how to live the last of it."

Henry drew in a breath, hoping wisdom would come with it. "It's not up to us to choose the time, George. It's up to God."

George flipped a hand. "God schmod. He and I aren't on the same wavelength since He decided to take Irma from me. We weren't doing anything wrong. We were living a good life. There was no reason for Him to break us up like that. Didn't He have anything better to do than mess with us?"

"Why do bad things happen to good people?"

"Exactly." George squinted one eye and wrinkles formed a star burst at the corner. "If you've got an answer to that one, Mr. Henry Smith, I'll forget my plans and marry this husband hunter next to me."

Henry's stomach contracted. "Your *plans?*"

George banged the palm of his hand into his own forehead. "Now I'm a dumb fool!" He pointed at Henry. "Why can't I keep my mouth shut?"

Henry decided it was time for bluntness. "Are you really planning on suicide?"

George blinked once, then lifted his chin as if he were telling Henry he'd just won first place in a contest. "Sure am."

Henry did his own blinking, trying to blink the knowledge away. *Now what?*

Do what you do best. Sell to him. Sell him on life.

Henry shook his head, wanting the idea to go away. Who was he to sell anyone on life when his own was so up in the air? So unexciting? So unfulfilling?

George slapped his leg and sat back, laughing. "You don't know what to say, do you? Talk about a conversation killer."

"Don't do it."

"Now *that's* original."

Henry's mind swam, trying to think of something profound. "God wants you alive."

This earned him a raised eyebrow. "Oh, He does now, does He?"

Hoo boy... "He does."

"And how do you know that?"

"Because you're alive right now."

George snickered. "Alive? Barely. Hardly."

You got me there. "God said 'you shall not murder.' That includes murdering yourself."

"I hate to tell you, Mr. Henry Smith, because I can tell you're a believing man, but God's not in charge of my life. I am."

"No, you're not. If you were, your wife would still be alive."

George opened his mouth to speak, shut it, then opened it again. "I—"

A male voice came over the speaker system. "Attention, ladies and gentlemen. This is your captain speaking. As you may have noticed, we've had a slight delay in takeoff. It seems we continue to have a weather problem. We'll keep you informed."

George clapped his hands together once and glared at Henry, triumph in his eyes. "See? None of us are in control. None of us. Chaos reins."

Henry looked out the window where snow buffeted the glass. He could barely see the terminal. Maybe George was right. Chaos ruled outside the plane—and inside too. If he was honest with himself, what he really wanted to do was hide in a corner where he didn't have to deal with bad weather, air travel, suicidal seatmates, or the turmoil in his own heart. In fact…

I have to get out of here! Now.

Henry unbuckled his seat belt and began to stand.

George tugged at his arm. "Hey. Where you going?"

"I have to leave. I can't be here. I'm not supposed to be here!" Henry saw the panicked eyes of the widow by the window. He took a step into the aisle and reached for the overhead bin. A flight attendant hurried to his side, her arms waving.

"Sir! You'll have to sit down."

He shook his head, an absurd fear welling up inside him. "I have to go. I have to get off this plane. I have to—"

"You have to take your seat and wait like the rest of us. We have delays like this all the time. There's nothing to worry about. The captain has everything under control and he—"

George raised a finger and interrupted. "You're wrong there, miss. According to Henry here, God's the one in control."

The woman looked at Henry with new understanding in her eyes. *She thinks I'm a religious fanatic.*

Her voice became patronizing, as if he were a deranged sicko who needed talking back from the edge. *Hey, I'm not the one who wants to kill myself; George is.*

She smiled and continued her placating monologue. "Take a seat, and I'll get you a glass of water. You'll feel better then. Would you like a pillow? Or a blanket?"

Henry looked around the cabin. All eyes were on him. Some were puzzled as if they, too, wondered if they should be asking to get off; others looked disgusted, as if they resented having to witness a lunatic. A few showed compassion. Perhaps doubt seeped into their sanity too?

He allowed the flight attendant to direct him back into his seat while George pulled him from the side.

The attendant watched until he buckled his seat belt. *That's it; strap yourself into the straightjacket like a good boy.* "There now. That's better. I'll be right back with your water."

Henry looked at his lap rather than the eyes of those closest to him. He saw George's wrinkled hand pat his. "There, there now, Henry. It seems that of the two of us, you're the one needing the help."

Henry couldn't argue with him. He folded his arms around his chest, feeling suddenly cold. And with the cold came the feeling God was very far away.

It scared him to death.

Three

Listen to advice and accept instruction, and in the end you will be wise. Many are the plans in a man's heart, but it is the LORD's purpose that prevails.

PROVERBS 19:20–21

1:55 P.M.

Roscoe Moore pointed to the worry line between Sonja's eyes. "It's gotten deeper."

She laughed nervously, looking at her watch. It was already forty minutes past their scheduled takeoff time. "Yeah, well, hearing we have a problem with the flight tends to do that."

Roscoe shrugged. "Let it go."

"Huh?"

"Don't worry about things you can't fix. And you and I certainly can't fix the plane's problem or the weather."

"The question is, can they?"

"The question is, why was Sonja Grafton worried before there was trouble with the flight?"

"You're not going to let me out of this, are you?"

"Nope."

Sonja studied him a moment. His looks were handsome but not hunky, his grooming impeccable but not showy, his voice vibrant but not pushy. She had the absurd notion she could tell him anything, and he would understand—and maybe even advise. She could use some advice.

"Do I pass muster?"

She felt herself blush and looked away. "I didn't mean to stare... I was just—"

"Sizing me up? Determining whether or not you could trust me?"

She laughed. "You're good."

"Listening is my job."

"What do you do?"

He shook a finger at her. "Uh-uh. You first, Ms. Grafton."

"This isn't fair."

"Tough. Spill it. With the delay, all we've got is time."

The possibility that Roscoe could help made her stomach quiver in anticipation. Maybe it was a good sign. Maybe her trip would be a breeze. She took a cleansing breath and began. "I'm worried because I finagled my way onto this plane, this trip."

"Finagled?" His right eyebrow raised.

"It's a good word."

He smiled. "But not the most precise one?"

She rubbed her forehead, hiding her eyes from his for just a moment. *He* is *good*. She put her hand down. "How about...schemed?"

He rubbed his hands together. "Ooh, the plot thickens."

Suddenly, Sonja got cold feet. To admit out loud what she'd done...

"You did it to get ahead in your company, right?"

"How did you—?"

He shrugged. "That's the reason for corporate intrigue, isn't it? Getting ahead? Leaving others in the dust?"

"I'm not leaving—" She thought of Geraldine back at the office, definitely in the dust. She sat up straighter. "What's wrong with trying to get ahead?"

"Nothing. Nothing at all. But at what cost?"

"It's not costing me anything."

He waved a finger at her forehead. "Except some worry lines."

She ironed them but knew as soon as she removed her finger, they'd spring back. "You're a man. You wouldn't understand."

"I'm a black man. Believe me, I understand."

Sonja had never thought of that. "Maybe you do."

He put a hand on her forearm. "Listen, Ms. Grafton, you don't need to confess anything to me. I've been there. And I've probably done that."

"You've—" she smiled—"finagled things to get ahead?"

"I was one of the finest finaglers in Phoenix."

"Did it work?"

"Yes. Very well."

She blinked.

"That's not what you expected me to say, was it?"

"Actually, no."

"Finagling—scheming—does have its moments." He shook his head, as though something weighed heavy on him. "But the cost, the cost is high."

"Oh, so you got caught."

His eyes were intense. "No, I didn't. I rose to the top of the company, became its president. Had an office suite right out of a movie. Four cars. A house so big we didn't have to see each other if we didn't want to. Vacations whenever I wanted."

"Sounds good."

"It was—as the world defines good."

"What other definition is there?"

He sat silent a moment, and Sonja watched his own worry line etch its way between his eyes. Then it faded and he looked up. "There's God's definition."

She sighed inwardly. She didn't need a sermon. She thought Roscoe could really help her.

"Don't turn off the ears because I said the *G*-word, Ms. Grafton."

"I'm not."

"You are." He pointed at her eyes. "Watching your reaction…it's like I saw little shades being pulled down in order to keep out the light."

"I didn't—"

"But He is the Light. You don't want to keep Him out."

"I'm not—"

"I'm not judging you. I can only judge myself. All I know is when I was at the pinnacle of my success, my blinds were the blackout kind. All I wanted to see was what I could get from the world. Gimme gimme more more. It didn't matter what people said, what warnings I received. I was content on my side of the blind. Not even my wife could get through to me, though God knows she tried."

"So what happened to change things?"

"Our little boy was killed."

She drew in a breath, not expecting anything so awful. "That's terrible. I'm so sorry."

He looked at his lap. "Yeah, me too."

"What happened?"

Roscoe put a hand to his mouth as if he wanted to cover the words. "I backed over him."

Sonja couldn't restrain the shock. "What?"

"I'd stopped home one evening—I did a lot of 'stopping home' back then, and I was in a hurry to get back to work. Eddy was play-ing in the driveway on his tricycle." Roscoe's hands jerked toward his ears as if he wanted to cover them. "I can still hear the thud, the crunch. His scream."

Sonja put a hand on his arm. "I can't imagine."

Roscoe closed his eyes. "You wouldn't want to." It was an acci-dent." It was a true statement that sounded incredibly lame. "An accident that could have been prevented if I had my priorities straight, if I had my focus on my family instead of my finances and fame." He opened his eyes, and she could sense the effort it took to clear them. "After Eddy died, I looked at everything—I mean, *everything*—in my life and found it wanting. What was I working for if not to make a better life for him and my wife?" He shook his head. "My wife had warned me, but I didn't listen. You should meet her sometime…quite a woman. *Quite* a woman." His eyes locked on to Sonja's. "Listen to me now, Ms. Grafton. Don't let your focus on getting ahead force you to ignore what is right in front of you."

"But I don't have a family. There's just me. The shortcuts I take now won't hurt—"

"They'll hurt *you!*"

Roscoe's voice had risen. They both looked around to see who heard. A few people glanced in their direction but quickly looked away.

Roscoe took a deep breath. When he spoke, his voice was normal. "You might gain material, visible success, but what you lose, Ms. Grafton…what you lose is more precious than any of that. 'A good name is more desirable than great riches; to be esteemed is better than silver or gold.'"

Then it hit her. *Good name? Have I ruined my good name? For what? A few days in Phoenix?*

Roscoe slapped his hands against his thighs. "Things are different now; *I'm* different."

"Do you still have the business?"

He shook his head. "Sold it. Now I work with poor kids, helping them stay in school and on track. I help them pinpoint their talents and strengths and find jobs. My wife, Eden, works with me." He laughed. "We live week to week. We sold the big house, the cars…"

"You gave it all up?"

"I gave up a few things and gained my soul."

A thought burst through Sonja's lips. "But since you *had* things, it was easier for you." She looked away. "I mean, you got to experience success and wealth. It probably was easier for you to give it up than for someone like me who's never had any of it. My office is a six-by-six cubicle, and my car is held together by rust and dust."

"It's been said, 'It is easier for a camel to go through the eye of a needle than for a rich man to enter the kingdom of God.'"

"I don't get it."

"People who are rich—whether in regard to money, talents, or even intelligence—tend to depend on themselves."

"What's wrong with that?"

"Everything."

Sonja looked out the window of the plane. The snow tatted against the glass. The reality of its properties was a fact she could understand. Roscoe was talking gibberish.

She felt his hand on her arm again. When she turned toward him, his eyes were soft with sincerity. "Ms. Grafton—Sonja—please hear me. I know you're not comfortable with my God talk. But you've got to know that God's Son, Jesus, died for you—for all of us who mess up and finagle." He smiled. "He's taken the hit for our bad doings. And if we believe in Him, we'll live forever. Sounds like a good trade to me. A little faith, a little surrender, while gaining heaven."

Oh, please.

Roscoe nodded as if he sensed her reaction. He turned forward in his seat. "Just think about it. I know such decisions don't come easy. I must have heard a hundred times what I just told you before I let it sink in. And if it weren't for Eddy's death, maybe I'd still be in that fancy office, finagling my brains out and losing my soul."

"But I—"

He raised a hand, stopping her words. "I know. I know every thought you're thinking. And go ahead and think them, Sonja. Think them hard. But don't make God do something drastic to get your attention. Don't make Him reach down and shake you. Look up, away from the world, for just a moment. That's when you'll see Him, waiting there for you." His words caught in his throat. "You'll see Him. I promise." Suddenly, Roscoe unbuckled his seat belt and stood. "If you'll excuse me…"

He headed toward the lavatories, leaving Sonja alone.

Or was she alone? Was Roscoe right? Was God waiting for her to acknowledge Him? Wanting her to relinquish control?

You can do it.

She was immediately confused. Did those four words mean she could surrender to God? Or did they mean she could do it—life—on her own?

She looked up to see Allen coming down the aisle toward her. She shoved the decision into a corner of her mind and applied a smile.

"How you doing back here, Sonja?"

"Fine."

"Bad luck, having the delay and all. Less time in Phoenix."

She shrugged.

He took a second look at her. "You look upset. You nervous?"

She shook her head, wishing her emotions would leave her face alone. "I'm fine. I've got everything under control."

He hesitated a moment before turning to leave. "Good. I'm glad someone does."

Sonja watched him go. Control…she had everything under control?

She flipped the doubt away, thought about bringing the reflections of God out of their corner, but decided against it. She was fine. Everything was fine. There was no reason to change now.

2:10 P.M.

The pilot's voice interrupted all conversation. "We're sorry for the delay, folks, but the weather…Mother Nature's feeling pretty wicked today. Visibility is nonexistent, and the runways are drifted. Hopefully, she'll ease off soon. Thank you for your patience."

Merry looked out the window and saw snowplows heading toward the runway. *They have to plow the runway?*

This whole thing was a fiasco. If only they could be home enjoying a normal Saturday, with Justin making a mess in the family room while he watched TV, his Goldfish crackers scattered all over the carpet. Lou would be puttering down in his workshop, making nothing but noise. And she would be doing laundry and sewing a batch of charity lap blankets for Justin's school. They wouldn't have to leave the house all day if they didn't want to. They could be snug as a bug in a rug. She'd feel safe at home. Bored, but safe.

Safe. *You didn't miss being safe until it was gone.*

Lou must have sensed her thoughts, for he reached above Justin's head and gave her shoulder a squeeze. "Don't worry, Mer. Things will be all right. Airlines have to deal with stuff like this all the time."

She was going to ask how he knew such a thing since this was only the second time he'd flown. "Don't kid yourself. It's bad, Lou. I've heard of airports being 'socked in' but this—"

"That's for fog. They do have to be able to see."

Merry tried to see the plane in the gate next to them but could only see the orange of the logo on the side. "They can't see through this."

He leaned over her to look for himself. His aftershave was woodsy, and she caught the scent of shampoo in his hair. He sat back, taking the scents with him. "Yup, you're right. It's bad. You can worry."

She laughed. "Thanks a lot."

"Don't mention it."

They both watched Justin color a picture. It was beyond odd how her family was sitting in the seats beside her on what was supposed to be a vacation to get away from them. The best laid plans…

"By the way," Merry asked, "how did you manage all this? How long have you been planning it?"

"It's amazing what you can accomplish at five-thirty in the morning."

Merry had a vague recollection of Lou's rummaging through drawers while she slept. *This* morning?"

"I couldn't sleep. I was desperate to do something nice for you." He shrugged. "Unfortunately—according to you—I chose wrong."

There was still enough anger present to prevent her from contradicting him just to make him feel better. Maybe she'd done too much of that—locking her feelings inside in order to keep the peace, saying the right words instead of the true words.

And yet…she thought of a verse Lou had made her memorize for Bible study: *"Whatever is true, whatever is noble, whatever is right, whatever is pure, whatever is lovely, whatever is admirable—if anything is excellent or praiseworthy—think about such things."* But what if the things that were true in Merry's heart were not pure, lovely, or admirable—and devoid of all nobility? Was she a bad person? Was that the truth? Thinking good thoughts was not something she could turn on like water in a faucet.

Lou was talking. "…I found your ticket in your purse and got on the computer, never imagining the two seats beside you would be vacant."

Lucky me.

"Actually, they weren't. There were no tickets available. But I wouldn't take no for an answer." He smiled as if he were proud of himself. "So I took a chance and bought two standby tickets. I even prayed two people couldn't go. I felt a little guilty about that, praying that other people's plans would be ruined so we could go." He sighed. "But here we are. God must have wanted us on this trip seated right next to you."

Or maybe you're merely an ace at pushing your will on a situation. She'd seen it before. Once Lou got something into his head, he made it happen, and they often paid for it with consequences.

"Once I printed up the standby tickets, I packed us each a suitcase and put them in the back of the van, ready to go before you even got up."

Merry touched Justin's arm. "Did you know about this?"

"Not until after Daddy dropped you off. Then he told me we were going too. He even remembered to pack my coloring book." He turned to his father. "But you could've told me, Daddy. I would've kept the secret."

Lou gave Justin a look. "Remember Mommy's birthday present?"

He turned back to his coloring. "I didn't mean to tell. It just slipped."

Booking tickets, packing. "But what did you use for money, Lou? We had to dip into the vacation fund to get my tick—" As soon as she said it, she realized what he'd done.

"I used the vacation fund and put the rest on a credit card."

The family vacation fund was being used for a family vacation a little sooner than expected. Not what she had in mind. Not at all. And now they were in debt too. "What about your work?"

He squirmed in his seat.

"You *did* tell them, didn't you?"

He took a crayon and colored a flower blue. "They weren't too happy about me taking time off, but I told them it was important."

"Lou, you shouldn't have risked your job."

He stopped coloring and met her eyes. "I'd rather risk my job than risk losing you. I'd do anything for you, Merry. Don't you know that?"

Sure. Anything except let me go.

2:15 P.M.

Tina looked at her watch. "This is ridiculous. I didn't plan this getaway so I could sit on the tarmac in a snowstorm."

Mallory laughed. "It's okay with me. I'm in no hurry to get back to school." She laughed again. "Hey, we're the same."

Not hardly.

"You don't want to be in school and neither do I. But it's worse for you."

"Why do you say that?"

"Because you're a teacher. You're supposed to be into that learning junk. Remember your passion for books?"

She let out a huff.

"But you don't like teaching, do you?"

Tina felt her cheeks grow warm. It was none of this child's business whether she liked teaching or not. It was her job.

"You're not going to tell me the truth, are you?"

Tina nearly choked. "Why do you say that?"

"You hesitated."

She looked at the girl. How could so much insight be stuck under that absurd mass of hair, makeup, and messy clothes? Mallory looked like most of Tina's students, but she certainly didn't act—

"Did I hurt your feelings?"

Tina realized she'd waited too long to answer. "Let's just say it's a little disconcerting having a kid tap into my brain."

Mallory laughed. "Don't worry; I won't stay long—mostly because I don't know what disconcerting means." She pulled at the elastic in her beaded bracelets. "So what's the truth? Do you like teaching, or don't you?"

Tina let a full breath fuel her statement. "Actually, I don't."

"Why not?"

She snickered. "I can't tell *you.*"

"Here we go again. You're thinking of me as a student instead of a seatmate. Students are not the enemy, you know."

"Wanna bet?"

Mallory snapped a bracelet against her skin. "No wonder you

hate it so much. You hate them. Us."

Tina felt herself redden. She'd gone too far. "I don't hate—"

"You must. You're the one who started the 'us' and 'them' talk. I'm not one of them. I'm me."

Tina reached out to touch Mallory's arm, then pulled her hand back. "I'm sorry. I shouldn't sound so harsh. I've just been doing a little searching lately, trying to figure out what I'm supposed to be doing with my life."

"Hey, just like me!"

Just like you.

Mallory traced a finger around the perimeter of the armrest. "Grandpa says I should pray about it—the searching, I mean—but I…I don't know much about that." She met Tina's eyes. "Do you believe in God?"

"Well…yeah."

"Do you pray?"

"Sure."

Mallory shook her head slowly. Then stopped. Now was the perfect opportunity for Tina to tell her more about God. Hadn't they talked about this very thing in church? *If we come across someone who's truly searching we need to be ready to speak.* How hard could it be to tell her God loves her, tell her God's got a plan for her, tell her God's actively pursuing her?

Tina glanced at Mallory. The girl's eyes were expectant, and with a wave of trepidation, Tina realized that Mallory truly wanted to talk about God. How rare was that? All Tina had to do was quit being such a chicken and do it. *But who am I? I don't have all the answers. What if she asks more? What if—?*

Mallory twirled a cornrow around her finger. "Does God know about…does He care about—?"

The pilot's voice interrupted the moment. "The airport has been reopened. We will be taxiing onto the runway in just a moment, though there still might be a delay due to the backlog of airplanes scrambling for position. I'll keep you informed. Again, thanks for your patience."

Mallory sighed. "I'm not very good at being patient. Are you?"

Tina shook her head. The moment to talk about God was gone. Oh well, it wasn't very nice of God to just spring it on her like that. Besides, the girl would have probably rejected her words. Nothing lost, nothing gained.

2:30 P.M.

Anthony wished he hadn't put his jacket in the overhead bin. He felt the need to clutch something soft and warm to his chest like a child holding a blankie. He was a seasoned traveler, but with the delay, and the snow, and the wind, and the—

He looked toward the window. They'd claimed a spot in line now, but the snow swirled around the wings as if a mere plane couldn't stop its rush from point *A* to point *B*. Maybe the smartest thing to do would be to give up on going today. If they took a vote, Anthony would vote to stay. But unfortunately, no one was asking him.

"Boy, you're scared, aren't you, Doc?"

Anthony whipped his face toward his seatmate. "I am not scared."

She pointed to the death grip he had on the armrests.

He let go. She laughed.

Anthony felt heat on his face. "Don't make fun of my fear, lady."

"The name's Belinda Miller, as if you care."

He didn't, but found it interesting. The name did not suit her at all. She should have been named Bertha or Gertrude or Brunhilde.

Anthony parried. "And you aren't feeling a bit nervous about the situation?"

"I may be nervous about an airplane flight, but at least I'm not scared about life in general." She shifted in her seat. "My kind of fear may save me, but your kind will kill you."

She was talking nonsense. "What are you talking about?"

"You really want to know?"

"Actually—"

"Well, I'll tell you. My shrink says—"

"You're getting therapy?" *Why does this not surprise me?*

"I prefer to think of it as counseling, but yes, I'm getting some professional help to work through a few things." She bobbled her head. "Anyway, my shrink says arrogant people—I'll leave it up to you to put yourself in that category or not—tend to be that way because they're hiding a deep-down fear they don't even know about."

He pulled his briefcase onto his lap. "I think this conversation has gone far enough."

Belinda made clucking noises.

"Stop that!"

She stopped, but even out of the corner of his eye, Anthony could see her smirk.

"You don't know me, lady."

"I know your type."

"I am not a type."

"Neither am I."

Touché.

She tapped a pudgy finger against her lips and studied him like a specimen in a cage. "If I had to guess, I'd say you're afraid of taking chances."

"That's absurd. Taking chances is how I got where I am today."

"Only to spend all your time being scared of losing everything."

Anthony looked down the aisle, wishing a flight attendant would come along and save him. Then he thought of a good comeback. "At least I have something worth losing."

Her eyebrows twitched and she looked away.

He'd hurt her. He felt bad for a moment, but then pushed the conviction away. Served her right. Who was rude to whom first? The lady had a chip—a plank—on her shoulder. Could he help it if he was the one to push it off?

He got out a report he needed to read for the convention. As their silence lengthened, he let himself relax. Maybe it was good she'd been offended. At least now he could have some peace and—

"I have a good life." Belinda's voice was very small.

He risked a glance. She was not looking at him but at her own hands, which were busy finding interest in each other.

"I'm sure you do."

"I'm a good wife and mother. And I volunteer at the homeless shelter twice a week and—"

"I travel overseas and do plastic surgery for free. It's been written up in the papers." As soon as he said it, Anthony wished he could take it back. What was he doing, trying to one-up a stranger? A pathetic stranger?

She turned her head toward him, a devious sparkle back in her eyes. "You're quite a pharisee, aren't you?"

"Excuse me?"

She laughed, shaking her head. "You don't even know what that is, do you?"

He thought about testing her on the names for the muscles but flipped a page on his report instead.

She got comfortable for her next attack by adjusting her position, pushing her hands against the armrests. He braced himself.

"I know you aren't interested, but I'm going to tell you anyway. I figure you owe me for that last barb you hurled at me. The Pharisees were a group of religious leaders who thought they were hot stuff. They did everything for show. They prayed big—and in public—and when they gave their offering, they made sure everyone knew about it. Just like you, huh?"

He hadn't planned on answering her. "I didn't call the papers about my trips. They just found out."

She nodded. "I bet."

"Now you're calling me a liar?"

She shrugged.

"You're the one who brought up your acts of charity first. Sounds a little pharisaical, doesn't it?"

She waved a hand at him. "I'll judge my motives and leave you to judge yours."

"Thank you."

"But the least you could do—if you're doing charity surgery—is help some people close to home."

"What *are* you talking about?"

"People like my grandson. He could use plastic surgery, but we can't afford it. He could use a little of your philan…philian…"

"Philanthropy?"

"Yeah, that."

Anthony hated to ask. "What's wrong with him?"

"He has a port-wine stain over half his face. Kids make fun of him, call him scab-face." She shook her head. "Ronnie acts like he doesn't care, but he does. He's only ten." She shivered. "Kids are bad enough at that age; I cringe to imagine what he'll have to go through as a teenager. My son and daughter-in-law try to make him feel all right about himself, but it's hard."

Anthony felt sorry for the kid. And it was a fixable problem. He would simply use his yellow dye-pulsed laser that was heavily absorbed by the hemoglobin that caused the red color and—

"But that's that," she said, slapping her ample thigh. "I suppose trips to Africa and Bosnia make better news than a charity case in Murfreesboro, Tennessee."

"I—"

"Oh, never you mind, Doctor Do-da. Don't let it bother your conscience one iota. We've done fine enough without you up to now, and we certainly wouldn't want to cut into your quest for fame and fortune."

"You're extremely rude."

"Probably am, but I'm too tired to get out my white gloves or raise my pinky." She let out a breath. "I guess this means we aren't going to be best friends, huh, Doc?"

"Guess so."

"So be it."

"So be it."

He went back to his report. He read the same paragraph over and over and over…

2:40 P.M.

George Davanos pretended to read a magazine. He was relieved the widow next to him had gotten the hint and remained silent. She stared out the window at the blizzard.

Actually, it was his other seatmate who concerned him. Why had Henry panicked like that? Acting as if leaving the plane were a matter of life and death?

Henry clutched the plastic cup of water the flight attendant had brought him, fingering the sides, threatening to spill its contents on his lap. He looked straight ahead, but his head was shaking back and forth as if he were repeatedly telling himself no. When one leg started bobbing up and down, making the water slosh from one side of the cup to the other, George took action.

"I assume your watch is shockproof and waterproof?" He pointed to Henry's fancy gold watch, which was worn on his right wrist and in imminent danger of a bath.

Henry popped out of his daze. "Actually, it is. In four time zones. Why?"

George closed his magazine, put a firm hand on Henry's thigh, and rescued the cup.

"What are you—?"

George pointed to Henry's leg, then the water. "I had to stop the earthquake before we had a flood."

"Oh. Sorry."

"No problem."

Henry's leg started its bounce again. They both looked at it. It stopped.

"Anything I can do to help?" George asked. "Call your therapist? Contact the National Guard? Sing you a lullaby?"

"I'm fine."

"Sure you are."

For the first time since returning to his seat, Henry looked at him. "You should talk."

George shrugged. "Yeah…well…it appears we're at an impasse, you and I. I want to die, and you're afraid to."

"I am not!"

George let Henry's ridiculous statement hang in the air. "So you wanted to leave the plane because you forgot something at home?"

Henry's shoulders relaxed. "I refuse to answer on the grounds it may intimidate me."

Now that George had been proven right, he wasn't sure what to do—or whether he wanted to do it. Talking about nothing with the widow seemed more and more appealing. But when Henry pressed a hand into his forehead as though he were restraining pain, George had no choice. "Spill it, seatmate. What got you so riled? I really resent you interrupting our delightful conversation about my suicide by having a panic attack. And here I thought I was being a fine conversationalist by keeping things interesting. It's time for quid pro quo, Henry."

Henry hesitated. "I'm not sure *interesting* is the right word. Suicide is serious business."

"Duh."

"I meant everything I said. God does not want you to die."

"Ah. That again."

"It's the truth."

"According to you." By the tilt of her head, George could tell the widow was listening, so he angled his body to cut her out of the conversation. *Mind your own beeswax, lady.* "Face it, Henry. My situation was not to blame for your surge of adrenaline, and you can't be that worried about the airline's delay." He raised a finger. "'Neither snow nor rain nor gloom of night…'"

"That's for mail carriers."

"It applies to airplanes too. You've never heard of airmail?"

Henry shook his head. "It's complicated."

"Try me."

Henry sat silent a few moments, then pointed at his water. "Can I have that back?"

"As long as you drink it." George was amazed when Henry downed the water like a troubled man downing a shot of whiskey. "Feel better?"

"Not really. But I am ready to explain myself." Henry looked at George, his eyes confused. "Maybe you can help."

"I'll do my best." But George didn't mean it. He didn't want to help. He had enough to think about without taking on someone else's problems.

"It all started last night when I nearly had a one-night fling."

George raised an eyebrow. "This is getting good."

Henry shook his head. "No, it's not. It was bad. Really bad." He looked up. "But I didn't go through with it—I came close, but stopped."

"Too bad."

Henry cocked his head, and George didn't like his scrutiny.

"You don't mean that, do you?"

George looked at his lap. "No, I don't."

"Were you faithful to your wife all those years?"

"Hey, this conversation isn't about me."

"But were you faithful?"

George's mind zipped back to the summer of 1963. A raven-haired beauty. A hot day. He shook the thought away. "Pretty much."

"You weren't."

George pointed a finger at him. "Don't go judging me—"

Henry raised his hands in surrender. "I'm not. Believe me, I'm not. I was there too. Or on the edge of there. I understand."

"Good."

"I'm not judging you."

"Good."

"Can I continue my story now?"

"Gladly."

Henry took a deep breath. "Anyway, I came close to giving in to the temptation of this woman. Even had her at the door of my hotel room when I got this sudden burst of decency and shut the door in her face."

"You get an A for ethics and an F for manners."

"But even though I'd done the right thing, I was still upset. I tried distracting myself with TV."

"That might do it."

"But it didn't. Not completely. What got me calmed down was the verse."

"The verse?"

Henry squirmed, and George guessed why. *He means Bible verse. This story is going to turn into some praise-the-Lord testimonial. Great. Just what I need. Maybe the widow still has photos to show.*

"You know the Bible that's in the nightstand of hotel rooms?"

"Sure. I use it as a coaster sometimes."

Henry's mouth dropped.

"Just kidding… Yes, I know the Bible. Sheesh, don't get so serious."

"But it is serious. It changed my life. Or at least I feel it has the potential to change my life."

"The Bible in a hotel nightstand changed your life." George shook his head. "This I gotta hear."

"I was upset about what I'd just been through—"

"I prefer a cold shower—"

Henry gave him a scathing look. *"Anyway...* I was looking for comfort, for guidance, and I opened the Bible and noticed there was a verse highlighted."

"By what? Glowing lights from heaven?"

For the first time, Henry smiled. "By a yellow highlighting pen."

"I like my version better. More drama. What did the verse say?"

"It was Isaiah 30:19–21."

George sighed, not in the mood to be preached to.

Henry hesitated for a moment. "They were good verses about God having a plan for us. They ended with 'This is the way; walk in it.'"

"What is the way?"

"That's the part I didn't know—don't know. I've been waiting for God to give me details, to tell me what to do next. I have this enormous feeling of anticipation, as if I'm on the verge of something big." He looked at George. "Does that sound crazy...or presumptuous?"

Yes, and yes. "That depends."

"On what?"

"On what God's told you to do."

Henry raked his fingers through his hair. "Nothing! Don't you see? This feeling of anticipation has grown stronger since it happened, but there aren't any details. It's like I'm being brought to the edge of a cliff, and I don't know if I'll find a bridge there, a parachute, or be expected to fly."

"Or if you'll be pushed off."

Henry sucked in a breath, and George regretted his words. "Don't mind me. I'm suicidal."

"But I'm not!"

George put a hand on his arm. "But you're afraid…of death. You must think this 'way' has something to do with death."

"No, I don't." He lowered his voice. "I think the way will have something to do with how I'm supposed to live my life. Something I'm supposed to accomplish. I've tried to be a good person, tried to stay out of trouble, tried to be a good father and husband, but as far as doing anything huge or monumental, I can't imagine what it would be." He put a fist to his gut. "And yet the feeling is so strong."

"Hey, Henry, none of us have all the answers. None of us know the future."

"You do. You're going to take the future by the horns and—"

"Flip it over, dead."

Henry rubbed his face. "I shouldn't have told you. This conversation isn't helping either of us."

"Sure it is. This conversation reminds you that you have a distinct destiny to play out."

"God has a plan for your life too."

George shook his head. "I'll talk destiny; you can talk God. God's never given me a verse. He's never told me—in any way— what to do with my life. Guidance, even confusing guidance, is better than silence."

"Have you asked Him for guidance?"

"Why would I do that?"

"You've never prayed?"

George fingered the top of the magazine in the seat pocket. "Sure I've prayed. I was brought up praying. And don't think I didn't pray buckets when Irma got sick—little good it did."

"God said no."

He'd never heard it put so bluntly. "You could say that. God said, no way, no how, uh-uh, see you later. Don't call Me, I'll call you."

"He must have had His reasons."

George shook his head. "Can't think of a single one."

"Sometimes we don't understand—"

George laughed. "That's an understatement." He pointed at Henry. "And you are further proof. God gives you this direction, but He doesn't have the decency to tell you what it means."

"I'm sure He will. When He's ready. God is never late and never early."

"I bet you have that gem cross-stitched and hanging above the john, right?"

"It's the truth."

George had enough. "The truth is, God's confused you by making you dwell on this mysterious way. He's got you so messed up you're like a bead of water on a frying pan, jumping around, trying to get off the plane and not knowing why."

"I stayed, didn't I?"

"Only because the stewardess strapped you in. Not 'cause of anything God did to comfort you."

Henry stared into space. Then he turned to George. "Maybe He sent you to comfort me."

George laughed. "Me? Surely you jest."

Henry took in two controlled breaths. "I *am* calm now. I do feel more at ease about things."

"I can assure you it isn't because of me. Must be something in that water you drank."

Henry laughed, and the worry in his face seemed to disappear completely. "You're right; it must be the water."

Henry was relieved when the widow diverted George by asking a question about the further delay—it had been over a half hour since they'd left the gate. The snow was so thick he couldn't see the terminal. With the snow isolating them from the world, Henry felt as though they were *too* alone. Too vulnerable.

Don't get yourself worked up again. Not when you've just calmed down.

He closed his eyes and willed peace to envelop him. He did feel better after talking with George. He needed to concentrate on that. Funny how a suicidal man could help him. And in a way—though Henry had no proof—he believed George would not take his own life.

Thanks for George, Lord. And forgive my panic. The uncertainty got to me, but I'm okay now. And I'm ready for whatever You want me to do. Just give me the strength to do—

The voice of the pilot interrupted his prayer. "It's finally time, folks. Flight attendants, please make ready for takeoff."

Henry sighed. Finally. It was time.

Four

Yea, though I walk through the valley of the shadow of death,
I will fear no evil: for thou art with me;
thy rod and thy staff they comfort me.

PSALM 23:4, KJV

2:57 P.M.

Sonja Grafton looked out the window—as best she could. A fine snow blew past the plane at a near-horizontal angle. It was the kind of blizzard that would make a person bow low against the wind. "It doesn't look good, " she told Roscoe.

He leaned toward the window to look for himself. "I'm sure it'll be fine. Certainly a little wind and snow can't stop a plane this big."

"You wouldn't think so."

They spent a moment watching the snow whip around the wings. "I wanted to tell you, Sonja, I had a feeling something important would happen today. And it did."

"How so?"

His smile was both sincere and mischievous. "I met you, didn't I?"

She rolled her eyes.

His face turned serious. "I mean it. Rarely do I have such insightful conversations with my seatmates. Most people can't get past the latest ball scores. You're different...you've got substance."

Sonja felt a surge of pride. She barely knew this man, and yet

71

his words filled her up like those of a close friend. "Thanks, Roscoe. I've enjoyed meeting you too. You've given me a lot to think about."

"Can't ask for more than that." He held out his hand for her to shake.

She hedged. "This isn't good-bye; we're not in Arizona yet."

He pulled his hand back, as if catching his faux pas, and chuckled. "I guess we've been stuck here so long I forgot our journey was only beginning."

Sonja smiled with him, but something about his words struck her wrong. Her stomach clenched, and she looked out the window at the weather raging around them.

2:58:15 P.M.

Merry Cavanaugh wanted to throw up. Between the nerve-wracking delay, the horrible weather, and the confusion of her personal life… She fingered the contents of the seat pocket in front of her. Yes, there it was, the barf bag.

"You feeling okay?"

"Not really."

Lou reached across Justin, took Merry's hand, and pulled her to a kiss above the head of their son. "I love you."

Merry hesitated only a second. "I—"

She didn't have time to say more. The engines surged and the plane began its trip down the runway.

2:58:30 P.M.

"Here we go!"

Tina McKutcheon noticed Mallory grip the armrests and tense her body as if she could physically aid in the takeoff.

Tina purposely crossed her legs and acted nonchalant, hoping it would reassure the girl. Any second now they would be airborne, and her vacation could really begin. She was tired of talking, of thinking, of doubting.

A few seconds later, Mallory looked to Tina, her eyes intense. "Isn't this taking a long time? Shouldn't we be in the air by now?"

Tina felt a twinge of fear. It *was* taking a long—

The plane lifted a few feet but seemed hesitant, like a hand on the ground was holding on. It lifted a little more but felt heavy.

"What's happening?" Mallory grabbed Tina's arm.

Tina grabbed back.

2:58:50 P.M.

Anthony Thorgood braced his feet on the floor as the plane struggled to gain altitude. The nose was up sharply as if straining to touch the sky. "This isn't good."

He looked to Belinda, who had her eyes clamped shut. She started shaking her head, repeating a mantra that mimicked the truth that had shot into Anthony's heart: "We're going down, we're going down, we're going…"

Anthony looked out the window and saw buildings much too close. *Oh, dear God. No! It can't be!*

But it was.

2:59:01 P.M.

So much for suicide.

The nose of the plane strained toward the sky. The engine battled. The plane shuddered. An overhead bin popped open, spilling its contents. *We're not going to make it. We're going down.*

People started to scream. George Davanos looked to his right.

The widow had her eyes closed, her lips moving in prayer. He looked to the left. Henry was doing the same.

Oh well, if you can't beat 'em...

He reached for his seatmates' hands. Their eyes opened for an instant, then closed in recognition of their bond. They gripped each other, holding on to life, their hands intertwined.

Just like their prayers.

2:59:04 P.M.

Henry Smith felt the plane stall. And he knew...

He sucked in a breath.

Lord, be with us. Help us!

The tail of the plane slammed hard, propelling his legs into his chest.

Crunching. Scraping. Wrenching apart. Screams melded together in a unified explosion of fear. A baby wailed. Henry's mouth was open, but he couldn't hear his own scream above the scream of the plane trying to survive.

An instant of relief.

He took a breath. His eyes shot open. *I'm alive! That wasn't so—*

The scraping sound had stopped. The screams fragmented as hope made one last, valiant—

Piercing wind stung his face. He saw sky. *No! No! We're breaking ap—*

The front of the plane fell away and left them behind. Snow needled Henry's face.

Is that water?

The tail section hit. The impact tore through him. The plane slid.

Grinding metal. Ripping skin. Rushing water.

Searing cold.

Pain.

And horrible silence as death laughed.

Five

"Rise up; this matter is in your hands.
We will support you, so take courage and do it."

EZRA 10:4

2:59:10 P.M.

Tina's boyfriend interrupted his work on the computer long enough to glance at the clock. 2:59. She had probably landed in Arizona by now. It was odd that so much of David's future was riding on a trip *he* wasn't even taking. If only she had reacted favorably to his proposal this morning. What was wrong with her? Why couldn't she accept the fact that he loved her and adored her. It was hard being soul mates with someone when she didn't even know it.

Suddenly, a horrible feeling of dread gripped his insides like a hand grasping out of a grave for air. He buckled over, his hands making fists at his midsection.

One word formed in his brain, a word as big as a billboard: Tina!

Was something wrong? Had something happened to her?

David closed his eyes, seeking clarification. But there were no handy visions or images to explain away his dread. Just a feeling...

He found himself holding his breath and letting it out, nearly gasping for fresh air.

He shivered and said a prayer. *Keep her safe, Lord.*

He forced his hands back to the keyboard. They were shaking.

2:59:22 P.M.

"Flight 1382? How do you read?"

Silence. Again.

The air traffic controller had called for the plane three times with no answer. He looked to the screen. The blip that represented the plane was gone, and there was no answer. That only meant one thing.

"Oh my…" He flipped a switch that connected him with the emergency broadcasting system. "Attention! We have a disaster involving an aircraft…"

Air!

The freezing water sent Henry's body into instant panic. He flailed his arms, seeking the surface, but as the tail section dropped, he dropped with it.

I'm gone.

Then suddenly, the tail twisted and Henry was propelled to the top of the water. He gasped for air, bracing himself for yet another wrenching. But the contorted plane stopped moving with a final yank that ripped through him.

He opened his eyes and fought to get his bearings. His upper body was above the water. He tried to move his legs, but they didn't cooperate. They were heavy with his wet shoes, and numbed by the biting, icy cold. Cables and jagged metal bound him like evil hands keeping him captive.

With another jolt, the tail section adjusted itself. Henry dropped a few inches deeper in the water. He snatched the torn edge of the plane and wrapped his arms around the serrated metal at eye level. He tasted blood and risked letting go with one hand to check his head. His hand came back bright red.

Lord, help!

The snow stung his face. He squinted and saw a mangled tennis racket floating by. A child's shoe. Such chilling symbols of what was alive a few moments before; *who* was alive.

Hold on. Just hold on. You're alive. Just hold on.

He had to get oriented. He looked around. The rest of the plane was gone with bubbles marking its place in the river. Chunks of debris spotted the water, mixing with the ice: insulation, luggage, a maga—

Screams!

He tried to see through the snow. The screams weren't coming from the water. There were dark images through the blizzard. Dots of color. Movement? Cars and people?

He remembered the first impact. Had the plane hit a building? His mind shivered, just as his body lost its ability to do so.

"Hold on!" the voices called.

He didn't need to be told twice.

Sonja opened her eyes and realized she was under water. So dark. So cold.

Her lungs threatened to burst. She was still buckled in her seat, which had become a cushioned anchor holding her down. She managed to push the release button and set herself free. She had to choose a direction. She swam toward the light, her shoes like weights yearning to find the floor of the river. She forced her legs to move, to propel her away from the dark.

There was no more air. Her lungs constricted, hunting for every last atom of fuel. Suddenly, she burst through the top of the water. She tried to see, but her eyes were blurry and stung with jet fuel. She rubbed them. Her forearm rejected the pressure. Was it broken? "Help? Help!" The words came out in pitiful bursts of breathiness.

"Here!"

She looked over her right shoulder. A bearded man held onto the wreckage of the tail section. She swam toward him as best she could. He extended an arm. She got a hold, and he awkwardly pulled her close, making the water surge onto his chest and face.

She lunged for the plane. Her hand stuck to its frozen metal and she pulled back.

"Grab it!" he told her.

She had no choice. She took hold of the plane, feeling her skin meld to its iciness. The chattering of her teeth echoed in her ears like an inner jackhammer.

"Sirens…"

Sonja turned toward a woman's voice. A few feet away, an older woman wearing a bright magenta sweater held on to the plane, her head barely out of the water. Her eyes turned toward the sound.

Sirens wailed in the distance, and Sonja saw people running down the slope of the river toward its edge. Their voices carried over the water. The silhouette of a parking garage could be seen, the top level punctuated by flames. A sign advertised a car rental company: Rapid Rentals. *Did we hit that?*

"Hold on!"

"Help's coming!"

With a jolt, Sonja let hope enter. But as she looked at the shivering people nearby, she knew it wasn't over.

If they didn't get out of the water soon, they'd be dead.

Anthony came to under water. His mind flit past the denial of *this isn't happening* and zoned in on the facts.

Crash. Water. Breathe.

But he couldn't breathe. He propelled his arms downward, keening toward the light above. He saw legs dangling in the water. Life.

He swam toward it.

Even as she swam—even as Merry reminded herself that she didn't know how to swim—an irrelevant thought came front and center.

When I get home, I really should take some swimming lessons with Jus—
Justin! Lou!

Suddenly, she sensed more than saw a form beside her. She reached out and felt flesh. She grabbed on, finding an arm. It was a small arm. A child's arm... With a surge of purpose, she burst through the top of the water, dragging the child with her. Her mind screamed the prayer, *Please let it be Justin, please—*

She sucked in frigid air and pulled the child's head above water. Justin's eyes opened for a moment. "Mommy...help." His eyes closed. She struggled to hold his head above water, as well as her own. She couldn't do this long. She needed to hold on to some—

The tail of the plane loomed before her, its happy orange logo an indecent splash of normal like a birthday cake at a funeral.

"Grab on!" The voice came from a woman with very short hair plastered to her head like a sticky red-and-black helmet. *Blood and jet fuel?* She yelled from the jagged fuselage and held out a hand.

Merry took it and let herself and Justin be pulled toward the plane. The woman took Justin's other side while Merry grabbed hold of the plane, the cold biting into her fingers. A life vest floated by. She yelled to the other woman, "Hold him a minute!" Merry grabbed the life vest and, with the woman's help, got it on her boy. Her hands barely worked, her fingers thick and useless. She fumbled, yet managed to open the inflation valve. The vest came to life and Merry held on to the plane with one hand while she kept the floating Justin close with the other. She told herself to relax.

But the water wouldn't let her. Her body wanted to pull in on itself and make a ball to get warm, like Justin making himself cozy in a blanket cocoon or snuggling between her and Lou— She gasped.

She scanned the water, squinting against the snow and the sting of jet fuel. "Lou!" She needed to swim. Find him. *God, I'll do anything. Just help me find him!* She let go.

The woman pulled her back. "Don't let go! Hold on to the plane. Hold on to the boy."

"But my husband—"

"Hold on!"

Merry looked around the tail section but only saw the short-haired woman, a woman in a bright pink sweater, a handsome man, and a man with black hair and a beard. *Where are the others?*

Suddenly, another woman popped through the surface of the water, gasping for air.

The cold air both relieved and seared Tina's lungs. She coughed the water away.

"Over here!"

She turned in the water and saw six people clinging to the tail section. But where was—?

"Mallory! Where's Mallory?"

The people ignored her question, leaning out into the water toward her. "Come on. Grab hold!"

The handsome man got her arm and pulled her close, grimacing as if the action caused him pain. A woman in a pink sweater helped until Tina hooked a hand over the ragged edge of the plane. Icicles hung from the survivors' hair. Their skin had a bluish cast like the Lladro figurines she coveted but could never afford. The little boy in a life vest appeared to sleep, his head lolling against the vest.

This was all?

But Mallory was in the seat beside me. Tina whipped her head, once again looking for the girl. "Mallory!"

"Save your strength, lady. Help's coming."

She looked to the shore where people scurried around, tying things together, trying to create a makeshift lifeline. They were pitiful extensions across the expanse that separated them from safety. And then Tina knew.

"We're going to die."

What scared her the most was that no one argued with her.

He woke to darkness and cold and wet.

I'm under water!

The cold constricted every part of George's body, an icy vise that pushed inward so he couldn't move. He found himself still in his seat.

That's it. Just sit here. You wanted to die, didn't you?

He looked toward the light above him. His bursting lungs forced the issue. *Not now. Not yet.*

He pushed the button of the seat belt with a leaden finger. It released him to the light. But it wouldn't be that easy. His left leg hung like a useless rudder. The muscles of his arms burned at the effort. *Almost there…almost—*

His hands broke the surface, but his head met opposition. Something was in his way. He scraped at it and jabbed, desperate for air. The block of ice relinquished the space and floated aside. He burst through the surface and gasped. The snow bit his face, feeling like salt in the wound of his frigid skin.

He frantically grappled for something to hold on to. A suitcase came close, but when he tried to grab it, it sank. He saw the tail section of the plane twenty feet away. He treaded water and made a decision to reach it. But twenty feet…it could have been twenty miles due to the sluggish way his body moved and the dead weight of his injured leg. He had to stay where he was. A piece of the fuselage floated close, and he clung to it.

Odd how a piece of the very plane that had betrayed him might save him now. A man who had wanted to die, but whom God had chosen to live?

3:07 P.M.

Upon getting to work at River Rescue, Floyd Calbert popped the back of his coworker's head as he passed his chair. "Seems we're going to be grounded today, eh, Hugh?"

"Unless you want to play Santa Claus. Hey, maybe we'll be lucky and have a quiet shift."

"Sounds good to—"

The red phone rang. Hugh reached it first. Floyd watched his face turn ashen. Hugh hung up and stood in the same motion. His face stared out the window at the snow. "A plane's down. In the river."

"Down?" Floyd joined his stare out the window, knowing what they were being asked to do. "But we can't go—"

"We've got to. They said it's hard for rescue vehicles to get through. The plane hit a parking garage. The highway next to the river has traffic backed up. They're trying their best, but we've got to do the same. There are survivors in the middle of the river. Even if the rescuers had boats, the ice floes would get in the way. And the current... No one can get to them."

Floyd shivered. "Except us."

Hugh looked at him, his face pulled with concern—and fear. "Except us."

Reporter Dora Roberts knocked and entered the office of the news editor in one motion.

Her boss looked up. "Hey, I thought you were going to Phoenix."

"There's been a plane crash. It hit a building. It's in the river."

"Go!"

She went.

3:27 P.M.

How long had they been in the water? Henry pried open a frozen eyelid and looked at his watch. Nearly a half hour. How much longer could they last?

Not long.

The other male survivor nodded to the shore where dozens of people were scrambling about, getting nowhere. "At least we're going to die with an audience."

Henry wanted to laugh but couldn't find the energy or the charity. *Why hadn't someone come to help?*

The survivors around him slipped in and out of consciousness, and it took extreme effort for him to remain awake. Yet maybe they had the right idea…just fall asleep and let death take—

Stay awake.

He didn't question the inner urging. Henry suffered a deep breath and willed himself to live.

At least for now.

3:28 P.M.

George heard the sound of a helicopter. He looked up and saw it come closer, a lifeline dangling from its body.

Thank you, God!

With all his energy he waved at it, sinking in the water every time he sacrificed a hand from the job of staying afloat. But it moved past him to the tail section.

They're not going to see me!

It would serve him right.

Floyd could tell that Hugh was having trouble keeping control of the helicopter in the blizzard. Their jobs at the River Rescue usually dealt with rescuing summer boaters. They'd never been out in a blizzard before.

Floyd yelled at Hugh from the open door, his body craning to see through the snow. "I see a kid. Go after the kid!"

"Roger."

Hugh brought the helicopter over the tail section, angling the open door toward the child. It fell next to a man with a beard. He looked up at them expectantly, but instead of wrapping it around himself, he passed it to a woman with blond hair, the one holding on to the child. At his nudging, she took it. He helped her wrap it around her torso, looping it under her arms. Then she pulled the boy to her chest. He seemed to come to and weakly lifted his arms around her neck. The man said a few words to the woman, she nodded, then he looked up to the chopper and waved.

"Go! Go!" Floyd said.

Hugh pulled up and they watched as the man guided the woman and boy away from the twisted fuselage into the air. The two appeared to be glued together. Floyd prayed they stayed that way. The helicopter raced to shore. "Hold on, you two…we're almost there."

The wind and snow stung Floyd's face, and he couldn't imagine how cold the survivors must be. *And they won't be survivors much longer if you don't hurry and get them out.*

As they neared the shore, Floyd was relieved to see so many people ready to take hold of the woman and the boy. Everyone wanted to help. But their actions were agonizingly slow in the slippery snow and cold, and the coordination of so many was awkward.

Floyd cupped his hands. "Come on. There's more out there. Give me back the line."

Someone looked up and dedicated himself to getting the line free.

"Clear!"

George heard the helicopter come close again. Was he getting a second chance?

He waved furiously. *Come on, see me, see me! I'm all alone out here.*

The helicopter hesitated from its flight toward the tail section and turned toward him. His heart raced with appreciation.

George grabbed the line, the roughness of the rope cutting his brittle skin. He held on to it, but the man standing in the open chopper shook his head and waved his arms. "No! Around. Put it around yourself."

A glimmer of logic entered his brain, and George realized he had to move into the hoop of the lifeline. Once he did so, he nodded he was ready.

"We gotcha."

George felt himself being lifted, and the river sucked at him, trying to get him back. *Help me, God.*

The blizzard swirled around him, the wind caused by their movement freezing his skin on contact. The pain intensified as his arms and shoulders rejected being asked to use frozen muscles.

Hurry, hurry, hurry. I can't hold—

He heard shouts all around him, reminding him of his football days. Voices of support, urging him on.

"You're almost there!"

"Hang on!"

"Come on, come on, you can do it."

He tried to see the source of encouragement, but his eyelids had frozen shut. Then the words of comfort became action, and he felt arms encircle his legs, then his body. And his weight was lifted up and held strong and fast.

"Let go. You can let go now."

He told his hands to let go of the rope's loop, but they would not respond. Someone pulled the lifeline away and he was free of it. Free of the bitter wind, the greedy water, the traitorous plane.

His saviors hurried him to an ambulance, the jostling of their running sending jolts of pain through his body. But he didn't care. He could take the pain now.

Voices yelled directions. George let himself slip away to a quieter place. He didn't need to listen.

Not anymore.

Three down… As they made their way back to the tail, Floyd had an idea. "I'm adding another line."

Hugh glanced back. "But the weight. We're only meant for five under normal conditions and the weight of the wet—"

"I know, I know…but time's running out. We've got to try."

Hugh shrugged and nodded at the same time. Floyd knew the brunt of it would be on his shoulders. To maneuver in these conditions with two dragging weights was dangerous. The odds of them crashing into the river themselves…

Floyd shook such considerations away. The people had been in the water nearly an hour. That they were even alive was a miracle. He hoped God had a few more miracles in His pocket.

Anthony Thorgood had had enough. This rescue was ridiculous. From what he could see, there were only eight of them. Surely the helicopter could move a little faster to get them out. He looked around the tail section at the remaining survivors—such as they were. A man and three women, including that Belinda person. They were all drawing into themselves, their shoulders at their ears. They wouldn't last long, and who knew? Even if they got out of the water, they probably wouldn't survive.

But he would. He was not going to die.

Take your chance!

He mentally nodded at the order and planned to do exactly that.

The helicopter positioned itself overhead and dropped the line to the other man. *Why do they keep giving it to him?* But as the man caught the rope, he handed it to the woman with bloody short hair.

Idiot! Now's not the time to be a fool.

The woman took it, and Anthony felt a surge of disappointment. But then, suddenly from the sky, another lifeline fell. The man caught it and again handed it toward the others. But it was caught by the wind and bobbled over their heads, landing in Belinda's range. She reached for it. But when she fumbled the line, when it moved past her to the space within Anthony's grasp, he grabbed hold.

There was a moment's hesitation as Belinda looked at him, her hand extended, wanting the line back. But Anthony quickly looked away and placed the rope around his body.

His adrenaline surged. "Go!"

The chopper rescuer seemed to hesitate a moment, but then Anthony felt himself being lifted. He did not look down at the water where he'd been. He did not look down at Belinda.

He was alive. That's all that mattered.

I should dump him in the river.

Floyd tried to calm his anger with the man who'd taken the line from the woman. He knew the survival instinct was strong—by necessity—but to witness such a blatant act of selfishness made his heart pump in a way that had nothing to do with the heat of the moment.

You'll get yours, buddy. People saw what you did. They saw.

Henry closed his eyes. The cold lured him toward sleep. But he couldn't give in. Such sleep would be eternal. And there were two more people to save.

To save?

The thought shocked Henry into wakefulness. Save? He needed saving too!

This is my *way; walk in it.*

The words came to him so clearly that for a moment, he wondered if they had been audible. Then he knew: They weren't words for all to hear. They were words for him alone. Words from God.

Henry sucked in a breath, ignoring the pain that came with it. In this one moment everything was clear. *This* was his purpose. *This* was his destiny. *This* was the road God had been leading him toward. The road of a plane crash. The road of man against nature. The road of life against death. The road of sacrifice.

But he still had a choice. God wouldn't force him to do it. God was big on free will. He gave opportunities; He gave chances for excellence. He gave encouragement for goodness. But God did not push. He offered.

*This is the way…*will *you walk in it?*

It was odd to hear the words formed as a question. A slice of pain shot up Henry's arm, urging him to think of himself. *Don't do it, Henry. You have a right to live as much as any of these other people do. You don't know them. You don't owe them a thing.*

The whap-whap of the helicopter cut through the air. The rotors made the wind and water blast Henry's body as it hovered above them. A lifeline was thrown. And then a second one.

Henry caught the first one.

I don't owe them, but I do owe Him.

And with a clutch to his throat, knowing full well what he was doing, once again Henry Smith handed the lifeline to the woman who should have gone the last time; the woman who had the line stolen from her.

With a look of shock she nodded her thanks and placed it around herself.

The second lifeline brushed past Henry, grabable, takeable, but he let it go, directing it toward the young woman who'd called out to Mallory. She took the line weakly.

The helicopter moved away with two people holding on to two lifelines.

Henry watched as it left him alone.

But not alone. He smiled. Never, ever alone.

"No! No!"

Floyd watched in horror as one of the women lost her grip and slipped away as she was dragged over an ice floe. The helicopter couldn't gain much altitude with the weight of two, and the victims were being towed through the water. He couldn't imagine their pain. He didn't want to imagine their pain.

"We lost one!"

And then, within seconds, the woman in pink on the other lifeline lost her grip and fell back into the water. Both lines bobbed free and useless.

"What do you want me to do?" Hugh asked.

Floyd had to make a split-second decision. *One was on top of an ice floe; the other was in the water.* "Back to the one in the water."

As soon as they reached her, Floyd could see she wasn't going to be much help. She lay nearly dead in the water, weakly gripping a seat cushion that had floated by.

"Go lower. I've got to put the loop around her."

"Put it...?"

"No choice." Floyd positioned himself in the open door, setting his feet on the skids. *Please God, please let me get her.*

As they neared the top of the water, the woman opened her eyes and her eyes met Floyd's. She nodded. There was life there. And a will to live.

Floyd held the loop of the lifeline over her, as if he were attempting a ring toss. "You have to get this," he yelled above the whir of the rotors. "Put your arms through."

He thought he saw a flash of understanding. The helicopter was only five feet above the water. Floyd balanced on the skid and tossed the line. It landed perfectly over her head. She awkwardly put one arm through, then the other, the seat cushion bobbing away. Floyd took up the slack as much as he could.

Hugh was struggling to keep control. The skid dipped toward the water, then raised. They had to go. Now. The woman looked ready, but was she?

"Okay, Hugh. Go. But go slow."

As they moved through the icy air, Floyd locked on to the woman's eyes. "Look at me! Look at *me*. We're almost there. Hold on."

As they got to within a few feet of the shore, she could hold on no longer and plunged into the water. Rescuers on shore waded in and pulled her to safety.

It wasn't pretty, but it worked.

Floyd called to Hugh. "Get to the woman on the floe."

When they reached her, the woman appeared dead. She lay on her stomach, gripping the chunk of ice like a person sprawled face first on a mattress. She appeared to be asleep.

Is she dead? "Hey! Lady!" She stirred and managed to turn her face enough to see him. "It's your turn. I'm throwing you the line."

He was shocked when she actually turned over to receive it, but her actions were the stilted movements of an old, old woman. The ice floe teetered dangerously. Floyd threw her the line, and she caught it.

"Yes!"

She slipped the loop around her torso and they pulled her up. The ice floe broke in two beneath her. They were about thirty feet from shore. "Come on; you're almost there..."

Warily, the helicopter made its way back to the shore. As they got close enough for their success to be imminent, Floyd let his thoughts race back to the one last survivor still in the wreckage. He could hardly wait to meet the man who'd handed over the lifeline three times. He had never, ever witnessed such selflessness—

Once the line was free he said, "Clear! Let's go get him."

In the far corners of his mind, Henry could hear voices, sirens, and even the helicopter. But they were of no use to him anymore. They were not of the world where he was going.

A small part of him held on to the hope that the helicopter would return in time. But as the minutes passed, Henry let even that hope slip away. A bit reluctantly at first, but then with the peaceful joy of full surrender. God loved him. God would take care of him—even in the end.

Henry tried to adjust his body against the fuselage, but his grip was slipping. His hands were like two bricks, incapable of movement. Plus, the tail was sinking, and his lungs had tightened around his heart, which beat ever so slowly like a windup toy winding down.

His heart...

My lovely Ellen...my boy, Joey. I love you.

With that final thought, the tail shifted, and Henry Smith was pulled beneath the black water.

Floyd strained to see through the blizzard. Strained to see that familiar head and torso held erect against the fuselage.

Where is he?

Hugh called from the cockpit. "Do you see him?"

"No. Go around again!"

"It's been so long, too long."

"I know, I know. Go around again. He has to be here!"

The helicopter dove and circled, making figure eights above the sinking tail section of the plane. Floyd searched the water for a body. If only they could see him floating somewhere and go down and scoop him up as they had done with the woman.

"Come on, be there." *Lord, make him be there.*

But he wasn't there. The man with the black beard was gone.

The man who'd given everything had lost it all.

But death would not win. In the final moments of his life, as he descended into the blackness of the river, Henry Smith, an ordinary man, laughed at death. And as he died, he smiled ever so slightly.

For Henry knew a secret. A secret known to him and to God: "Greater love has no one than this, that he lay down his life for his friends."

And when the final breath left his body, when death tried to grab hold of his soul, the angels of the Lord shoved death away and said, "You may not have this man. Not this special man." Then they lifted him out of the dark coldness and took him to a place where the warmth of the Father enfolded him. And then Henry heard the words he'd been longing to hear; the words that made everything perfect.

"Well done, good and faithful servant."

Six

Ellen Smith put the sack of groceries on the counter and flipped on the kitchen TV. Her attention was drawn to a special report. She stopped to watch with a carton of eggs in her hands. She'd gotten all the fixings for the best omelet Henry would ever eat. In just a few days he would be home.

A reporter stood in the midst of a blazing snowstorm, yet his parka hood was down around his ears. *Vanity, thy name is television.* Behind him was an icy river. The tail section of an airplane stuck out of the water, an awkward testament to a catastrophe. A helicopter circled overhead, whipping the water with the wind of its blades. Ellen shivered.

"God be with them."

The camera zoomed in over the shoulder of the reporter as he spoke. "Sun Fun Flight 1382 headed for Phoenix went into the water right before 3 P.M. Witnesses say it strained to gain altitude then clipped the parking garage of Rapid Rentals with the tail, the landing gear still down. It broke in two and slid into the water. The front section of the airplane disappeared immediately. Passengers were seen still strapped to their seats. The tail section fell away and landed where we see it now. Seven survivors have been plucked from the icy water by a helicopter lifeline. We are told that one remains. Witnesses say one survivor—a man in his forties with black hair and a beard—repeatedly handed off the lifeline. Now, finally, it is his turn."

His turn. She remembered Henry's words that morning. *"Bill's son is getting married. He covered for me last year when Joey graduated from high school. Now it's my turn."*

Fortyish. Black hair. Beard. Phoenix. Snow.

My turn.

"No!"

Ellen's hands flew to her mouth. The eggs broke. As did her heart.

Ellen hurried to the couch in front of the living room TV, grabbing the phone on her way. She dialed information.

"The number for Sun Fun Airlines, please." She thought of their absurd jingle, *"Come fly with us; we're having sun fun now."*

A recording gave her the number, and she realized that she didn't have anything to write with. She found a pen and scribbled on the back of a magazine. She hung up and called. It was busy. She hit redial. Busy.

She took a moment to watch the news programs, flipping from one station to another, looking for one that had close-ups of the tail section. In the meantime she took in the disaster: the flashing lights of emergency vehicles; cars on the highway; swirling snow; people on either shore, waiting, hoping, needing something to do. That was the core of all disasters. Once she'd witnessed a car accident and experienced that awful feeling of helplessness, of wanting to help but not knowing how.

Maybe it wasn't Henry's flight. He'd never told her the flight number, and there were dozens of flights to Phoenix every day.

She dialed Henry's office. Maybe they'd heard from him. Maybe he'd called from Phoenix, faithfully checking his messages, being the conscientious man she loved. Maybe—

"Cosgolds. May I help you?"

"Hi, Amy, this is Ellen Smith, can I speak to—?"

"Oh, Mrs. Smith," said the receptionist. "Have you heard any-thing yet? We've been watching on TV. It's just awful. Simply awful. We—"

She disconnected the phone with her thumb, not wanting to hear. The phone rang, sending her heart to her toes. "Amy?"

"Mom? Have you been watching the news? Wasn't Dad going to Phoenix today?"

"It's his flight."

A moment of silence. Then the sound of Joey's tears cut through her. "Ahhh… Mom, what can we do?"

She glanced at the screen. The helicopter hovered over the wreckage. "There's one man left, Joey. They said so. The heli-copter's come back for him."

"Black hair, beard…I heard. I even saw footage of him hand-ing off the line to one of the other survivors."

"Was it your dad?"

"Do you think it could be? Oh, Mom, do you really think…? If only the pictures were closer…the snow makes it blurry. They say he's handed the line off to six people. It came to him, but he gave it away. Over and over! Ahhh…if it *is* him…"

Ellen slumped in the chair, a horrid certainty flowing through her veins like acid. "It's him."

"I didn't hear—"

She cleared her throat and tried to get the words out again. "It's your father."

"How do you know?"

How *did* she know? Was her Henry the type of man who would hand off the line, letting someone else go first? Yes. Absolutely. But would he continue to do it when it was a danger to his own life?

"Don't do it, Henry."

"What?"

She blinked herself back to reality. "We have to pray, Joey. Pray that the last survivor—whether it's your father or not—is saved and is brought back to his family."

"But if it isn't him? Mom…what if Dad is already dead?"

All the tenets of their faith rushed forward like eager children wanting to be chosen to answer the teacher's question. *Death is not the end; it is a new beginning in heaven, with Jesus. God is in control.* Henry believed. His eternity is assured. Even if…even if…

"If he's already dead, we pray for us, Joey. We pray for us."

David walked past the break room at work and saw a crowd gathered around the small television on the counter. He stepped inside. "What's up?"

"Where you been, David? A plane crashed in the river. They've been pulling people out—by helicopter."

A cold rush swept over him. He pushed his way through the crowd until the television screen came into view. He saw a tail section of a plane in the water. The Sun Fun logo laughed at him.

"Tina!"

Everyone turned around.

"What's the flight number?" David asked.

"What?"

"My girlfriend… What's the flight number?" As he screamed the question, he reached into his shirt pocket and pulled out the piece of paper on which Tina had written—

"Flight 1382."

Sun Fun flight 1382. He stared at the note and mouthed the words but nothing came out.

"David? Are you all right?"

He handed the note to the questioner and bolted from the room.

As David ran for the exit, he heard the commotion behind him as his coworkers realized what had happened.

And what *had* happened?

The impossible. Tina's plane had crashed.

"Where is he? Bobby? Where's the hero?" Reporter Dora Roberts screamed at the photographer who'd come with her and pointed to the sinking tail section.

Bobby turned his 35mm to the area beneath the helicopter, adjusting the zoom. "We were so busy watching the rescue of the others that we didn't pay any attention to him."

Dora stepped closer to the water's edge, on the shore down a ways from the rescue operations. The circling helicopter told the story. "They can't find him. They've gone back for him, but they can't find him."

"No!"

The exclamation came from a couple standing nearby. The man's head was buried in his collar, a stocking hat pulled to his eyes. The woman who'd screamed was burrowed under his arm.

Dora moved close. "Did you see what happened to the man in the water?"

The woman put a mittened hand to her mouth, and Dora saw tears on her face. "I should have been watching him. But I was watching the other rescues… Oh, they *have* to find him. They have to! He gave up the line. Over and over. We saw him."

Dora agreed with every word she said. *Come on, helicopter, find the hero. Bring him home safe. We* need *him to be safe.*

Bobby moved along the edge of the water. Dora wasn't sure if he was taking pictures or merely using the zoom to do his own search. They all scanned the river, aching to help. It was growing dark, plus it was hard to see through the blizzard and chunks of ice. The blocks of white floated like pieces of glass in a church window with the blackness of the water serving as the leaded seams. Everything was gray and darker gray. The only hint of color was the logo of the plane on the tailpiece, a splash of happiness among the desolation.

A shiver coursed through Dora, and it had nothing to do with the weather. The thought of that brave man, finally realizing he would not be saved…did he feel resigned? Scared? Did he pray? Or did he merely lapse into a frozen unconsciousness until his grip loosened, and he floated down into the dark—

She shook the image away, knowing it was one that would remain with her for days—if not years. The last lonely moments of a man who had given everything so others might live. *Lord, bless him… Bless him…*

Suddenly, Bobby sprinted to the right and pointed frantically. Others closed in on him, trying to see. The chopper pilot must have seen the commotion, for he turned and hovered over the area where Bobby and the others were pointing. But as the whirring blades churned the water, the object was revealed to be a seat cushion that must have loosed itself from the wreckage below.

There was a groan from the crowd as the chopper moved back to the tail section to resume its search. But as darkness fell and the minutes passed, it was evident that the last survivor of the crash had become its last victim.

Dora's body was leaden—from the cold and from the shock of knowing the hero was gone. She felt as if she'd lost a loved one.

The woman beside her sobbed, and Dora heard sniffs from the man. Suddenly, she wondered who they were and needed to know their story. She put a hand on his shoulder.

"Excuse me…where were you when the crash happened? Did you see it?"

The man nodded and pointed up the embankment. "That

blue car there. We're hemmed in. Can't move. We were just driving by on the highway when we saw the plane struggling. We see planes come close to the highway all the time, but not low like that."

The woman's eyes flashed with a memory. "It was so loud we couldn't hear ourselves cry out."

"And it hit!" The man let go of his wife and slapped the palm of one hand into the other; his fingers tilted upward like the nose of the plane seeking the sky. "The tail just ripped into the parking garage, then the plane broke apart and fell into the water. If it had been to the north just a hundred feet, it would have landed on the highway. Maybe on us." He shook his head.

His wife squeezed his arm. "But it didn't, honey. We're safe. But the passengers… We swerved onto the shoulder, got out of our car, and raced down the embankment to help." She put the mitten to her mouth and the sobs started again.

"Can I have your names, please? I'm a reporter for the *Chronicle.*" They gave their names and a phone number. Bonnie and Ted Gable.

Mrs. Gable continued, her voice under control again. "There was so much noise. Then quiet. Unearthly quiet."

Mr. Gable nodded. "Then came the screams from the water. There was nothing we could do. Some people tied scarves and belts and jumper cables together, but with the river's current… Even if we could've gotten it long enough, we had no way to get it out to them." He shook his head. "That's the worst of it. There was nothing we could do. Nothing anybody could do for the longest time." His voice softened. "Nothing we could do…"

"Except pray."

He nodded at his wife.

Dora looked to their vehicle. It was undamaged but blocked in by other witnesses and the curious. Their nice warm car. "Why aren't you waiting in your car? It certainly would be warmer." As she asked the question, she knew the answer.

"Warmth isn't important. Not with those people out there. They were cold. And we decided we could be cold too, to support them by being here." He shrugged. "I know it seems stupid, but—"

"No, it doesn't seem stupid. It seems right. I understand, truly I do." Dora noticed how the crowd that had gathered along the water's edge had moved closer to each other, as if they were unconsciously pooling their wills and their strength to help the man in the water. Strangers stood shoulder to shoulder, touching, hugging, talking, crying, praying. Their emotions and the overpowering desire to survive bound them. Without understanding what they were doing, they had created a community out of suffering—a community *of* suffering.

Mr. Gable looked to the sky and seemed to notice for the first time that it was nearly dark. "I suppose we should try to get home."

"I suppose." Mrs. Gable sighed.

Their attention was drawn to a man, stumbling down the embankment toward the water. He slid on the snow and tumbled the last few feet. A police officer tried to stop him because he gave every impression that he was going to jump into the river, but the man shook the restraint away. He came toward Dora and the couple, his eyes focused on the water—eyes that streamed with tears.

At the river's edge, his legs buckled beneath him and Dora ran to grab his arm. "Are you all right?"

His head shook no with a rhythm that seemed to have no end. "My brother's down—" He pointed to the black water and covered his face with his hands. He collapsed to his knees. The Gables got on the other side of him and offered what comfort they could. "I have to help, have to do something. He was taking a vacation to Phoenix. A much needed vaca—"

Phoenix? Dora's heart stopped. She looked at the tail section in the water. Sun Fun Airlines. The airline she was going to use to visit her mother in Phoenix.

She felt a hand on her arm. "Ms. Roberts? Are you all right?"

Sun Fun Airlines, an afternoon flight, Phoenix. The full implications of the information raced through her mind and crashed into the wall that protected her emotions from such knowledge. "I...I was supposed to be on that flight."

The Gables and the man looked at her, their faces sharing an incredulous stare.

Dora's voice gained strength as she pointed at the tail section, jabbing the air with her finger. "That might have been me in that water!"

"Or under the water." Mrs. Gable slapped a hand to her mouth and looked apologetically toward Dora and the man who had lost his brother. "I'm sorry. I shouldn't have..."

The man stared at Dora as if she were guilty of something. Maybe she was guilty of living when his brother had died. "Maybe your brother is one of the survivors."

The man's jaw tightened. "You mean like you?"

"I'm not a surviv—"

"You're here, aren't you? You were supposed to get on that plane but fate kept you off."

"I'm so sorry." It was a stupid thing to say, but Dora couldn't think of anything else.

The man stormed away, up the embankment, as if the sight of Dora disgusted him. She turned to the Gables. "It's not my fault I didn't get on that plane. He's acting as if I did something wrong by not dying."

Mrs. Gable put a hand on her shoulder. "He's mad. Like he said, fate kept you off. You should be thankful."

Oh, she was; she was. But not to any vague notion of fate. *Thank you, Lord Jesus, for saving me.*

She'd allow herself to think of the whys of it later.

Without a word, the couple turned to leave. Dora followed. There was nothing else to do. Nothing else to say. But plenty to think about.

David drove over the speed limit when he could—which wasn't often. Traffic was terrible and grew more congested the closer he got to the crash site.

Finally, it slowed. And then stopped. He craned his head, trying to see. Horns honked. He added his to the mix and rammed the palm of his hand into the steering wheel. "Come on, people!"

But nobody moved. And after five minutes of immobility, he realized he was stuck—mentally, emotionally, and now physically—in a limbo land where nothing was certain. Nothing was known. And worse, there was nothing he could do...except...

"God, help them. Oh, dear God, help them."

If Dora heard her photographer, Bobby, say one more time, "I can't believe you were scheduled for that flight but didn't go. And to have your mother's condition be healed..." there would have been one more casualty due to the crash of Flight 1382. The guy was a broken record. Dora knew the coincidence was amazing, and she needed time to let it fully sink in—time alone. Unfortunately, she did not have that luxury, and wouldn't have, for quite some time. She had a job to do—with an angle unlike anyone else's. How ironic that her first big break in a story involved herself.

By the time Dora dropped him off at the paper so he could develop his pictures, the lobby of the hospital where the survivors had been taken was crammed with news cameras and reporters surging and vying for position in a feeding frenzy.

She drew on her adrenaline reserve and scanned the room for a friendly face, a sympathetic rival who might fill her in. She spotted Jon Cunningham, a TV reporter. Since their mediums were not in direct competition, he was a good choice. She waved at him. "Jon!"

He looked up and motioned her over. As she snaked through

the crowd, one question hummed from every island of conversation: What was the name of the hero?

She reached Jon and shook his hand. "What's the news?"

He was not offended by her lack of pleasantries. He tilted a notepad in her direction. She pulled out her own, along with a pen, and wrote as he talked. "The original survivors are Tina McKutcheon; Belinda Miller; George Davanos; Merry Cavanaugh and her son, Justin; Sonja Grafton; and Anthony Thorgood."

"You said original survivors. Have some of them died?"

"The grapevine says two, but we haven't been told any details yet."

"Anything going on back at the river?"

"We have a crew there," Jon said. "The rescuers set up searchlights, but the ice is refreezing around the wreckage. And the truth is, there isn't anyone else to search for. They've called it off." He tapped his list. "This is all there is. Was. Seven survivors, and only five of those are left."

"Out of how many on the plane?"

"Ninety-five."

"Anyone hurt in the parking garage?"

"No one. I expect some people will find their cars demolished like a pop can in a can smasher, but no one was hurt."

"That's a miracle."

He nodded.

"And the name of the hero?"

"No one knows."

Dora scanned the room. "I've got to find out. I've got to. I watched him…" Her eyes filled with tears, and she angrily flicked them away. "It's just not fa—"

"Hey! Anybody!"

All eyes turned to the area in front of the entrance. An elderly man in a navy parka pulled a chair across the floor and, with the assistance of those around him, stood on it.

"What is he doing?" Jon whispered.

Dora had no idea.

The man extended his arms and called over the heads of the media. "Does anyone know the names of the survivors? My son, Cameron Smiley, was on that plane and…" As his voice faltered, so did his legs. He was helped to the floor where he sank onto the chair, his head in his hands. News people surrounded him, offering their lists.

"Poor—"

There was a sudden wail as he learned his son was not among the living. It sliced through whatever professional restraint Dora had left. "Oh dear, oh my… Excuse—" She ran out of the gaggle of reporters and took refuge in a rest room. It was blessedly empty. She slammed the door of a stall and locked it, leaning her head against the cool metal. How could she detach herself from the pain of over ninety families, each with stories of loss and devastation? How?

The door to the rest room swung open, and Dora heard the scramble of another woman dashing for solace. The door to the next stall slammed shut. Dora heard sobs much like her own. A comrade in pain.

She touched the shared wall between them. "It's so sad," Dora offered.

"Huh?"

"Covering this crash…the people… It's so sad."

"Wrenching," the other woman said.

"To witness such pain."

"It rips me apart."

"It hurts."

The woman answered with her cries. Dora joined her.

When traffic finally started to move, it was dark, and David heard on the radio that the search had been called off. All survivors—and there were reportedly five—had been taken to Mercy Hospital. Was

Tina there? David didn't know. And the radio hadn't released any names.

At the first exit, he turned off the highway and headed to the hospital via side streets. They'd mentioned four women, a child, and two men. *Please let one of them be Tina.*

The hospital parking lot was jammed, so David double-parked and ran into the building. A group of media people filled the lobby, but David rushed by them to the front desk.

"My girlfriend? She was on Flight 1382. I need to know if she's one of the survivors."

The older woman bit her lip and looked at a very short list. "What's her name?"

"Tina McKutcheon."

Suddenly she beamed and held the list so he could see it. "She's here! She's alive."

Some reporters overheard and peppered him with questions. "You know one of the survivors?"

"Who are you? What's your relationship?"

"Tell us—"

David leaned toward the woman. "Can I see her?"

"No, I'm sorry. They're not allowing any visitors right now, but soon only immediate family, though as yet there haven't been any immedi—"

"But I'm her fiancé."

She looked at him as if she were very aware that he had just upped his status. Let her think what she wanted; he had to see Tina.

"Truly, sir, they aren't allowing anyone in to see them, but you could go up to six and wait—"

David didn't have to be told twice.

David went to the nurses' station on the sixth floor and realized he'd have to be even more assertive to break through their wall of protection around the survivors.

A redhead looked up from her computer. "Yes?"

"I'm Tina McKutcheon's husband. She's one of the sur—"

The nurse eyed him warily. "Mr. McKutcheon, is it?"

David had lied once but found this eyeball-to-eyeball scenario more difficult—but not impossible. "Yes. May I see her? Please?"

"I'm afraid not. Your wife needs a little more time before she can accept visitors. We want her condition stabilized. We're administering warm oxygen to try to slowly raise her body temperature."

"But how's she doing? Is she going to be all right?"

The nurse patted his hand. "Yes, she will. She's proven herself to be quite a survivor." She pointed to a room across from the nurses' station. "You can wait if you like. We've set up a special room for the patients' families."

David went inside. A television blared to the empty room. News of the crash assaulted him. He turned it off and sat in the opposite corner. To wait. To pray. And to give thanks for Tina's life.

George opened his eyes.

I'm alive.

Those were two simple words that voiced the ultimate declaration. *I think, therefore I am.* If only it were so simple.

The thing was, he shouldn't have been alive. Not when he'd wanted to be dead. There were so many dead who wanted to stay alive.

Sorry, Irma, I'll be a little late.

He closed his eyes but quickly opened them when memories of the crash filled the dark. He did a quick inventory of his body. To say he felt as if a truck had hit him was a comparison that was totally lacking creativity. A truck? Try a plane slamming into ice. Try waking up under water, still strapped to your seat. Try being in water so cold it nearly made your heart stop as it fluttered as fast as your shivers.

He moved his arms. Sore, but all right. He moved his legs and felt a sharp surge of pain. *The left one is broken.* He remembered kicking toward the surface and acknowledging that fact, yet dismissing it as irrelevant to that particular moment. Who cared about a broken leg when lungs were bursting from lack of air?

He allowed himself a quick scan of the horrible events, testing his memories to see what he could handle. Speeding down the runway, the plane shook like a carton of chocolate milk being made ready for pouring. It felt…heavy. They rolled on forever, never going quite fast enough. He remembered thinking that perhaps the pilot was considering aborting the takeoff. It was just a feeling, as if he'd sensed a moment's hesitation on the part of those in charge, like the scene in Hitchcock's *Vertigo* when the police were leaping from rooftop to rooftop. They'd take a run at it, relying completely on faith, luck, and speed. Yet there was always that moment of hesitancy at the edge of the abyss where they'd have to make a split-second decision to pull up or fly. If they let that hesitancy take over for a moment past its allotted time, the danger was that they wouldn't have the speed to make the jump even if they wanted to. It was that kind of decision-moment on the plane. "Do we go for it? Or back off?"

Obviously a wrong decision had been made.

George remembered taking Henry's and the widow's hands and praying just as the tail section hit, only to have their prayers answered with the terrible sound of tearing metal, scraping, fractures, screams, cries.

George whipped his head toward the other bed in the room. It was empty. After a disaster shouldn't the hospital be crammed with casualties?

Maybe you're the only one, George. Maybe God let you live, and the rest are gone. Wouldn't that be a horrible joke? Let the suicidal man be the lone survivor?

George closed his eyes against the sting of tears. *God, no. Don't let me be the only one.*

Get this thing off me. I can't breathe! Merry shuddered out of her dream as if she were shrugging off a wool coat on a hot day.

She left Justin and Lou behind, their arms outstretched, reaching for her, calling to her. Yet they were too far away. She couldn't reach—

The dream was so vivid, it took her a moment to focus on reality. She was in a bed, but not her own. There was a TV on a high shelf attached to the wall. Soft whispers filtered in from outside.

"…she doesn't know. And the doctor doesn't think we should—"

A nurse peeked in the door, then seeing her awake, came in. "Well, well. This is good. After what you've been through, we expected quite a sleep."

What I've been through?

Suddenly the dream was real. Merry bolted upright, her body screaming at the effort.

The nurse rushed to her side. "Hey now, slow down a bit. Take it easy."

Merry shook her head, searching the room. "Justin! Where is he? How is he? And where is my husband?"

"Now, now…"

"My husband. My baby. Where are they?"

The nurse pressed a call button with one hand while restraining Merry with the other. "You need to rest. There's plenty of time for—"

Merry shook the nurse's hand away, not caring about the jolt of pain that wracked her body with the sudden movement. "Where's my family?"

The nurse glanced toward the door, her hands trying to pat Merry's concern away. But when Merry caught the panic in her eyes, she knew the answer to her question. *No. It can't be. It can't.*

Another nurse rushed in, her face assessing the situation in a glance.

"She wants to know where her husband and son are," said the first nurse.

The new nurse nodded and put her hands firmly on Merry's shoulders. Then she looked her straight in the eye and said, "I'm sorry, Mrs. Cavanaugh, but your husband was not one of the survivors. And your son... I'm afraid he never regained consciousness. He passed away a half hour ago."

Merry stared at the nurses, and the nurses stared at her, waiting.

Then Merry took the deepest breath she could manage, tapping into each vein to find every vestige of air left in her body. Then she hurled it out of her mouth, melding it into a wail that emptied her heart.

The nurses backed away, unwilling witnesses to the death of a wife and mother.

Sonja smelled the starch of fresh linen. She loved when Mom changed the sheets. But she hated her mother's choice of music. Elevator music.

Sonja opened her eyes and pulled her hands to her face to rub the sleep away. One forearm was in a cast.

What?

This didn't make any sense. The last thing she remembered was getting coffee at the airport, calling her parents, and—

A sudden rush of images flashed. The concerned eyes of Roscoe Moore in the seat beside her, the ice on the wings, the way the seat in front of her shook as if they were on an old-fashioned roller coaster. The sight of her own hand bracing against that seat as the plane changed from straining up to falling down. Dark water. Light. The tail section. Ice. A man. A lifeline. The interior light of an ambulance, its siren wailing.

We crashed. But I'm safe. I'm alive.

She shivered at the memories and remembered being so cold that it was impossible to shiver, as if the shivers were so intense they turned into a constant state that became the norm.

But crashing wasn't the norm. Being in the water wasn't the norm. Being dragged through the air by a helicopter wasn't the norm. She closed her eyes and remembered voices intersecting and a company of hands grabbing her from the air, her desperate body absorbing the meager warmth of their closeness, drawing it to herself. The pain was secondary.

She remembered screaming for help, and then eventually a calm voice—with its accompanying warm breath—spoken directly in her ear, "You're safe now. We've got you."

That was the last thing she remembered. Until now.

But where were the others from the water? And where was her seatmate? Where was Roscoe?

She remembered the intensity of his eyes and his small smile as the plane struggled for the sky. A smile of comfort—and even acceptance—as if everything would be all right, no matter what happened. But it wasn't all right. She grabbed his hand and together they braced the armrests, urging, imploring, beseeching the plane to climb, as if the tension of their muscles would add power to the plane.

But suddenly climbing was not an option. Nor was landing. Like a cartoon character jumping off a cliff and running a few steps in midair, the plane hung for a moment between up and down, success and failure, rise and fall. And then the shell of the plane cracked open like an egg, and the front fell away to reveal sky. Then Roscoe fell away, his hand ripped from hers.

"No!"

A nurse popped her head in and took one look at Sonja. "I'll get the doctor."

Roscoe was dead. That good, good man…dead.

She tried to remember the other survivors huddled around the tail. Roscoe wasn't one of them. How could he be beside her one minute and gone the next? Their seats had been attached, their hands touching. They had been connected, then torn—

A white-haired man tapped on the door. "May I come in?"

Sonja nodded and used her good hand to push herself up. The man hurried to assist her. "Here, let me do that." He pressed a button on the bed and it lifted her torso to a seated position.

She saw a cross on the lapel of his suit. "You're not the doctor."

"No, she'll be here in a few minutes. In the meantime I thought I'd keep you company. I'm Pastor Rawlins. And you're Ms. Grafton?" He held out a hand.

"Sonja." She lifted her right hand, showing the cast. He dropped his arm and gave her left hand a pat.

"Glad to have you with us, Sonja."

"What about the others?"

"They rescued seven survivors from the water."

"That's it?"

He nodded. "I'm afraid so. And sadly, two of those have since died."

"Two? Which ones? Who?"

"Belinda Miller and Justin Cavanaugh."

She realized the names meant nothing to her. "What did they look like?"

"You need to concentrate on getting better, on—"

"Which ones were they?" Sonja was adamant.

Pastor Rawlins looked to the ceiling, then down. "Ms. Miller was in her fifties and had very long hair."

Sonja thought back. "Was she wearing a magenta sweater?"

"Magenta?"

"Bright pink?"

He nodded. "Yes, I guess she was. She died of cardiac arrest in the ambulance."

"And the other?"

"Justin was a little boy."

Sonja closed her eyes and saw the young woman clutching the boy to her chest being lifted into the sky. She'd touched that boy. Held him for a moment while the life vest was put on. And now he was gone.

She did a mental count of the survivors in the water. "There were eight of us, but you say only seven were pulled out?"

The pastor nodded again, but this time his eyes filled with tears.

"Who didn't make it?"

"We don't know his name."

She nodded, trying to think logically. "There were four women, the boy, an old man separate from us, a handsome man, and the guy who gave me the line."

The pastor nodded.

The implications assailed Sonja like a blast of cold air. She sucked in a breath. *"Him?* The man who gave me the line instead of taking it himself? He didn't make it?"

The pastor took Sonja's left hand in his. He had difficulty swallowing. "That man handed off the lines three times, letting the rest of you go first. When they went back for him, he was gone."

Sonja ripped her hand away from the pastor's comfort. "Why'd he do that? Why didn't he take his turn?"

"I don't—"

"I wouldn't have taken the line from him if I'd known he was going to do a stupid thing like that."

"It wasn't stupid. It was a wonderful—"

"What's wonderful about it?" She shook her head, remembering the line being handed to her and the man's kind but determined face urging her to take what he had to give. "Now I'm going to go through the rest of my life thinking I shouldn't have gone. I should have said, 'It came to you; you go first.'" She looked at the pastor and suffered a torrent of panic. "I don't want to live with that guilt. Why didn't he take it? He had blood all over his face. He was hurt. Why didn't I let him go?" Amid her ramblings, the bottom line surfaced: "I shouldn't have taken the line!"

"No one blames you for living, Sonja."

She turned her face away from him, clamping her eyes shut. "Go on. Get out of here."

"Sonja—"

"Go!"

He slipped quietly out the door, but his words lingered in the air. *No one blames you for living, Sonja.*

They didn't need to. She blamed herself.

Tina felt a presence in the room and opened her eyes. A white-haired man stood in the doorway as if deciding whether or not to come in.

"Hi," he said. "I'm Pastor Rawlins."

She removed an oxygen mask and tried out a breath. "Where am I?"

He moved to the side of her bed. "You're in a hospital. You're safe. But we almost lost you. They say your body temperature was way below normal. A few more minutes…"

Tina looked past him into the air where her memories could find a screen. "I remember being pulled through the water, trying to hold on to ice." She looked at him. "I lost the line. My hands wouldn't work."

"They were frozen."

She looked to the window. The shades were drawn, and there was no light coming between. "Is it night?"

"Yes."

"Did they get them all out?"

"Not all."

"How many?"

"They saved seven."

Tina's throat constricted. "Out of that whole plane?"

He nodded. "It's a tragedy."

"Mallory wasn't one of them, was she?"

He thought a moment. "No, I'm sorry; there wasn't a Mallory. Was she your daughter?"

Tina let the tears come. "No, she was a stu—" She stopped herself, her throat constricting, then started again. "She was my seatmate."

Anthony opened his eyes and within two breaths made a self-diagnosis: *I'm alive.* It was a good start.

He was glad to see he was in a hospital room—a private room. He checked his body. His injuries—multiple gashes and bruises, and perhaps some cracked ribs—were not life threatening. If he could reach the chart, he would know for sure. He hit the switch on the bed, and it hummed to life.

There was a tap on the door.

"Yes?"

"My, my, you're alert," said an old man in a suit.

"A condition I intend to maintain."

The man smiled and entered the room. Anthony saw the cross pin on his lapel. "You're the chaplain."

"Guilty as charged."

Anthony adjusted the sheets around his legs. "Well, I'm fine—or I will be." He pointed above the bed. "Hand me my chart."

"That's not for you to look at. That's for the doc—"

"I *am* a doctor, and I am very capable of reading my own chart."

The chaplain nodded, his smile gone. "Sorry. It's not here."

"When will the doctor be in?"

"Soon."

"Tell him I want to see him ASAP."

"Her."

"Whatever. How many made it?"

He hesitated. "Five, including yourself."

Anthony shook his head. "Too bad." The man raised an eyebrow like he disapproved. *Hey, you want a sideshow? Go to a circus.* "I suppose you're here to comfort me?"

"Do you need comforting?"

"Not really."

"That's what I thought."

Anthony suddenly realized it was in his best interest to keep the hospital staff on friendly terms. "So…how are the others? You having a busy day with them?"

"They feel a lot of guilt."

"For what?"

The chaplain cocked his head as if it were a dumb question. "For living. It's a normal reaction. Guilt…and questioning, 'Why me?'"

Anthony touched the bandage on his head. The skin felt tight, as if there were stitches. "You won't need to go that route with me."

"Why not?"

"Because I know why I lived."

He raised an eyebrow again. "And why is that?"

"Because my life is worth more than theirs."

The chaplain jerked his head as if he had been slapped.

"Don't look so shocked, Father or Pastor or Reverend or whatever you call yourself. I always knew I would live. I have a lot left to do with my life."

"And those who died didn't?"

Anthony shrugged, and the movement hurt his shoulder. "I'm not one to judge—"

"But that's exactly what you're doing. Raising up your life as more worthy than theirs." The chaplain shook his head like a bobbing dog in the back window of a '68 Mustang.

"I refuse to go on a guilt trip just to fall into your handy-dandy post-tragedy package. I'm a doctor. I—"

"So you said."

They looked at each other a moment. "You can move on, your holiness. I'm sure you're needed elsewhere."

The chaplain headed toward the door, then turned back to Anthony. "By the way, we don't know the name of the hero yet."

"What hero?"

"The man in the tail section who handed the line to the rest of you. They went back for him, and he was gone."

"Really."

"They don't know his name yet." He smiled smugly, reminding Anthony of a professor he once had in biology class. "Perhaps you can help identify him? Give the man the honor he deserves? Especially since you took a line that was meant for someone else. That *he'd* given to someone else. A woman."

"Hey, it was every man—and woman—for himself. Besides, you can't blame me for going when I had the chance. You don't know what it's like to be in a position like that. You have to make split-second decisions. She lost the line; I took it. Self-preservation takes over."

"It didn't take over for the hero."

"Maybe it should have."

The chaplain took a step back, then lowered his jaw, his eyes taking on a decidedly nonchaplain-like glare. "Well, then. I guess since the hero's dead, you'd say his life wasn't worth much, right?"

Anthony opened his mouth to reply, but before he could think of a response, the chaplain left him alone.

So be it.

Dora hit the send button on her article, then sat back in her chair, drained. And though she felt as if she didn't have the energy to type another word, in many ways it was the easiest article she'd ever written. Actually, two articles. Although her boss had not approved it ahead of time, Dora had to find a way to release her feelings. So in addition to her news story of the crash and rescue, she wrote a first-person essay entitled "That Could Have Been Me." She hoped it would be printed, but she truly didn't care if it wasn't. It was therapeutic just writing it.

Actually, her initial title had been, "That Should Have Been Me," but *should* pulsed on the page, demanding attention like a black speck on a white dress. At first she couldn't understand why that one word bothered her so, but then she realized that her choice of that particular word was an affront to what had happened. And a lie.

She shouldn't have been on Flight 1382. The miraculous event of her mother's recovery had prevented her from going. *Prevented* her, not enticed or nudged. Once that event had fallen into place, she never even considered going. The strength of the facts behind her decision not to go made it clear that God had not wanted her on that flight; He had taken care of circumstances to make sure she wasn't on it. Which meant, for whatever reason, God wanted her alive.

It was heady stuff that found no place in her jumbled brain to land and take root. And so the *should* was changed to *could*. Yet even the weighty possibilities of *could* made her thoughts play bumper cars and sent shivers up her arms. She wondered how long it would be before she stopped thinking about what-if.

What if she had died? Or maybe harder to take, what if the hero had saved *her?* What if—?

The ringing of the phone startled her. "Hello?"

"What's this essay you sent me, Dora?"

It was her boss, Clyde. "I know it's extra and you didn't expect it, but I'd really like you to include—"

"Hey, you won't get an argument from me. Why didn't you tell me you were supposed to be on that flight?"

"I didn't know until I was at the scene and found out the plane's destination. And then—" She changed the phone to the other ear—"then I had to live with it a while. Get used to the idea. Get my feelings down on paper."

"Well, it's good. Real good."

Dora warmed to the praise. Praise from Clyde's lips was as rare as chocolate on a lollipop. "Actually, what I'd like to write next is something about the hero. My chest is heavy with thoughts about him. And soon, those thoughts will need to come out."

"Good. Get on it."

"I can't. Not yet."

"Why not?"

It was hard to explain. "I've given you an article highlighting the hero's actions; you've got the facts. But the deeper aspects of one man saving others…I haven't worked through that yet."

"The story's hot now, Dora. It won't wait for you to psycho-analyze the world."

Not the world, just one man. "I know that. But we don't even know his name yet, so there's still a chance for it to be timely."

A moment of silence lingered. "Tell you what. You get in and talk to the survivors. See what they think about being saved by the guy, and then you'll have some fuel to feed your story."

"But the hospital…so far they've allowed no visitors except family."

"But you're nearly family."

"How's that?"

"You should have been on the plane with them. That's a bond. Use it."

"But I *wasn't* on the plane. They might resent how God saved me from the experience they had to endure."

"And God saved them from death. That's a link. Go with it. Be their friend."

"That sounds so cold. As if I'm using my experience to get a story."

"You are. So what?"

She didn't have a ready answer for his flip question.

"Dora? Will you do it? Or do I have to assign it to someone else?"

Low blow. "I'll try."

"You do that. You've done good, Dora. Don't stop now."

She hung up but kept the phone in her lap. She wasn't sure she could do this. How could she combine being a good reporter with being a decent human being who respected the survivors? For whatever reason, she *hadn't* had the same experience they had. And only they knew what it felt like to live when their savior died.

Dora took a cleansing breath. Then she looked at the phone and realized something she could do to help move past the emotions that threatened to pull her under. She dialed a number she knew by heart. It rang and was answered.

And then Dora let herself stop being the reporter, the survivor of a close call, or even a grown-up. Dora Roberts became a kid again and let herself be comforted.

"Mom?"

Hugh and Floyd entered the warmth of the River Rescue office. The next shift had come on and looked to them expectantly.

"Hey, you two. That was some flying you—"

Floyd didn't want to hear it, didn't want to hear any words of congratulation. Without a word, he headed for an empty office. Hugh followed and closed the door. They each slumped in a chair without removing their coats. They stared at nothing and yet Floyd saw everything. Saw the tail section. Saw the man in the water. Saw the ice and the blowing snow and the wobbling lifelines, and the expectant, frozen faces looking to him for help. For life. And then saw nothing. The man was gone. The man who had helped the others in a way no one else could had disappeared beneath that fuel-covered, debris-laden, deathly dark water.

Floyd slammed a fist on the desk, willingly accepting the pain.

"Hit one for me." Hugh sat forward, balancing his elbows on his thighs, his hands clasped, eyes to the floor. "I really wanted to meet him, you know? I wanted to shake his hand, to ask him what he was thinking about out there." He looked at Floyd. "You know, a fellow could learn a lot from a guy like that. Life lessons. Deep thoughts."

Floyd nodded. "I've never seen anyone with such dedication. It's like he took it upon himself to play this part, to be the savior of the others."

"And he had to know," Hugh said. "At some point, he had to realize giving off the line one more time would mean his own death."

Floyd's throat tightened, and he put a hand over his face to hide the tears. He was glad Hugh let him cry in silence. Floyd wiped his face with the back of his sleeve. "That's what gets to me the most. The *decision* in it. I can see lots of people handing it off the first time. I mean, the law of the sea is 'women and children first.'" The words caught in his throat, and he waited until he could swallow again. "But when the cold started to get him, when he knew time was running out, he still gave it away."

"Gave his life away."

Floyd pressed his fingers into his temples, then opened his eyes. "What was he thinking, Hugh? When he saw us fly away with the last load, leaving him all alone in the wreckage?" Floyd shuddered, then hit a fist on his thigh. "If only I would've added the second line right away. If only we could have taken more load. If only the people would have been able to hold on so we didn't have to go back for them."

"We risked our lives too, Floyd. By going down so close, the jet fuel in the water could have blown. And the skids could have iced up, destabilizing the whole thing. I could've lost it." He blinked and looked away. "Nearly did, more than once. We did what we could—but it wasn't enough." His head shook with the words. "It wasn't enough."

Floyd let the silence settle between them. He had something to ask, but he wasn't sure how Hugh would take it. Funny how you could work with a fellow—risk your life with him—and not know much about the guy. Not the deep stuff anyway.

"You're going to ask me something," Hugh said, pointing at Floyd's face. "I can see it brewing. Out with it. Do you think we could have done more? Is that it?"

Floyd waved his hands in front of his face. "No, no, nothing like that. We did good, Hugh. Five people are alive because of us."

"Then what is it?"

Floyd took a deep breath. "Do you believe in God?"

Hugh sat back in his chair. "Sure. I suppose. Do you?"

Floyd nodded.

Hugh unzipped his coat and shrugged it off. "And yes, disasters like this get me thinking about God, if that's what you're asking. I'm wondering why He lets things like this happen. You know, if God is love and all that…"

Floyd agreed with Hugh's statement, but that wasn't what he had been thinking about. "I was thinking more of the hero. Being out there alone, but not alone, you know? Did he feel God's presence before he died? Was he comforted in some way? Did God take the pain away and let him go easy considering the sacrifice he'd just made? Did God approve?"

Hugh considered this a moment. "What that man did…it *is* kind of a God-thing."

Floyd nodded. "That's what I thought too. And somehow, the thought of him not being truly alone makes it a little easier to take."

"Yeah, I suppose."

Floyd had one more question. "Would you do it, Hugh? I mean, we risked our lives to save them, but that's our job. He was probably just an ordinary guy. An ordinary hurting, needy guy. Would you give up the line?"

Hugh put a hand to his mouth and stared out the window at the darkness. His reflection stared back. "I don't know. I honestly don't know. How about you?"

The intercom buzzed. "Floyd, your wife's on two."

He picked it up and let his wife's concern flood over him. "Yes, honey, I'm okay. *We're* okay." He exchanged a look with his partner and they shared an understanding. They may have been physically okay, but emotionally?

Hugh left the room, closing the door behind him…leaving Floyd alone with the answer to Hugh's question.

Ellen Smith had been glued to the television all afternoon—until the helicopter gave up looking for the hero. Then she turned it off, unable to watch any longer. It was as though with the death of the hero, a little bit of her had died too.

What if it's Henry?

She tried not to think about it. She'd strained to see every shot of the hero as he handed off the line, over and over. She listened to the commentators describe her Henry. If he *was* the hero, so be it. If he wasn't, then what did it matter? Either way he was dead. Joey was on his way from college to be with her.

She sat on the couch, looking at the dark TV. Although she'd been able to turn it off, she could not seem to move too far away from it. For in this magic box contained information—information she wasn't sure she wanted to have, yet information she needed.

She pulled the phone onto her lap. If only they'd call. If only someone from the airline would call and end her awful waiting.

She'd tried calling them repeatedly but gave up. Let them do the calling. Why should she make it easy for them? She wanted it to be very, very hard. After all, they had killed—

Not yet. Allow yourself just a few more minutes of believing in miracles. Maybe Henry will call and tell me he took a different flight. "Sorry for taking so long to get back to you, Elly, but I had to run onto the plane at the last minute, and we were so late getting in by the time I found a cab to the hotel..."

The phone rang in her lap. Ellen had it to her ear before the sound completed its tone. "Yes?"

"Is this Mrs. Henry Smith?"

"Yes."

"I'm sorry, Mrs. Smith, but this is Sun Fun Airlines, and we regret to inform you that we have confirmation that your husband was on Flight 1382 today and—"

She forced herself to take a breath. "Are they trying to recover the plane?"

"Yes, ma'am. As we speak."

The harder question. The stupid question. The last-ditch question. "Do you think anyone could still be alive?"

"I...I'm sorry, ma'am. I just don't know."

Ellen took down the information about where to go to identify her husband—when he was found. She kept nodding to the phone, feeling silly for having a conversation about flight times, hotels, and taxis when Henry was dead.

She hung up with that thought resounding through her soul.

Henry was dead. Henry was dead. Henry was—

She heaved the phone into the television set, shattering both. Horrified, she scrambled to the floor and began picking up the pieces, trying to fit one to another.

"No, no, no... Fix it, fix it."

She suddenly realized the absurdity of what she was doing and let the pieces fall from her hands to the carpet. She stared at the broken, jagged fragments and noticed a small stream of blood snake its way down the palm of her hand. The wreckage of a phone and a television set. A little blood. Inconsequential wreckage compared to—

With an expulsion of breath, she fell over on her side and pulled her knees to her chest, the broken pieces crackling beneath her.

She let the sobs come and, with them, felt her heart do its own breaking. Unlike the television or the phone, her heart couldn't be fixed. Not ever. For all the king's horses and all the king's men couldn't put Henry together again.

Seven

*Do nothing out of selfish ambition or vain conceit, but in humility
consider others better than yourselves. Each of you should look not only
to your own interests, but also to the interests of others.*

PHILIPPIANS 2:3–4

The next morning, Dora was on the road early. The airline was going to give a statement at nine, and she wanted a front-row seat. But it turned out her early start didn't matter. The conference room was packed with people waiting for an official to appear. Dora had to settle for a seat halfway back.

"Did I miss any—?"

A door opened near the podium and a group of three men came out. The crowd quieted. The oldest of the three approached the microphone. "Good morning. I am Malcolm Evers, spokesman for Sun Fun Airline, and these two gentlemen are Simon Wallin from the National Transportation Safety Board, and Chad Reese from the Federal Aviation Administration. I have a brief statement to make before we open the floor to questions."

He cleared his throat, donned reading glasses, and lifted an index card. "We at Sun Fun, wish to express our sincere…"

Dora shook her head at the subtle faux pas. If he couldn't give a heartfelt show of condolence and regret without notes, he was in trouble. She readied her pad and pen for some *real* news.

"As of yet, we have not determined what caused yesterday's crash, and I hazard to speculate. But certainly weather was a possible factor."

Duh.

He turned to the FAA man. "Mr. Reese?"

They exchanged places. "Although the weather is beyond our control, each pilot has the choice of taking off or not taking off."

"Are you saying he made a mistake?" asked a reporter.

There was an awkward silence. "That is a possibility."

Chaos erupted. Questions were hurled across the room. Dora felt sorry for the man, whose head whipped from one question to another, not knowing what to do.

"...pilot error?"

Reese made calming motions with his hands, and the questions stopped. The main question *had* gotten through. *Was it pilot error?*

"We don't know," Reese said. "But there is a saying: PIC. Pilot in Command. A pilot always has the option to abort a flight until he reaches the point of no return."

"Had Flight 1382 reached that point?"

"Apparently."

Mr. Wallin stepped to the mike, sharing it with Mr. Reese. "As you know, the airport was closed for nearly an hour and a half yesterday because of inclement weather."

"Have you recovered the black box yet?"

"Not yet. We haven't found the flight data recorder yet, either. Both of them will help us determine what happened to the plane and what was said in the cockpit before the time of the crash. However, preliminary examination of the communication between the cockpit crew and the control tower appears to be normal. There was no distress call." Mr. Wallin took a deep breath. "Of course our first priority is recovering the victims so accurate identification can be made. As we speak, relatives are arriving and are being taken to area hotels."

Dora resisted the impulse to run out of the room to head to nearby hotels. *Cause of crash first, reaction to crash second.*

"Please keep in mind there are many factors to consider, and all these take time to investigate."

"Such as?"

Wallin held out a hand and began listing them. "Runway conditions; the weight of the plane; the condition of the engines; mechanical failure, since it appears the plane did not receive the thrust it needed for takeoff; pilot error; and, of course, the weather. Visibility when the plane took off yesterday was minimal."

"Another question, Mr. Wallin. Why did the plane sink so fast? Aren't they supposed to float so people can be evacuated?"

Wallin opened his mouth, then closed it again. He looked to Reese and Evers but got no help. He turned back to the microphone. "They will stay afloat for some time unless the structural integrity of the cabin has been compromised."

This was all very interesting, but no one was asking the most probing question Dora wanted answered. She took a chance and stood.

"What about the hero?"

Silence. Then murmuring. *"Yes, what about the hero?"*

"We all witnessed the sacrificial actions of the eighth person in the water and were deeply moved. All efforts will be made to identify this man and give him the honor he is due. We can only wait and see—and hope he is identified." Mr. Wallin looked to the other two men. It was a good way to end. "Let's get back to work."

George woke to find a nurse taking his blood pressure. The Velcro band ripped apart, the sound yanking him from the last remnants of sleep.

"Good morning, Mr. Davanos."

Morning? He groggily glanced at the blinds.

"You want these open?"

Whatever. He didn't protest when she opened them and adjusted the light. His eyes skimmed the empty bed beside him.

I'm the lone survivor.

He felt like asking for more drugs. The ones they had given

him last night, for the pain had been great. Hours and hours of dreamless sleep—only to be wakened in the morning to the reality of *his* life and *their* deaths.

The nurse took his water pitcher and filled it at the sink, chattering in a happy monologue. "We are so glad you slept well last night. Some of the others had a harder time of it. They tossed and—"

He perked up. "Others?"

She set the pitcher on his tray table and turned the handle to his right. "The other survivors."

He shoved the table aside and sat up. "Survivors? So all the people in the water lived? How many?"

"Hold on a moment, Mr. Davanos." She moved the table and its water pitcher close again as if a glass of cold water would make everything better.

I've had enough cold water, thank you very much.

"Tell me, woman!"

She lifted both eyebrows and let a brief glare escape before couching it in nurse-happy again. "There were originally eight survivors; seven were airlifted to safety. Two of those have died." She tucked the sheet on the side. "And, of course, the one man in the water who didn't make it. The one who kept handing the lifeline to the others."

"What are you talking about?"

She hesitated, then her face lit up with an aha-moment. "Oh, that's right…you weren't hanging on to the tail section. You didn't see, you weren't there." She told him about the hero and his sacrifice.

"I'll take that water now."

She poured him a glass and he downed it.

"Are you all right, Mr. Davanos? I didn't mean to upset you."

He shook his head. As soon as she left, he called her back, but it was too late. He asked the next question to his empty room. "What about the widow and Henry? Were they among the five?"

The phone rang and he answered it. Suzy's voice flowed through the line like an elixir. "Dad? Is that you? Are you all right?"

For now. At least for now.

"But you need to eat something, Mrs. Cavanaugh. Your body needs fuel to heal."

With a swipe of her hand, Merry shoved the breakfast tray to the floor. "Don't you *get* it, lady? I don't *want* to heal. My family is dead! I don't want to heal."

The orderly picked up the dishes, then fled the room.

Good riddance.

Merry stared at the mess on the floor. A disheveled blob of green Jell-O looked like mint jelly without the Easter ham. A piece of meat lay dead amongst its brown gravy blood with baby carrots strewn on top as if they were bold strokes from an orange pen writing a special message just for her.

Here's the message, Merry: Your family's dead. What would you like for dessert?

Merry sank into the pillows even as the aroma of the meal lured her to climbing off the bed to eat. She turned her head away from it. How dare she think about fulfilling her own desires or needs when her family would never desire or need again? If she could cut off the other aspects of life her body craved—breathing, water, sleep—she would. She'd just lie there and let time swallow her up as if she had never existed.

She saw the light streaming through the blinds. How dare the sun shine. And flowers…her room was full of flowers and cards. Who would do such a thing? She was not allowed to enjoy beauty or a flower's fragrance or the warmth of the sun. They were off-limits. She glanced at a framed picture on the wall across from her. It was a desert scene, with large-armed cacti dotting a many-layered peach-colored vista. A blue and pink sunset silhouetted the low hills. A desert. Phoenix. She was supposed to be in Phoenix right this minute, enjoying a break.

Serves you right, Merry. You wanted to run away from your life? Now your life has been ripped away from you forever.

Merry looked at the picture a moment longer, then laughed. Why couldn't she have been placed in a room that offered a mountain scene? Or a French marketplace? Or a still life of perfectly arranged flowers? Why had God placed her in a room with a picture of a desert—her destination that God had cut short?

She desperately looked around the bed for something to throw at it, to banish it from her vision, from her conscience. But there were no more throwables at hand. She'd already swept them to the floor with her food.

It was appropriate. She was stuck with the desert scene mocking her, condemning her. And so she stared at it, letting it do its work. If it made her feel bad, so be it.

She deserved worse.

Merry heard a commotion outside her hospital room. She wrapped her body tighter around her pillow and wished them away. *Didn't people have any manners? Didn't they realize hospitals were a place to rest and find—*

Merry's eyes shot open as she heard her mother's voice. The moment she glanced toward the door, it opened wide, and a stream of family filed through. Her mother-in-law, two sisters-in-law, and their spouses, Uncle Jerry, and—

Her mother made a beeline for her bed, her face a puckered mask of sympathy. "Oh, my poor baby, my poor baby."

Before Merry could protect her injuries from the onslaught of Anna Keenan's hugs, she had two pudgy arms wrapped around her torso.

"Ouch!"

Her mother jerked back. "Oh, baby, I'm so sorry."

Merry pushed the controls to the bed, propelling herself to a more seated position. She scanned the faces of her family and realized they had no idea what to say. The feeling was mutual—especially when Merry glanced in her mother-in-law's direction. What could she possibly say to Mabel Cavanaugh, who suffered a pain equal to her own?

Mabel's eyebrows warred against each other as she tried to keep her composure. It was a losing battle. Within seconds, she flanked Merry's mother on the other side of the bed, her hand clasping Merry's, her head shaking no with such a furious rhythm that Merry wondered if Mabel would ever be able to stop it without divine intervention.

"Oh, Merry… My boy, my boy. And my little Justin."

Across the bed, Anna joined in with her own head rhythm. "Oh no, no, you can't think of them. Merry is alive. She's only one of five to be a—"

"But my boy is dead. My grandson is dead."

"He's my grandson too."

"But your daughter is alive."

Merry's mother leaned toward the center point of the bed. "So you're saying it would be better if Merry had died too?"

Mabel met her stance, their faces separated by mere inches.

"Certainly not, but you can't possibly say your grief is deeper than mine. My heart is ripped in two. My—"

"And mine's not?"

"Not like—"

The other relatives took sides and pulled the two women away from the war zone above Merry's bed. A nurse suddenly appeared, assessed the situation in one glance, and ordered, "Everybody out. Now!"

As their voices faded down the hall, Merry expelled the breath she'd been holding and took a fresh one. *So much for relatives.*

Then she turned over on her side and pulled a pillow to her chest. At the moment it was all the comfort she could tolerate.

Sonja hadn't slept well. She found it ironic that hospitals were supposed to be places of rest and yet they were probably the hardest places to get any rest with nurses in and out and the clattering of trays and carts.

She had breakfast and let herself doze while waiting for the doctor to visit. The half-sleep was the hardest to take, for that was when her mind ran a mental video of the events of the crash and rescue. If only she could reach deep sleep, maybe she'd find some peace there. She would even settle for the hard nothingness of drug-induced sleep. Anything but this laundry list of events that replayed itself on an endless loop.

Suddenly, her eyes shot open with a new memory. *Dale! Allen!*

She put a hand to her chest, trying to calm her breathing. They were dead. They were lying at the bottom of the river, cold and hurt and dead. She hadn't thought of them before—why *hadn't* she thought of them before? She didn't want to know what character trait that omission revealed. And Geraldine… Geraldine must be laughing in her Bandolinos right now. Her nemesis was safe and unhurt. Sonja, because of her own finagling, was traumatized and broken.

Then Geraldine's words returned, clear as if she were in the room. *"Just wait, Sonja…some day…"*

Some day was here.

Sonja remembered Allen coming back to her seat to check on her while they'd been waiting to take off. What had she told him? She closed her eyes and snickered. *"I'm fine. I've got everything under control."*

What a joke. If nothing else, the crash had proven she had *nothing* under control. It was the most out-of-control, violent, drastic thing that had ever hap—

She saw Roscoe's face in her mind's eye, heard his voice. *"Don't make God do something drastic to get your attention. Don't make Him reach down and shake you. Look up, away from the world, for just a moment. That's when you'll see Him, waiting there for you."*

Had God crashed the plane to get her attention?

She shivered and shook her head vigorously. Surely He wouldn't let dozens of people die just so she would maybe, possibly, by chance, turn to Him?

Look up, away from the world...

Sonja tentatively let her eyes move upward, but when she realized that all she saw was the water-spotted ceiling tiles of a hospital room, she looked away.

Roscoe may have been a nice man, but he was over the top when it came to God. None of this happened because God was thinking about Sonja, wanting her to turn to Him. No way. She couldn't even fathom such a thing. For to do so would mean that there was a reason she lived—and others died.

She clamped her eyes shut and willed herself to sleep, choosing to face the disturbance of her half-dreams rather than the disturbance of her soul.

Tina let the tendrils of warm tea flow through her body. She would never take warmth for granted again. She set the mug down awkwardly. Her fingers still didn't work well because of the frostbite.

There was a tap on the door. It was Pastor Rawlins. "May I come in?"

"Sure."

He pulled a vase with one yellow rose from behind his back. "This came for you."

"How nice of you."

He laughed. "Not me. I'm just the flower boy." He handed her the card.

"Can you take it out? I'm all thumbs." She read it: *They wouldn't let me see you. I'll get off work early and try again. I love you, David.*

The pastor tucked the card in the envelope. "From someone who cares?"

"My boyfriend."

"Boyfriend?"

"It isn't that odd, is it? For me to have a boyfriend?"

"Well, no," the pastor said, glancing at the door. "I met him earlier. He's been waiting all night in the relative's waiting room but had to go home to change before he went to work. He said he was your husband."

"No way!" She was shocked at her vehement reaction.

"I must have misunderstood."

Suddenly it became clear. Hospital rules. David had *become* a relative in order to see her. "You didn't misunderstand. But he's not my husband. He's just being pushy, trying to see—"

"You don't sound pleased."

"He's a complication."

"That's an odd term."

"He wants to get married."

"And you don't."

She shrugged, realizing it was an imperfect gesture. Her feelings were more complex than she could express. And she wasn't being fair. David's attempts to see her were good. He was concerned. That was normal. "You'll have to forgive me. I'm confused; I don't know what I think about anything right now."

He put a hand on her arm. "Going through a disaster such as this does complicate things. Perhaps that's what you meant?" He looked hopeful.

Was that what she'd meant with her rude comments about David? "There was a lot to think about before, much less now." She shook her head, wishing she didn't have to think about anything for a while.

The phone rang and he handed it to her.

"Tina! My little girl. Are you all right?"

At the sound of the voice, Tina started to cry. She was suddenly a child again, a child who only wanted to hear one voice when she was hurt or scared.

"Oh, Mom…"

Pastor Rawlins nodded with understanding, handed her a tissue, and slipped out of the room.

"We love you, sweetie."

"I love you too."

Tina sank into the pillows, letting them surround her like her parents' hug.

After talking with her parents, Tina sat in silence trying to hang on to the glow of their concern. They'd apologized for not coming to visit, but their health wasn't good, and neither were their finances. She understood and accepted their voices as comfort enough. She'd always been able to depend on them.

But something her father said stuck with her. He asked if she'd met the other survivors, or the men who flew the helicopter. She hadn't, and the trouble was, she wasn't sure she could. Was it healthy to relive such a crisis? She wanted to say hello and thanks, but she wasn't ready. Not yet. It was obvious she had some healing to do first, and she feared a few days in the hospital was only the beginning. Bodies heal more quickly than bruised memories.

As Tina let her eyes fall shut, she reconciled herself to the fact that there was only one man she really wanted to meet—and he was dead.

Perhaps it was better to leave the rest alone.

Tina felt someone stroking her hand. *The nurses sure go overboard on the personal atten—*

"I love you, Tina."

Huh?

Tina opened her eyes, and David smiled down at her. "Hi there."

She adjusted her shoulders against the pillows. "So…I hear we're married. You shouldn't have said we were married."

He took a step back. "Nice to see you too." He shoved a vase of yellow roses into her arms. "Here's the other eleven." He pointed to the bud vase on the windowsill. "I see you got the one I sent with the pastor." He eyed the other huge arrangements and cards from strangers. "Do I have competition?"

"Maybe."

He turned toward the door. "I'll see you la—"

Tina sighed. "David…come back. I'm sorry. Those flowers are from my parents, friends, work, and complete strangers. There's no competition."

After a moment's hesitation he returned to the bed, and Tina could tell she was forgiven. That was just like him. He never held a grudge. Unlike some people they both knew…

She extended her hand, and he took it, scanning her body. "You broke a leg?"

She nodded.

"I was at work when I saw everyone watching the news. I saw the tail section with the logo, and then, when I heard the flight number…" His forehead ruffled. "Oh, Teen. It's such a miracle you survived."

"I know."

"I tried to see you last night and this morning, but they wouldn't let me."

"Pastor Rawlins said my 'husband' was here."

He blushed. "Sorry about that. But I wouldn't have had any chance without lying."

"Thou shalt not lie."

"Even if I hope it will be true someday?"

"David…"

He nodded. "I know. Now's not the time. You have to concentrate on getting better and getting out of here."

"The doctor said soon. But I want to go home now." She handed him the flowers and he put them on the bed tray.

"You're so matter-of-fact about all this, Tina. Shouldn't you be going through some post-traumatic stress something or other?"

For some reason this incensed her. "No one has a right to tell me how I should or shouldn't feel. *I'm* the one who went through it. *I'm* the one who's dealing with it the best I can. *I'm*—"

She suddenly realized the core of her anger. It had nothing to do with David or their possible engagement or even her physical condition. *I'm the one who had the chance to tell a searching girl about God and didn't. And now she's dead. There are no more chances. No more opportunities.*

She covered her face with her hands.

"What's wrong? I'm sorry; I didn't mean to upset you."

She shook her head against his apologies. It wasn't his fault. She was the one who was out of whack. What was wrong with her? She *wasn't* acting like a person who'd been snatched from death. She was acting as nonchalant as someone who'd broken a leg while running after a missed bus.

You certainly missed this bus, Tina. You had a chance and blew it, but good. She clamped her jaw. It was time to face this, one way or the other.

"I need you to do something for me, David."

"Anything."

"I need you to find the parents of the girl I sat next to on the plane. Her first name was Mallory. I don't know her last name, but she had a grandfather Carpello, Carpelli, something like that. He lives in town. She was from Phoenix."

"But how will I find them?"

"I'm sure her parents have to come to town to identify the body."

He pushed the hair away from her eyes. "Why do you need to find them? And what do you want me to say to them when I do?"

She hadn't thought that far. What *did* she want to say to the family of a dead girl she'd only known a few hours? What comfort could she give them?

What comfort can they give me?

The selfishness of the thought shocked her like a bolt of electricity.

"You're getting that look again."

She wanted to turn away but held fast. She needed to face this—all of it. The truth was, she didn't want to talk to Mallory's parents to offer them comfort or to tell them about their daughter's last hours. Tina wanted to be assured that what she hadn't done—what she hadn't said—wouldn't matter.

She reached for her water, but David had it in her hands before she could even complete the movement. *I don't deserve him.*

He pulled a chair close and looked at her with concerned eyes. "You can tell me, Teen. You can tell me, whatever it is."

She wondered if that was true. Would he still profess his love when he found out what a slacker she'd been—a slacker for God? A coward? An arrogant, selfish woman who'd only thought of herself and the small discomfort of Mallory's possible rejection of her words?

Her thoughts got sidetracked by a new one. "I only talked about myself."

"What?"

She replayed the conversation she'd had in the plane with Mallory. The girl talked about herself, but not because Tina had shown any interest. Most of the conversation revolved around Tina—Tina's thoughts, Tina's hates, Tina's needs. Even when Mallory did talk, Tina managed to turn the conversation around to me, myself, and I. It was pitiful. It was disgusting.

"I am the most selfish, arrogant, insecure, insolent, selfish—"

"You said *selfish* twice."

"Don't stop me; I'm on a roll."

He sat back in the chair, crossed his arms, and grinned.

"And don't laugh at me. This is serious."

He erased the grin and touched her arm. "I'm not laughing, but I've heard this before."

"No, you haven't. I've never felt like this before."

"Oh, yes you have. Remember six months ago when you nominated yourself for that church office and then felt bad for doing it? You recited a similar list then. But I think *prideful* was included on that one."

She closed her eyes, hating the memory of the past humiliation. She had withdrawn her name from the selection process more out of a fear of not receiving any votes than contrition, though she'd been through that too. Hadn't she dealt with all those nasty character traits back then? Then why did she have to deal with them again?

"What weaknesses do you deal with, David?"

"You tell me."

"Not fair. I recited my list; now it's your turn."

It only took him a moment to begin. "I'm too passive, nonconfrontational to a fault; I procrastinate, daydream far too much, and I don't like surprises."

"That's pitiful."

He hung his head. "I know—"

"No, I mean your list is pitiful. I'm sorry, but daydreaming and not liking to argue does not measure equally with being insolent and selfish."

"Sorry," he said. "I'll work on it."

"You do that."

He traced a finger around a bruise on her forearm. "You still haven't told me why you want me to track down Mallory's parents. I assume it's linked to your tirade against yourself?"

She nodded and together they watched his tracings. It felt good, and with little effort, she knew she could slip away into sleep. Not have to deal with it. Escape.

No. She pulled her arm away and lifted her chin. "Have you ever witnessed to anyone before, David? Told them about God?"

"Not as often as I should—"

"But you *have* done it?"

"Sure."

He said it so casually, as if sharing God to a stranger should come easily. Maybe it should. Maybe that was the root of the problem. Maybe if she were a godlier woman, then talk of faith would simply flow out of her, without effort.

"Did you talk to Mallory about Jesus?"

Tears followed a puff of air and the word *No!* She grabbed a tissue. "No, I didn't. Don't you get it? Mallory, this sweet, open girl, asked me about God, and I didn't answer her."

"Why not?"

"Because I wasn't sure how to say the right thing, didn't feel like trying to figure it out, and basically was afraid she'd reject what I *did* say."

She sniffed loudly. "Ah, David…I had a chance to make sure a fellow human being was on her way to heaven for all eternity, and I blew it off. And now she's dead. Who would have thought that God would depend on me in that way? I mean…*me.*"

"And you want to meet her parents to do what?"

"To find out if she already knew the Lord; maybe she was just searching for more information. Maybe her soul wasn't hanging on that one question."

"What question?"

Tina looked at him, the aches of her body nothing compared to the ache within her soul. "She asked me—and these are her words—'Does God know about…does He care about…?'"

"Her?"

"Her. She was searching. She wanted to know if He loved her. If He cared about her plans. She wanted to know if she was important. And I didn't tell her." Tina sobbed, shaking her head. *Guilty, as charged.*

David wrapped his arms around her. "I'll find them, Tina. I'll find Mallory's parents."

Anthony flipped the channels, devouring the reports about the crash. As each video clip replayed the rescue, he kept thinking, *I lived through that?*

It was a miracle. *His* miracle. He was a celebri—

A spasm of pain ripped through his torso and lingered, bringing a tear to his eye. A nurse happened in and rushed to his side. "Are you all right?"

He nodded and looked back to the screen. A reporter was doing a gig about the hero and the search for his identity.

The nurse nodded knowingly. "Oh, I get it. You shouldn't feel bad about that."

Anthony expelled a breath, relaxing as the spasm retreated. "About what?"

She nodded to the screen. "About living when he…you know… You shouldn't feel bad."

He blinked at the absurdity of the idea. "I wouldn't think of it."

She gaped at him, looking very much like a codfish. Why couldn't he get a pretty nurse?

She pointed to the screen. "But the hero—"

"Died. I know. We all know. It's plastered all over the news, the media's latest baby to burp. He died, and that's too bad, but five of us lived. I haven't seen a single interview with any of us. We have a story to tell too."

"The hospital won't allow—"

So that was it. "The hospital has kept the reporters away? Whatever for?"

"So you can rest. Recover. And forget."

He leaned against his pillows, nodding. "No doubt the airline's lawyers have influenced the hospital administration, wanting us to lie dormant—or maybe waiting for us to die too—so there'll be one less lawsuit, one less report of wrongdoing, mechanical failure, or culpability. I'm a doctor; I know how lawsuits go. I know the psychology of lawyers and the guilty."

The nurse's jaw was set. She glared at him. "I bet you do."

"What's that supposed to mean?"

She looked to the door, as if checking to see if they were alone. "I wouldn't think you'd want to see reporters."

"Whyever not?"

She nodded toward the television. "You *were* on the news this morning. Didn't you see it?"

Anthony tried to sit up straighter. "What are you talking about?"

The nurse hesitated. "They had video of the rescue."

Talking to her was like extracting a splinter from a finger. "And?"

"People saw what you did…what you did to get the line."

Anthony rolled his eyes. "Not that again."

The nurse's jaw dropped ever so slightly. "*That* was grabbing the line when it wasn't your turn."

"I didn't grab anything. The woman next to me—"

"Belinda Miller."

"Whatever. She couldn't hold on to the line. It came to me. I didn't rip it out of her hands. There hardly was time for a polite 'no, you go first' discussion."

"She died."

He paused.

"Don't you have anything to say about that?"

"That's too bad."

"You took her place. She might have lived if she'd gone when she was supposed to."

Anthony had had just about enough. "If you're waiting for me to feel bad for living, take a seat and get comfortable, because it isn't going to happen anytime soon."

The nurse shook her head. "You're hopeless, aren't you?"

"Indeed not. I am full of hope. I lived because I was supposed to live. And that's why I insist on seeing a reporter. Now. I want to tell my story."

"I'm not sure that's possible, Mr. Thorgood."

"*Doctor* Thorgood."

She didn't correct herself.

"I'm sure it *is* possible. What's the name of the man in charge?"

"I don't want you bothering, Mr.—"

"It's his job to have people bother him. What's his name?"

She gave it to him and he made the call. Less than sixty seconds later, Anthony was assured by a very accommodating administrator that the floodgates holding back the media would be opened immediately.

He could hardly wait. It was time the world heard from Dr. Anthony Thorgood.

Eight

D ora couldn't believe her luck. After attending the press conference from the airlines, she dropped by the hospital on a
whim, hoping against hope that the ban on interviewing
the survivors had been lifted, and she could follow her boss's instruc-
tions. She was just walking in the door when the excitement started.
A crowd of reporters swarmed a suited man wearing a hospital ID
badge. They raised their arms, vying to be chosen like kids choosing
up sides for a kick-soccer game. *Me! Me! Choose me!*

Dora rushed forward, vying for her own spot. The hospital
administrator held up his hands, trying to calm the ruckus. "One
television, one newspaper."

"That's it?"

"That's not fair."

"It's that or nothing," he said. "Only one patient has expressed
any interest in talking with the press, and even with his permission,
we are wary and mindful of his ordeal." He looked right at Dora.
She'd interviewed him once for an article about the new trauma
unit. He was some assistant to the administrator... Aaron? Arnold?
Arnie, that was it. She smiled at him, waggled the tips of her fingers, and mouthed, *Please, Arnie...*

He smiled back. "Dora? Let's have you and..." He looked to a
TV reporter Dora didn't recognize. "And you. Let's go." He hustled

the two reporters and one cameraman through the crowd toward the elevator.

"But when will we have a turn?" asked one of the less fortunate.

Arnie called over his shoulder. "When I say so." They got in the elevator, and as the doors closed, he laughed. "I've been wanting to say that my whole life."

Dora and the others laughed dutifully. She held out her hand. "Dora Roberts. We talked a few months—"

His smile flirted. "I remember." He seemed reluctant to break eye contact but was forced to when the TV reporter made his introductions. "Stephen Brady, WDIU. And this is Wayne." The cameraman nodded, obviously not offended that his last name wasn't given. "Who are we getting to see?"

"Anthony Thorgood—*Doctor* Anthony Thorgood, as you will soon find out if you dare call him otherwise."

"Whoa," Stephen said. "This should be interesting."

"I think that's a given."

"How about the other survivors?" Dora asked.

"Soon."

"Are they that badly injured?"

"Not any worse—"

"Then why is he—?"

He smiled and winked. "I'll leave that for you to discover."

They exited the elevator, and Arnie led them to Dr. Thorgood's room. He knocked on the door. "May we come in?"

"Enter."

Dora and Stephen exchanged a look. *Yes, your majesty.*

Dr. Thorgood sat in bed wearing a blue hospital robe. The top of a torso bandage could be seen. He clasped his hands on his lap and lifted his chin as if sizing them up. "Who's who?" he finally said.

Dora and Stephen introduced themselves.

"Hmm."

Was that a good hmm or a bad hmm?

Wayne set up the camera and nodded to Stephen that he was ready. Stephen cleared his throat and spoke into the mike. "So, Mr.—Dr.—Thorgood, how do you feel—?"

"How do I feel?" Thorgood laughed. "Now that has *got* to be the most inane question I've ever heard." He pointed to Arnie. "If these are the best reporters…"

Stephen interrupted. "I was saying, how do you feel about being one of only five survivors out of a plane carrying one hundred?"

Dora expected to hear the word *lucky* or even *blessed*—

"Vindicated."

She did not expect that. Her initial mental reaction was not kind. And the answer took Stephen by surprise so much that he didn't know what to say. Dora stepped in. "Would you care to explain yourself, Doctor?"

"Of course." Thorgood took a cleansing breath. "It's obvious since I was chosen to live, there must be more for me to accomplish in my life. My survival is vindication that my life is worthwhile."

Stephen pounced. "So all those people who died…are you implying their lives were *not* worthwhile? They died because they had nothing more to—as you say— 'accomplish' in their lives?"

Thorgood thought a moment, then shrugged. "The facts speak for themselves."

"But—"

He waved the question away. "But the reason I called you here is that I feel it is my responsibility to bring to light the appalling disregard for life by Sun Fun Airlines. They should never have taken off in such horrendous conditions. By doing so, they sealed the fate of—" He looked to Stephen. "What's the death count?"

"Ninety-five."

"The deaths of ninety-five people, not to mention causing the rest of us extreme pain and suffering. I for one intend to sue, and if I have my way, Sun Fun Airlines will never see the sun again."

Dora was in shock. She had never witnessed such arrogance. She decided to go ahead and ask the question she'd tucked away out of sympathy for the survivors' ordeals. *This man doesn't deserve any sympathy.* "Back to the rescue, Dr. Thorgood. The entire world saw you grab the lifeline away from Belinda Miller, who later died. How do you account for your—?"

He threw his hands in the air. "For the umpteenth time, I did not *grab* anything. It virtually fell into my hands. I merely took it, as anyone would have done."

"Not everyone," Dora said.

"Yeah, yeah. The hero. If he were here I'd thank him. But I bet his family isn't putting him on a pedestal like you reporters are doing. They'd much rather have him alive than canonized."

"But if *he* were alive, you might not be," Stephen said.

"Oh, I would have survived, one way or the other."

Thorgood's last statement said it all. Dora felt further questions die. Apparently so did Stephen. And Wayne. For with only a slight glance at each other, Wayne shut the camera off, and Stephen put away the mike. Dora agreed completely. The three of them started to leave.

"Hey! What about my story?"

They were desperate for a story but not that desperate. *Get yourself another pawn, bucko.*

Anthony felt his blood pressure rise. How *dare* they leave like that? They had no idea—

The administrator—Arnie something or other—returned to his room and entered without knocking.

"You sure know how to pick losers," Anthony said. "What did you do, take a poll on which reporters were the most inept?"

Arnie slowly closed the door, and Anthony had an odd notion

he was going to get slugged. *Just try it, peon. Speaking of lawsuits...*

But the administrator did not hit him. The man deliberately leaned against the doorjamb with his hands cushioning his tailbone. He looked down and was silent, which was almost more disturbing.

"Cat got your tongue?"

Arnie looked up and smiled. The last time Anthony had seen such a smile was when he'd just been handed a speeding ticket by a quota-hungry cop who loved his job a bit too much.

Anthony sighed. "Either say something or leave me alone."

"I just have one thing to say to you, Mr. Thorgood. And if you repeat it to anyone, I'll deny it."

"Ooh, this sounds good."

Arnie sniffed a laugh. "It *is* good. But you are not. Good, that is."

"You know very well it's Doctor Thorgood, and you have no right—"

Arnie raised a hand and nodded. "I've digressed. Let me say my piece and leave you to...yourself."

Anthony crossed his arms, ignoring the pain in his ribs in order to gain the effect. "Sounds like a plan."

"I may not be an extraordinary man, or worthy, or wise. But I do have an opinion and that counts for something."

Anthony rolled his eyes. This was taking forever. "And...?"

The little man stood upright and squared his shoulders. "You were one of five chosen to be saved. And yet...all things considered, I think God made a mistake."

With that, he left, closing the door behind him.

After traveling down the elevator to the lobby, Dora excused herself from the TV crew and slipped into the rest room. Her heart pumped double time. Although her interview with Thorgood was a wash, Dora's appetite for talking with the survivors was whetted.

Big time. She had to get back up there, and now that she knew the layout...

They'll stop me. They know I'm not a relative.

It didn't matter. She had to try. She checked the mirror and attempted to remove the frenzy from her face and replace it with calm assurance, but she could not rid her eyes of their fire. Oh well, it would have to do.

Dora left the rest room, walked around the throng of reporters still in the lobby, and headed down a long hall. She found an obscure stairway.

Six flights. It would be good exercise.

Dora paused on the sixth floor landing and caught her breath. Now came the hard part. If only she could make herself invisible long enough to get into one of the survivor's rooms.

She bit the top of her notebook, thinking. Then she had an idea. She stuck her reporter's notebook in her purse and passed through the door into the sixth floor ward.

As expected, a nurse walked by and did a double take. "I thought you were through with Dr. Thorgood."

Dora kept walking, hoping she looked more confident—and innocent—than she felt. "I forgot my notebook in his room. I'll just be a minute." She felt a twinge of guilt at the lie.

The nurse gave a nod that indicated Dora had better be telling the truth.

Dora walked faster.

Sonja listened as visitors talked in the hall. She perked up and arranged the blankets over her lap. How wonderful to have people from work stop by. She'd even take a visit from Geraldine rather than this convicting silence.

Her mother and father had called to say they would be down tomorrow when she was scheduled to be released. And they sent a beautiful philodendron plant, which Sonja was sure she'd manage to kill within weeks. She tried to take joy in the gesture, and yet…her mother knew she was terrible with plants, so why hadn't she sent fresh flowers that weren't supposed to live instead of shoving another of Sonja's inadequacies in her face by sending her a plant to kill?

Sonja closed her eyes and thought happy thoughts. She was being too sensitive. She had survived a plane crash. It was a time of second chances, and because of that, it was wrong to harp on past slights—or new perceived ones. Besides, there were visitors in the hall. Certainly she could claim a few of them?

But the visitors passed by. No visitors for Sonja. Uh-uh. No visitors for a conniving woman who didn't care about the feelings of other people before the crash. No, sir, she didn't deserve to have visitors. She didn't even deserve to be living at all, not when so many good people died.

"Excuse me?" A woman stood in the doorway.

"Yes?"

The woman took a step into the room. She was more handsome than pretty and wore an air of kind confidence like a well-worn but classic coat. "I'm Dora Roberts. I'm a reporter for the *Chronicle*." She glanced outside as if expecting some administrator to pull her away. "I know I should have made an appointment, but with the media mob downstairs…" She shrugged. "I snuck in here."

"You want to talk to *me?*"

"If you're up to it."

I'd be up to talk to a bedpan man if it would mean company. "Come in."

Dora motioned to a chair. "May I?"

"Sure."

Dora settled in, removing a notepad from her purse. "We can make this as long or short as you like. You're the boss. I don't want to wear you out."

Sonja smoothed the blanket. "I want to talk. I could use a friendly ear."

"Funny you should say *friend*... My boss..." Dora shook her head as if she hadn't meant to say it aloud. "Maybe we can help each other," she said. "I mean that."

Sonja looked at Dora with new eyes. This was more than a reporter; this seemed like a genuinely nice person. Sonja had met so few *nice* people in her life.

"Is there anything *you'd* like to talk about?" Dora asked.

Sonja thought of her high school journalism class. *When, where, who, why, and how.* Odd how only two of the five were known. "Actually, I'd like to know why."

"Why it happened? What went wrong? That sort of—?"

Sonja shook her head and stroked the word. "*Why?*"

To her credit, Dora hesitated only a second. "You mean the deeper, philosophical, purpose-of-life why."

"Exactly."

"I don't know."

Her honesty made Sonja smile. It felt good to smile. "I guess if you could answer that one, you'd win the Pulitzer or something, huh?"

"At the very least." Dora clicked her pen on, then off, then on. "The why question interests me too because it's something the rest of us—those of us who *didn't* go through the crash—don't completely fathom." She looked down as if she had to get her emotions under control. "Actually, I was supposed to be on that flight. Your plight could have been mine."

Sonja raised an eyebrow. "What kept you off?"

"God."

Sonja raised the other eyebrow. "You're sure about that?"

"Positive. My mother, who lives in Phoenix, needed an operation; then suddenly she didn't."

"Could be good medicine."

Dora shook her head. "It was God. He didn't want me on that flight."

"Then does it follow that He *did* want *me* on that flight?"

Dora sucked in a breath. "Oh dear…I'm so sorry. I didn't mean to imply—"

Sonja waved her concern away. It all made sense. It's just like Roscoe had said. She was on that flight because God wanted to get her attention.

Dora poised her pen above her pad, all business again. "Let's get back to you. How do you, Sonja Grafton, handle the why question?"

"I don't know."

Dora laughed. "It appears we're even up on the 'I don't know' answers, one apiece."

Sonja rubbed her face, avoiding the cut on her forehead. "I lost two of my coworkers on the plane. They were sitting up front. I was alone in the back. Was it luck? Or was it fate?"

Dora made a face that hinted of disapproval. "You don't think you deserved to live more than—"

"Oh no, no. I don't think that at all."

Dora let out a breath. "Good."

"But living when so many others have died does make me wonder." She shook her head. It was hard to explain. "I'm not expressing this very well."

"You're doing fine."

Sonja thought of the real question she wanted answered, yet it wasn't a question she could ask anyone else—especially not a reporter who might use it against her.

"You have some regrets?"

Sonja stared at her, incredulous that two strangers—Dora and

Roscoe—had both sensed Sonja's unease. Was she that obvious? "You're very intuitive."

Dora shrugged. "It's part of my job."

"I have the feeling it's more than that... Beyond the job, perhaps?"

"Maybe. I'd like to think so."

I hope so. I don't need a reporter right now.

As if sensing Sonja's thoughts, Dora put her pad and pen away. She crossed her legs and gave Sonja her full attention. "What's eating at you, Ms. Grafton? Off the record. I know you don't know me from Eve, and if you don't feel comfortable confiding such a thing to me, then don't. I don't want to pressure you. But I know if I went through what you went through, I'd need someone to talk to." She looked around the room. "And since I appear to be the only one here at the moment... It's your call."

More than anything, Sonja wanted to spill it. And yet she wasn't an open heart-on-her-sleeve person. At least not usually. Yet she *had* confided to Roscoe on the plane. Maybe Dora could be trusted too.

Dora waited patiently, her foot making figure eights in the air.

Why not? Sonja took a deep breath. "I'm not a very good person—and yet I lived."

"I'm sure you're overreacting."

"No, I'm not. I'm too ambitious, conniving, and selfish. I've gotten where I am in my career by taking every advantage—some deserved and some not deserved."

"Ah, you're one of *those.*"

A brief stab of pain sliced into Sonja's confidence.

Dora waved a hand. "Sorry. I didn't mean that in a judgmental way, as much as to say that I understand what you're talking about. And let me assure you, all successful people have probably done a bit of...whatever you've done."

"But I did a lot."

Dora smiled. "Well, that certainly makes it interesting."

"You want to hear the whole thing?"

"If you want to tell me."

Sonja did. So Sonja did. When she was through, she waited for the reporter's reaction.

"Well then..." Dora took a moment and reversed her legs. "You know what I would think if I were you?"

"What?"

"I would think I was getting another chance. The very fact you see the error of your past is significant. I know some..." She looked to the hall again. "Some who don't seem to be changed by this whole ordeal. And yet you have allowed it to move you. To open your eyes. To get your attention."

Sonja sucked in a breath. "That's what my seatmate said! Roscoe said sometimes God has to do something drastic to get our attention."

"And so it appears He has." Sonja nodded, and Dora put a hand on hers. "I'm going to let you rest now." She retrieved a business card from her purse and scribbled a number on the back of it. "This is my card with my number at work and at home. Please feel free to call if you want to talk more. About anything. Off the record or on."

Sonja suddenly realized something. "But I didn't give you anything you could use for an article. I—"

Dora shook her head. "It doesn't matter. Sometimes the story has to take second place to just being there. I like you, Sonja. We can talk more whenever you like."

Sonja studied the business card and found herself smiling. Things were definitely looking up.

"The identity of the hero is still unknown. Channel 5 news has blown up the video images of the hero as he clung to the wreckage, but the blinding snow and the dimness of dusk prevent us from seeing his face clearly. All that can be seen of the man in his forties is his black hair and beard and a gold watch on his right wrist."

The fork full of green beans stopped midway to George's mouth. *Henry had a gold watch.*

He put the beans in his mouth and chewed. So what? Most people wore watches. Just because the man wore a watch didn't mean he was Henry. *But most don't wear it on their right wrists.*

Black hair. Beard. Forties. Two, three, four matches for Henry Smith.

George squinted at the newscast image. Could that blurry man be his seatmate? Or, more importantly, did he think Henry Smith was the sort of man to give his life for others? George hadn't known Henry well enough to make such a determination. And yet maybe it wasn't something a person could predict of others, or even of himself. Who knew what well of strength might be tapped into during a time of crisis? Some people revealed cowardice or selfishness, so why not heroism?

A woman with lovely eyes knocked, then came in his room. "Excuse me a moment, Mr. Davanos. My name is Dora—"

George jumped at the audience. He pointed his fork at the screen. "I think I know that man!"

The woman looked at the TV. "That man?"

The video of the hero was over. The camera focused on a reporter. "No, not him. The hero. The eighth person in the water."

The woman stepped to the foot of his bed. "Really? Everyone's talking about him, about what he did. But nobody knows who he is."

"But maybe I do." George counted off on his fingers. "The man I sat next to on the plane was about forty, had a beard, black hair, and wore a gold watch on his right wrist."

"Do you know his name?"

"Henry Smith."

The woman shook her head. "Sounds too ordinary."

George was amazed that such a stupid statement made an odd sort of sense. Shouldn't a hero's name be Alexander or Solomon or something grand? Not Henry. And not Smith, *the* most ordinary of surnames.

The woman pulled George out of his thoughts. "Have you told anyone?"

"Huh?"

"Have you told anyone else about knowing the name of the hero?"

"No. Not yet."

"You should."

"Yeah, I suppose I should."

The woman looked down and then up again, as if she'd made a decision. "I need to complete my introduction. My name is Dora Roberts, and I'm a reporter with the *Chronicle.*"

George clamped his lips together. *Oops.* "Well, I guess you're pleased. I just gave you the scoop of the century."

"It's not a scoop until it's a known fact. Would you like me to get you the number of someone to call?"

Her nonpiranha-like attitude made George reassess his opinion of her. "I'm not sure. It's just a feeling."

"But if it's true, they need to know. The family needs to know. And don't *you* need to know?"

"He didn't hand the lifeline to me. I was separated from the—"
She nodded.

"I didn't see the hero. I wasn't in that group."

"But you may have sat next to him. Talked to him. Gotten to know him. Think of the odds of that."

A moment of silence sat between them during which George thought about how different things would have been if he had been on the tail section with the others. If he had recognized Henry and seen what he was do—

He put a hand to his chest.

"What's wrong?" Dora asked.

George stared into space, trying to collect the thought that had nearly knocked the wind out of him.

"Mr. Davanos? Are you okay?"

Finally, George was ready to talk. Maybe voicing it out loud would make the seriousness of the implications fade into a perspective that was easier to take. "If I'd been hanging on to the tail section, and if the hero *is* Henry Smith—" He clamped a hand over his mouth. "You can't write any of this. Not until we're sure."

"It's okay," she said. "Continue. I want to hear your thoughts."

"If I'd seen Henry give the line away, over and over again…since I'd talked to him before, since I knew him…" George looked up, hoping for comfort. "Would I have talked him out of it? Would I have said, 'Don't be stupid, Henry. Take the line'?"

Dora nodded, obviously following his train of thought. "Then he might not have handed the line to others. He might have gone first. And everything might have changed."

"We still could have lived…"

"But maybe not all of you." Dora put a finger to her mouth, thinking hard. "Your arguing with him could have wasted precious time. There wasn't time for discussion. There was only time for the hero to make a decision and act on it."

"You may be right." The what-ifs were complicated and staggering.

Dora touched George's arm. "Perhaps God knew what He was doing in having you be the only one separated from the others in the tail section."

George put a hand to his forehead, the thoughts cumbersome.

Dora continued. "Only by having the hero—a stranger—help other strangers could the plan have played out."

George snapped out of his shock. "The plan? How could there be a plan in all this? Other than the obvious saving of seven—now five—lives, how could Henry's heroism be a good thing? How could anyone's death be a part of a—?" He stopped short. *You planned to die, George. That was your plan. But you're alive and Henry is dead. Obviously God had other—*

George snickered. "Life is what happens while we're making other plans."

"What?"

He'd forgotten Dora was there. "Nothing. Just an observation."

Dora left George's room totally discouraged. Three strikes. She'd interviewed three of the five survivors and still didn't have any article material. She *wouldn't* write Dr. Thorgood's story, and she *couldn't* ever write Sonja's, or George's now. Clyde would not be happy.

But there was hope. Three down, still two to go.

She made a beeline for Tina McKutcheon's room and slipped in.

Tina had a leg in a cast.

"Who are you?"

Dora felt herself blush. "Sorry. I didn't mean to make my entrance look so James Bondish."

"If you've got Sean Connery out in the hall, bring him in."

They laughed. Dora took a step toward the bed. "I'm Dora Roberts, Ms. McKutcheon. I'm a reporter for—"

Tina's face darkened. "I'm not sure I should talk to you."

Dora pulled her hand away. "Why not?"

"Have the other survivors talked?"

"Some." Dora shook her head. "Though in truth, I can't use what they've said."

Tina angled her head. "Now that sounds interesting. Care to explain?"

"I'll talk if you will."

Tina smiled, but there was a sadness behind her eyes, a discontent. "How can I refuse? Have a seat."

Dora didn't have time to wallow in her luck. She was in. Maybe this conversation would be different.

Maybe she'd get something she could actually use.

Tina was surprised she felt like talking to a stranger. So far the only visitor she'd had was David. But the fact this reporter had snuck in gave a hint of adventure to her...adventure.

She adjusted the slant of her bed to a more upright position.

"Do you need help? A pillow or something?" Dora asked.

"No, I'm fine." She smoothed the sheet and clasped her hands in her lap. "So. What do you want to know?"

The reporter seemed taken aback. Tina had expected her to whip out a notebook of questions. Instead, Dora sat on her hands. "What feelings do you have about Dr. Thorgood?"

"Who?"

"Doctor Anthony Thorgood."

"My doctor's name isn't Thorgood."

Dora shook her head. "He was one of the survivors. He's the one who took the lifeline from one of the other women, forcing her to wait while he went first. She later died."

Tina's mind was blank.

"Don't you remember? The hero handed her the line, and it slipped out of her hands, then Thorgood grabbed it and went when she should have gone."

Tina put a hand to her head, starting to remember.

"Haven't you seen it on the TV reports? They've shown the rescue a hundred times."

Tina shook her head. "I haven't wanted to watch. It's still too fresh."

"You don't remember that he took that woman's line?"

Tina didn't like the direction this interview was going. "Ms. Roberts, are you trying to stir something up? Trying to make me say that I hate this Thorgood fellow, maybe because that woman isn't here to hate him herself?"

Dora put a hand over her eyes and sighed. "Oh dear...what *am* I doing?"

"Acting like a sleazy reporter?"

"Ouch. I deserved that."

"Yes, you did."

Dora pinched her lower lip. "Is there anything you'd like to tell me about *your* ordeal?"

Tina considered talking about Mallory but decided against it. "No. Actually, there isn't. At least not yet."

Dora nodded and stood. "Then I'll let you rest. I'm sorry for bothering you, Ms. McKutcheon. My boss wanted a series of interviews with the survivors, and so far I've struck out."

"Oh yes, you were going to tell me about that, about the interviews you had but couldn't use. What did they say to you that you can't repeat?"

"Private things. Actually, we usually ended up talking about God. My boss may not be a bad guy, but I work for a secular paper, and I'm pretty sure they would have no place for an article about Him."

"You never know. Miracles happen."

Dora laughed. "Not with my boss."

"But they do happen. The five of us are living proof."

Dora nodded. "Yes, you are." She turned toward the door, then back to Tina. "I'm sorry I tried to make you angry at Dr. Thorgood when you weren't."

Tina shrugged. "I guess it *would* be nice for him to apologize for the sake of that woman's family, but who knows what I would have done if put in the same position?"

"Actually, I think we both know the answer to that one."

Tina felt her throat tighten. "Thanks. I needed that."

"You're welcome. Maybe we'll talk again."

"Maybe you'll get to write your articles. All of them."

"We can only hope."

Dora gave a salute and left her. Tina was sorry to see her go.

One to go...

Dora stood outside the hospital room of Merry Cavanaugh. She meant to knock and go in, get this last one done with, but then she heard crying. She was torn between running away from the tears and going in to comfort—

"Miss? May I help you?"

Dora's heart flipped as she turned to face a stern nurse. "I... she's crying."

"You family?"

Dora shook her head. *Don't ask another question about who I am; please don't ask...* "Shouldn't someone be with her?"

"Sometimes it's best they're left alone. You'd cry too if your family had been killed, especially when your little boy had initially lived."

Dora nodded. She feared she'd do more than cry. She'd scream and throw things and—

The nurse cocked her head, giving Dora the once-over. "If you're not family, then who—?"

Dora turned away. "I'll come back later when she's feeling better."

"But miss..."

Dora hurried away, turning into the stairwell. The door clanged shut behind her, echoing in her ears. She sank onto the top step and tried to imagine Merry's pain of gaining her physical life while losing her heart.

Dora flicked a tear away. Some reporter she was. A blubbery, weak mess.

It could have been me.

Why couldn't that thought leave her alone?

She ran down the stairs trying to get away from the truth.

Medical examiner Conrad Tills was weary. He and his team had worked overtime, completing autopsies on the casualties from Flight 1382. There were grieving families waiting, investigators to be appeased, and questions to be answered. Up until now the process had been distressing by its very harrowing quantity, and yet also routine. Cause of death? Blunt trauma. Over and over and over, until...

"Sally, come here a minute." His assistant came to the other side of the table. "Look at this." Dr. Tills spread open the lungs.

Sally looked at the evidence, then met his eyes. "Water."

"Exactly."

"He drowned."

"Exactly."

"None of the others drowned."

"Exactly."

"He was alive for a while."

"Exactly."

Dr. Tills turned over the hands of the man. "Look at the fingertips."

"Frostbite?" Sally's eyebrows wrinkled, and Dr. Tills watched as the knowledge of the truth washed over her face. "This is *him?* This is the hero?"

Dr. Tills gently placed the man's hand at his side, lingering a moment, warm skin against cold. "Look on his face, Sal. Look on the face of the hero."

"He doesn't look like a hero."

Dr. Tills nodded. "Then maybe there's hope for us all."

Nine

For you have delivered me from death and my feet from stumbling,
that I may walk before God in the light of life.

PSALM 56:13

B ut you've got to listen to me! I sat next to the man on the plane. I think the hero is Henry Smith."

George ran a hand through his thinning hair and listened as the woman on the other end of the line went on and on about needing to be sure and blahde-blahde-blah. George had already supplied the same information to three different people. It was like repeatedly being shoved back into the starting gate of a race, never getting to finish. Never getting to hear, "That's wonderful, Mr. Davanos! Thank you so much for your input."

Enough of this. The woman could have her own talk show. "Excuse me? Ma'am?"

Blessed silence.

George refrained from yelling at her and applied his most sickly sweet tone laced with the subtlest tinge of pain for best effect. "As I told you, I'm one of the five survivors, and I happen to be severely injured and still in the hospital. Yesterday I got your number from a good friend of mine, Dora Roberts, a reporter for the *Chronicle.*" If the woman found a threat in that piece of information, so be it. "So if you could be so kind as to pass my information on to whoever needs to hear it, I would be forever grateful."

The woman gushed nervously, then assured George she would do what he asked. He hung up the phone. "Insipid no-mind!"

"My, my, a little ol' plane crash didn't do anything to pale your opinions, did it, Dad?"

George looked up. "Suzy."

His daughter moved to the side of the bed and kissed her father's cheek. "What was all that about?"

George set the phone aside. "I think I know who the hero is, and I was trying to tell the airlines."

"Didn't they want to hear what you had to say?"

"They think I'm a crank."

"You *are* cranky."

"Very funny."

"So what's his name? The hero's? And how did *you* figure out what everyone else hasn't?"

George waved a hand. "I'll tell you the details later. For now, get me outta here."

"You're free to go?"

"Doctor approved my dismissal as of this morning."

Suzy looked around the room. "I suppose you don't have much to take with you."

"Just the nifty items they bought to replace my crash clothes. I guess it's tough getting a decent dry cleaner anymore. Jet fuel can be such a pesky stain…" He swung his good leg off the bed. "Now help me get dressed."

As soon as she felt a hand on her wrist, Merry turned it so the nurse could easily take her pulse. She found there was no need to even open her eyes in order for the nurses to do their duties. She didn't need to be mentally present for them to check on her body's progress. Her body would heal.

Traitor.

"Well, well, you're doing real fine today, Mrs. Cavanaugh."

Merry didn't recognize the voice. Obviously this nurse didn't realize closed eyes were a nonverbal order for silence—or at least a ban on small talk.

"The doctor will be checking in soon, and we all hope you'll be discharged today."

Merry's eyes shot open. "Discharged?"

The nurse looked confused. "Well, yes… You should be very pleased with your progress."

Merry let out a snort. "Pleased? You want me to be pleased that I am well enough to go home? Home to what? An empty house?"

"I…"

"You people, with all your cheeriness and smiley faces. You make me sick. There is nothing—absolutely nothing—to be cheery about."

The nurse put a hand to her chest. "But…but you're alive."

"And my family is dead! Don't you get it, lady? My husband and child are dead. My boy who I held in my arms… I couldn't make him live. I have no life anymore. I have no home to go to. All I have is a house. *They* were my home." The nurse extended a comforting hand. Her lips began to form a word that Merry couldn't bear to hear. "Lady, if you tsk-tsk me, I'll have you fired."

The nurse pursed her lips together.

"That a girl. Now we're *not* talking."

She fled to the door. "I'll send the doctor in as soon as he's available."

"You do that."

Merry folded her arms and grimaced as pain slid under her anger. She looked at the clock. It was an hour until they'd give her more medication.

Boy, am I two-faced. One minute I bemoan the fact my body will heal, and the next I want more painkillers to make my life easier.

Hypocrite.

It wasn't the first time she'd claimed this character trait. Wasn't it the essence of hypocrisy to go on a trip to get away from her family and then grieve over the fact that God had taken them away for good? *Be careful what you wish for.*

Her doctor appeared in the doorway and offered a concerned smile. Obviously the nurse had blabbed. He came to the bed. She noticed he wore a name tag, but she purposely looked away. She didn't want to know the name of the man who had brought her back from the edge of death. She could only forgive him if she pretended he was an anonymous stranger who didn't know any better, just a man doing his job.

The doctor read her chart. "Are you ready to go home? Because we're ready to let you go. Do you feel up to it?"

"Which question do you want answered?"

He tilted his head. "Aren't they one and the same?"

"Not at all," Merry said. "Am I ready to go home? No. I never want to go home again. Do I feel up to it? No. And from all self-examination, I doubt I will ever feel up to anything again."

He cleared his throat and avoided her eyes by looking at the chart. "Perhaps we should have Dr. Gillespe come in and speak with you?"

"And why would *we* want to do this?"

"Dr. Gillespe is good at helping patients deal with—"

"He's a shrink."

"Psychologist."

Merry tapped her head. "No thanks, Doc. What I have up here is mine alone."

"But I'm sure things are very confusing right—"

She had to laugh. "Confusing? Confusion equals uncertainty. I am alive. My family is dead. I don't see anything uncertain or confusing about that."

"Yes, well… Unfortunately, there's more. I wasn't going to tell you this, but—"

"Something more than death? Oh my, what further news do you

have to brighten my day? Out with it, Doc. I don't see how anything you have to tell me could be worse than what I already know."

He hesitated, and Merry's stomach grabbed at the possibilities. Maybe it was best that she didn't know. She pushed such weakness aside. She'd started this thing; it was time to finish it. She lifted her chin. "Out with it. Give me your best shot."

The doctor replaced her chart in its slot. He faced her. "The body of your husband has been pulled from the wreckage."

All breathing stopped. Merry hung in limbo until her body took emergency action and jump-started by sucking in fresh air.

"They found him yesterday. Your mother identified him. And also your son, whom you, of course, brought in."

Brought in only to die. Some mother I was. I couldn't save him. I couldn't keep him warm. Keep him safe. And the visualization of her mother looking at a lifeless Lou and Justin. Cold Lou. Cold Justin. Wet from the depths of the river Lou and Justin.

Merry jerked her head back and forth, denying such a picture could be reality. Her lips closed tight, her chin hardened.

"I'm sorry, Mrs. Cavanaugh. I know this is hard."

Hard? That word was no representation of how she felt. Falling from the sky was hard. Waking up under water was hard. Holding on to the metal of the plane was hard. Holding on to Justin as they flew through the air was hard. But the vision of her mother seeing in death the two people who were her life? That wasn't hard.

Was there a hell?

Absolutely.

"Mrs. Cavanaugh?"

Merry stopped brushing her hair. A man in a suit stood at her door. "Yes?"

He came in, his hand extended. "I'm Dr. Gillespe, a psychologist on staff. Your doctor asked me to stop by."

Merry didn't answer. Nor did she shake his hand. The last thing she wanted was to have her head shrunk by a shrink.

"I hear you're upset."

Merry had never heard a more idiotic understatement. This guy called himself a doctor? She resumed brushing. "No, not a bit."

He blinked twice, and in his confusion, Merry found strength. *Maybe if I act as if I'm all right, he'll leave me alone.* She slapped the brush against the palm of her hand. "Will there be anything else, Doctor? Otherwise, I'd like to finish getting ready to leave."

"You don't want to talk?"

She cocked her head. "Well, let's see, since I'm not into basketball, and baseball hasn't started yet...no. I don't think so."

He smiled. "Your humor is a good sign."

"Glad to hear it. If you care to wait, I bet I could think of a doctor joke."

He locked his hands in front of himself. "Nice wall you're building."

"Excuse me?"

"Nice wall you're building around yourself, Mrs. Cavanaugh. Before you can work through this, you'll need to knock it down."

"I don't know about any wall, but you know what might make me feel good?"

"What?"

"Knocking *you* down."

She watched him put on his tolerant face. "There's no reason for you to get violent—"

"No reason?" Her voiced edged into its shriek mode. "No *reason?*"

He glanced toward the door. "I think it's best if you calm down. If you would like a tranquilizer to help you—"

"No!" Being drugged out of her pain was the last thing she wanted right now. What she *did* want was to be rid of this man.

Then be calm. Tell him what he wants to hear.

Merry ran her hands over her face, pressing sanity into place. When she removed them, her panic was absent—at least in her outer appearance. She even managed a smile. "Well, that was quite a fit I had there, wasn't it?"

The doctor blinked a few times, gauging her new persona. "It *is* understandable."

You bet it is, Doc.

"I want to apologize for my outburst." She sighed for effect. "I just want to get home so I can begin to deal with my loss."

"But your doctor said you didn't want to go home."

Caught in the truth. She forced an apologetic smile. "That was then, this is now." She clasped her hands in her lap like a teacher's pet vying to get her way. "May I please go home now?"

The doctor studied her face intently, and Merry nearly lost it under his gaze. She felt her right cheek twitch at the effort, but luckily, the doctor looked away and didn't see it.

He fished a business card from his pocket. "If you want to talk…" He nodded a good-bye and left.

Merry stared at the card. *That was easy—and telling.* A few witty comments, a confident facade, and people left her alone. The doctor had been eager to accept her normal mode over her panic. Interesting.

But maybe it made sense. In spite of their good intentions, people didn't want to talk about bad things, be reminded of bad things, or be around people who were suffering through bad things. Perhaps because it made *them* feel bad and vulnerable and inept.

If Merry wanted to be left alone in her grief and pain, then the best course of action was to pretend she was fine. Act strong. Put on a face of acceptance, tinted with a blush of regret for good effect. People would be so relieved they would flee to escape even the shadow of what she'd been through. Truth be told, they didn't want to know how it felt. And they didn't want to witness it, either. Ignorance was bliss.

But if she was going to pull this off... Merry held a mirror to her face. She looked awful, her face scarred from cuts, bruises, and the aftereffects of frostbite. She'd lucked out with the doctor. Fooling her extended family would take more effort. She lifted her chin and immediately noticed a change for the better. With difficulty she relaxed her forehead until the lines went away, and she pressed a finger against the crease between her brows until it dissipated.

Her smile needed work. Actually, it wasn't her mouth's problem but her eyes. For even when her lips were curled in the right direction, her eyes betrayed the mask.

With a deep sigh, Merry took one last look at the reflection of her facade. It was doable. She'd work on it.

"You wait right there, Mrs. Cavanaugh. Your mother called and said she'd be here momentarily to take you home."

The nurse left Merry sitting in a wheelchair in her room. There were no belongings to collect. She wore a complete set of new clothing, a gift from the hospital or airline or some Good Samaritan. She had no purse, no money, no nothing. And that was fine with her.

If only she could proceed with her life without its other encumbrances. There was no picking up where she left off, either in terms of her activities, her possessions, or her home. Maybe if she worked hard on her "I'm okay" face, she could somehow con her mother into dropping her off in the middle of nowhere and driving away, leaving Merry to fend for herself. If that involved crawling off in a wilderness corner to curl up and die like a wounded animal, so be it.

She maneuvered her wheelchair into the doorway and looked down the hall she'd avoided in spite of numerous attempts by the nurses to get her to take a walk. All the noise and hubbub were disturbing, and she pulled the wheels back, making sure she wasn't sticking out into the fray. Her domain since the crash had been so small. Safe. Isolated. To venture into the world…

An old man in a wheelchair was pushed past. "Whoa! Back up there, girl."

His wheelchair reappeared in her sight line, and he looked at her. "You one of the five?"

"The five?"

"The five survivors? One of us?"

There were others? Why have I never wondered if there were others? "I guess I am."

"Me too." He extended a hand, then turned it into a salute when the doorway and their chairs prevented contact. "George Davanos. And you're…Sonja?"

"Merry. Merry Cavanaugh."

"That's right. Taken first."

"How do you know that?"

"I've been watching the news reports." He did a double take. "Haven't you?"

Merry shook her head. It had never occurred to her to watch coverage of the crash. Why would anyone want to see it again and again and—

"You'll have to take a look sometime. It's a weird experience seeing yourself in the water and then being rescued. Obviously at the time I was pretty focused and had no clue what was going on around me. Did you?"

She shook her head again. He studied her a moment, reminding Merry of the questioning looks her father used to give her when he knew she was keeping something from him. George must be a father himself.

"Too bad we didn't have a chance to compare notes, Miss Merry, but the hospital was pretty tight with visiting privileges. Protective as a mama hen covering her brood." He leaned closer.

"Speaking of chickens…I bet they thought our meeting would cause more emotional trauma than they were ready to deal with. Or maybe they're worried about lawsuits or something." His eyes twinkled. "Or maybe they're in cahoots with the airlines. Now there's a company that would rather not see *us* again." He took a deep breath. "But maybe we can get together once we're mended. You think?"

She didn't answer. The last thing she wanted was to rehash the destruction of her family with strangers.

He swatted the arm of the woman pushing his chair. "Well then, I guess we'd best be going, Suze." He looked at Merry. "This is my daughter, Suzy. You got family coming to get you?"

Don't mention family to me, old man. But as soon as Merry felt the anger threaten, she remembered her new resolve and tried out her happy mask. It took a little effort…but… *Yes, there it was.* She grinned a moment, letting the muscles find their places. "Of course they are," she said. Her voice broke a little, but she hoped he wouldn't notice.

He noticed. "Oh, shoot…you're the one who lost her husband and son, aren't you? I'm so sorry. I didn't mean to be flip about things. Don't take no nevermind about me. I'm just an old coot who should know better but doesn't."

The daughter spoke. "But do you have a way home, Mrs. Cavanaugh?"

So much for my acting abilities. Merry nodded. "My mom's coming."

"Well, that's good anyway," George said.

Merry shrugged. George kept looking at her. It made her squirm. *My face green, old man?*

Finally he pulled his eyes away. "Home, Suze."

As he moved on, Merry turned her chair inward toward the room. Why hadn't her cover-up worked with George? She was so sure it was the answer to dealing with people. But maybe it didn't work because he wasn't an outsider like the rest. George and Merry shared something unique, and that made the mask unnecessary— almost an act of bad manners.

And yet, as nice as George had been, Merry didn't want to meet any of the other survivors. Although they had this shared experience, there was no way they could ever bond. They were not the same. The others had lived and were eager to go on with their lives.

Merry had lived only to want to die.

As they waited for the elevator, George looked over his shoulder toward Merry's room.

"What?" Suzy asked.

"I'm worried about that girl."

"You don't even know her."

Suzy was right. There was no reason for George to worry about a woman he'd met for thirty seconds, a woman who had spoken less than a dozen words. And yet there was something about Merry's eyes, something about the way she shrugged when George had mentioned how good it was that her mother was picking her up. As if her mother was not enough, as if what she had to go home to wasn't worth leaving the hospital for.

She's just lost her husband and *her child. You lost Irma. You know how that feels. You know—*

George tossed his hand backward and whacked Suzy's arm. "Go back!"

"What?"

"Go back to Merry's room. I have to talk to her. There's something wrong." He tried to turn the wheelchair on his own, but his hands wouldn't prevail against Suzy's solid stance.

"Dad. Enough. Leave the woman alone. You could tell she didn't want to talk—"

"But that's the point. She's depressed. I could see it. And I can help."

"How can you help?"

"I...I know..."

"She's probably just tired and hurting from her loss. You know how you felt when Mom died. She doesn't want a stranger butting in."

"But—"

The elevator dinged. "We'll get her phone number. You can call her later, okay?"

George was pushed inside the elevator. His stomach grabbed when the doors closed between him and Merry Cavanaugh.

The doctor standing beside her wielded the ultimate power over her immediate future. With this knowledge, Sonja was on her best behavior. She was *willing* herself to be pronounced well.

"What's the verdict, Doctor? Can I go home?"

The doctor peered over the top of the chart. "Do you want to go home?"

"Where's the door?"

"I see no reason—"

"Super." Sonja flipped back the covers.

The doctor stopped her. "I don't want you driving. Can someone come and pick you up?"

"My parents are flying in."

"Then you need to wait until they get here."

"I can get a cab."

"You could, but I'd rather you have more personal help." She patted Sonja's hand. "You deserve a little pampering, Ms. Grafton. There are so few times in life when one gets it. I'd enjoy it if I were you."

Sonja wasn't sure her parents were the pampering types.

Although she wanted some attention, the thought of having them with her, in her apartment, was not restful. Especially since she hadn't cleaned up before she left for her trip. Her kitchen was full of dirty dishes, there was laundry to do, and newspapers were strewn all over the floor—

"I'll tell the nurses you can go as soon as your parents get here. Agreed?"

Do I have a choice? "Agreed."

The doctor adjusted her stethoscope around her neck. "Have a nice life, Ms. Grafton. You're a very lucky woman."

"I know."

A candy striper came to the door with magazines and news-papers. The doctor nodded a good-bye and let the girl in.

"You want something to read?"

Sonja looked at the clock. It was two hours before her parents' flight got in. "Sure. Give me a newspaper." She thought of her new friend, Dora. "The *Chronicle* if you have it."

Sonja's attention was immediately drawn to a front-page pic-ture of a crane lifting a twisted piece of fuselage from the river. It was a ghastly reminder. *It's a miracle any of them had survived. If the crash could do that to metal, what chance did a frail body have?*

She found a story about the helicopter rescuers, Floyd Calbert and Hugh Johnson. It was a wonderfully written piece, but more than that, Sonja found she could not take her eyes off the two men. Her saviors. Two men propelled into heroic action by cir-cumstances beyond their control. *All logic told them not to go, and yet they did. And saved us. Saved me.*

Sonja pulled the paper to her chest and closed her eyes. *If I haven't said this before, and I know we haven't talked much, but thank You, God. Thank You for giving me this second chance. Thank You for men like Floyd and Hugh.*

She ended the prayer feeling better—and more than a little

shocked that just a few words to God would have such an instant effect on her. Maybe this God-stuff wasn't all bad.

She turned to page two. A headline caught her attention: *Funerals Set for Sanford Industries Crash Victims.* She held the page close. Allen and Dale were being buried tomorrow. To think she nearly missed it. If she hadn't read about it in the paper…

Which brought to mind something that irked her more as each hour passed: Why hadn't anyone from work called her? Not just to tell her about the funeral, but to check on her? On the plane, Roscoe had spoken of her reputation. Apparently things were worse than she thought. Did people resent her for living when Allen and Dale died? Did they think she'd done something shifty to bring about their deaths?

That's absurd.

Perhaps. Yet why hadn't anyone called? Why was she being treated like a persona non grata? Was she being punished for living?

With a sudden burst of energy, Sonja crumpled the newspaper into a wad and tossed it toward the wastebasket. It fell short.

Join the club.

If Sonja's body hadn't been so sore, she would have paced. What was taking her parents so long? They'd called from the airport to tell her they arrived and were renting a car. But maybe her father didn't like the car they'd gotten and was arguing about getting a better one—while his daughter was going crazy in a hospital room, waiting to go home.

She'd seen him do such a thing many times. No transaction was easy when Sheffield D. Grafton II was involved. Dinners were sent back, hotel rooms refused, traffic tickets disputed. When she still lived at home, Sonja had made it a habit to go to the rest room or wait in the car when such confrontations loomed. And it wasn't that he had the power of money on his side. No, her parents were definitely middle class, but her father's name *sounded* like money, so he played the part.

Sonja found comfort in knowing she wasn't like him. Not in this respect anyway. Or was she?

She heard a commotion outside and recognized its source immediately. The booming bass of her father's voice demanded attention as he asked where his daughter's room was located.

Sonja put a hand to her chest. Why had her heartbeat suddenly shifted from a livable two-step to a polka rhythm?

They're here to help you, Sonja. You have nothing to apologize for or feel bad about. You're the victim.

Her parents swept into her room, her father in the lead. He took the power position at the foot of the bed. "Well there you are."

Where did you expect me to be? In the lobby, waiting so you wouldn't have to bother finding a parking space?

Her mother made a beeline for her side, studying her, assessing the damage. She lifted a hand to touch the forehead bandage but withdrew it before it could be contaminated by the wound's imperfection. "My, my, you *are* worse for the wear, aren't you, dear?"

"I just went through a plane crash, Mother."

The woman cocked her head, making further assessments. "No need to be rude, Sonja. Is that a bruise on your neck there? And your skin…"

Sonja put a hand over the black and blue welt that decorated the right side of her neck. And her skin… She knew her cheeks were still suffering the aftereffects of frostbite. "Nasty, nasty crash. We'll have to sue."

Her father nodded. "I've already started proceedings."

Sonja shook her head, incredulous. "I was kidding, Daddy."

"Being compensated for such a huge misjudgment and failure is no kidding matter. People have to pay for such things."

Sonja knew he was probably right. A lawsuit by the families of the victims was inevitable. "But I lived. I'm all right."

He waved a hand the length of her body as if it disgusted him. "You are not all right. You are broken and bruised and—"

"I'm damaged goods?"

"Don't be cute, Sonja. You know what I mean."

Indeed I do.

Her mother continued giving her the once-over. "Where *did* you get those clothes, dear? They're atrocious."

"*My* clothes were ruined and reeked of jet fuel. These were a gift from the hospital." She looked down at herself. Although they weren't something she'd choose, they were fine—to anyone but her mother. "Perhaps you should have offered to shop for them? Or at least shown them the acceptable stores?"

Her father pulled out his cell phone, checked the display, then obviously seeing no waiting messages, put it away. "It was a simple question, Sonja. No need to treat your mother so unkindly. She— *we* only want what's best for you."

Sonja was suddenly weary and wanted nothing more than to have them leave so she could snuggle under the covers and take a nap until some nice nurse wanted to draw blood or poke and prod. Anything was better than the mental drawing of blood and the emotional poking and prodding that were her parents' specialties.

She drew on what little energy she had and tried to focus on today's goal. "Please take me home now."

"Of course, dear."

As her father commandeered some nurses to help her into a wheelchair, Sonja realized she was the victim all right—and had been for twenty-six years.

Tina heard the whir of wheels in the hall and an odd thump-thump sound. Her curiosity was answered when David pushed a balloon-bedecked wheelchair into her room. The balloons took a moment to adjust to the sudden stop.

"Ta-da!"

"David, what are you doing?"

He put the brakes on the chair. "I've come to take you home."

"They said it was all right?"

"You have been cleared and are ready for takeoff." He suddenly clamped a hand over his mouth. "Oops, sorry. Bad choice of words."

She waved his concerns away. "If you think I'm going to break down every time someone mentions flying, you're wrong. How weak do you think I am?"

"It wouldn't be a sign of weakness, Teen. It would be totally understandable."

"Not to me." She threw the covers off her legs and carefully maneuvered her cast to the floor. David rushed to help, but she shook her head. "I can do it. I *have* to do it."

"Actually, you don't *have* to. The world won't disown you if you admit you need help."

She adjusted her crutch and hobbled to the closet where the nurse had hung the new clothes donated for her trip home. "That's all very dandy, but I'm not going to admit to something that isn't true. I am very—"

"Rude."

She turned to look at him. His cheeks were mottled pink. "I was going to say I am very capable of handling things for myself."

"Maybe so, but you're also very rude. Did it ever occur to you that people take pleasure in helping other people? That by being so disgustingly self-sufficient, you are denying other people—denying me—of a feeling of worth and the feeling that my actions can do some good?"

She handed him the hanger so she could close the closet door. "So I'm supposed to act weak and weary just to make you feel strong and macho?" He looked at her without speaking. "David, don't look at me like that."

He extended the hanger and dropped the clothing to the floor. "Your wish is my command." He left the room, the sound of his footsteps fading fast.

What have I done? Why did she fight a constant battle between mind and mouth? What Tina thought, Tina said—right or wrong, loving or hurtful.

She remembered a proverb: "Even a fool is thought wise if he keeps silent, and discerning if he holds his tongue." She snickered, remembering a down-home quote: "It is better to keep your mouth closed and let people think you are a fool than to open it and remove all doubt." Two quotes from two great men: King Solomon, the wisest man to ever live, and Mark Twain, the wittiest. Against wisdom such as this, she had no defense.

There was no doubt. She was a fool. The empty room was proof.

Lord, help me only say things You approve of.

It was a tall order.

Since David had walked out, Tina was forced to get dressed and into the wheelchair by herself. A heart-shaped Mylar balloon proclaiming "I Love You!" kissed the top of her head. David loved her.

Past tense?

She wouldn't blame him. How could she be so rude as to shove away the one person who'd been at her side through this entire ordeal—and everything that had come before?

And everything that would come after? That was less certain.

She looked at her watch. It had been twenty-five minutes since David walked out of her hospital room, dropping her clothes on the floor. All during the process of getting dressed—when she *could* have used some help—she kept expecting to hear his knock on the door. He'd come in and apologize for leaving. *He* would apologize, and his willing act of regret would spur her own reluctant apology. Then things would be normal again until the next time David got in the way as she battled her own private demons of insecurity and pride.

It was disturbing to realize that most of the arguments between them were arguments between Tina and Tina, two sides of herself duking it out with poor David, the innocent witness. How could he still profess to love her when she repeatedly put him through such turmoil? It was beyond—

"Hi." David stood in the door, his hands in his pockets.

Tina nearly cried at the sight of him. She avoided his eyes but held out a hand. He bent to kiss it. Then he moved to the back of the wheelchair.

"Let's get you home."

Anthony listened to the television newscasts with a pad of paper in hand. There had to be someone to blame, and he intended to be first in line.

He'd already called his lawyer and flipped past his polite questions of concern. The point was this: "How much can we get?"

He had not received a satisfactory answer, and Anthony came to the conclusion that he might need a special kind of lawyer to handle such a lawsuit. Or maybe they would go the class-action route and file jointly with the other survivors and the families of the deceased.

He was not going to let this go. It was his duty, his responsibility, to make people pay for their mistakes, and from what he'd heard on the news so far, some whopping human errors had been made. The bottom line was that Flight 1382 should never have taken off. And who knew what errors had contributed to this fatal lapse of judgment?

Anthony heard a commotion in the hall and turned up the volume on his set to cover it. He saw a hoard of people file by, their eyes searching for a room number. Pesky visitors. Probably relatives of one of the other survivors coming to hug and cry and listen to the stories of rescue and fear.

Showing their love and concern.

Anthony shook such weak interpretations away. Although it was true no one had come to visit him in the hospital, the office did send a vase of flowers. And strangers had filled his room with other floral offerings.

He had no family. He supposed there were some distant cousins, but any contact now would be construed as an act of desperation or a desire to share in his notoriety. *Yes, I'm Tony's third cousin on his mother's side, and he was always such a good boy...*

And he wouldn't let himself be disappointed that one of his lady friends—Sarah, Bridget, or especially long-legged Marta with her intoxicating scent—hadn't stopped by to fawn all over him and kiss his owies. Marta had called and informed him she didn't *do* hospitals. So much for her. He didn't need commiseration. He needed action. Legal action.

A candy striper peeked in his door, then pulled her head away when their eyes met. He waited a moment for her to fully emerge, but she didn't.

"Come in, girl. Do you have my paper?"

She appeared, newspaper in hand. "Sorry you had to wait, Dr. Thorgood, but I was late getting to work because my alarm—"

Anthony raised a hand. "I don't accept such excuses from the people in my office, and I won't accept them here."

"Yes, sir." She stopped far short of the bed, which forced her to lean awkwardly in order to extend the paper within his reach.

He grabbed the paper. "I don't bite."

She blushed but did not move closer.

He flicked a hand, dismissing her. She escaped into the hall. Why was it so impossible to get decent help anymore? Either they acted like frightened peasants or they had a cocky attitude that no amount of discipline would break through.

Anthony removed the want ads and fluffy social sections from the *Chronicle* and concentrated on the real news. He scanned the first few pages quickly for articles about the crash and its aftermath. There were other articles by Dora Roberts, updating the progress of the retrieval, but not the one he was looking for. Not the one about him.

He went back to the front page, scanning again. *It's not here!* He crumpled the paper and tossed it to the floor. He reached for the phone and drilled his finger into the number zero.

"Get me the *Chronicle.*"

"The who?"

"The *Chronicle,* the newspaper."

"Just a moment, sir."

Anthony watched TV while he waited. Twenty more bodies had been recovered. It was exasperating how slow the retrieval was. The experts weren't able to concentrate on recovering the majority of the wreckage until the bodies were out of the way. And until they recovered the wreckage, they wouldn't know whom to blame.

"The *Chronicle.* May I help you?"

"Dora Roberts."

"One moment, please."

The operator returned. "I'm sorry, sir. She's out of the office. Can I give you her cell number?"

Perfect. "Do it."

He memorized the number and dialed it immediately.

"Roberts here."

"This is Dr. Anthony Thorgood—"

"Yes, Dr. Thorgood. What can I do for you?"

Her voice was flat and Anthony noticed a slight emphasis on his title. "What can you do for me? You can write the article you promised. The one written from our interview. I just got the paper and it's not there."

"And it won't be."

"Excuse me?"

She cleared her throat. "I know you're a survivor, Dr. Thorgood. And I know you've been through a terrible ordeal."

"You bet I have."

"But the truth is, I'm just not interested in your story."

"And why not?"

There was a pause. "Because there are better stories to be had."

"You mean the stories from the other survivors?"

"That's really none of your business, but the truth is, the other survivors *do* have interesting stories to tell. Plus the stories of the rescuers, the airline personnel, the people working on the salvage of the plane…"

"But not me?"

Another pause. "But not you."

"You're singling me out?"

"I'm singling you out."

"Why?" She didn't respond. Anthony muted the television. "I didn't hear your answer."

"That's because I didn't give you one."

"And why is that?"

"Because my mama taught me to be polite."

"Dora…"

"*Ms.* Roberts."

Touché. "*Ms.* Roberts. I really don't have time to play games. I am a man of facts, so tell me the facts. I insist."

She let out a small laugh. "Well, if you insist."

"I do."

"The truth is, Dr. Thorgood, I chose not to write an article about you because I found you to be an arrogant, egotistical man with a skewed opinion of yourself and your position in the world."

"You have no right to judge—"

"But *you* judged. You judged all those people who died in the crash. You said you lived because you were better than they were, because your life had more meaning, because you were more important. You took the lifeline of another because of that belief."

And your point is?

Anthony had to admit his philosophy of "I deserve it" sounded brash coming from another person's mouth. And though he still believed it was true, he suddenly had a stab of insight. To believe a truth was one thing, but to share a truth with people who were not able to comprehend it was foolish. Especially when the said truth was proof of their own mediocrity. He'd have to be more careful.

"Will there be anything else, Doctor?"

Anthony shook his head, then realized the reporter couldn't see through the phone. "No, I'd say I've had quite enough from you."

"My dear doctor, the feeling is definitely mutual."

Anthony pressed the call button two more times. What was taking them so long?

Finally a nurse appeared, though by the nonchalance of her entrance, she should be fired.

"Where have you been? I've been calling and calling and—"

She appeared unimpressed. "What can we do for you, Dr. Thorgood?"

"*We* can speed up the paperwork so I can go home like the others."

She let a grin escape. "I'm sorry, but the doctor has determined that, unlike the other survivors, you need to stay another day."

"I what?"

"You have a temperature—which as you know, *Doctor,* indicates infection. Unless your temperature is normal you can't go home."

This is unbelievable.

"Is there anything I can get for you?"

"Everyone else gets to go home, and I have to stay?"

She didn't respond.

"You're enjoying this, aren't you?"

Her smug look vanished, and her eyebrows dropped. "I assure you, we'd like nothing better than to see you discharged."

"You are a whiz at the double entendre, aren't you, nurse?"

She pivoted on one foot, then spoke over her shoulder. "Why, Doctor, I have no idea what you're talking about."

"What do you mean you can't do the articles?"

Standing in front of her boss, Dora wished she had called in the bad news. But that would have been the chicken's way out. Since Clyde trusted her for the articles on the survivors, he deserved the chance to yell at her face-to-face.

"I interviewed four of the five and—"

"Which one wouldn't give you an interview?"

"Not wouldn't," Dora said. "I never even approached Merry Cavanaugh, the woman who lost her husband and child. I didn't want to bother her. I thought it would be in bad taste."

He stared at her incredulously. The veins in his nose rose to attention, looking like a map of a river delta. "I'll take bad taste over reading about her ordeal in some other paper."

Dora's stomach clenched. "Have you seen anything?"

"No. But if I do…" He shook his head. "So that explains the one. What about the four you *did* get?"

"They considered me their friend, just like you wanted."

"Good. Then write the—"

"They spoke off the record a lot. They confided in me. I can't betray that."

"What's so hard about getting a few lines like, 'I was petrified' or 'I thought I was going to die'?"

Dora was stunned that she had never asked any questions of

the survivors that would have elicited such quotes. "We never talked about that kind of thing."

Clyde snickered. "You never...? What *did* you talk about? Their favorite dessert? The Super Bowl game?"

He wasn't going to like this. "Mostly we talked about God."

Clyde rolled his eyes. "I've been very tolerant and patient with all your God-talk, Dora. Hey, I believe in Him too. But you take it too far. When your faith starts to affect your work..."

"But it's natural for people who've faced death to think about God, to talk about Him."

"But it's not natural for a secular newspaper to print testimonials, and it sounds like that's all you got."

What could she say? "I'm sorry, Clyde."

"Yeah? Well, me too." He turned back to his computer screen. She was obviously dismissed. "Why don't you go talk to Jean. Maybe she has a dog show you could cover. Or a sewing circle. Those seem to be more your speed."

"That's not fair."

"Life's not fair. But if you don't give me any news fit to print, then you don't give me much choice, do you?"

"I'm working on the article about the hero."

"Oh, really? I'll believe it when I see it." He flipped a hand at her. "Now go on. I have work to do."

Floyd and Hugh approached the building that housed the remains of the crash victims. They walked shoulder to shoulder, their hands in their pockets, their eyes on the sidewalk.

"I don't want to do this," Floyd said.

"It shouldn't be that bad," Hugh said. "They use TV cameras now. It's not like they lift up the sheet and make you look."

"But why do we need to be involved? If they think they've found the hero, they must have their own clues. Besides, I'm not sure we can help. During the rescue we were busy and conditions were lousy. It would be terrible to identify the wrong man."

"We can only give it a shot, Floyd. If we're not sure, we're not sure. Agreed?"

"Agreed."

They reached the front door and the helicopter crew proceeded to the viewing area. They checked in and waited in a small room with a television overhead. A white-coated man joined them.

"Thank you for coming down, gentlemen. This will only take a moment. If you'll look at the screen."

A face appeared. Ashen, with a cut on his upper forehead. But otherwise undisturbed, as if asleep. Floyd had trouble swallowing. How many times had he looked into the eyes of the hero as the man raised his face expectantly toward the helicopter? Were those the eyes—now closed? Was this the man who'd made a conscious decision to die in order to save the lives of others?

"It's him," Hugh said. "The hair. The beard. As near as I can tell, it's him."

The technician turned to Floyd. "Do you agree?"

Floyd's throat tightened so he was forced to nod. He could not take his eyes off the face of the hero. He felt Hugh and the technician looking at him, but he didn't care. He cleared his throat. "What's his name?"

"Henry Smith."

Nice to meet you, Henry. You don't know it, but you changed my life forever.

"Well then, thanks for coming in." The technician left them alone. A few moments later, the screen went to black.

"Just like that, he's gone again," Floyd said. "We finally see him, and then he's gone."

Hugh put a hand on Floyd's shoulder. "Hey, take it easy—"

Floyd let the tears come. "I wanted to meet him, you know? I wanted to shake his hand and tell him how I found his actions astonishing." His voice cracked. "Do you think he knew people were proud of him? Or did he just slip into that water feeling as if he failed?"

"Floyd…"

"*We* were the ones who failed, Hugh. We were the ones who couldn't get back in time."

Hugh squeezed his shoulder and nodded. "I know. I know."

"They're calling us heroes too. But what kind of heroes are we to let a man like this die?"

The black screen was their only answer.

Ten

My comfort in my suffering is this:
Your promise preserves my life.

PSALM 119:50

We have begun to make our descent. Please make sure your seat belts are fastened."

Ellen Smith didn't move to put on her seat belt or secure her tray table or put her seat in an upright position. Since they'd taken off two hours before, she had not stirred. She hadn't read a magazine, slept, eaten, or talked to the person in the seat beside her. She was relieved that her seatmate was not the talky type, but one of those businessmen who took out his laptop at the first chance and spent the entire flight working.

Until now… Having to stow his computer, he suddenly had nothing to do. He turned to Ellen. "I wasn't too keen on flying this airline after their crash—especially going to that same airport. How 'bout you?"

Ellen considered remaining silent. Why stop the zombie act now? But then her anger and frustration met somewhere in the pit of her stomach, and she felt words clawing toward the surface. She slowly turned her face toward him and waited until his eyes met hers. "My husband died in that crash. I'm on my way to identify the body."

The businessman sucked in a breath, his eyes wide. "I'm so sorry. This must be awful for you. I can't imagine such a—"

"Lucky you."

With another short stutter, he wisely shut up and turned his face toward the window. Ellen would have to remember that line. It was obviously a conversation killer. And why shouldn't it be? What could people say in response to such a blatant reminder to count their own blessings?

Ellen closed her eyes and felt the engines decrease their power. How bizarre that she was being flown in a Sun Fun airplane in order to identify the body of her husband who had died in a Sun Fun Airlines crash. And first class, no less. She'd never flown first class, though she and Henry had talked about doing it to splurge. He certainly had the frequent flyer miles. But during his brief times off, the last thing Henry wanted to do was fly. He usually ended up giving his perks to coworkers. But now—alone—she was living like the rich and famous. *Henry? Look at me! I'm riding in first class. Aren't I special?*

Special? Not in a way Ellen wanted to be special. And not even in a unique way. For ninety-five other families were coming together, taking a special trip to handle the special task of identifying the bodies of their special loved ones.

It wasn't even a sure thing that they'd found Henry's body yet. But Ellen had been assured that recovering the deceased was Sun Fun's first priority. *How about flying a safe plane? Shouldn't that be your first priority?* It was like having a teenager trash his house during a party and then tell his parents that his first priority was picking up the shards of Waterford crystal they'd broken. Too little too late.

Her worst fear was that they'd never find his body. The plane crashed in a river. A river has a current. What if Henry was swept downriver, never to be seen again? What if she waited and waited, day after day, only to be told, "I'm sorry, Mrs. Smith, but we can't find him." Now that would be a special situation.

Can't find him? Can't find the man I've been married to for twenty years? Can't find the man who had the ability to make me laugh, drive me crazy, and fill my soul like no one else in the world? Isn't it bad enough you made him lose his life? How dare you lose his body!

But maybe lost was lost. Ellen knew Henry wasn't in his body anymore. The soul that was Henry, the essence of his being, was with God. Ellen knew that and found comfort in it. She wondered if Henry was looking down at her now with the glories of heaven all around him. Smiling, laughing, glowing with God's peace and true happiness, whispering to her, "Come on, Elly. I'm fine. Really. You should see it up here. I'm the lucky one. And I'm waiting for you, Elly. When your time comes, I'll be the second face you see."

When your time comes.

Such a strange phrase. People tossed it around at times of death, attempting to make each other feel better. *It was his time.* Ellen didn't ask the question, "Who says?" She knew God was in charge, and it was His choice—though such ends were certainly affected by man's choices too. People often sealed their fate by their own stupidity, and God allowed it. He was big into free will—which was both a blessing *and* a curse.

No, the question Ellen wanted answered was not "Who says?" but "How come?" Why did Henry have to die? Why did ninety-five innocent people perish in the few split seconds where everything that was right went wrong?

Yet what good would it do to know why? If they could tell her today that the plane crashed because it was too cold or because it ran out of gas or because it was Friday, what difference would it make? Henry was dead. Would knowing that by the absence of some error he would still be alive make that fact better? Or different? Would having someone to blame make her feel better?

Ellen heard the landing gear descend. It was time to find Henry.

A flight attendant came down the aisle and stopped beside Ellen's row. Ellen looked up expectantly. They were within minutes of landing. But the woman had tears in her eyes. What could possibly—?

"Mrs. Smith? Mrs. Henry Smith?"

"Yes?"

The woman's chin quivered. "I just got word from the gate. They just announced that your husband was…" Her voice choked.

Whatever could be wrong?

"Out with it, lady," Ellen's seatmate said. "You're torturing the poor woman."

The attendant took a deep breath. "Your husband was the hero of Flight 1382."

Ellen felt a quiver start in her diaphragm and travel up to her throat. She drew in a shaky breath. "Henry?"

"Yes."

"Oh my…oh my…" Ellen closed her eyes and leaned her head against the headrest. *I knew it. I knew it was him.*

She heard whispering around her and then louder talking. Then came applause. She looked at the attendant who stood in the aisle, tears streaming down her face, wearing a bittersweet smile. The attendant spread a hand toward the rest of the plane, then began clapping herself. "It's for him," she whispered toward Ellen. "It's for Henry."

It took a moment for Ellen to absorb the implication of the applause. People were proud of her Henry. They were applauding his final act. They—

The attendant put a hand on her arm. "Would you stand for a moment, Mrs. Smith? Acknowledge them?"

Somehow it didn't seem right for Ellen to take a bow for her husband's deeds. And yet—

Her seatmate leaned toward her. "Do it for your husband, Mrs. Smith. He can't be here, but you can."

And so, with the help of the flight attendant, Ellen Smith unbuckled her seat belt and stood. And the applause soared. She looked back at the rest of the plane and saw faces full of awe, compassion, and a shared combination of sorrow and joy. And she wanted to clap herself.

Bravo, Henry. Bravo, dear husband.

"There."

David stood over Tina and tucked her in. She was cocooned in the Queen Anne chair in her apartment, her feet on the ottoman, her legs swathed in an afghan. On the table to her right sat a cup of hot chocolate, and in her lap were three new books waiting to be read.

"You comfy?"

"If I were any more comfy, I'd hibernate for the rest of the winter. I certainly hope I don't need to go to the bathroom soon. I wouldn't want to ruin your handiwork."

"Then hold it."

"I'll do my best." She noticed David check his watch for the third time. "You have to get back to work?"

"Nope. I took the day off." He moved to the front door and looked out the side window. Something was up. Surely he wasn't having more balloons or flowers delivered.

"David, what's going on? You're acting like a nervous lookout."

"In a way, I—" He glanced out the window, then clapped his hands. "They're here!"

"Who's here?"

"Your surprise."

Tina felt a wave of nervous knots grip her stomach. She couldn't imagine whom David had invited over. Fellow teachers? Not likely. Students? No way.

The doorbell rang. David put his hand on the doorknob. "You ready?"

"How can I be ready when I don't know who—?"

He opened the door. A couple stood shoulder to shoulder as if they did not want to be separated. The man was slight and reminded Tina of the weak brother Fredo in *The Godfather*. The woman had the beautiful unmarred skin of the Orient. Within moments, Tina knew who they were.

Mallory's parents.

Tina took advantage of her stagnant position in the chair and the time it took David to usher them in to try to get her bearings. She'd asked David to get ahold of them, and now he had. As a surprise. To please her. But now that she was confronted with them, what was she going to say? She closed her eyes. *Lord, help me.*

David made the introductions. "Mr. and Mrs. Carpelli, this is Tina McKutcheon. Tina, Mr. and Mrs. Carpelli."

Tina extended her hand, and Mr. Carpelli shook it. Mrs. Carpelli nodded a greeting. They did not smile—which wasn't too surprising. And yet…

"Have a seat," David said, indicating the couch across from Tina. "I've made some hot chocolate. Would you like a cup?"

"We won't be staying that long," Mr. Carpelli said. His wife shook her head.

Tina homed in on the *won't* in his statement. Not "we can't stay long," but "we won't. " Maybe this wasn't such a good idea.

Mr. Carpelli adjusted himself on the couch cushions while Mrs. Carpelli perched herself on the edge as if ready to flee. *From her husband or my house?* He sliced through Tina with a look. "We didn't want to come."

Tina's breath stopped. She and David exchanged a look. Finally she found some words. "Then why did you?"

"It seemed like the right thing to do."

Tina couldn't remember witnessing such a blatant example of people doing the right thing wrong. "If you'd rather go…"

Mr. Carpelli glanced at his wife. "Maybe we should."

David rushed between them. "No, no…stay. I know this is

awkward for everyone, but Tina got to know your daughter on the plane and was impressed with the girl. That's why she wanted to meet you."

"To gloat?"

Tina let out a puff of air. "Excuse me?"

Mr. Carpelli took his wife's hand. "You lived. Our daughter died. You're a teacher. You're supposed to help and protect children when their parents aren't around. Why didn't you save our daughter?"

David moved to Tina's side. "Mr. Carpelli, I don't think that's fair. Tina—"

Tina stopped him with a hand. She could handle this. She *had* to handle this. "Mr. and Mrs. Carpelli, I cannot begin to imagine the grief you are going through, and because of that, I will forgive your horrid and insensitive outburst. As with most of the world—including myself before this experience—you have no concept of the forces involved as a plane crashes." She adjusted herself in the chair and grimaced against the pain more than she needed to in order to make her point.

"If you must know, I *was* holding Mallory's hand when we knew things weren't right. But there is no way I could have saved her as the plane ripped apart. If I could have, I would have. Perhaps your accusation comes from the question of whether or not I would have given my life to save hers—like the hero did for the rest of us." She shook her head. "And the answer to that is, I don't know. I don't think anyone knows the full extent of the heart in regard to sacrifice until the time comes."

Tina felt the sting of tears and was strengthened by David's hand on her shoulder. "Speaking of the hero…should I have refused the lifeline from him? Should I have insisted he go first?" She sniffed loudly, knowing this was a question that would haunt her like a shadow. She lifted her chin and gained strength with her next breath. "Though you might want to condemn me for that too, I won't let you. That's between me and God."

She saw tears in Mrs. Carpelli's eyes. Her husband stared straight ahead, but Tina could see the tendons in his neck tighten as he struggled for control.

Suddenly, Tina remembered why she wanted to meet them. Had her blown chance to tell Mallory about Christ resulted in eternal consequences? This was going to be delicate. How could she segue from yelling at Mallory's parents to asking them about their relationship with God?

Tina decided to emphasize the positive. "Mallory was an interesting girl, Mr. and Mrs. Carpelli. As you mentioned, I'm a high school teacher so I know the kind of kids who are out there. To be truthful, I suffer through teaching them. But your daughter..." Tina remembered the thought-provoking discussions they'd had on the plane. They were extraordinary. If only she'd realized it at the time. "Mallory mentioned wanting to go into the military?"

"A stupid idea," Mr. Carpelli said.

Couldn't the man say *anything* positive? "I don't think a person's desire to serve her country is ever stupid. She was very inspired by her Grandpa Carpelli."

"My father brainwashed that girl."

Mrs. Carpelli squeezed her husband's knee indicating she did not have so harsh an opinion. *Doesn't the woman talk?*

"From what I could tell, your father had a good influence on Mallory. He made her interested in history, in honor, and..." *Here goes.* "And in God."

Mr. Carpelli stood, drawing his wife up with him. "Don't you dare speak that word again. It was God who made me lose my job, it was God who made my wife lose her breast to cancer, and it was God who took our only child. My father's opinions of a loving God go against every bad thing that's ever happened to us. If Mallory was such a good girl, where was God when she needed Him?"

"I—"

He pulled his wife to the door. "Thanks for nothing, Miss McKutcheon. I hope you enjoy this life our daughter *won't* be living."

The slam of the door echoed. Tina stared straight ahead, incredulous. "What just happened?"

David knelt by her side. "They didn't mean it, Teen. None of it. They're upset. You shouldn't feel responsible for Mallory's death."

"Oh, I don't," she said. "I know there was nothing I could have done differently. At least not in saving her life. But the God-stuff, David... If what they said is any indication, Mallory didn't know about God or Jesus or heaven or anything. When she asked me about Him, it was from a sincere need to know—a sincere need to balance out the anti-God sentiment she got her whole life. And I didn't tell her. I missed my chance—and there were no others."

David wrapped his arms around her, but she noticed he didn't offer any words of comfort.

Because there weren't any.

Tina had insisted that David go home. For the first time since the crash, she was completely and positively alone. Alone with her thoughts, her pain, and her guilt.

Her apartment assaulted her with a cloak of normalcy. Rows of stuffed bookshelves looming against the walls, framed photos of places she hoped to visit someday: Rome, the Alps, Paris. A three-tiered stack of vanilla-scented candles that made the apartment smell homey and warm even in the coldest weather. A glass jar stocked with wrapped candy from peppermints to butterscotch to root beer barrels. Her apartment was a place of comfort, fulfillment, and hope for the future.

And yet, suddenly she felt like an alien. How could she take a book off the shelf and read it? How could she dream of faraway places or light a candle just for the sheer deliciousness of the smell?

And how could she indulge in sweets, choosing a flavor to suit her mood?

Mallory Carpelli was dead. If her soul was in heaven, Tina had lucked out. But if her soul was in hell...

There was hell to pay.

Merry watched her mother scoop coffee into a filter, then empty it back into the can, then scoop it out again, only to repeat the process a third time.

"What's wrong, Mom?"

Her mother blushed. "I can't seem to concentrate. I can't count."

"You want me to do it?"

"Don't be ridiculous. You shouldn't have to do this."

"It's just coffee, Mom."

And yet Merry knew it was much more. Making coffee, doing dishes, getting the mail...these were the trivia of life. How many thousands of trivial acts did a person perform throughout the day without thinking? And what was the sum of those parts? Mere existence? Or true meaning?

Her mother switched the coffeepot on. She sighed as if she'd just accomplished a milestone. "There. That's done."

Whoopee. Should we have a celebration? Merry put a hand to her head, trying to block further sarcastic thoughts. Her mother was only trying to help.

"Would you like me to press your navy dress, baby?"

Merry was lost. "What?"

"Your navy dress? Would you like me to press it for the...you know..."

The funeral! The funeral was tomorrow. The thought of seeing Justin and Lou in their coffins, of standing emotionally naked before hundreds of family and friends. She would rather go through the plane crash again than do such a thing. "I can't go."

Her mother's widened eyes betrayed her shock. Merry braced herself for the requisite hug, which soon engulfed her.

"There, there. I know it's hard—it will be hard for all of us. But funerals are an important part of grieving. They help us let go. When your father died, I—"

"It's not the same, Mom. Dad was old. He died of lung cancer because he chose to smoke."

Her mother stepped away from the words. "Are you saying your father deserved to die?"

What *was* she saying? "He died because of a choice he made—a bad choice. What did Lou and Justin ever do wrong? Tell me that."

Her mother looked to the coffeepot as if wanting it to be through so she'd have some other busywork to attend to. "Don't ask me hard questions, Merry."

"Then who should I ask? Dad is gone. Lou is gone. You're all I've got."

Her mother sat on the couch and picked up a magazine. Merry stared at her. "That's it? Where are the words of comfort, Mom? The 'I'll always be here for you, Merry' line?"

Anna Keenan's page flipping stopped at an ad for Valentine's Day. Merry's mind registered the fact that there would be no more Valentines in her life.

Her mother looked up. "I'm hurting too, baby."

You could have fooled me. Merry fell into the recliner, beaten. "Why did God let this happen?"

"Don't ask me about God-things. You know I've never known much about Him."

Merry laughed bitterly, thinking of her childhood that had been devoid of God. "No, you're right. God was Lou's department. Everything I know about Him is because of Lou."

Her mother raised an arm and dropped it, as if the subject were taken care of. "Well then…"

"Well then, what, Mom?"

"Lou taught you all about God."

It was a ridiculous statement. With Lou gone, Merry realized how little she knew. She even remembered tuning Lou out on occasion. How many times had she pretended to be sick on a Sunday morning so she could sleep instead of go to church? How many times had her mind drifted when Lou took her hand and prayed with her, while Merry—in her selfish stubbornness—chose to be a pious bystander instead of a sincere participant? Why hadn't she paid more attention? Why hadn't she jumped into Lou's faith and made it her own?

"Things will work out, baby. They always do."

Merry shook her head. That was the best she could do? Her mother wasn't getting it at all. And her blasé attitude confirmed Merry's previous decision not to share her precrash discontent with her mom. Yet maybe if she had, she and her family wouldn't have been on Flight 1382 at all.

No. Don't think that.

Sitting in her mother's kitchen and spilling her messy troubles on her mother's Pledge-shined table wasn't an option. Merry had never been able to confide in Anna Keenan. She always had to keep up the front of the perfect daughter. *Is everybody happy?* And so Merry kept her restlessness to herself, not wanting a lecture about accepting life as it came.

Funny…her previous suffering was nothing compared to now. A scratch compared to a gaping wound.

Merry placed her hands around her middle, feeling her bruised muscles ache. It was time for another pain pill. Maybe it would alleviate another kind of pain. "I'm tired, Mom. I need to take a nap."

Luckily, Anna was never one to make a nuisance of herself. Although she had offered to stay over instead of going home to her own house, Merry had refused. There was only so much mothering she could take.

"I'll be going then," Anna said. "But I thought of a God-thing."

Oh, dear. "I'm really tired, Mom."

"No, you asked for God-stuff from me, and I just realized I do know something I can share with you."

"Mom..."

She looked like a pouty child who wasn't being allowed to share what she did at school that day.

Anything to get her gone. "Fine. Shoot."

The older woman straightened her spine. "All this must be God's will." She smiled tentatively at her daughter.

Merry wanted to scream. *God's will? The death of my family is God's will?*

"Well? Does that help?"

Just leave me alone. Please. Go. "Sure, Mom. Thanks."

Apparently satisfied she'd done her duty, Anna gathered her things and left.

Merry escaped to her room and sat on the edge of the bed. Her mother was either amazing or pitiful—she wasn't sure which.

Without warning, Merry shouted to the empty room, shaking her fists at the ceiling. "Lou! How dare you leave me! Tell me what to do. Tell me why."

Her words fell away, and the silence of her empty house pressed against her. She looked at the two prescription bottles by her bed. Both were for pain, but one made her sleep.

Sleep. That was the ticket.

She took two, wrapped herself in the scent of Lou's pillow, and prayed for oblivion.

George let Suzy use the key on the front door and swing it open.

"Dad? Come on. It's cold out here."

George froze on the front sidewalk—and it had nothing to do

with the cold weather. The sight of his home assailed him in a way he had not anticipated. The home he had left, just a few mornings before… He had not expected to return. Ever.

"Dad? What's wrong? Do you need help with your crutches?"

Don't blow it, George. Don't let your daughter know what you intended to do. He made himself move and hobbled through the door. The sights and smells swept over him like a wind. A distinct smell of oak and aftershave and past meals cooked in the microwave. *His* distinct smell? Why had he never noticed it before?

Because you've never forfeited your life only to regain it.

Suzy moved into the kitchen. "You want some coffee? I'll make a—"

She came out of the kitchen flipping through a pack of papers. "What are these doing out? Your will, your insurance policies, your—"

George thought fast and tried to act nonchalant. He maneuvered his crutches close to his daughter, balanced on one, took the papers, and tossed them on a chair. "Your mother and I always did that when we traveled. Got the important papers together so if anything happened to us—"

"I don't remember seeing them out when I used to water your plants."

"Your mother was better at putting them neatly in the desk. I was running late so I never got them that far. Where's that coffee?"

Suzy filled the coffeemaker while George lowered himself onto the couch. He was glad he'd decided to stash the $68,392 he'd withdrawn from his account in a desk drawer instead of leaving it out in plain sight. He never would have been able to explain that one away.

"How about a snack, Dad? You got any crackers and cheese?"

"I don't know, you'll have to—" Then he remembered. He'd emptied out most of the food in preparation for his suicide trip. "Actually, I'm not hungry, Suzy. I don't want—"

George heard the refrigerator open and braced himself.

Suzy appeared in the doorway. "Where's all your food, Dad? The fridge is practically empty."

"I eat out a lot."

"Now you make me feel bad. If we'd known you weren't eating decent, Stan and I would have had you over for dinner more often."

"I've been eating fine. It's my choice. I'm not helpless, you know. I make a mean meat loaf."

"You *know* how to make a mean meat loaf, but do you do it?"

Actually, no. What was the use of it? Cooking for one was a bore. George managed to get the remote from the coffee table. He flipped on the television in time to see the opening announcement for a special report.

A reporter looked seriously at the camera. "We have just received news that the hero of Flight 1382 has been identified. Henry Smith, age forty, was the man who handed off the lifelines."

"Suzy, come here! That's him. That's Henry. That's my seatmate. I was right."

Suzy ran from the kitchen. "They confirmed—?"

"Shh."

"A visual confirmation of the identity of Henry Smith was made by the two helicopter rescuers, Floyd Calbert and Hugh Johnson. Added to that identification are the unique autopsy results that revealed only one victim of Flight 1382 died from drowning. All others died from blunt trauma—injuries caused by the impact of the plane crashing into the river." The reporter looked behind his own shoulder, then turned back to the camera excitedly. "We are here at the airport to greet Mrs. Henry Smith, who has just arrived. Only minutes ago she was notified that her husband was the brave man who gave his life for others."

A distraught woman appeared on the screen, her face drawn, her eyes filled with tears. Reporters surrounded her.

"Look at those vultures," George said. "The poor woman comes to town to claim her husband's body and is assaulted by those—"

"But she should be happy. He's dead, but at least he died a hero."

George swung in his daughter's direction. "He survived the crash, Suzy. He had the same chance we did, and he gave it away. I'm sure she's torn between being proud of him and being furious."

"I never thought of it that way."

"Well…you should."

George knew all about mixed feelings.

Sonja felt like a guest in her own living room. She sat in the armchair while her parents took the other points in the triangle: one on the couch and the other on the love seat. Although Sonja had wanted to go to bed first thing—for numerous reasons—her father had made that impossible within three seconds of entering the apartment.

"Let's sit down," he said.

And so they sat. And so started the dialogue, or rather two monologues that shared equal billing. Her parents didn't talk *to* each other or even about each other. They talked about themselves and their own concerns, assuming other people in the room would be as enraptured by the subject matter as they were.

Sonja was polite for the first fifteen minutes—after all, her parents had come all this way to see her safely home—but after her mother shoved a stray newspaper to the edge of the love seat as though it were a defiled object, Sonja had enough of polite. This was *her* apartment and she needed to regain control. Blocking out her mother's rambling about the J. C. Penney's decorator who had presumed to suggest burgundy for the redecoration of their dining room, Sonja planned her strategy.

There were three ways to handle the elder Graftons. The easiest way was to ignore them. But Sonja had tried that, and her silence only increased their preoccupation with themselves.

The second way was to fight. Sonja wasn't sure if she felt up to it.

Which left the third way, the method Sonja most often employed: She would cajole them—or at least give it a good shot.

She interrupted her father's monologue. "Daddy, would you like some hot tea? Or maybe I could run to the store and get some of that brandy you like?"

"No thank you, dear. We're fine."

A laugh escaped. Sonja clamped a hand over her mouth to keep it contained. Were they totally clueless as to who should be doing errands for whom?

Apparently, Sonja's mention of libations made her mother think of the kitchen because she migrated to the edge of the linoleum and peered in. "Oh dear."

"Sorry, Mom, I wasn't expecting company."

"Obviously."

Her mother moved on to the doorway to Sonja's bedroom. Various Phoenix rejects littered the bed and floor. "Sonja, you know it doesn't take you any more time to hang up—"

So much for cajoling. Sonja pushed herself out of the chair with her good arm. "Okay. That's it." She winced as a pain shot through her midsection.

"Are you all right—?"

Sonja pointed a finger at her mother. "Don't suddenly act as if you care how I feel, Mother. It's been over an hour since we left the hospital, and not once have you or Daddy asked me about the crash or about my experience in living through it."

"Now, now, dear—"

Sonja's voice broke. "Do you have any idea what it's like to fall from the sky? To experience that *moment* when you know that all your thoughts of such things always happening to the other guy are a lie? Do you know what it's like to hear people screaming all around you and then realize you're screaming with them?"

Her mother came toward her, but she waved her away. "Get away from me!"

"Sonja, I won't have you speaking to your mother that—"

"Shut up, Daddy!"

He drew back and put a hand to his chest as if he'd been assaulted. She didn't care—and she found that knowledge both terrifying and wonderful.

A deep breath calmed her, yet Sonja still found herself fueled to say what was bursting from her heart. "The plane cracked in two beneath us. Do you understand that? I was holding on to the hand of the man seated beside me, and then suddenly he was gone. Everyone was gone! And I thought I was gone too." She shook her head, staring at the ground. The solid, carpeted, neutral ground. How could anyone take for granted such an important element of life?

When she looked up, her mother had found solace under her father's arm. Two against one. So be it.

"Those of us who didn't dive-bomb into the river, who weren't crushed by the collision of plane and water, were hurled free— through the ice. Think of the coldest you've ever been in your life and triple it. Quadruple it." She shook her head, unable to come up with an example cold enough. "We plunged into that water *without* taking a deep breath to hold. We went in with only the air in our lungs that instinct told us to grab. And pain…such pain." She couldn't stop her hands from shaking.

"I hurt from the impact. I hurt from broken bones and cuts. And I hurt from the cold. Yet I didn't have time to think of any of that. I had to get to the surface or die, but I was still strapped in my seat, held prisoner at the bottom of the river. I had to make my body move through all that—or die right there. Somehow I got free and broke through the water. I sucked in the air, such as it was. It was cold and snowing and the water was doused with jet fuel, and it tasted awful and was in my eyes…"

"Honey…"

She shook her head, once left, then right. "Let me finish this." She was surprised to hear how calm her voice had become. Oddly calm. "Getting to the top of the water was just the beginning. I found myself by the section of the plane that I had been sitting in moments before. It was now ripped to shreds, sticking its awful tail out of the water." She laughed softly at the surreal memory. "And there was a man—*the* man. The hero, though we don't even know his name yet." She swallowed hard. "He called me over and told me to hold on to the plane, even though just to touch the cold metal hurt my hands and ripped at my skin."

"But then you were saved," her father said.

Sonja caught a breath and then laughed at his succinct summary. "Yup, I guess that's it. And then I was saved. After all, everything always works out for the Graftons, doesn't it, Daddy? Life wouldn't dare outsmart one of us, would it? It better not, not unless it wanted to feel the full wrath of the Grafton anger."

"Don't be sarcastic, dear."

Sonja stared at her parents, huddled together in their oblivious block of ignorance. "You want sarcasm, Mother? I shouldn't have been on that flight at all. In true Grafton fashion, I forced my way on. And also in true Grafton fashion, I didn't die. Do you get the irony of it? I shouldn't have been there, and yet I was one of the five to live. Did Sonja Grafton have to pay the consequences of doing whatever it took to get what she wanted? No way. Sonja lived! Sonja was even the fourth one saved—right after a mother and child and an old man." She pointed to her father. "Even you would agree that, in the case of a rescue, a Grafton should let mothers, children, and the elderly go first, wouldn't you, Daddy?"

He cleared his throat.

"You should be proud of me for letting them go. But then, when the hero handed me the line—*his* line—I acknowledged the fact that I was special and worthy to be saved, and I took it."

"Certainly you're not implying you should have died?"

"Oh, heavens no. I have too much ego for that." She looked her parents straight in the eyes. "But just because I won't admit it doesn't mean it isn't so."

Sonja suddenly realized her energy was gone. Her reserve was gone. She nodded toward the door. "I'd like you two to leave now."

"What?"

"We came to help—"

Sonja shook her head. "You came to fulfill a duty so you wouldn't suffer guilt later. Now it's done. You've gotten poor Sonja home safe. But poor Sonja is tired and wants to be alone so she can maybe, possibly, but probably not, deal with all this."

"You want us to go home? We just got here."

"I don't care where you go—to a hotel, or home. Just go."

She turned her back on them and was relieved when she heard them put on their coats and open the door.

"Call if you need us, dear."

It was too late for that.

Anthony didn't know if his temperature had gone down because he was truly better or because of an act of will. He didn't care. All that mattered was that he had been discharged. Since it was so late in the day, they said he could stay until morning, but Anthony wouldn't hear of it. He was going. Now.

He tucked his shirt in, minding his sore ribs. The shirt they'd bought him was slick to the touch. Polyester city. And the pants did not hang right at all. But what could he expect from a blue-light special?

He turned toward the sound of a wheelchair only to find Lissa in the doorway. "Your chariot awaits, sire."

He was alarmed to find himself smiling with genuine pleasure at the sight of his head nurse. He pulled the grin back to its proper place in storage. "Lissa. Finally a visit."

"Yeah? Well, I got stuck in traffic for a few days."

"But I'm checking out."

She moved the wheelchair forward an inch. "Duh. I called to check on your condition, and that's what they said. That's why I'm here. I didn't want you taking any cab home." She grinned. "So I brought my '67 Impala with the leopard-fur seats."

He stared at her. Certainly her taste wasn't that bad.

She laughed at his expression. "Give it a rest, Doctor. I'm kidding. How's a honeybee yellow VW sound?"

He raised an eyebrow.

She let go of the wheelchair. "Hey, I refuse to have my mode of transportation disparaged in any way. Especially from someone whose last mode nearly killed him."

"Touché."

She angled the wheelchair for him to sit. He eased his way into it, and she expertly flipped the footrests into place. "Care for a seat belt, Doctor?"

"I think I'll skip it. I like to live dangerously."

"I'll remember that."

She pushed him into the hall. Anthony looked around for the nurses who'd taken care of him. He remembered the chatter and good-byes the other survivors had received upon their discharge. Nurse Double Entendre looked up from her paperwork at the nurses' station.

"Bye, Doctor." She went back to work.

That's it?

The elevator door opened immediately, and Lissa pushed him inside and punched one. They had the elevator to themselves.

"You alienated them too, huh?"

214 N A N C Y   M O S E R

He tried to see her face, but she was behind him. "What are you talking—?"

"You know what I think I'll do for you, Doctor? As soon as you're well, I'm going to sign you up for a Dale Carnegie course: How to Make Friends and Influence People."

He stopped trying to see her. Now she was being disrespectful. "I influence people plenty."

"Ah yes, but in what way? And what about the making friends part?"

The elevator doors opened. Just in time.

"You're quiet," Lissa said as they neared his house.

Anthony shrugged. What was there to say? Nothing was working out right. He'd expected some kind of fanfare when he left the hospital but barely got a nod. Then for Lissa to imply it was his own fault? Perhaps it stemmed from his asking those reporters to come to his room. In retrospect that had been a mistake. And perhaps he shouldn't have been so open regarding his true feelings about living when others had died. Definitely a miscalculation. And the press was pouncing on the fact that he'd taken the lifeline, citing all that "it wasn't yours" bunkum. But he could handle that. He was okay with that.

But to have no recognition at all, to anonymously slip out of the hospital and back to his house—riding in this absurd lemon drop of a car. What had he done to deserve such treatment?

They neared his neighborhood, and he did a double take as a TV van drove by. Maybe they heard he was coming home and were camped in his yard? Maybe—?

"My, my, what brightened your day so suddenly?" Lissa said. "You look positively hopeful. You remember some socialite who might be available for dinner tonight?"

He was in no mood to have her harp on his love life. "This

seems to be a reoccurring theme with you, Lissa. What's so wrong with my dating a lot of women?"

"Nothing. Not a thing. I date a lot myself."

He started to laugh, then caught himself. "Sorry."

She glanced at him while driving. "You think you're the only eligible single person on the planet?"

"Fighter, take your corner!"

She wagged her head. "You infuriate me."

"So I've noticed."

"I came to take you home because I thought you might need a little sympathy, a home-cooked meal, and some nursing." She looked at him. "I *am* a pretty good nurse, you know."

"I know."

Her look was suddenly pitiful. "You do?" She caught herself and was cocky again. "First I've heard of it."

"An oversight to which I humbly apologize."

She sniggered at him.

"What's that sound supposed to mean?"

"The great Dr. Thorgood? Apologizing? You just cost me ten bucks."

"Excuse me?"

"I bet Candy that you would never apologize to anyone, for anything."

The gall. "But Candy bet *for* me?" *I'll have to be nicer to the girl.*

"Yeah…well…she's new. And not too bright."

He laughed. "You are a piece of work, Nurse Conklin."

"It's about time you noticed."

She turned onto his street. He could see his house. The street was empty. So much for reporters. Yet maybe it was a blessing.

She pulled into his driveway, and a question surfaced, "How do you know where I live?"

She shrugged and got out of the car. "It's about time you realize I know everything."

Anthony closed his eyes and let the rich aroma of spaghetti sauce fill his senses. It was odd to hear the sounds of someone else working in his kitchen—especially someone who sang as she worked. He didn't recognize the tune, but the subject of the lyrics was love. With a start he wondered if all this attention was part of a romantic plan.

Surely not. Nurse Conklin? A love interest? The idea was absurd. He was filet mignon; she was fried chicken. He was Armani; she was Target. He was opera; she was… He listened to her singing and wasn't sure how to define it.

"What *is* that song?" he finally asked.

She popped her head out of the kitchen. "You like it?"

"I wasn't saying that. It was merely unlike any love song I've ever heard."

"That's because it's a love song to God, not to a man." She pointed a wooden spoon at him and changed to a song he knew— "You're So Vain."

He felt himself redden. "Cute."

"Absolutely. But the point is, *did* you think my previous love song was about you?"

"Don't flatter yourself."

"If I don't, who will?" She eyed him a moment. "Care to volunteer?"

"That sounds…dangerous. Is that an apt word?"

She turned on her heel. "You said you liked living dangerously." She turned back. "Or would you rather lay low on the danger for a while?"

The crash had supplied him with enough danger to last a lifetime, but he couldn't tell her that. "All I want to do now is get back to work."

"Hold that thought. You can tell me your plans while we eat."

She disappeared into the kitchen and returned bearing two plates of pasta. She set them at the dining room table, on which she'd already placed a green salad and bread.

She held out his chair for him. "Thank you. This looks good."

"It *is* good. My last name may be Conklin, but my mama's name was Figatoro. I made my first sauce at age five."

"You're not married?"

She made a disgusted face. "You know, it wouldn't hurt for you to get to know some of us. No, I'm not married. How long have I been working for you?"

He had no idea. "A while."

"Six years. Six *long* years."

He put his napkin in his lap and reached for his fork. She diverted his motion by taking his hand. She bowed her head, and before he could react…

"Bless this food, O Lord. Thank you for bringing Dr. Thorgood home safely. Help him use this second chance to do good work for You. Amen." She looked up. "There. Doesn't that make it better?"

"If you say so."

She sprinkled Parmesan on her sauce. "My, my, doesn't the good doctor believe in the Almighty?"

"Actually, the good doctor has never thought about it much."

She gawked at him. "How can you not think about it? You have a God-given talent; you help people feel better about themselves; you help people who've been injured regain their lives. God gave you that gift. He's made you privy to medical truths that make everything you do possible. He's—"

"I learned what I know from medical school and medical books, not any god."

"We're not talking just *any* God. We're talking the one and only."

Anthony spun his spaghetti on his fork. "Whatever."

She dropped her own fork with a clatter. "I knew you were cocky and confident, but I never took you for blind."

He didn't need this, home-cooked dinner or not. "I think you're overstepping your authority, Nurse Conklin."

"Perhaps I've been negligent in not making clear the One I hold in highest authority." She raised an eyebrow. "And for your information, Doctor, that isn't you."

"If you want to let yourself be deluded by believing fairy tales instead of the facts of science, go ahead, but don't bring your ignorant views into my home. I've been through enough. I—"

She put her napkin on the table beside her plate. "Perhaps you haven't been through enough."

"What do you mean?"

"Generally when people go through a tragedy, it's called a life-changing experience. For good reason. People use the event as an impetus to assess their lives and change—for the better. Apparently, you see no need for such a change."

"Absolutely not."

She shook her head. "You're planning to go on as you did before, with no change in attitude, purpose, or growth?"

Now he got it. And the knowledge of her intentions incensed him. "So that's what all this do-gooder attention has been about? You wanted to be around to witness some hallelujah change?"

She crossed her arms. "A woman can hope, can't she?"

"So by this action, I assume there is something about my life that offends you? Something you disapprove of?"

"I can think of one or two things."

"Would you care to elaborate?"

"Would you care to listen?"

He wasn't so sure.

She took his hesitancy as a no. "I thought so."

It was his turn to toss a napkin on the table. With difficulty, he stood. "I think you'd better go, Nurse Conklin."

She pushed back her chair. "I think you're right." She collected her coat and shoved her arms in the sleeves like bullets being shoved into a gun's chamber. She tossed her purse onto her shoulder.

He sat back in his chair. "I assume you won't mind if I don't see you to the door?"

"I wouldn't expect any less, Doctor." She slammed the door behind her.

The chore of getting to bed was difficult, but Anthony took comfort in the fact he wouldn't have asked Nurse Conklin to help even if she had stuck around. He didn't need a nursemaid—or a conscience.

He sat on the edge of the bed and noticed his answering machine for the first time. He hit the button to get his messages. The mechanized voice proclaimed, "You have no new messages."

That couldn't be. He'd been gone for days, his name had been splashed across the news, and he had *no* messages?

Whatever. Who needs them anyway?

He switched off the bedside lamp, held his ribs as he stretched out, and drew the covers up to his chin, wincing at the effort. He planned to go to work tomorrow, but with the pain, it wouldn't be easy.

You don't have to go. It is your own practice.

Then he thought of Lissa's harsh words and knew he would have to go in as a show of strength—mental, if not physical. How dare she presume to know how he would react to the crash? True, most people found such occurrences to be life-changing events, but he was not most people. Certainly there was nothing wrong in having his previous view of life vindicated. He was important. His life was important. He knew that before, and he knew it now.

He closed his eyes and tried to expel all thoughts of Lissa from his mind.

Dora tossed the TV remote on the couch. She hated having the television scoop her story on the hero's identity. But it couldn't be helped; she'd given George her word.

Henry Smith.

As she'd discussed with George, it was such an ordinary name. But was he an ordinary man?

How she would love to meet Mrs. Smith. Yet the sight of the widow's distraught face on the news had quelled any thought of bothering her for an interview. But how could Dora write what she wanted to write *without* talking to her?

How can I betray my own boundary of decency?

She leaned her head against the couch cushions and sighed. *But my heart, Lord... I want to write about this man. I want the world to truly give him his due, not just report on his actions, but delve into what You see as important in his sacrifice. I want to somehow answer the question of why You chose him.*

Her thoughts spun against each other, not staying still long enough to form a solution. Yet perhaps she couldn't clarify her thoughts because there *was* no solution.

Would there ever be?

Eleven

The LORD redeems his servants;
no one will be condemned who takes refuge in him.
PSALM 34:22

Tina sat alone in her classroom, waiting for the first period bell to ring. She'd come back to the concerned voices of her fellow teachers, but she quickly felt the need to have a few moments alone before meeting up with her students.

So much had changed in her life. And yet, had anything *really* changed regarding her attitude toward teaching? Did she want to be here? Did she feel a renewed passion for the profession? She closed her eyes and waited for some profound wave to rush over her and spur her toward being the best teacher she could be.

Nothing happened.

She glanced at the notes the substitute teacher had left but found herself rereading them multiple times without letting them sink in. It was Mallory's fault. Through innocent but keen insight, the girl had made Tina realize that she was a mediocre teacher. And in return? Tina had failed the girl. Just as she had failed all the students she'd ever tried to teach?

I can't do it. I'm a flop before I even get start—

The ringing of the bell made her muscles jump and her heart beat double-time. Within seconds the sounds of conversation, footsteps, and banging lockers grew closer.

Her stomach flipped over. *They* were coming and there was nothing she could do to stop them.

Not a single student asked to sign her cast. Tina didn't understand why that bothered her so much, but it did. Fellow teacher Tom Merit had broken his arm once, and his cast had been covered with students' signatures, funny notes, and pictures. In fact, Tom had it displayed on a bookshelf in his classroom like a trophy, an expression of affection and respect. Tina felt the old opinions and points of envy return. Perhaps they were never dead. She wondered how long God would continue to take her over the same character road.

She knew the answer: Until she got it right. Yet it was such a struggle, and at the moment, she didn't feel up to it.

Just do the job and go home. Forget about being a beloved teacher. It ain't going to happen, Tina.

"Ms. McKutcheon?"

Tina looked up from the copy of *The Scarlet Letter* that lay open on her desk. Ashley had her hand raised, her elbow supported by the other hand. How long had she been trying to get Tina's attention?

"Yes, Ashley?"

"Can we not talk about the book today?" Ashley scanned the room, looking for support. "We can talk about that anytime. What we want to know about is the crash."

A chorus of agreement. Tina's heart lightened. They were truly interested. In *her!* Maybe things *had* changed.

She closed the book and received whoops of joy. She looked across her class. "So…what would you like to know?"

Mack raised his hand, and Tina was so shocked at his participation that she called on him. "Did you see any bodies?"

Tina paused in shock. "No, I did not. The only people I saw were alive, in the water."

Mack's face fell. "I thought there was supposed to be blood and stuff when a plane crashed."

Jon reached across the row and swatted Mack's arm. "That's only if the plane crashes into the ground, not when it goes in water. All the people went in the water. Slid right in." He made a swooshing sound and a sliding motion with his hand.

"Did you see the pictures of the cars in the parking garage?" Duncan said. "Smashed like this…" The boy swigged the last of his cola, then stomped on the can. *"Wham!"*

Some laughed. Others groaned.

The kids angled toward each other and continued the discussion.

"Did you see them haul those pieces out of the river? And the rows of bodies on the shore?"

"My dad's friend works for the medical examiner, and he saw tons of them. Had to touch tons of them."

Tina had had enough. She wasn't needed in this discussion. They had not asked her to delay their schoolwork to talk about *her* experiences. They didn't care about her. They only cared about the flash and crash. They were interested in the stuff of tabloid head-lines, not in the heady emotional effects of her survival. Their dis-cussion was an affront to the memory of Mallory, the hero, and all the others who had died.

She stood and gathered her crutches. A few students glanced in her direction, but they didn't miss a beat of their discussion. As soon as she was steady on her feet, she grabbed her teacher's com-mentary of Hawthorne's book. The weight of it felt good in her hands.

Then, without further consideration, she heaved it over their heads until it hit the back wall of the room. All talking stopped. All eyes were finally hers. She wanted their attention? She had it.

"Good arm, Ms. McKutcheon."

Nervous laughter. Tina's heart pumped in a heady rhythm she hadn't felt since the crash. If she'd had another book handy, she would have thrown it too—and not so high. She grabbed a breath and pointed a finger at them. "You people don't care a thing about anyone but yourselves. You don't care about me, you don't care about learning, and you've just brazenly proved you don't care a whit about showing respect for the people who died. And because you're so good at taking care of yourselves, you certainly don't need me. I quit."

She walked from the room, slamming the door behind her. The hall echoed with it.

I just quit. I quit!

Her entire body shook. Tina looked back at her classroom and heard voices. No doubt they were discussing their crazy teacher. Or maybe not. Maybe they had already moved onto the next topic of discussion. The mere thought of that possibility sealed her decision.

She headed down the hall toward the exit.

A door opened. Ashley's voice called out, "Ms. McKutcheon, where are you going?"

She had no idea. Tina did not look back but continued on the road she'd chosen. God help her.

Anthony drove to work feeling on top of the world. Maybe Lissa was partially right. Surviving the crash *had* given him a chance to start fresh. If his life was good before, it could be even better now.

He pressed the accelerator of his red Corvette to the floor, wallowing in its surge of power. He turned a corner as if he and the machine were one. A few minutes later he pulled into the parking space marked, "Dr. Thorgood." He was back. Life was good.

However, he *was* thankful there was no one else in the parking lot to witness his awkward exit from the car. A sports car was great for taking curves—and attracting women—but an obstacle to overcome when one's body was injured and sore. He shut his door and paused a moment to catch his breath and shove the pain aside. He'd considered milking his injuries but discounted such a plan as only marginally providing him with the attention he deserved. Besides, to do so would be a sign of weakness. Instead, he'd chosen to be a bastion of strength, a true survivor worthy of being chosen to live when others had died.

He adjusted his camel-hair topcoat across his shoulders and walked to the entrance. With each step his bruised ribs reminded him of their presence. Through the glass doors he spotted some bright oscillating colors in the lobby. Balloons? And was that a banner on the wall?

This is going to be great.

He raised his chin and entered, allowing himself to limp slightly for effect.

Candy saw him first and raced to his side. "Dr. Thorgood. You're here! You're here!"

Her exclamation brought the others from the back: nurses Sandy and Emma, and three other women who were past recipients of his surgical skills: Tummy Tuck, Face Lift, and Nose Bob. The women applauded, and he bowed as much as his ribs allowed.

Emma pointed to the banner. "Welcome back, Doctor."

Sandy moved to a food table that was crowned with balloons. She tilted a cake so he could see the icing. It had a plane drawn on top, flying amid blue sky. "See? We had this made just for you. And there's punch, and I brought in some of the mints left over from my daughter's wedding."

Anthony wasn't sure an airplane cake was in the best of taste, nor did he find leftover mints appealing, but he accepted the intention behind it. "Thank you, ladies. You do me great honor."

Candy jumped in with the response he had hoped for. "Oh, we're the ones who feel honored, Doctor. After all you've been through." Her eyes skimmed his torso. He hadn't realized he'd put a hand to his ribs. He lowered it. "But look at us. Standing here jabbing when you need to sit." She raced toward a chair and turned it around for him.

As soon as his bottom hit the cushion, Sandy got him a slice of cake, while Face Lift poured him a cup of punch. Its pink color looked sickeningly sweet.

Face Lift winked at him. "We're *so* glad to have you back, Doctor."

He realized he didn't know her name. And hadn't they dated? She held on to the glass of punch a moment too long, as if waiting for a special acknowledgment. "Thank you…"

"April, quit making eyes at the doctor," Tummy Tuck said. "You need to share."

April. I was close. I was thinking June…

As his fans fawned over him, Anthony noticed Lissa standing on the edge of the waiting room. Alone. She leaned against the wall, her arms across her chest. Why wasn't she out here with the others?

He smiled at her, but instead of returning his smile, she merely shook her head as if she were disappointed in him. *How dare she ruin my triumphant return.*

Candy pulled a chair close and sat, her cheap perfume offending his nose. "Oh, Doctor Thorgood, tell us all about it. Tell us about the crash." The other women gathered their own chairs until he had a circle of admirers.

At least someone was interested. He looked up, prepared to give Lissa a smile of victory, but when he did, she was gone.

He dismissed the subsequent wave of regret as ridiculous and turned back to his appreciative audience.

Anthony sank into the leather chair in his office. Although his staff had limited his appointments, he was still exhausted—and it was only noon. But he wasn't about to show them that. To them he was a god, risen out of the icy waters of destruction. And gods didn't get tired.

There was a tap on the door. He looked up and shoved the

exhaustion aside. Lissa came in and eyed him far too knowingly. "You look wasted, Doctor. It's tough being master of the universe, isn't it?"

"What do you care?" As soon as he said the words, he wanted them back. He sounded like a bitter teenager.

They shared a moment of silence.

"What can I do to help?" she asked. Her voice was surprisingly kind.

Confronted with mercy, Anthony didn't know how to respond.

"We're ordering in for lunch. Do you want me to get you something? You're on call at the hospital starting at one, but until then you can close the door, eat in peace, and even lie down for a bit. How does that sound?"

Anthony took a breath, prepared to maintain his omnipotent role. But the sincere look in Lissa's eyes stopped him. It might be nice to have one person with whom he could just be himself, weak or strong. "That would be great."

She smiled. "Turkey or pastrami?"

"Pastrami with lots of hot mustard."

"You *do* like living dangerously."

Sonja buttoned the top button of her black dress and smoothed it across her hips. Classic but subdued. Perfect.

It had taken her over an hour to get dressed and her broken arm was only part of the reason. She wanted to look perfect as she made an appearance at Allen and Dale's double funeral—and then when she went into work right after. But not too perfect. At first she did a good job of covering her facial bruises and cuts with makeup, but then she thought better of it. Her injuries were a badge of honor for all to see. Off with the makeup. Black and blue looked good on her.

And yet she wasn't exactly sure why she was going through all this. Did it stem from a feeling of guilt for living when they had died? Was it a way to assuage her guilt for forcing her way on the trip? Was her attendance a form of penance? It really didn't matter. What mattered was going and being seen—

She stopped looking for her other gold earring. *Did I really just think that? Am I that cold?*

She waited for the desire to be seen to subside, or at least be handily pushed away by a character trait such as compassion or genuine sorrow, but it remained where it was. That was the trouble with most truths. They didn't budge an inch. *You can run, but you can't hide.*

She moved her cast around, determining whether or not she would have trouble driving. The last thing she wanted to do was call someone from the office to pick her up. For one thing, she couldn't think of anyone she'd like to spend one-on-one time with, and for another, she didn't want to dilute the power of her entrance by having a companion.

She could call a cab, but going to a funeral in such a way would be awkward. She wasn't about to pay it to wait for her to come out, but if she didn't, she'd have to call another cab to take her to the graveside service. And it was important to go to both sites to employ the full extent of her public sorrow and personal trauma.

It still bugged her that no one had called to tell her about the funeral.

No, she would have to drive. Perhaps there was power in surprise? She hoped so. Attending the funeral was part of her job—PR in its most poignant form. She'd gone into this thing alone; she would finish it alone. She looked in the mirror. "Right?"

As if she had a choice.

She was late. Because Allen didn't belong to a church, his family had agreed to combine his funeral with Dale's at his church. Sure was convenient.

Sonja steeled herself as she walked up the front steps. Her body was still sore, but she tried not to show it. After all, she had something to prove. The men from their office had died. The lone female lived. Strength be to women!

She took a deep breath and entered the church, bracing herself for the attention that would surely be hers—along with sympathy, concern, tears, and hugs.

Two caskets crowned the top of the aisle, and for a brief moment, Sonja found it oddly shocking. Her stomach roiled, and she reached for the edge of a pew. *They're really dead. They're up there. The last time I saw them they were on the plane and—*

A few heads turned in her direction. After the requisite widened eyes at her cast and bruises, those people she didn't recognize turned forward again. But those from work…the gazes of her coworkers hung a few seconds too long. And not one person smiled or showed pity. Not one person stood to come to her aid. Not one person even scooted down in the pew to make room for her.

Then the whispers began. Raised hands, darting eyes, nodding heads.

What's going on?

She spotted Geraldine, and Geraldine spotted Sonja. The look the woman flung across the sanctuary was enough to drive Sonja into the back wall. Geraldine rolled her eyes, shook her head, and her lips turned up in a snarl. Utter contempt. Hatred. Not an ounce of sympathy or compassion. Not even the cool friendship of working acquaintances. Hate.

A man at the end of a pew tugged at her sleeve. "Do you want to sit down, miss?"

Sonja shook her head. She had not expected to be treated like a conquering hero, but neither had she expected to be shunned.

"Are you all right?"

Things were *not* all right, not right at all. White was black, and black was white.

Sonja turned her back on the condemning crowd and left the church as fast as her injuries would allow. She got in her car and shut the door.

Then Sonja cried.

George saw the notice in the paper. Louis Grange Cavanaugh and Justin James Cavanaugh. Services at one. Wife and mother, Merry.

He closed the obituaries. *I should go. For that girl. For Merry.*

And yet he didn't want to go. He hadn't been to a funeral since Irma's. He hated them.

He laughed at the absurdity of his thought. "Nobody likes funerals, George. It's not something to like; it's something to attend out of respect."

He nodded at his own argument. Though the next funeral he'd planned to attend was his own, he'd have to make an exception. For Merry.

Merry walked in the crook of her mother's extended arm through the double doors of the funeral home, past the solicitous words of a greeter, and toward the viewing room. She was getting her own private viewing of the bodies. Just her mom and Merry; Lou's mother getting her own time an hour before. Merry held her back straight, pretending only reluctantly to let her mother comfort her. But in truth, the support was needed. Everything up to now had been rehearsal. This was the real thing.

Merry saw an open door ahead to their left. Just a few more

feet and she would be face-to-face with her husband and son. Although her entire being wanted to see them again, there was one small stipulation to her wish: She wanted to see them alive. And that wasn't possible.

She knew their silent faces would condemn her. Even in the funeral home's applied mask of peace, she'd be able to see what they truly felt about her. Their disappointment, their accusations, their anger.

If it weren't for you, we'd be alive. Can't get much plainer than that.

The fragrance of flowers wafted toward her, luring her in. *See? It's all right. There are pretty flowers in here. You love flowers. Come smell them. Come closer and see the pretty—*

It was a trick. An awful trick.

Merry stopped walking, pressing back against her mother's guiding presence.

"Merry? Come on… You know this is part of it. We have to go in. You have to see—"

Her veil of strength ripped apart, leaving her exposed. "No, I don't. I don't have to see. I can't see them. I can't!"

Reinforcements appeared, touching her, cajoling her.

"It's important, Mrs. Cavanaugh. It's part of the grieving process."

"It's a chance for you to say good-bye, baby."

"It will make you feel better."

Merry turned toward the person who'd dared to utter the last argument. It belonged to a somberly-dressed stranger. A funeral worker. "Seeing the dead bodies of my family will make me feel better? Do they pay you to say such drivel?"

"Now, now, baby. Don't take it out on Mr. Patterson. He's been very helpful to me in planning the funeral, especially since you weren't any…since you were indisposed."

Now I have to suffer the guilt of not being able to plan my family's funeral? Is there anything else? Perhaps my relatives will blame me for making them take time off from their jobs or for the burden of having to pay travel expenses? Yes, indeed, it's Merry's fault.

All restraint left her. Her guilt cup overflowed, and yet the flood brought a certain relief. *Bring on some more. It doesn't matter anymore. My cup runneth over, so let it run.*

She enjoyed a sudden realization that she didn't care what anyone thought about her today. Their opinions couldn't be any worse than the opinions she had of herself. And so, she had three choices: She could try to regain her strong act; let herself be led through the day like a zombie—a choice which *did* have its merits; or she could just let it happen and feel what she had to feel, say what she had to say, and do what she had to do.

She chose the latter.

With a wave of her arms, she swept away the cloying hands of her comforters. "Get away from me!"

They stepped back as if she spat on them. It *was* a thought…

Her mother extended a hand. "Merry, baby…we're only trying to help you through—"

"Don't you get it, Mom? I don't want help *through* anything. Part of me wants to wake up and have it be a horrid dream; while another part of me wants to wallow in it, rut in it, sit myself down in the dirty, slugging mess of it and never get up. Unfortunately, I'm coming to the conclusion that neither choice is going to make it go away. And so I'm going to face reality and, as you keep telling me, move on."

She felt her lip curl. "I have never heard such a ridiculous set of words. Move on where? I don't have a destination anymore. I don't have a job—I was a wife and mother. I don't have an identity—I was a wife and mother. I don't have a purpose—" She clutched the neckline of her dress and screamed the rest. "I was a wife and mother!"

She felt her heart break in two. A definite pain. A crack she knew would never heal. It scared her, comforted her—and condemned her.

Merry had no more words. She looked around the lobby. She was surrounded. Her mother was crying, her hands to her mouth. Two funeral workers took the other points of the triangle, exchanging visual, unspoken strategies to prevent her escape. And to her back…she was up against a wall, or rather, up against the open door of the viewing room.

She could either burst through the mortal barricade or escape to the land of the dead. Inept words, irritating hands, and ignorant minds? Or condemnation and just punishment?

She turned on her heel and fled into the viewing room. She closed the door behind her.

She locked it.

The pounding started within seconds.

"Merry! Let us in. You can't be in there."

Merry had to laugh. She put her forehead to the door and stroked the barrier that was saving her from such idiocy. "You wanted me in here, Mom. And so I'm here. Now leave me alone."

Another voice. "Mrs. Cavanaugh. We do want you to have time with your family, but we'd prefer if you kept the door open—"

"No."

"But what…what are you going to do in there, baby?"

Merry stared at the door, just inches away. What *was* she going to do? What were they afraid of? That she'd snuggle down beside Lou and slam the lid?

Say, that's not a bad…

Merry blocked out their pleadings and slowly turned around. Her husband and son lay in front of her in matching white coffins—one big, one little. A spray of red roses lay on top of Lou's and white roses on Justin's.

Lou didn't like roses! He always said they were a huge waste of money because they didn't last. He preferred carnations. You could buy one carnation, and it would last for weeks, long after any rose had wilted to nothing.

Who made this decision?

With a single movement, Merry approached Lou's coffin and shoved the spray of roses toward the back where they slipped off the coffin to the floor. She looked around to the sides of the room. Multilevel stands held dozens of fresh flower arrangements and plants. She spotted carnations. She ripped them out of the water and returned to the coffin, laying them on top. Beads of water ran down the slick sides of the white lacquered wood.

She smiled. "There, that's better."

She moved to confront Justin's flowers and was within inches of giving them a similar fate but couldn't bring herself to shove them away. The white of innocence. She touched a tender petal.

Then, only then, did Merry allow herself to look on her family. Justin was so handsome in his corduroy pants, his Christmas vest with a reindeer on it, and his little red tie. Merry remembered him bowing like a real gentleman when he first wore the outfit for church saying, "Can you be my date, Mommy?"

You'll always be my little man, sweetie.

Justin's blond curls were a golden halo. But his skin…it had a waxy look to it. Gone was the iridescent glow of her son's perfect skin, a glow that came from the inside out. Yet perhaps capturing that glow was impossible once the life behind it had exited the body.

Because of you, Merry. Because of you.

Merry put a finger on his cross tie tack and tried to remember the essence of comfort she knew could be found in that symbol of faith. But comfort eluded her—yet she didn't mind. Now was not the time for comfort. This moment was the essence of *dis*comfort, and knowing that was in itself comforting.

It can't get much worse than this.

Merry kissed her son's forehead and, with difficulty, pulled her eyes away. Then she moved back to her husband. Lou was dressed in his only gray suit, wearing the maroon tie she'd given him for his birthday. His hands were clasped across his midsection, his wedding ring an eternal reminder of their bond. *A ring. No beginning and no end. With this ring, I thee wed.*

He'd taken their vows very seriously. *For better or worse.* She'd certainly given him worse lately. Why had she done that? Why had she shoved aside the better and allowed herself to grab up the worse, like an obnoxious banner she was proud to wave? Why hadn't she realized what she had until it was gone?

She put her hand on his but removed it when its lack of warmth registered. His hands, his wonderful hands that had caressed and helped and held on and worked hard and... The very hand she had grabbed as the plane went down.

"I'm sorry, Lou. I'm so sorry."

Merry heard the fumblings of keys outside the room and knew her time was short. She kissed her husband on the lips and faced the door, straightening her shoulders against the invaders who would soon take her captive again.

The door opened and her mother burst in. Her eyes scanned the room, and Merry realized these people had expected desecration of some sort.

Sorry to disappoint you, Mom.

Without a word, Merry walked past her mother, past the funeral employees, and out the door. Let them scurry to catch up. She had a funeral to attend.

Merry saw the old man from the hospital standing on the outer rim of mourners. Their eyes met and he gave a short salute as a greeting. What was his name? Joe? No...George. Another survivor like herself.

Funny, she didn't feel like a survivor. Yet to everyone who saw her she was putting on a great performance. Academy Award time. *Nominated for Best Actress in a feature-length life...*

Merry's senses wrestled for attention. The sea of black against the white snow and green pines of the cemetery. The drone of the minister's words like a buzzing bee caught in the wrong season. The smell of her mother's and Mabel Cavanaugh's perfumes as they stood on either side of her—musk meets magnolia. The feel of the shredded tissue permanently gripped in her hand. And the acrid taste of grief that threatened to close off her throat so that she, too, would die.

This strong-woman number was exhausting. She glanced at George again. He had been so upbeat at the hospital when she saw him with his daughter. Hopeful. Grateful. Rejuvenated.

Looking down at the caskets of her family being lowered into the ground, Merry felt none of those things—and doubted she ever would.

Twelve

For the foolishness of God is wiser than man's wisdom,
and the weakness of God is stronger than man's strength.
1 CORINTHIANS 1:25

Sonja looked at the clock in her car. She'd been driving around for an hour. Surely the funerals were over. Surely people were heading to work. Surely she should join them.

She could not get Geraldine's face out of her mind. Was the woman still holding a grudge because Sonja took the trip? If anything, Geraldine should be grateful. She could have been killed like Dale and Allen.

And what did Sonja's finagling matter anyway? The bottom line was their boss, Allen, was dead. Certainly the whole Barston merger had been put on hold until Sanford Industries could regroup and hire replacements for Allen and Dale. Geraldine was the only one who knew what she did.

Maybe she was overreacting. The double funeral had been an emotional situation, not an easy thing for anyone to bear. The feeling of rejection Sonja had felt might have been the result of her own nerves and uncertainty and, yes, even sorrow. She was only human.

Sonja looked at the street signs, getting her bearings. She couldn't hide forever. She had a job to claim. After all, she'd proven herself to be a survivor.

Hadn't she?

Sonja got in the crowded elevator and pushed the button for the Sanford Industries floor. The man to her right eyed her cast and face.

"Boy, what happened to you?"

"Plane crash."

The man's eyes widened, and Sonja smiled—inside. It was kind of fun shocking people.

It took the man a moment, but then he clapped a hand on his mouth and pointed. "You're one of the survivors! You were on Flight 1382."

"Yes, I was."

"I heard about you."

The other people in the elevator started talking at once, offering their sympathy, sharing their shock regarding the tragedy, and detailing where they were at the time it happened. She'd heard her parents talk about where they were when President Kennedy was shot, or when the Challenger blew up. Wow. She had become a part of history.

The door opened to Sonja's floor, but she was reluctant to leave her admirers, especially since what lay ahead was so uncertain. Her stomach tested its limits. She was grateful that her nerves had been sidetracked by the kind attention in the elevator, but now… This was it.

"Bye."

"Good luck."

The doors closed and Sonja was face-to-face with reality. The receptionist applied a receptionist smile even before looking up. But when her eyes showed recognition, her smile faded and, after a beat, returned falsely. "Ms. Grafton. How nice to have you back."

"Thank you." Sonja started toward her office but then returned to the desk. "Do I have any messages?"

The girl checked. "Sorry. None."

Sonja nodded. *Don't panic. They had to have someone cover your work while you were gone. It doesn't mean—*

"Ms. Grafton, is it?"

Mr. Wilson stood at the edge of the corridor. She'd never met him but had seen him many times walking through the office, usually in deep conversation with Allen or other superiors. He was a vice president. A lifer. And at the moment, he didn't look happy.

And yet he did know her name. That was a good sign. Maybe.

"Hello, Mr. Wilson."

He stepped toward her. "I thought that might be you." He pointed to her cast. "You recovering all right?"

"Yes, sir."

"Terrible thing, terrible."

"Yes, sir."

He checked his watch. "I have a few minutes. We might as well get this…" He cleared his throat. "I'd like to talk with you."

"Now?"

"If you please."

Sonja glanced at the receptionist. The girl bit her lip. When their eyes met, she looked away.

This wasn't good. This wasn't good at all.

Mr. Wilson proceeded down the corridor toward his office. Sonja followed after him. Neither one spoke. She was concerned over his lack of small talk and yet also relieved. Her insides were knotted so tight she feared if he did talk to her in any way that required a response, she would throw up. Now wouldn't that be impressive on her first day back?

Mr. Wilson's office was lush and old world. No tan land here. Rich navy blue colors and brown leather heralded his status as one of the big guys.

He moved behind his desk. "Have a seat."

Sonja sat. And waited. *Maybe he's going to offer the company's support in my recovery? Maybe he's going to tell me I can take as much time off as I need? Maybe—*

He cleared his throat and picked up a pen, though she could tell he had no intention of using it to write. "Well, Ms. Grafton, we didn't expect you back so soon."

"I was at the funeral." *But I got scared away.*

"Oh. Were you? That's good. I mean it was good you were there to say good-bye."

She nodded. Now was the time he would ask about her injuries, inquire about the horror of her experience, or share where he was when he first heard—

"I'm sorry, Ms. Grafton, it seems we have a problem."

That's when she knew this was not a courtesy meeting. The way Mr. Wilson's eyebrows dipped, the way his chin jutted forward as if he were attempting to fortify himself. Fortify himself to do what?

Somehow, Sonja managed to find her voice, or rather, *a* voice, since the words that came out sounded strained and odd. "What problem, sir?"

He looked her straight in the eye. "The problem of deceit."

Sonja's first thought was almost comical. Instead of letting her mind zero in on the meaning of Mr. Wilson's words, she marveled at the classy way he had found to say it. Not "Your lying" or "Your cheating" or even her own personal favorite, "Your finagling," but "the problem of deceit." Very highbrow.

She decided to lie. "I don't understand."

At this ludicrous statement, he raised his left eyebrow. "I think you do. We at Sanford Industries know what you did in order to go on the trip to Phoenix."

"I didn't do—"

A raised hand stopped her denial. "And though it is true you didn't break any laws or even do anything particularly blatant like changing the numbers on a report, you *did* do something that is just as reviled at Sanford Industries. You violated our team concept. You forced yourself front and center as a Me-player instead of a We-player."

The cards were faceup on the table. "I was only trying to make sure the work was done correctly."

"That was your only consideration?"

Sonja felt herself redden. "I don't see what's so wrong with pointing out an error that might have cost this company tens of thousands of dollars."

He nodded, tenting his fingers under his chin. "Ah. So your first concern was with the bottom line of the company."

Although she wanted to, Sonja couldn't bring herself to blatantly lie. Not anymore. "It was *a* concern."

"And what were the other concerns?"

That I go to Phoenix instead of Geraldine, that she be showed up, that I finally get some recognition in this stinking company. That my parents finally be proud—

"Ms. Grafton?"

She took a breath. "The other concerns were personal."

"I see."

She looked at her lap and put a hand under her cast, supporting it as if it hurt. Actually, at the moment the pain in her arm was the least of her worries. Yet perhaps if she got the sympathy vote…

"We're going to have to let you go."

Sonja's throat intertwined with her intestines. "Go?"

"You're fired."

Nothing highbrow about those two words. She shook her head against the impossible. "But this isn't fair. I just lived through a plane crash. I almost died. I…" She knew none of the things she mentioned had anything to do with her job performance, a matter for which she had no defense.

"I know you've been through a horrible experience and I feel bad for you. But you are obviously a survivor, Ms. Grafton. You've shown a knack for looking after yourself."

The way he said it was not complimentary, and his tone irked her almost more than the firing itself. At that moment she stopped pretending. She remembered the freeing aspects of the episode with her parents and sought to duplicate it. She had nothing to lose.

She straightened her spine. "Face it, Mr. Wilson. You don't care about the crash. All you care about is this company. How ironic I'm being penalized for being aggressive, for doing the same types of things that are done every day in this office by men—by Allen, if you must know. His slate was far from clean."

"We know. And if he had lived through the crash, he would have faced his own Waterloo. Eventually."

She laughed. "I'm supposed to find comfort in that?"

Mr. Wilson shrugged. "Living through a close brush with death offers a chance for new beginnings, Ms. Grafton. Considering the hard feelings you've left behind here, perhaps you can look upon this as a blessing. A fresh start. A chance to get it right."

Sonja stood and moved until her thighs touched the edge of his desk. She loved it when he leaned back in his chair in order to create more space between them. "In that case, I thank you for releasing me to my destiny."

Releasing me to my destiny? What was that? Sounds like a blurb from a cheesy self-help book.

Sonja drove home, her speed increasing and decreasing with the sway of her emotions. She'd already traveled through anger, skirted past disbelief, and was now headed on a collision course with acceptance—a state of mind she desperately wanted to avoid. *Fight or fail.* Acceptance was the end of fighting. Acceptance was akin to failure.

Sonja stopped at an intersection and rested her head upon the steering wheel. She was beyond weary. If only she could go home and sleep for a week. She knew she ought to be making plans, formulating a strategy for the rest of her life.

She raised her head to check the traffic light and noticed she was right in front of the *Chronicle*. Dora Roberts worked there. The friendly reporter. She needed a friend.

Clyde leaned over the top of the cubicle. "Dora, hop to! There's someone here to see you."

"Who?"

"One of the survivors." He pointed a pencil at her. "It's a chance to redeem yourself." He tapped the pencil twice on the partition. "Get the story. Now."

She called after him. "But who—?"

He answered over his shoulder. "Sonja something."

Sonja? Dora rushed to meet her. Was she ready to talk on the record? That would indeed be a coup.

But when Dora saw Sonja, she pulled up short. Sonja was dressed impeccably in dark clothes, but her face looked worse now than it had in the hospital, and it went beyond the bruises. Dora could tell Sonja was suffering from another kind of pain. A worse kind.

She extended her hand. "Sonja. How nice to see you. Let's go in the conference room." She led her into the room and closed the door. "Can I get you some coffee? Tea?"

"Nothing, thanks." Sonja didn't just sit on the seat but seemed to let the inanimate cushions swallow her up. "I remembered at the hospital…you…you were so nice to me. You listened."

So there still wouldn't be an interview. Dora shoved her disappointment aside. "So what's up? How are things going? It's nice to see you've been released."

Sonja offered a bitter laugh.

"Uh-oh. That bad?"

"Today's been…a bad day. I tried going to the funeral of my coworkers and—"

"Oh, dear."

"Actually, I *tried* to go but got the most awful vibes in the church, and the strangest looks from people, and whispering behind hands." She traced the edge of the conference table.

"What was all that about?"

Sonja looked up. "They hate me. They blame me. They—"

"They can't hate you or blame you for their friends' deaths. It wasn't your fault the plane—"

"No, no, not that. Not directly at least. But remember when I told you about what I did to get on that flight? The deception and conniving."

"Oh yes, I remember."

"They found out. I was just fired."

Dora fell back against the chair. "That seems pretty cruel, considering what you've been through."

Sonja's shrug was full of defeat and resignation. "All in all, I'd say I got what I deserved. Ever since the crash, when I look back at my job, it all seems so tainted." She took a deep breath but seemed to gain no strength from it. "Besides, I've passed through the angry and incredulous stage. Right now I'm trying to figure out what to do next. As you told me in the hospital, this is a chance for me to start over." She laughed. "Neither crisis was one I would have chosen, but God didn't ask me."

Dora felt a wave of hope. Although they'd mentioned God during their first meeting, it made things easier that Sonja brought Him up again. This was good.

"You'd mentioned your seatmate. Roscoe, wasn't it? He talked to you about God getting your attention?"

"Yes, he did, and I haven't forgotten it. He said he'd gone through a similar experience in his life—not a plane crash, but a big event that forced him to reassess things." Sonja looked down, then up. "He ran over his little boy and killed him."

"Oh my goodness. That's terrible."

Sonja sighed. "I know. I can't imagine."

"But he turned his life around?"

"Completely. Up until then he was consumed with his work. But after that he gave up being head of the company and worked with his wife helping high-risk kids."

"Wow. I admire people who can do that—get their priorities straight *and* work with kids who need them."

"He said it was all due to his wife. She'd been trying to make him see things clearly for years, but he never listened to her. Until their son's death."

"She sounds like a neat lady."

"He wanted me to meet her someday."

An idea flashed into Dora's head. "Then you should do it. Meet her. Find her."

"What?"

Dora was surprised by the intensity of her idea. "You said Roscoe helped you, and his wife helped him. He wanted the two of you to meet."

"But I don't even know where she lives."

"Did he say if he was heading home on Flight 1382?"

Sonja brightened. "Yes, yes, he did."

Dora stood. "Then let's go find her."

Sonja sat in her living room with the phone on her lap. She stared at the address and phone number of Eden Moore. Would Roscoe's widow want to hear from her? Or would the knowledge that Sonja, a woman sitting right next to her husband, had lived when he died upset her?

There was only one way to find out. Sonja took a deep breath and dialed the number.

A woman with a deep alto voice answered. "Moores."

"Hello…you don't know me, but my name is Sonja Grafton, and I sat next to your husband on the plane and—"

"You sat next to Roscoe?"

"Yes."

"On Flight 1382?"

"Yes."

"And you survived?"

Sonja braced herself. "Yes."

"Praise the Lord!"

"What?"

"I've been wanting to know what happened; I've been aching to know what Roscoe went through, and now to have someone call who sat next to him and talked with him. I want to meet you, Sonja Grafton!"

To expect anger and receive enthusiasm… Sonja's voice was tight, but she managed the words. "I want to meet you too."

"I can't get away again right now. I've been away from our work too long, but—"

"I'll come down there," Sonja said, totally surprising herself.

"You will?"

"I'll fly down tomorrow."

"You don't mind flying?"

Sonja had never thought about it. "I'll do it. I'll be there."

"Bless you, dear girl. You are a gift from God."

Funny, she didn't feel like one.

Anthony's pager vibrated. He looked at the number. *911.* The code meant he was needed in emergency. Just his luck. If only he'd canned the superdoctor bit and stayed home another day. But it was too late now. He couldn't refuse.

He reached for the phone and called back. "Dr. Thorgood here."

"Yes, Doctor, we have a hand injury. Bar fight. The patient's been bit pretty badly, plus there's some glass—"

Yes, yes, don't drone on about it. "I'll be right there." Anthony hung up and closed his eyes in disgust. This was one of the reasons he'd veered away from reconstructive plastic surgery and toward cosmetic. He hated dealing with the lowlifes who got injured through exposure to drunk drivers, domestic abuse, or sheer stupidity. He liked dealing with people who chose surgery as a means toward bettering their lives.

The truth was, some people got what they deserved.

Anthony found the patient sleeping, or out cold from the booze that seemed to emanate from every pore. His shirt was covered with blood. Various cuts on his face had already been treated. *Must have been some fight.*

The man pulled out of his stupor, saw Anthony, and got agitated. "My hand! You have to fix… I must play…"

At that moment the attending physician, Dr. Andrea Margalis, came in and rushed to the patient's side. "Shh, shh, Mr. Harper. Calm down. Everything will be all right. We've brought in a specialist to look at your hand."

The man glanced at Anthony, then, when consciousness seemed too much for him, lay back down, mumbling a few times more about his hand before going silent.

Well then. Anthony donned a pair of gloves and lifted the patient's hand, assessing the damage. Andrea moved close. Her perfume was delicious. She waited patiently until he finished his examination. "You can see why we called you in."

Anthony set the hand down. "Actually, no. This is a stitch-up job, pure and simple."

Her eyebrows furrowed, taking nothing away from her beauty. Anthony purposely glanced at her left hand as she donned a pair of gloves. There was no ring, which indicated no husband. Usually. Though that detail wasn't necessarily a problem.

"Not to disagree, Dr. Thorgood, but look at this." Dr. Margalis turned the hand over and pointed to a particularly vivid set of teeth marks. "There could be deeper damage here. I thought you might want to go in to make sure."

To appease her, Anthony took a closer look. She could be right, but probably wasn't. After all, he was the expert. She was used to quick fixes, not the finesse work that was his hallmark.

The man groaned.

Andrea put a calming hand on his arm. "Poor man. When the police brought him in—"

Anthony nodded, his judgment of the patient complete. "The police broke up the fight?"

"Yes, but Mr. Harper was the only—"

"Then he's no poor man. He's an arrogant fool."

Andrea flashed him a look. "That's uncalled for."

Anthony shrugged and felt a wave of fatigue threaten. His ribs throbbed. He arched his back, adjusting to the pain.

"Are you all right, Doctor? Considering what you've been through, I was a little surprised to see you back on call. If you'd rather I call Dr. Burrows—"

"No, that won't be necessary." Anthony despised Dr. Burrows. Compared to himself, Burrows was a meatball surgeon hiding under the guise of an elite plastic surgeon. Yet at the moment his professional opinion of his colleague wasn't the point. The vital point was Dr. Margalis's questioning Anthony's opinion. "It comes down to this, Andrea. Either you trust me or you don't. Or did you call me in here on my first day back from being in the hospital to ignore my prognosis?"

She reddened, and Anthony thought she looked quite cute when she blushed. As soon as he felt up to it, he'd ask her out. "Of course not, Doctor. I defer to your expertise. But would it hurt to take a deeper look? Personally, I've never seen so much damage."

"Well, I have. Stitch him up, and get this brute on his way."

Andrea bent over the hand, looking close. "But this part right here—"

Anthony sighed deeply. "Come on, Andrea. This is not a life or death matter. Stitch the drunk up. Get him home to beddie-bye where he can sleep it off. Either you do it, or I'll do it. What's it going to be?"

After one last look, Andrea gently set down the hand. "As I said before, I defer to your expertise—and your workmanship. I'll get you what you need."

Tina raced from her car to the front door of her apartment as fast as her crutches would take her. Ever since walking out of the school—and her job—she'd put her emotions on hold, not daring to let them out while driving. And now they were on the edge of enveloping her. If she didn't get release soon…

She fumbled the keys in the lock. "Come on. Come on." Finally the key did its work and she was inside. She closed her apartment door and took a cleansing breath. And then…

She tossed her keys into the air like they were confetti. "Yahoo!" If she had two good legs, she would have clicked her heels together like Gene Kelly singing in the rain.

As the keys clattered to the floor and her shout died, Tina laughed. It was a wonderful, foreign sound. How long had it been since she felt such joy? The answer took her far back in time, way before the crash.

She removed her coat and flung it toward the couch in a hook shot, enjoying the awkward arc. Then she fell onto the cushions with a satisfying *umph*. She couldn't stop smiling.

Settled in, she allowed herself to say the words that had been forming since she walked out of the school. "I'm not supposed to be a teacher. I don't *have* to be a teacher."

Tina had never felt so free in her life. It was as if a weight had been lifted from her soul; it was like flying through the air with her arms outstretched; it was like running through a field with the wind whipping through—

The phone rang and she answered it. "Hello!"

"Ms. McKutcheon?"

It was her principal's voice. She ignored the quick flip of her stomach. What's the worst he could do to her? Hire her back? She let the joy remain in her voice. "Well, hello, Mr. Dall. How are you doing today?"

"How am I? Ms. McKutcheon, why aren't you in your class-room? Some of your students came to the office and said you'd quit, walked out. They were concerned. *We* are concerned. This isn't like you."

No, it wasn't. Until now. Now she was AWOL. Truant. A deserter from duty. An escapee of education.

Free.

"Ms. McKutcheon, what do you have to say for yourself? We know you've been through a lot, but this kind of behavior is unac-ceptable."

"I agree."

"You—?"

"It *is* unacceptable. Students should have teachers they can admire. Not a teacher whom they merely tolerate; not one who epitomizes the axiom, 'Do as I say, not as I do.'"

"So you *are* quitting?"

"Indeed I am." How long had it been since she meant anything so sincerely?

"Are you going to another school?"

Tina hadn't thought about it until this moment. "Nope."

"You're giving up teaching for good?"

"Yup."

"But your career? You have tenure. You can't just throw that away."

Tina felt an inner flutter as the full consequence of her action became clear. Was she sure? Was this the right decision? *Lord, help me see.*

"You've put us in a bind, Ms. McKutcheon. I suppose Mr. Merit can cover one of your classes, but the others…"

Tina smiled. Tom Merit. Super teacher. He was the perfect person to take her students and make them shine. Teaching was his calling.

But it isn't yours.

Tina's soul locked onto this truth as if it were a magnet making contact with metal. She had never been so sure of anything in her life. She asked for God's help and He *did* help—within seconds of her asking. With these four words her world changed from closed and ominous to open and promising. The freedom she felt swelled like a sponge expanding with water. For those words *were* the water of her life. Those words made everything possible. *"What is impossible with men is possible with God."*

That's my problem. I've been depending on myself and not on Him.

She embraced this other truth with a smile that dispelled all flutters and doubts. Then she made her proclamation into the phone, "I am very sorry for the inconvenience, Mr. Dall, but my decision is final. I am not supposed to be a teacher."

"Not supposed…?"

"You'll have to trust me on this one."

"Well then, good luck, Ms. McKutcheon. I fear you're going to need it."

She laughed and hung up. He couldn't be more mistaken. Tina wouldn't be needing luck. Luck didn't save her from the crash. Luck didn't force her to quit her job. Luck didn't make her feel like the whole world was suddenly open and good and promising.

Luck was a fantasy. God was real.

❧

Tina bounced on the couch as she waited for David to answer his phone. *Come on!*

"Calloway here."

"David, my dear man. Sorry to bother you at work, but you *have* to come to dinner tonight."

"Tina, what's wrong? You sound…odd."

She laughed. "Oddly happy. I know that emotion is rare in my regard. But no more. No more."

"What's going on?"

"Not now. Come to dinner, and I'll tell you all about it."

"You're going to cook?"

She laughed again. "Actually, I was thinking of ordering in Chinese. Sweet and sour chicken okay?"

"Add some crab rangoon and you're on."

David arrived a few minutes after the restaurant delivered the food. She met him at the door with a kiss, then backed away. It took him a moment to open his eyes.

"Wow. Now I *am* curious. You're kissing *me?*"

She kissed him again for good measure, then headed for the table. "Come eat, and I'll tell you everything."

He grabbed her hand and stopped her. "Before you tell me anything, I want you to know you've made me incredibly happy."

"How?"

"By being happy yourself. So whatever it is, I'm all for it."

She touched his cheek and let her brown eyes stroke his blue ones. "You are too good, David Calloway. I've done absolutely nothing to deserve you. If there's anything I can do for you—"

He kissed her nose. "Feed me. I'm starving—for food *and* your news."

They took a seat at the table, and Tina let David take up their portions. When all was ready, she grabbed his hand for grace before he could grab hers. And for once she led the prayer. "Lord, thank You for this food we share, and thank You for the chance to be together. And most of all, thank You for showing me a glimpse of Your plan for my life. Amen."

"Ah, the plot thickens."

Tina took a bite of chicken. "I quit my job."

David's bite didn't make it to his mouth but skipped down the front of his shirt. She handed him a napkin. "You quit? Why?"

She told him about the students' preoccupation with the morbid side of the crash and her realization that there was no bond between them. "Yet if it weren't for their lack of interest… It was a veiled blessing. It forced me to act and do what I should have done a long time ago. I've been living my life in neutral, David. My faith too."

"But your degree. Your teaching certificate. Your tenure."

She was a little disappointed he'd homed in on the practical side of things. "What about my faith and finding my true calling?"

He blushed. "You're right. Of course you're right. But you've got to admit it's drastic. And haven't you gone through enough drastic lately?"

She pushed her plate aside and clasped her hands on the table. "Have you considered maybe all this happened so I *would* change my life and get on the right track? Think about it. I was on my way to Phoenix to make a decision. I was seated next to a student, traveling alone. What are the odds of that? And not just any student, but a brilliant, kind girl who talked about discovering her purpose when all the time I was supposed to be discovering mine."

"You're not saying her purpose was to help you pinpoint yours, are you?"

He made it sound so cold. "I don't know, David. And there's no way *to* know. Not for sure. But the point is, Mallory *was* instrumental in helping me see the light." She frowned. "Even if I was negligent in helping her see *the* Light."

"So what are you going to do now?"

"I have no idea."

"You don't seem too upset about it."

"I'm not. The uncertainty frightens me, but it's also extremely exciting. And faith, David, don't forget about faith. God will show me what to do next."

He nodded, then kissed her hand. "Of course He will."

The phone rang and Tina's insides grabbed. "I don't want to talk to anyone. It's probably some teacher at the school. I don't want to defend myself. Not tonight. Tonight is for celebration."

David nodded and answered the phone. He talked for a while, then handed it to Tina, covering the mouthpiece. "You have to take this one. You'll never believe who it is."

"Who?"

"Vincent Carpelli, Mallory's grandfather. He wants to meet with you."

"How did he get my—"

David handed her the receiver. "Mr. Carpelli? This is Tina McKutcheon. You want to see me?"

"Indeed I do, miss. I found out from my son that you were the last person to speak with my Mally. And I..." His voice broke. "I need to talk with you. Find out about her last moments. I thought we could meet at Johnny's Diner for breakfast tomorrow? We could go real early so you could get to work."

Tina smiled. "No need for the early hour. I'll meet you there at eight."

The door closed on the last well-wisher, and Merry leaned against it. Just in time too. She had approximately ten minutes of civility left. She'd put up an excellent front throughout the day. Once she left the viewing room, she wrapped herself in a cloak of feigned strength. It was not a heavy cloak, and it threatened to slip from her shoulders on more than one occasion. Only with acts of great will had she kept herself covered so no one knew the horrible, weak, worthless creature who hid beneath. People had even complimented her on her fortitude.

Yes indeed, she handled the hundreds of well-wishers as aptly as a politician at a fund-raiser. Shake hands, nod your head, smile, and say thank you. Then hug. Lots of hugs. *If I never hug another person...*

But afterward, everyone came to the house to eat and chat. And eat. And chat. And as the time neared for her to be left alone, people's comments changed from words of condolence to words of concern. For her.

"Are you going to be okay?"

"If you need anything, *anything*, just let me know."

She knew they meant it sincerely. And she realized there were only about ten appropriate lines to say at such events. But once she'd heard the ten lines a dozen times each, the cloak began to suffocate, and she felt desperate to shrug it to the ground. She longed for silence and whatever it would bring. Letting the strength die and the weakness take over was another step in the process, and she wanted to get it over with.

And now she was alone.

Merry looked at her kitchen. The counters were covered with nine-by-thirteen pans of brownies and apple crisp, and the refrigerator was stocked with endless containers of Jell-O, lasagna, and shaved ham. She'd be able to eat for a month on the leftovers.

Or not.

She forced herself to leave the support of the door behind and ventured into the living room. Everything had been tidied up. There were no stray cups or plates. And no stray toys either. Or Lou's work shoes. Or Justin's mittens. Or...

She had a realization. Without a son or husband in the house, it would rarely get messy. Merry was the type of person who had an obsession for cleaning up after herself. Perhaps she'd done so to make up for her family's penchant for messiness. But now as she looked around the perfectly clean room, the reality of never having to clean it again, never having to make a meal for the whole family, never having the burden of wet towels on the floor, sand in the carpet, or shirts on the ironing board, was too much. Too stark. Too high a price to pay for her survival.

You're nothing anymore. You have no purpose. No use. You're worthless.

She put a hand to her temples, shocked at the strength of the inner accusations.

You've done your duty. You got your husband and son put in the ground. Now it's time you joined them. Do what's right, Merry. Pay the price for your own mistakes. Don't let them pay it alone.

She nodded. It made perfect sense. Being a survivor had given her a second chance—a second chance to die.

She didn't die when her family did because she didn't deserve to die like they did. Or die with them. They were together in death as they had been in life. Two against one. Now that she had suffered, now that she had felt the guilt of her sin, *now* it was her time to do the right thing.

She calmly walked toward her purse and took out her prescription. She jingled it and held it to the light. Blessed, blessed pills. There were still plenty left. Plenty enough to finish the job the crash had begun.

George heated a can of chili on the stove. He knew it was late for him to eat such a thing, and he would surely pay for it during the night. But the nice thing about living alone was that he was able to eat what he wanted when he wanted to eat it.

The chili began to bubble and he stirred it, then switched on the television. Commercials. He shook his head as a local station showed a leftover commercial from the Christmas season. Didn't anybody check these things?

"So have a merry, merry Christmas with Landon's Furniture Warehouse."

Merry.

He stopped stirring. Her name returned to his consciousness. *Merry. Call Merry.*

The feeling was so strong… He stood over the pan and waited. Maybe it would go away.

Call her.

He shook his head, not understanding what was going on, but not willing to ignore it either. He flipped off the burner, turned down the television, and took out the phone book. He got her number. He dialed. It rang.

It rang and rang and rang and rang.

And suddenly he knew. Something wasn't right. He ripped the page from the phone book, grabbed his coat, his crutches, his keys, and left the house.

George jabbed Merry's doorbell until his finger hurt. He'd already pounded. And yelled.

She's not home.

It was a handy answer to the situation, but he knew in his gut that it was not the truth. She *was* home. And she wasn't merely asleep. George had made enough ruckus to wake the—

Enough of this. I have to get inside.

He felt around the top of the doorjamb for a key. He looked under the mat and the icy planter in the corner. Nothing.

If only he had heeded Suzy's advice to get a cell phone. If only he had called 911 the moment he felt something wasn't right. But would they have taken his feelings seriously?

There had to be a back door. Would it be open? People were often negligent about locking their back doors.

George eyed the snow warily. To trudge around the house with two good legs would have been an iffy venture, but with crutches? He wasn't a kid anymore. He wasn't even middle-aged. He was an old, injured man. He had no right risking further injury over something that was so uncertain.

And yet the idea of *not* trying everything to get inside… What if she was hurt? Maybe he was her only chance. He turned toward the snow. "Here goes."

The crutches proved to be helpful in the snow as they provided him something to hold on to and lean against to keep his balance. The snow found its way under his pant leg and into the top of his shoe. It also bit into the bare skin above his sock and across the opened toes of his cast. The cold brought back bad memories.

He stopped to rest a moment. *What if the back door isn't open? You'll be doing all this for nothing, and you'll have to walk back the same way you came.*

He couldn't think of that.

Save her!

He was nearly bowled over by the intensity of the inner voice. Rest time was over. Now.

He turned the final corner and spotted a patio. Although no one had shoveled it, it *had* been trampled with footprints. Stray cigarette butts dotted the white. At least she'd had company. For a while. But now no one answered. Had they all gone and left her alone?

Alone's not good when you're depressed, George. You know that from experience.

He hurried to the sliding glass door. *Please let it be open.*

It was.

He slid the door to the side and stepped in, stomping the snow away. The smell of Italian food lingered, and one lamp lit the open

spaces, revealing covered dishes on the counter. *Condolence food.*
He remembered now. Family and friends bringing food in a welcome—but desperate—attempt to do *something* to help.

George saw crayon drawings on the fridge. Family photos
filled the walls above the kitchen table. Father, mother, child. Three
reduced to one. His heart buckled and he felt a wave of familiar
depression return, and yet he knew its intensity was minor league
compared to Merry's. *I lost a wife near the end of my life. Merry lost
her family in their prime.*

"Merry? Merry, are you here?"

When his call was answered with silence, he realized if she hadn't
answered the door she certainly wasn't going to answer a strange
call from within her house. He had to find her.

There was only one hallway leading past the living room into
the bedroom area. He flipped on its light and peeked in a darkened
children's room, a teddy bear marking the bed. A bathroom. And
one other room.

The door was ajar. The light from a bedside lamp cast a warm
glow. George pushed the door open with his crutch. It swung free
and revealed a woman on the bed. Near her hand was a prescription bottle.

He didn't wait to see more. He called 911.

George felt for a pulse behind Merry's ear. Faint, but there. At
least help was coming.

He remembered the locked front door and hurried to open it
wide for the paramedics. Then he went back to Merry and lifted
her torso into the crook of his shoulder, jostling her with purpose.

"Come on, Merry girl. It's not time to leave us yet. Wake up,
wake up. It's morning. You're going to be late. Breakfast, Merry."
He knew the chatter was false and meaningless, but who knew
what would elicit a reaction in a comatose mind? George still had
nightmares about being late for work and not being able to find
two shoes that matched.

George slapped her cheeks and willed her eyes to open and her slack jaw to suddenly suck in a deep breath and ask for water. He found himself rocking her. "Please, God. Help her live. Help her live."

George heard footsteps. Then a shout: "Paramedics!"

Finally. "Back here, in the bedroom!"

A man and a woman appeared in the doorway carrying equipment. They assessed the situation in moments and took Merry from his arms to do their work. George stepped back and watched. "What's her name?" one of them demanded.

"Merry. Merry Cavanaugh."

The paramedic talked to her as his partner worked by inserting an IV. "Hiya, Merry. We want you to come back to us now." They read the label on the prescription. They talked to each other and to the hospital. Finally Merry's eyes fluttered. "Thata girl, Merry, you can do it."

The woman stayed behind while the other paramedic left. He came back with a wheeled stretcher he placed out in the hall. He carried Merry toward it as easily as if she were a child. They covered her with a blanket and strapped her in.

"You family?" he asked George. "You want to ride with us?"

"Absolutely." On both accounts.

Thirteen

The LORD will fulfill his purpose for me.
PSALM 138:8

Tina walked into Johnny's Diner and spotted Vincent Carpelli immediately. Now she knew where Mallory had gotten her beautiful olive skin. The man was old-world Italian with a bushy white mustache and matching eyebrows. He stood as she approached.

"Mr. Carpelli?"

His smile reached his eyes. "Miss McKutcheon. It's so nice of you to come." He pulled out her chair and set her crutches in the corner. He held up a carafe. "Would you like some coffee?"

"Definitely."

A waitress came with menus, but Mr. Carpelli put out a hand stopping their distribution. "Do you like cinnamon rolls, Miss McKutcheon? Because Johnny's has the best cinnamon rolls, as big as a plate, with icing that looks like snow on a mountain."

Tina was charmed by the man's ease of expression. It was quite a contrast with the other male Carpelli she'd met in her living room. "Count me in."

After the waitress left, there was an awkward moment when they looked at each other, yet tried *not* to look as if they were looking at each other. Finally, Mr. Carpelli's hand bridged the space between them but did not touch. "Tell me about my Mally. If only I hadn't insisted she come visit…" He pulled his hand—and his eyes—away.

"Oh no, you mustn't say that. I mean it's natural for you to have regrets about her being on the plane, but as for your visit? You had a profound influence on her life."

"She told you about me?"

"You were the number one topic."

His eyes softened and the wrinkles eased. "She was a good girl. She tried hard to do the right thing. She was searching so hard."

"That's what she said. She told me about your stories of the military and how they made her think about joining some branch of the service herself."

"Yes, well…"

Tina was surprised by the doubt in his voice. "I thought you backed her choice."

"I wasn't sure. Although *I* had a good life in the service, and although Mally certainly had a heart to serve her country, I wasn't sure it was right for her."

"She acted as if you approved—as if you were the only one who approved."

He shrugged. "I didn't disapprove, but there was more to Mally's willingness to sacrifice and serve than the military would…" He searched for the right word. "Cultivate. She has so much to gi—" His hand moved toward his mouth. "Had. She *had* so much to give." The hand shook and his face crumpled.

The waitress came with the cinnamon rolls, hesitating as she saw the man's pain. "Sir? Are you all right?"

He nodded and drew a breath through his nose, which seemed to calm him. He dug a handkerchief from his pocket and dabbed at his eyes. "I know it's customary to apologize for public displays of sorrow, but I won't say I'm sorry for feeling pain over her death—or showing it. God allows our tears. 'Evening, morning and noon I cry out in distress, and he hears my voice.'"

That's a Bible verse! Without knowing it, Vincent Carpelli had made the perfect transition into the issue that was uppermost on Tina's mind. She unwound the outer ring of the pastry as she tried to unwind the outer ring of her thoughts.

"Your silence speaks of a question, Miss McKutcheon. Did my mention of God offend you?"

"No, not at all!"

He smiled at her fervor. "Glad to hear it. Then what's the problem?"

"Actually God is at the root of the problem."

"Oh dear. I bet He's not pleased to hear that."

Tina felt some of her nerves ease. Mr. Carpelli had such an interesting way of putting things. It was no wonder Mallory had felt connected to him. "I don't think God minds my having this problem—not if I'm sincere about trying to resolve it."

"And the problem is?"

Tina took a sip of coffee hoping the caffeine would spur her on. "On the plane…Mallory asked me about God."

Mr. Carpelli had trouble swallowing. He cleared his throat. "Did she now? What exactly did she ask?"

"She asked if I believed in God, if I prayed."

"And what did you say?"

"I said yes."

His shoulders eased. "That's good to hear. What else?"

Tina closed her eyes. She'd tried to reconstruct their conversation many times. Now, more than ever, it was important that she got it right—for Mallory's grandfather. "She was talking to me about trying to find her purpose, and she mentioned you'd wanted her to pray about it."

"That's true. But she found it hard. Her parents…" He shook his head. "I brought up my son to know God, but when he got on his own, he chose to reject Him. His wife being from the Orient and believing in the power of self rather than God didn't help. Then, when they had a few bad breaks he chose to blame God rather than his own choices and refused to see how good often comes from bad."

"He mentioned losing a job and his wife getting breast cancer."

Mr. Carpelli nodded. "At first Gerald used his faith like it was a security system. As long as he said so many Hail Mary's or remembered when to kneel and went to confession, nothing bad would get through. But God doesn't work that way."

Tina nodded, understanding completely. "People can get hung up on window dressing and ceremony instead of zoning in on a relationship with Him. And the hard times? Even though I don't like them any more than the next person, I know the struggles I've had have made me stronger because they've forced me to turn to Him. 'For when I am weak, then I am strong.'"

He applauded softly. "Bravo, Miss McKutcheon. It's nice to know Mally was sitting next to a Bible-knowing woman."

Tina stopped midchew. *Here we go...*

"Did I say something wrong?"

With difficulty she swallowed. "Can I be totally honest with you, Mr. Carpelli?"

"It's what I'd prefer."

Tina pushed her plate aside and clasped her hands on the table. She looked down at them, not wanting to meet his eyes. "I have a confession to make. When Mallory asked me about God, even though I knew it was the perfect time for me to share with her, even though I knew it was my duty to do just that, I...I..."

"You chickened out?"

She looked up. "Yes."

He nodded knowingly, and she waited to hear some much needed words of comfort. Surely this nice gentleman would make her feel better. She did not expect—

"Are you ashamed of God?"

Tina blinked. "No, of course not."

"Then why didn't you do it?"

She thought an answer would rush to her lips, but it didn't. Why *didn't* she do it?

His hand bridged the gap between them a second time, but this time it made contact with hers. "Forgive me. I don't mean to come down so hard on you, Miss McKutcheon. The truth is, I've been where you are. I've felt that regret, that shame at my own cowardice." His eyes suddenly filled with tears. "I share it now."

"Now?"

He withdrew his hand and fingered the handle of his coffee cup, shaking his head. "We're some Christians, you and me. God gave us a chance to reach His lovely child, Mallory, and we each chickened out."

No! Tina's head started shaking in rhythm with his. "She asked you too?"

His head stopped. "Yes, ma'am. When she was visiting, she was ripe to hear all of it—and I knew that but said little. Oh, I told her to pray for guidance, that sort of thing. But that's safe stuff—pabulum I could feed a baby. But I didn't tell her about Jesus and heaven and hell; I didn't tell her it was vitally important for her to make a decision in His favor. I thought there would be more time. Plus..." He looked up, his eyes drawn in an awful self-indulgence. "I didn't want to turn her off. We were having such a glorious visit. She was so open. We had great talks. I didn't want her to clam up and think I was a fanatic."

"Or have her reject it—and me."

He let out a laugh. "And there we have it, folks! Reasons number one and two why people don't share the gospel with others."

Tina was struck by his choice of words. "You said, 'share the gospel.' A lot of people don't know what that means. There are so many terms we believers use all the time that other people hear and block out because they don't understand the lingo."

"And we're not good at making it clear, are we? We like our lingo: our calls to be 'born again,' 'Jesus saves,' and 'repent.' It's like a physicist trying to tell a layman about gravity using the lingo of science. When all he has to say—all most people want to hear in order to believe in gravity—is that it pulls us toward the earth and prevents us from flying off into space."

Something clicked into place. "So what people want to hear about God and faith is what's in it for them?"

"Exactly. In words they can understand. That's what Mallory wanted to know."

It sounded easy. "So what should we have said—without using the lingo?"

Mr. Carpelli ate a bite of cinnamon roll, deep in thought. "I think it comes down to the facts."

"Which are?"

"There is a God and He loves us."

Tina remembered Mallory's final question. "Mallory wondered about that. She asked if God knew about her and cared about her."

"And what did you say?"

"Nothing. The pilot interrupted. We took off. We—" She couldn't finish the sentence.

Mr. Carpelli's shoulders sagged with the weight of it. "All she had was generic talk of God. She didn't know about Jesus. And now…"

Tina felt her own weight. "Why is it so hard to say the *J*-word? I can say God all over the place, but Jesus? His name catches in my throat."

"Because when we say His name, we're taking a stand. Just saying God is a good thing, but again, it's easy." He looked up. "I've heard that over 96 percent of the world believes in God. There's no risk leaving it there."

"But how do we explain that Jesus is God's Son, and that He was born with the sole purpose of dying for those sins we keep doing—on a cross? It's the most horrendous way to die. People have a hard time understanding such a sacrifice."

"Because they wouldn't think of doing it themselves."

Tina suddenly thought of Henry Smith. "The hero…the man

in the water who saved us and sacrificed..."

"Perhaps he achieved a bit of perfection in that last act?"

"I'd like to think so."

"I'm sure God and the angels celebrated."

"And Jesus."

He smiled. "And Jesus." He warmed their coffee from the carafe. "All you just said about Jesus was good. It was said simply. Directly. But you can't leave Him hanging on that cross. You have to get to the victory part."

"Easter."

"Resurrection. Rising from the dead. Coming alive like we will come alive in heaven—"

"If we believe in Jesus." Tina pegged her finger into the table. "That's the crux of it. That's what gets hard. Saying that Jesus is *the* way to heaven. Not *a* way. The *only* way." She thought of one of the verses she'd memorized. "In John 14:6, Jesus says, 'I am the way and the truth and the life. No one comes to the Father except through me.'"

"Pretty blatant. Pretty clear."

"Hard."

"Vitally important."

She couldn't disagree with that one.

Mr. Carpelli looked past her, and she could see an idea forming behind his eyebrows. "So do we not give people like my Mally the punch line because we're afraid of their reaction?"

"What?"

He looked right at her. "Does a stand-up comic not give the punch line because he's afraid the audience won't laugh at his joke? No. He goes for it. If they laugh, fine. If they don't? What's he out? A little effort?"

Tina liked this image and immediately got the connection. "And a person's salvation—their eternal, forever-after life in heaven—is no laughing matter. No joke."

"And just because there's a chance people won't respond how we want them to, doesn't mean we shouldn't say it. Go for it."

Tina agreed. But there was a small hitch. "The danger is in saying too much too soon. You and I both know that we never stop learning. There are definitely different levels of understanding all this—and it has nothing to do with chronological age. A person can be eighty and be a kindergartner in the school of faith, yet a ten-year-old can already grasp the essence of what we've said. So we need to be aware of our listeners' levels of understanding. You don't explain calculus to a person who's only ready for arithmetic."

"Point taken. And you don't take it personally if they don't kneel at your feet and want to pray with you on the spot—" he lifted his hands in a mock hallelujah stance—"and give their life to the Lord!"

"Lingo city," Tina said. "But your point is good. Free will prevails. We need to realize that maybe we're only supposed to plant a seed. Maybe it's up to someone else to do the watering or the fertilizing—"

"Or the harvesting. All are equally important."

"At least we'll know we did the right thing."

"Gave it our best."

"Yet even if our hands tremble and our voice wavers while we stumble over the words, or even if our timing isn't perfect, God can use our efforts. But He *cannot* use our silence."

Mr. Carpelli stared at her. Then he smiled. "That's very profound, Miss McKutcheon. You've hit it square."

They shared a moment of silence and both took deep breaths. Their time together had been so intense. And then, as if in concert, they made one final connection and acknowledged it to each other with a look.

"But Mallory…" Tina said.

"Did we fail her?"

"Did she choose Jesus?"

"Is she in heaven?"

This second silence spoke their answer. They didn't know. Only God knew.

Tina hugged Vincent Carpelli in the parking lot. They both seemed hesitant to let go.

When they parted he had a worried look. "I just realized we never talked about the crash. Your ordeal. And I don't know anything about you. Are you married? Do you have kids? What do you do for a living?"

Tina laughed. "We did the opposite of most people, Mr. Carpelli. We bypassed the small talk and got right to the important stuff."

"Indeed we did. But I still want to know more." He hesitated just a moment. "I'd like to be your friend, Miss McKutcheon."

She squeezed his hand. "My friends call me Tina."

Merry felt herself swimming toward the surface. *There's the light! Swim toward the light.* She was nearly out of air. Just a few more feet…

She opened her eyes, and the mental water dissipated. She found herself in a hospital bed. Pale walls. A TV looming near the ceiling. But the picture on the wall…it was all wrong. *I have a desert scene, not this barn, this meadow. Why did they change—*

Then she remembered. She'd been at the funeral. She went home. She got tired of pretending. She'd tried to die.

An old man with thinning hair peeked in the door to her room and did a double take. "Hey, you're awake."

A name clicked. "George?" Now she was really confused. Hadn't he been discharged too? Sure, he had. She'd met him in the hospital on his way out and had seen him at the funeral.

He came to the side of her bed. "That was a close one."

He knows. She looked away. She didn't want him seeing her like this. Weak. Pathetic. Not when he seemed so strong and together.

He took her hand, enveloping it between his. "Don't look away, Miss Merry. I'm not judging you. I'm just glad I found you."

It took a moment to sink in. *"You* found me?"

He nodded and let go of her hand, needing his own to be free when he talked. "Now if that wasn't a weird one. I was heating myself a pan of chili when I saw a Christmas ad on TV."

"It's past Christmas."

"I know. That's what got my attention. And when they said, 'Merry Christmas' I thought of you—Merry. And then my gut started acting up—and I hadn't even eaten the chili yet—and I knew something wasn't right. So I looked up your address and went to check on you." He waggled a finger next to his nose. "You didn't look too good the other day when I first met you in the hospital hall out here. You were putting on an act."

"I was?"

"Weren't you?"

He was smart. "I was."

"Thought so."

She creased the end of the sheet. "I thought if I pretended…" It was hard to explain.

"The pain would go away? Or the people would go away, or the guilt would go away?"

She looked up. "How do you know all that?"

He hesitated, then glanced at the door. "I've been where you are."

She didn't understand.

He let out a sigh. "Truth be told, I was on Flight 1382, heading to Phoenix to kill myself." He sighed again. "There, I said it."

A slew of questions came to mind. Unsure which should be asked first, Merry chose a statement. "But you lived."

He laughed. "Nobody can tell me God doesn't have a sense of humor."

Her next offering was delicate. "Do you still...you know...?"

"Want to die?"

Merry nodded.

"Nope. And neither do you."

She shook her head. "You presume too much."

He shrugged and turned toward the door. "Suit yourself."

"What?"

He stopped and faced her. "You heard me. If you're going to hold on to this notion of killing yourself, then I'm done with you. I did my good deed for the day in getting you in here—once. I'm not going to stand around and watch you do it again."

Merry sat up in bed. Her head seemed a beat behind the movement. "That's pretty cold."

"Yeah? Well, so be it. I figure I've earned the luxury of bluntness by sitting in your shoes—in more ways than one."

He had a point. Who else in the world would understand the scope of her ordeal—the crash *and* the suicide attempt? "What happened in your life that made you give up on living?"

"My wife died."

"I'm sorry." His loss reminded her of her own. Tears pushed their way to the edges of her eyes. She was relieved he didn't notice—or didn't mind.

"I'm sorry too. Irma and me were chocolate and peanut butter, cheesecake and cherries, Oreos and milk."

"I'm seeing a pattern here."

"Probably do. Our life together was the sweetest dessert."

She smiled in spite of her pain. "George, that's quite romantic."

He cleared his throat. "Yeah? Well, even I have my moments. Had. With Irma, that is. Without her, well...I felt like a dried-up scone with no butter."

"Felt? What made you feel differently?"

"Living when so many had died." He pointed at a tear that sat on the ledge of her cheek. "Don't go crying on me, Miss Merry. I know your situation is different, you losing your hubby and boy, but in a way it's the same." He returned to her bedside. "We lived, you and me. Through huge odds, five of us lived. There's got to be a reason for it."

"I can't think of what it would be."

He looked past her. "Well, when you think about it...I think I lived so I could save *you*. How can I throw that back in God's face?"

"Then why am I supposed to live?"

He studied the ceiling. "To be my friend?" He spread his arms as if presenting himself as a gift.

She had to smile. "Thanks, George. Thanks for being there for me. But I'm not sure what kind of friend I'll be."

"Don't worry about that. We'll work on it. All I know is that we can't throw away a gift God's given us. That would be down-right rude."

"I've never heard suicide described as rude."

He set his chin. "Until now."

"Until now."

He pulled a chair close and rested his arms on his knees. "The thing is, there's another reason you've got to go on living."

"And what's that?"

"Henry Smith."

"Who?"

"Henry Smith, the man who saved you."

"The helicopter man?"

"No, missy. The man in the water—the passenger like us. The man who handed over the lifelines."

She vaguely remembered the face of a bearded man hanging on to the tail section. Had he given her the line? She mentally saw the motion of his hand extending it toward her. The awful whir of the helicopter overhead, the gnawing cold, the—

"His sacrifice was a thing to behold."

"Sacrifice?" Merry shook her head, trying to clear her thoughts. "I'm still foggy; I'm not getting this."

George stood and clasped the side of her bed rail, as if in need of support. "Henry handed off the lines, but it took too long. When the helicopter went back for him, he'd already disappeared under the water. He drowned."

She put a hand to her mouth. To be told that a fellow passenger had given his life for her?

"Uh-oh," George said, waving a finger at her face. "There you go again. There will be none of that. And no guilt either."

"Those men in the helicopter…that Henry…they shouldn't have—"

"Saved you?" He swallowed with great deliberation. "I suppose you can go through the rest of your life feeling guilty and unworthy, but personally, I think that's a mighty waste of a hero." George's voice broke, and Merry watched his face fold in on itself. "Henry Smith died so you could live. Not so you can kill yourself and not so you can throw yourself some pity party and waste what time you've got left in this world." He threw back his head, pulling in his tears with a breath. "Do you want him to have died for nothing?"

"No, of course not."

His eyes flashed. "Then snap out of it! I know the doctors probably wouldn't approve of me sniping at you like this. They'll want to coddle you and have you talk for hours about why you thought you had to kill yourself. But I'm too ignorant and ornery to abide by such baloney. And when I'm yelling at you, I'm yelling at me. It takes guts to be happy. The two of us wanted to kill ourselves because we were cowards. That's a fact we can't deny. But what we also can't deny is that a man displayed the epitome of bravery for us." He looked away, then back again. "You know what Henry Smith said to me in the plane before we crashed?"

"No."

"He said two things I will always remember. One, that God didn't want me to take my own life. And two, that Henry felt like he'd been given a verse that directed his actions—only at the time he didn't realize how." George's eyes brightened. "He didn't realize it then, but now…the verse is perfect."

"What is it?"

"Isaiah something or other. But the words were, 'This is the way; walk in it.'"

"What way?"

George gripped Merry's arm. "Don't you see? God told Henry that verse as a kind of challenge. Getting him to think past himself to bigger things. Then the plane crashed, and Henry followed the verse. God showed him a *way,* and he took it—he *walked* in it."

"Wow."

George nodded, and when his eyes teared, hers did too. "You bet your bedpan, wow. People don't know they're heroes until God gives them the opportunity and they say yes. Heroes are not forced; they *choose.*"

Merry shivered.

George straightened his chin. "So considering all that, knowing what we know, I refuse to let either one of us taint the *choice* Henry Smith made. You hear me, little girl? You get where I'm coming from?"

Merry's lungs were suddenly empty. She gasped for air, then let out a sob. Everything he said was true. *She* had a choice to make. *This is the way; walk in it.* She reached out a hand. George took it and squeezed. "Help me get out of here, George. Help me get through this." She let out a breath. "Help me go home."

Merry's driveway was occupied so George pulled up front. A woman got out of the car in the drive, eyed them, and then rushed to Merry's door.

"Baby, where have you been? I've been sitting here twenty minutes. I knocked, I called you on the phone. I was getting worried." For the first time she looked at George. "Who's this?"

Merry got out of the car. "This is George Davanos, Mom. He's another one of the survivors. George, this is my mother, Anna Keenan."

The woman eyed him warily, as if her daughter's explanation weren't enough. Merry looked at George nervously, and he could read her mind: *Cover for me, George.*

He chose his words carefully. "I picked Merry up for lunch, Mrs. Keenan."

The woman's irritation turned toward her daughter. "You went out to eat the day after your family's funeral?

Merry headed for the door. "That's exactly what we did, Mom. I do need to eat, you know."

Good save, Miss Merry.

Merry stopped on the front step and turned back to George. "Care to come in?"

After checking the still-disapproving face of Anna Keenan, George knew the prudent thing would be to leave. But he wasn't in a prudent mood.

"I'd love to."

Merry waited at the door for him, then took his arm. "You coming, Mom?"

The woman's look changed from disapproval to the sad-sack face of a child who's received an invitation to a birthday party that's already in progress. "No, no thanks. I think I'll go home. I have things to do. Just so you're all right..."

"I'm fine. Or at least I feel the possibility that I *could* be fine. Maybe. Someday."

For the first time since meeting her, George believed it was true.

❧

Sonja hesitated at the edge of the airport metal detectors. She'd gotten this far from a sheer act of will, but suddenly, when faced with entering a gate, she shied like a thoroughbred on the edge of a fence. *What am I doing flying again?*

"Ma'am? Either come on through or step aside. You're blocking traffic."

Sonja stepped aside, aware of the puzzled looks of the other passengers, as well as the wary scrutiny of the security people who probably thought she was hesitating because she had a gun in her cast, her facial scars the result of a terrorist action gone bad.

This is ridiculous. Millions of people fly every day without incident. The odds of being in a plane crash are astronomical.

But I crashed…

Which means I'm done. Through. It's statistically impossible for me to experience such a thing again.

She saw a handsome African-American woman go through the line. The woman matched the mental image Sonja had of Roscoe's wife. Eden Moore would be waiting for her. The woman wanted her to come. The woman had called Sonja a gift from God.

She took a deep breath and straightened her shoulders. She had to do it. For Roscoe. For Eden.

And for herself.

Anthony's second day back at work was a little easier. He had a good night's sleep, fueled by the news that the black box had been recovered from the crash site. Soon they'd know who to blame, and his lawsuit could gain momentum.

Today he even had some surgery scheduled and felt totally up for it. Mrs. Wanda Saperstein was in for a face-lift. He'd worked on her before, and together they were methodically remaking her

body. With his expertise—and multiple thousands of her dollars—
she looked fifteen years younger than her chronological age. To be
honest, Anthony found it a little creepy when grandmothers
attempted to look the same age as their grown children, but who
was he to argue? If it weren't for his patients' vanity, he wouldn't be
able to pay his bills.

Anthony had just finished with Mrs. Saperstein in his office
complex's private operating room. He had a few minutes until the
day's remaining round of appointments started. He fell onto the
couch in his office. The promise of relief was not fulfilled. He
moaned. His entire body hurt, and he was exhausted as much from
the mental and emotional stress of keeping up the front of invinci-
bility as from any physical residuals from the crash.

He had just closed his eyes when the intercom buzzed. Candy's
voice filled the room, "Dr. Thorgood? Are you there?"

"Can't you leave me alone for a few minutes? Surely one of the
nurses can handle—"

"Sorry, but this can't wait. A doctor at the hospital has been
trying to get ahold of you. She said she's been paging you. I
explained that you've been in surgery, but she was insistent you call
her immediately. A Dr. Margalis?"

Lovely Andrea… "Fine."

Anthony groaned at the effort to move to his desk. As he
dialed the hospital, the smallest twinge of nerves teased his stomach. The only case he'd worked on with the beautiful doctor was
the bar fight the day before. Could her call stem from an urgent
desire to *see* him? Nah. Even his well-hewn ego couldn't hold on to
that one.

He got through to her immediately. "Dr. Thorgood here.
What's up?"

"We have a problem with the hand patient in ER yesterday.
This morning he went to his own doctor, who immediately sent
him to another specialist."

Anthony's pride surfaced. "Another...? That was pretty unpro-fessional."

"Forget your pride a moment, Doctor. Don't you want to know why?"

"Why?"

"Because Patrick Harper is a concert pianist. And when he regained full use of his senses this morning—and felt extreme pain when he tried to move his hand—he and his manager went to his personal doctor to have it looked at. That doctor called here to find out who had worked on him."

"So when's he coming back in?"

"He's not. At that point they purposely went to see another specialist. And that doctor—"

"Who? Who did they go see?"

"Dr. Burrows. Anyway, Dr. Burrows opened up the hand and—"

"He can't see my patient!"

"He can if the patient insists and if there is cause to believe the original doctor was negligent in stitching up a hand that should have been—"

Anthony's stomach clawed. "You sent him to Burrows? You went over my head? Do you know how insulting that is?"

"I didn't send him anywhere. When they asked for another sur-geon, I had an obligation to give them a name. And as far as that insulting you, insults are not the issue here. The primary concern must be for the patient, for his well—"

"Don't give me that. We both know Ed Burrows would sell his mother's soul to get at my patients. This is totally unethi—"

"Dr. Burrows took care of a desperate patient because of his concern for that patient, not to boost his ego, nor to injure yours."

"You're deluded."

"And you're arrogant."

What? Anthony found himself holding his breath. He let it out. "That was uncalled—"

"I'd say I'm sorry, but I'm too weary to lie."

So I suppose this means dating is out?

"Go back to your tummy tucks and breast implants, Doctor. Perhaps it's best you leave the more important situations to real doctors."

"Andrea!"

"But be warned there may be repercussions."

"What are you talking about?"

"If Mr. Harper doesn't regain the full use of his hand because of your misdiagnosis, your impatience not to be bothered past the quick and easy fix—which I warned you against yesterday—then I expect he'll sue."

"Why would he do that?"

"His occupation. Didn't you hear me? He's a concert pianist."

"But he got hurt in a bar—"

"Yes, in a bar. Defending himself in a bar fight. One he didn't start—and wouldn't dare start considering his profession."

"This is getting wearisome, Andrea."

"Your lack of empathy continues to astound me." Her sigh was heavy. "You'd better pray for a miracle, Dr. Thorgood, or you may lose your profession too."

The line went dead. Anthony froze.

This isn't happening.

Fourteen

No discipline seems pleasant at the time, but painful.
Later on, however, it produces a harvest of righteousness and
peace for those who have been trained by it.

<small>HEBREWS 12:11</small>

Tina drove too fast, fueled by her joy in meeting Vincent Carpelli. She had never had such an uplifting conversation, not even in her Bible study class. She felt like celebrating, and the best way to celebrate was to feed her passion. She needed a bookstore, and she needed it fast.

She saw a Christian bookstore to her right. Perfect.

This was Tina's favorite place, heaven on earth. The store—Feed the Need Bookstore—was huge and had a coffee bar and a large gift department. Rock music played in the background, the lyrics talking about a different kind of love than most rock songs. There were videos playing for kids. And books…definitely a reader's paradise. Biographies, picture books, self-help, Bibles, devotionals, and Tina's favorite: fiction. Shelves and shelves of beautifully presented inspirational fiction.

Tina spent the next half hour choosing five novels from different genres. It felt like Christmas. Perhaps it was, for in a way, today was the day Christ had been born in her again—thanks to Mr. Carpelli.

She went to pay at the counter. Behind the clerk was a sign: *Help wanted.* Tina's heart squeezed until her toes tingled.

Do it.

Without thinking a second thought she heard herself say, "I'd like to apply for the job, please."

The clerk smiled. "Your timing's perfect. The manager is in. Would you like to fill out an application and speak to her today?"

The clerk was right. The timing *was* perfect.

How will I recognize her?

As she exited the airplane, Sonja realized the inadequacy of her preparation for this trip. She had a mental image of what Eden Moore *should* look like, but nothing concrete. They had not exchanged physical characteristics, nor arranged a clue like *I'll be the one wearing a red carnation.*

The opening to the gate area loomed ahead. Sonja slung her winter coat over her cast and adjusted her carry-on on her other shoulder. She hadn't brought much. All the clothes she'd so carefully chosen for the convention in sunny Phoenix were gone. Roscoe's widow would have to deal with Sonja as is.

The jet way ended. The terminal opened up, and Sonja was assailed by the noise. She scanned the faces of the people waiting. No one's eyes locked to hers; no one offered a questioning glance. Then she saw a woman holding a bouquet of carnations with a card attached that had *Sonja* written on it. Eden Moore was even prettier than Sonja had imagined.

"Sonja?"

Before she could complete her nod, the woman engulfed her with a hug. "I am so happy to meet you. How was your flight? Was it hard being on a plane again? Is that all your luggage?"

Sonja laughed at the onslaught. "Fine, yes, and yes."

Mrs. Moore hesitated a moment, matching the answers with the questions. "Sorry. I get excited and talk way too much." She remembered the flowers. "These are for you."

Sonja held them to her face, inhaling. "You're very sweet."

"Just wanted you to feel welcome. And let me take that." Eden put a hand on Sonja's carry-on.

"You don't have to—"

"Shush now."

Sonja shushed and realized by Eden's aura of command that it was probably best to let the older woman have her way. She relinquished the carry-on and they started walking, with Eden linking an arm through hers, a move Sonja found a bit disconcerting, but one she didn't brush away.

Suddenly, Sonja saw a Welcome to Phoenix sign and drew back.

Eden noticed. "What's wrong?"

"This is the airport I would have come into for the convention, the trip I was on when we crashed. Seeing the sign…"

Eden patted her arm. "I thought of that when I was coming to pick you up. How it might be hard for you. It was a little hard for me too, remembering my Roscoe should have flown in here."

Sonja was horrified. She stopped and faced Mrs. Moore. "I'm so sorry. How selfish of me to think of myself, when *you* lost a husband. You probably think I'm the most insensitive, self-absorbed—"

"Nonsense." Eden started them walking again. Sonja was amazed at the strength in her forward movement; she had no choice but to go along. "If we can't be honest with each other, then you might as well get on that plane and go home. Honesty or nothing. That's my condition. Do you agree with it?"

Sonja felt the woman's eyes as they walked. She risked a glance. "I agree."

"Good. Then let's get on home."

Eden Moore's Oldsmobile was huge, old, and clean. A boat on wheels. Eden handled it with the offhanded ease of a professional driver; she was adept at talking while she drove, one hand always in motion.

"Now tell me about your experience. It must have been horrendous. Frightening. How are you doing? What can I do to help?"

Sonja had expected Eden's first questions to be about her husband. "Shouldn't I be the one comforting you, Mrs. Moore?"

"Call me Eden, and though that's very nice of you, dear, I'm doing fine in the comfort department. I know I'll be all right."

Sonja shook her head, incredulous. "Your husband said you were a strong woman, but—"

She laughed. "He said that about me? Fiddle-dee. He was the strong one. Though truth be told, we grew strong together. I always feel blessed to see how God uses our struggles in such positive ways."

Sonja expelled a breath loudly. *She calls losing a son* and *a husband "struggles"?*

Eden glanced at her. "Uh-oh. The sigh that spoke a thousand words. What's the problem?"

Sonja hadn't meant to express her feelings. "It was nothing…"

"It was not nothing. Honesty, remember?"

Sonja looked at the Phoenix landscape zooming by her window, bits of cacti and desert intermixed with lush lawns and palm trees. This woman was not going to let her get away with anything. Sonja wasn't used to being honest; in fact, she'd molded her life around her ability to be *dis*honest.

"I was just amazed at your choice of words," she said. "You mentioned your struggles. I know about your boy, and now your husband. Those aren't struggles, those are catastrophes, life-jarring disasters, tragedies worthy of Shakespeare."

Eden considered a moment, fingering a silver and turquoise earring. "I agree. And if I let myself concentrate on the loss, I would lose everything. That's the trouble with grief. It's cannibalistic. It makes you focus on yourself until you end up gnawing off your own foot trying to make the hunger pangs go away."

"But don't you need to focus on yourself in order to get through it?"

"Oh, I have, Sonja. And I do. I'm not a selfless person. But when Eddy died, and now my Roscoe... If I concentrate on *my* loss, then I miss the joy of thinking about *their* gain."

"Gain? They're dead!" Sonja didn't mean to shout. "Sorry."

"Shout if you must... Just a minute, I can't do this while I'm driving." She pulled into a gas station and parked. She rolled down the windows, letting in the dry air, shut the car off, undid her seat belt, and faced Sonja. "There. That's better. Roscoe used to tease me, saying if I didn't get to fully use my hands while I talked, I'd explode. The same goes for my need to see the person I'm talking to. Now where were we?"

"Your loss and their gain?"

She slapped her thigh. "Exactly. Of course I miss them. Of course I wish they were here. And some days I cry a river of tears. And I even went through being mightily mad about it. I gave God a good talking to those first few days."

"You yelled at God? Can you do that?"

Eden laughed. "Can? You bet. *Should* we do that? I don't think God minds. He wants all parts of us, and that includes the not-so-nice parts, even the downright nasty parts."

The few times Sonja had thought about God, she likened Him to a stern headmaster with a ruler, ready to whap the palm of anyone who displeased Him. A person would never ever consider yelling at a headmaster.

"You look shocked."

Sonja hadn't meant for her doubt to show. "I have a different view of God."

Eden nodded. "You want Him to be proud of you, right?"

"I guess."

"Like you want your parents to be proud of you."

Now *that* hit close to home. Too close. "So...you yelled at God. That still doesn't explain the win and lose part."

"It's the beginning of it. At first I only thought of me and my loss and the years we *wouldn't* have together. Then I thought of the pain they both went through." She put a hand to her chest and pressed. "That's still a tough one." She let out a breath as if releasing the image. "But then I remembered the promise."

"What promise?"

"God's promise that if we believe in His Son, we'll go to heaven when we die and be with Him—and each other." She closed her eyes, tilted her face upward, and smiled. "'He will wipe every tear from their eyes. There will be no more death or mourning or crying or pain, for the old order of things has passed away.'"

Sonja was totally confused. "No more death? What are you talking about?"

Eden opened her eyes. "Someday. When Jesus comes again."

"Comes again? You lost me."

Eden studied Sonja a moment, yet her look was not one of judgment but of assessment. Finally she nodded. "Tell me about yourself, Sonja. What's your background?"

Although Sonja didn't want to talk about her parents, at least it was a subject she knew. "I'm the only daughter and second child of Mr. and Mrs. Sheffield D. Grafton II. And it's not an easy job." She laughed. "I have no clue why I just said that."

"Because we were talking about making God proud. Unfortunately, a person's relationship with an earthly father often gets in the way of a relationship with the heavenly One."

"I never thought of that."

"Is it true?"

A headmaster with a ruler. Sonja was shocked by the comparison. "I think it is."

"Is your father demanding?"

Sonja had to laugh. "You could say that."

"Is he proud of you?"

"You *couldn't* say that."

Eden patted her arm. "I'm sorry."

Sonja was relieved that Eden didn't argue with her or ask for proof. In the few times in her life when she had confided in a friend about her parental problems, she had grown weary of their flip reaction of, "Oh, I'm sure you're wrong. They're probably plenty proud of you." How did they know? Now to have Eden accept Sonja's perception as real…it was a relief.

"God wants to be proud of you, and you should work toward that. But unlike flesh-and-blood fathers, He is very forgiving."

"That's *totally* unlike my father," Sonja said. "If I told him the truth about what just happened to me with my job—" She stopped herself and laughed. "You're a bad influence, Eden. I know you for a half hour and spill my guts?"

"Fiddle-dee. Spill away. That's what I'm here for. So what's this truth you don't dare tell your father?"

Go ahead. You might as well. "I was fired."

"Why?"

"Because of deceit and underhandedness and doing anything to get ahead."

Eden did a slow blink, as if looking inward at a memory. "Roscoe…we went through that. Doing anything…"

Sonja remembered. "He told me about it, how he gained success but ignored you and Eddy. He told me how Eddy's death changed all that, how *you* changed all that."

"Me?"

Her face was pathetic with hope. *Didn't she know?* "He said you were an inspiration to him, that you'd tried to get him to see the truth for a long time but never succeeded. It took the death of Eddy to get through to him, to get his attention."

"Make him surrender."

Sonja moved an inch toward the window. "I don't like that word."

Eden smiled as if she knew a secret. "But it's such a glorious word—if said in the right context."

"And that is?"

Eden put her seat belt back on. "I've got something to show you."

They pulled in front of an older strip mall at a busy intersection. A gas station occupied the second corner, a liquor store the third, and the fenced playground of an elementary school finished the cross. The strip contained a barbershop, a coin laundry, a pawnshop, and an office whose sign proclaimed, The Talent Track. Eden parked in front of the office and got out.

"This is the place. The evidence of our surrender."

This was the Moore's business? When Roscoe had told her that he and Eden had given up a life of wealth and had chosen a simpler life, she imagined a nice office in an office park, not…this.

Before Sonja could let it sink in, a teenager came outside. He waved a slip of paper. "Mrs. Moore! I just got a call from Tinnon's Printers. They're giving me a job. At first they were going to give me a delivery job, but when they realized it was you who sent me, and they saw my artwork that you sent…they gave me a real job in the printing department. They're going to show me how to design stuff."

Eden hugged the boy, then put a hand against his cheek and absorbed his eyes with a look. "I told you you could do it, Jose. I told you." She flicked the end of his nose. "But you know the rules. You go to work every day you're scheduled—on time. You listen to your bosses and no talking back. And don't you dare act like you know everything because you never will. You show them respect, and they'll do the same to you. Understand?"

"Understand." The boy eyed Sonja for the first time. His expression changed from one of joy to distrust. "Who's she?"

Eden drew Sonja close. "This is Sonja Grafton. She sat next to our dear Roscoe on the plane. She's one of the survivors, thank the Lord."

The boy's eyes grew sad. "I miss him."

Eden put a hand under his chin. "Indeed. But because we knew him we're going to go on and work all the harder, aren't we?"

The boy nodded, but the act was devoid of enthusiasm. He said his good-byes and left. They went inside. The room was furnished with mismatched desks and chairs and a couch in the corner. The walls were painted in bright colors and plastered with inspirational posters. A ballerina on pointe: Get the point. Follow your dream. A student hard at work at a desk with wads of crumpled paper surrounding him: God finds persistence irresistible.

A teenage girl who was huddled at a computer popped up when she saw Eden. "Can I see you, Mrs. Moore?"

"Certainly, Maria." Eden looked around. The girl was the only one there. "You minding the store for me?"

"Bobby had to go get copy paper. He'll be right back."

Eden nodded. "That's nice of you to stay, but don't you have a seventh period class?"

"Mr. Bates let me out early because I said I was coming here to talk to you."

"Nice try, young lady," Eden said, taking a seat behind a desk, "but next time stay in school until regular dismissal. You know I'm here for you anytime, and school comes first."

"Yes, ma'am."

"Now sit, girl." She turned to Sonja. "Care to join us?"

Sonja pulled a chair to the side of the desk while the girl sat across from Eden. The radio was on. Eden shut it off and turned her full attention to Maria. "What's on your mind?"

Maria looked at Sonja. "I can't talk with her…"

Eden smacked a hand to her forehead. "I must have left my manners in the car." She made the introductions, and Maria nodded as if reassured that Eden's friend Sonja was all right. She seemed totally unimpressed that Sonja had lived through a plane crash. Perhaps Maria had lived through some "plane crashes" of her own.

The girl twirled a strand of hair around her finger, revealing an ear that had been pierced four times. "I want to go to college, like you said I should."

"Should and could, depending on your grades. How are they? You doing your best? You're not still having trouble in history, are you?"

Maria took a deep breath as if unsure which question to answer.

Sonja broke the silence. "You need a notepad to keep track of her questions, don't you?"

Maria laughed. Eden feigned irritation with a hand on her hip. "Two against one. No fair."

"Sorry, Mrs. Moore. Luckily the answer to all your questions is the same. I'm doing good. Real fine. Mr. Moore quizzing me with those names and dates helped tons." She looked up, aghast. "Oh! Sorry. I shouldn't have mentioned—"

"Of course you should have mentioned Roscoe, dear. I want you to mention him often and with joy. Understand?"

"Yes, ma'am."

"If your grades are good, then what's the problem?"

The girl adjusted her bottom in the chair. "Mama says I don't need to go to no college; I shouldn't even think of it. She says it doesn't matter I'm good at math. She doesn't see why I need to take any calculus or differential equations or stuff like that. She says nobody uses that junk. She says the only math a body needs is adding and subtracting. The rest is for highbrow snobs."

Sonja had to intervene again. "You actually like calculus?"

"I've only had precalc, but yeah, I like it a lot. I like the way the numbers fit together with only one right answer."

Sonja sat back in her chair. "I admire you."

The girl's eyebrows raised. "Me?"

"Absolutely. I'm one of those people who can't balance her checkbook. You're one of those who can send a man to Mars, or invent a machine that can see inside our body, or design a tunnel under the English Channel, or…lots of neat things."

"With a math degree I could do that?"

"Of course you—" Sonja realized she'd taken over the conversation. She looked at Eden. "I'm sorry; I'm supposed to be a silent observer here."

Eden smiled. "Who says?"

"But I'm just visiting."

"Are you?"

"What?"

Eden winked at Maria and turned her chair to face Sonja. "It appears that you, Sonja Grafton, have a talent for inspiring kids to use *their* talents."

"What?"

Eden laughed. "You didn't have a clue you could do this. Am I right?"

Sonja was at a loss. "Me? Inspiring?"

Maria smiled. "Yes, Ms. Grafton, you. Until now I never really thought about what I could *do* with a degree in math. Everybody always told me what I could be—you know, a teacher or an accountant or a scientist. And I told my mom those jobs, and she just looked at me like she didn't get it. But if I tell her I could work on the space shuttle or in medicine or design a tunnel…" She moved to the edge of her seat, her eyes flashing. "She'd get that. She could understand that. And if I did that kind of thing, she'd…" Her voice broke. "She'd be so proud of me." She looked up at Eden and Sonja. "I just want her to be proud of me."

Sonja felt her heart melt with empathy. Earning the approval of parents. It was a universal quest.

Maria stood, leaned over, and hugged Sonja, taking her totally by surprise. "Thank you, Ms. Grafton. You helped tons."

This was so unexpected. "You're welcome."

Then she gave Eden a hug and left. Eden rocked in her chair, grinning.

"What's that look for?"

"This look is for you, dear Sonja, and is full of pure joy at seeing God's handiwork."

"What are you talking about?"

She stopped rocking and drilled a finger into her desk for emphasis. "God brought you here. To me. To Maria. He gave you an opportunity to share your expertise. You took it, and made one girl very, very happy."

"But I didn't share any *expertise.*"

"Sure you did. You have a fine organizational mind that sees through a problem and zeroes in on a practical answer. You are straightforward, honest, and inspiring."

Honest? Sonja wondered what Eden would think about her "honest" dealings with Geraldine. "I thank you for your encouragement, but I'm not the inspiring type. *Honest.*"

"Sure you are. You were just too consumed with other things to see it. Our job here at The Talent Track is twofold: to help the kids tap in to their God-given gifts and talents and to give them practical advice about how to use them. Turn them toward God and then turn them loose on the world to make it a better place." She scooted her chair toward Sonja's, not stopping until their knees nearly touched. She took Sonja's hands in hers. "You're supposed to stay in Phoenix, Sonja. I feel it. You're supposed to stay here and work with me."

Sonja pulled her hands away. "I couldn't…I…"

"You have some other plans?"

Back home she was faced with no job and humiliating disgrace. Here, there was a chance to start fresh. But the idea was crazy, totally out of left field, out of the question. Besides… Sonja looked around the minimal office. Eden followed her gaze.

"I know it's not much—yet. But Roscoe and I had big plans. We need to stay in the neighborhood. We realize that, but we planned to expand our services. We wanted to have a talent day at schools and offer some job-skills classes. All the talent in the world won't do these kids much good if they don't know how to fill out a job application or carry on an intelligent conversation in an interview."

"But back home…my apartment, my…" She hesitated, but then remembered Eden's vow of honesty. "My things. How could you pay me enough?"

Eden nodded. "There's the rub. The ever elusive enough."

"I had plans, big plans."

"I understand. Plans for promotions and raises and bigger apartments and maybe even a house?"

"Is that bad?"

Eden shrugged. "There was once a rich man who came up to Jesus and asked Him what he had to do to get into heaven. He'd been a good man and had followed all the commandments. But Jesus told him if he wanted to be perfect, he had to sell all his stuff and give it to the poor. Then he'd have treasure in heaven. Only then could he follow Him."

"Whoa. Tough order."

"It wasn't an order. It was an opportunity."

"What did the rich man do?"

"He couldn't do it. He went away sad because he was very rich."

Sonja supported her cast with her free hand. "That's what you and Roscoe did, isn't it? That's what you meant by surrender. You gave it up and followed Him."

"Yes."

"Do you regret it?"

"Never."

"Would I regret it?"

"You'll never know until you try, will you? Until *you* surrender."

"But I don't know *Him.*"

Eden smiled. "Oh, you will. Make a decision like this, and you will."

Anthony left work early, telling his staff he was feeling the after-effects of the crash—*not* confiding that his inability to work was caused by the threat of a lawsuit. But even that was only half the truth, for niggling at Anthony's body and mind was something completely foreign to him: guilt.

Did I make a mistake?

People make mistakes all the time.

But you don't.

But what if I did?

Impossible.

But what if?

The car behind him honked. The light had turned green.

Snap out of it. So your pride was hurt when the patient went to Burrows. Wouldn't you rather another doctor step in than the patient's hand be ruined for life?

"Not really."

Anthony was shocked to hear his own voice. He'd heard of people talking to themselves, but giving themselves verbal arrogant answers?

He remembered Andrea's words: *"You're arrogant."*

Was he? Had the character trait he attributed to confidence and determination turned into arrogance? Or had it always been arrogance, which he handily masked as those more admirable traits?

The man's a concert pianist.

If he'd only known.

Nope. He couldn't get away with that one. As a doctor he was supposed to treat all patients the same. No matter what. A rich socialite or a man hurt in a bar fight.

Anthony turned into his neighborhood, eager to get home, shut the door, and hide out. He knew the best thing to do would be to call Patrick Harper. Show concern. Mend fences.

He rejected the idea.

Why was it so hard to do the right thing? It was as if there were a wall between him and the right way, and he couldn't break through it. As if the path were before him but his shoes were bolted to the floor. He was deeply rooted in the self-image he had so meticulously created. To break away would be as painful as cutting off an appendage, and yet to remain where he was promised a kind of suffocation. Had arrogance been his air?

He was so preoccupied with his inner struggle that he barely looked beyond the bumper of his car. When he finally looked up as he closed in on his house, he was shocked to see his front yard covered with reporters, TV vans, cars, cameras, and microphones.

"There he is!"

Before he could think to stop, much less put the car in reverse or turn around, Anthony was surrounded by the media attention he'd craved. He locked the doors. But that didn't stop the words from reaching him.

"What's your response to the lawsuit by Patrick Harper?"

"Is it true you refused to do the necessary surgery that could have saved his hand?"

"What is your response to the comments of Dr. Edward Burrows regarding your negligence?"

"Is it true you once said you were saved from the crash of Flight 1382 because you deserved to live more than the victims who died? Is that the real reason you took the lifeline that wasn't meant for you?"

Anthony felt as if he were going to throw up. He pushed on the accelerator, forcing the reporters to make way. He drove into his garage and shut the door even before he shut off the engine. He escaped into his house, locking the doors. He closed the blinds.

Then he fell into his leather chair with the matching ottoman, which sat next to his Remington statue and beneath his Andrew

Wyeth print. He didn't turn on a light to illuminate his surroundings. He might never turn a light on again.

No comment. No comment.

David was coming over for another dinner, and Tina wanted to make everything perfect. They had a lot to celebrate. More than she'd ever dreamed.

He'd called to see how her meeting with Grandpa Carpelli had gone, and she told him everything—about *that* conversation. But not about the rest of her morning. And not about the other decision that had evolved throughout the day. She'd save those two surprises for dinner.

It was hard for Tina to tear herself away from reading one of her new books in order to cook. In fact, she had the book with her in the kitchen and opened it whenever the responsibility of cooking gave her a free moment. She *loved* books, and now, with her new job, her life could *be* books.

Tina adjusted her crutch for balance so she could open the oven to check on the cherry pie. The aroma engulfed the room, the cherries bubbling through the slits. *Perfect.* She took it out and checked on the roast, potatoes, and carrots in the Crock-Pot. Also perfect.

She heard a knock on the front door and then it opened. "Honey, I'm home!"

She used to be annoyed at David's reference to marital domesticity. But not tonight. Not anymore.

She hobbled to meet him, flung her arms around his neck, and lost her balance, nearly toppling them to the floor.

"Whoa, Tina!" David said, recovering from her kiss. "You should have breakfast with Italian grandfathers more often."

She felt herself blush. "I intend to. I like him. We're going to get together again."

David flung his coat over the back of the couch. "Should I be jealous?" She kissed him again, softer this time. It took him a moment to open his eyes. "I guess not."

"You'd better believe it."

He reached for her hand. "Please note that I'm not complaining, but I *am* curious as to what's got into you. You mentioned a surprise and a decision? They must be doozies."

"They are."

"And?"

She glanced toward the kitchen. Everything was under control. Why not tell him now? She led him to the couch and they sat. She angled her body toward his.

"First off, the surprise. I got a job this afternoon."

His eyes blinked his surprise. "Already? Where?"

"At a Christian bookstore."

"Not teaching?"

"Not teaching."

He looked past her, letting it sink in. "You *do* read more than anyone I know. You love books. But what made you apply there?"

"I didn't go in with any intention of applying. I wanted some new books to celebrate my breakfast with Vincent and happened to drive by that store. I bought some books, saw the help-wanted sign, interviewed with the manager, and I got the job. Assistant manager."

He laughed. "Assistant…? How'd you manage that?"

"I'd say it was my blazing credentials, but it wasn't. I think it's a God-thing. I think this is what I'm supposed to do."

"Not teach? Never again?"

"I can't say never, but I can't ignore the fact that this feels so right. To deal with people who like to read. To share my passion with them—for God *and* books."

"Sounds like your life is nearly perfect."

"It is. Nearly." She looked away from him, gathering her

strength. *Is this really what I want? Now's my chance to back out...* She looked up and saw him watching her. She took both his hands in hers. "I love you, David. Will you marry me?"

She wished she had a camera. The look on his face... His eyes widened in total shock, his jaw dropped, and he let out a short expulsion of breath. She thought of making a joke but restrained herself. This was a moment they would remember all their lives.

"Are you serious?"

"Completely."

"What brought this on?"

That was hard to explain, but she had to try. "I've resisted the idea of marrying you—of marrying anyone—because I felt unsure of myself. I grew up with people making fun of me for my weight, my brains, my obsession with books. I think I became a teacher out of spite. To get revenge on all the teenagers who made my growing-up years miserable and all the teachers who didn't come to my defense."

"Teaching shouldn't be a form of revenge."

"Exactly. That's why I wasn't good at it. And, as with all forms of revenge, it backfired the most on me, the instigator. And the more I hated the job, the more I hated myself, and the more unlovable I felt." She touched his knee. "Truthfully, I felt unsure about being loved by you—as if I wasn't good enough."

"Don't say such—"

She stopped him. "And I wasn't good enough. Mostly because I couldn't love you in return. But Mallory changed all that. Her interest in me, and then the crash and the larger kind of love those rescuers showed for me, and the hero's love for me..." She caught a tear before it escaped. "What I learned this morning with Vincent was that God allows our failures. He loves us in spite of them. He loves me so much I think *He* led me to the Christian bookstore, and *He* made the timing perfect for me to get a job there. If I hadn't quit my job yesterday, David..." She shook her head at the implications. "It's all worked out as it should have worked out—as He wanted it to work out." She smiled at his puzzled expression. "Ah, David, you're the last piece of the puzzle. I'm sure now. I'm flawed but finally willing to try. Will you take me?"

He said yes without saying a word.

"I've never had popcorn for dinner before," Merry said.

George handed her a heaping bowl. "Then you've missed out on one of the highlights of life." He sat at the other end of her couch. "I put extra butter on it. You need a little meat on you."

Merry knew she'd lost weight. Her kitchen was still full of food offerings, but she didn't feel like eating much. And yet the smell of freshly popped popcorn made her taste buds dance in anticipation. She ate a handful and sighed.

"Hits the spot, doesn't it?"

"I feel guilty for not eating all the food people brought."

"It'll keep. Freeze some. Throw some out. Or have some friends over for a feast."

Merry looked away. "I don't have many friends."

"Why not?"

"I've chased most of them away."

He looked at her sideways. "May I ask why?"

It was a good question. Merry tried to tuck her feet beneath her, but her sore muscles wouldn't budge. "They annoyed me."

"All of them?"

She loved how George got to the heart of things. "Pretty much."

"They had bigger houses, cuter kids, more romantic husbands?"

"Actually…no. They had exactly what I had. And that bugged me."

George tossed a kernel in the air and caught it in his mouth. "You lost me."

Merry bit her lip, trying to pin it down. "We were all living the American dream. A house, a family, a swing set in the backyard."

"But?"

Her heart began to pound as if she were on the edge of a precipice and had been asked to jump. "But...but they were content, and I wasn't." She took an extra breath, relieved to get it out. "They wallowed in their lives; they were happy. They thought it was enough. I got so sick of their...their perkiness that I wanted to slap them. Didn't they realize what they were missing?"

"What *were* they missing?"

"Reality. On TV, women work in fancy offices and have people hang on their words. They're important. They're contributing something."

George nodded. "Ah, I see. You're taking TV as the basis for reality? Hello? Surely you're not that naive?"

"It's not just on TV; it's in real life too. I know it is. My friend Teresa, who I was going to visit in Phoenix...she's free to spend money on what she wants and go where she wants, when she wants to go. She can party and not come home until two in the morning."

George tsked-tsked. "At the risk of sounding like a father, I've got to point out that what you've described as your friend's ideal life sounds like the yearnings of a teenager wanting to run away from home. Parties, late nights, buying things. Is this truly what made you discontent?"

It sounded so shallow. "I..."

George put a hand on her arm. "Listen to me, Miss Merry. Listen to the advice of one who's worked in a fancy office and has had people hang on my every word—and from one who's even felt a little important in my time. What the TV shows and even society at large don't tell you is that most of us successful corporate types would give anything to stay at home and have our *kids* hang on our every word and find a feeling of importance there. But we can't. At least I couldn't. As the man of the house, it was my responsibility to make the money, to provide for my family. You women have it made."

"Excuse me?"

"Now don't get huffy on me. Hear me out. A lot of women have the option of holding down an outside job or staying home with the kids, or a combination of both. Most men don't have that option. We're the ones who should be discontented with our lives. Maybe you felt that way because you had too many options. It was confusing, especially when the world tries to convince you that staying at home is the lesser thing. It's not. It's the greater thing. Maybe you resented your women friends because they loved what you were afraid to love: being a mom and a wife."

He was right. One hundred percent right. "Now I'm neither." She tossed the popcorn bowl on the table. It upset and spilled kernels across a magazine. "Oh, George. But now I'm neither!"

He moved close to comfort her.

George wished there was something more he could do for Merry. Popcorn and a willing ear seemed as ineffective as blowing on a burn to make it better. It was good that she'd realized the source of her discontent, but he was afraid the new knowledge might be too much for her. She seemed strong earlier, but was she really?

She'd gone off to the bathroom to freshen up. He heard the muffled blowing of a nose.

The phone rang. George got it. "Hello?"

"Who's this?"

George didn't like the caller's tone. "Who do you want it to be?"

"Is this the Cavanaugh residence?"

"Yes."

"Is Merry Cavanaugh there?"

"She can't come to the phone right—"

"Can you confirm that she was rushed to the hospital last night because of a suicide attempt?"

"Who is this?"

"Dan Craven, the *Probe.*"

"We have no comment."

"We? This doesn't happen to be George Davanos, does it?"

"How—?"

"We heard you were the one to find Ms. Cavanaugh. You saved her life. And now that you're home with her... Is there something going on between you two?"

George was so shocked he hung up the phone as if it were hot. He never even thought about the press finding out. And yet he shouldn't be surprised. He still got phone calls asking for interviews and even spotted TV vans driving through his neighborhood as if seeing him come and go was some huge piece of news.

Merry came out of the bathroom, her face freshly washed. "Did I hear the phone?"

She didn't need this new wrinkle in her life. "Wrong number." He stood. "I'd better be going."

Merry nodded. "We wouldn't want people to talk now, would we?"

She was *way* too close.

George scanned Merry's neighborhood as he went to his car. If only he'd parked a block down.

Don't be ridiculous. You haven't done anything wrong.

He spotted a blue car, parked on the street two houses away. A man got out and started coming toward him. He had a camera around his neck. His aggressive walk spoke volumes.

George glanced at Merry's house. He didn't want her to see that tabloid reporters were close, and he couldn't let the vulture bother her. He had to stop this. Now.

He hobbled toward the man, attempting his own aggressive stride in spite of the crutches. He was rewarded with a momentary look of surprise on the man's face. Apparently the reporter wasn't used to being on the defensive.

"What do you want?" George asked, as they met on the edge of Merry's property.

"You're George Davanos."

"Answer my question."

The man's grin was full of lewd thoughts. "You're a widower, right? And now Ms. Cavanaugh is a widow? I've heard of old guys like you going after young things but—?"

George shoved the man backward, making him fall onto a bank of snow. He pointed down at him with a crutch. "Listen to me, you dirty-minded cretin. You leave her alone! You leave *us* alone."

The man raised his camera. "Smile." He took a picture. George lunged for the camera, but the man scurried out of his reach and ran for his car. "Thanks for the interview, Davanos."

He sped away. Oh dear. Things were going to get dicey now.

Sonja and Eden sat on lawn chairs outside the Moore home, a white one-story concrete block house with yellow trim and cacti in the yard. Other neighbors sat in their front yards as the sun went down, watching the kids ride their bikes or play soccer in the quiet street. The evening was cool.

"This is so different," Sonja said.

"Different is bad?"

"I don't know. I don't know what to do about…about anything. Your offer to work with you…" She shook her head with the immensity of the decision.

"Maybe you need to let God push you out of your box, Sonja. Quit living the life you thought you ought to live, and live the life God wants you to live. Surrender and let Him do the work."

"My parents would never approve."

Eden nodded. "That's regrettable. But will that stop you?"

"Should it?"

Eden batted a fly away from her face. "We're supposed to honor our father and mother but, even more than that, bring honor to our heavenly Father."

"And you think He approves of me moving here?"

"Yes, *I* do. But more important, you need to feel that way. You need to pray about it. Ask for wisdom." She brightened. "Did you know wisdom is the one thing God always grants when we ask for it?"

"Really?"

"You bet. James 1 has been a favorite of mine for years. It says, 'If any of you lacks wisdom, he should ask God, who gives generously to all without finding fault, and it will be given to him.'" She raised a warning finger and continued. "'But when he asks, he must believe and not doubt, because he who doubts is like a wave of the sea, blown and tossed by the wind.'"

"I think I've been tossed a bit."

"We all get a little windblown at times."

"Surely not you."

"Just because I know God and can recite some Bible verses doesn't mean I'm even close to perfect."

Sonja smiled. "You're not?"

Eden shrugged. "Well, almost." She put a hand on Sonja's arm. "You don't need to give me an answer right now. Go home tomorrow and think on it—and pray about it. Okay?"

"Okay."

Sonja was willing to pray, but she wasn't too sure God would answer. Why should He?

Fifteen

But God chose the foolish things of the world to shame the wise;
God chose the weak things of the world to shame the strong....
so that no one may boast before him.

1 CORINTHIANS 1:27, 29

Anthony awoke to a pounding on his front door. It only took him a second to remember the reporters. He grabbed the arms of the chair, bracing to defend himself from the intruders.

Then he noticed the edge of light glowing around the window blinds. It was daylight. He looked at his watch: 9:32 A.M.?

"Dr. Thorgood? Are you in there?"

It was Lissa's voice. He eased his way out of the chair, his bruised body rebelling against its cramped night's sleep. He peered out the side window. The reporters were gone. He let Lissa in, along with a blast of cold air.

"What's going on?" she said. "We paged you; we called. You didn't show up at the office." She gave him a thorough once-over. "You look terrible."

"How appropriate." He turned toward the kitchen. He needed coffee.

She followed. "Did you see the news?"

He whipped around. "It's on the news?"

"Last night and this morning. In the papers too. The Patrick Harper thing *and* the Belinda Miller thing."

"Belinda?"

"Her family is suing you for taking the lifeline, saying that your act contributed to her death."

"There's no way they can prove that."

She shrugged.

His head swam, and he faltered like a drunk walking a line. She helped him to a kitchen chair and asked, "What happened with Patrick Harper? Is it true what they say?"

His initial reaction was to deny everything and even chastise her lack of loyalty and belief in his abilities. But what good would it do? She knew him too well. He ran his hands roughly across his face. "Is it true? Pretty much."

She sank into the seat nearby. "Why didn't you operate if he needed it?"

"I don't want to talk about—"

"Anthony, talk to me."

He did not miss her use of his first name. Could he have a discussion with her, friend to friend? The way he was feeling, he had to risk it. "I was in a hurry. I was tired. I didn't feel like it. I thought he didn't need—didn't deserve—the extra attention because he'd hurt his hand in a bar fight. I thought he was a low-life brawler." He met her gaze. "Satisfied?"

He waited for her condemnation. It did not come. Instead, she reached across the table and touched his hand. "I'm so sorry."

Her words didn't fit. He felt like he'd come in during the middle of a movie. "Sorry? For me?"

She nodded. "It's been a long time coming."

"What's been a long time coming?"

"Judgment day."

He pulled his hand away. He didn't need this from her.

"Uh-uh, stop right there, Anthony. Don't put your walls up. Not after it's taken this much to tear them down."

"I have no idea what you're talking about." But he did. He *did*.

She traced the edge of a place mat. "Everybody's life has these moments. It's not just you. We all get going down the wrong road, racing so fast we think nothing can stop us. We think everything's great. Oh, we might even realize it's inevitable we'll run off the road eventually, and yet we keep racing on, stubborn and willing to take the consequences of our actions any time, as long as it's later."

He looked toward the front door, wishing she'd use it. "I haven't been racing—"

"You have. The question is, what have you been racing from? Or what have you been racing to?"

He crossed his arms. "Since you know so much, why don't you tell me."

She made a face. "Why do you keep doing this? Making me tell you things about yourself instead of you figuring them out? Why do I have to be the bad guy?"

"Because you do it so well?"

"Don't use that sideways flattery on—"

"Or maybe it's because you enjoy it?"

When she clamped her mouth shut, he regretted his words. Although he knew this conversation had the potential to be painful, he was in the mood to hear it. He *had* to hear it.

"Sorry," he said.

Her smile started small and grew into a laugh. "Since the crash I've gotten two apologies from you. Maybe a dip in the drink did you some good after all."

"I don't see how a crash can do me any good."

She clenched her fists and groaned. "You are so... You may be brilliant, but you are dense as a London fog."

"Ah, now we're getting somewhere." He waved a hand. "Continue."

"You're insufferable."

He counted on his fingers. "Dense and insufferable. That makes two."

"Arrogant."

He flipped up a third finger. "Always a popular choice."

Her jaw clenched. "If you're going to make a joke of this…"

He dropped his hand. "Fine. Give it to me straight. Let's get back to road racing."

She studied him a moment, and he tried to apply his most sincere look. He was horribly out of practice.

She didn't buy it and stood. "This is a waste of time. I thought between this and the crash you would hit bottom, but apparently, it's going to take even more."

His mouth went dry. *More? He wasn't sure he could take any more.*

She suddenly smiled and pointed at his face. "What have we here? Is that panic in the eyes of the great doctor? Panic at the prospect of having to endure more? Could it be you *have* hit bottom but are too proud to admit it?"

Anthony turned away, hating that she'd read him correctly. He was appalled when he felt tears threaten. *This is ridiculous. I must be more exhausted than I thought.*

She returned to her seat, and he felt her constant gaze. "Anthony…let it go. Quit pretending you've got everything under control. It'll kill you—if not physically, then emotionally and spiritually. We all have choices, but none of us has ultimate control. Only God has that. And He'll wield it if we force Him."

He raised his chin, feeling an intensity he hadn't felt in years. "Don't tell me about God. I grew up going to church every Sunday, all dressed up in our country-club best. And all I ever heard from my parents about God—the only answer I ever got to any of my questions about this greater being everybody talked about—was a statement by my father to stop such nonsense. God was for the poor and the weak, not for us. He said he achieved his success on his own and so could I. And that's exactly what I did. *I've* got control of my life. *I'm* in charge of my destiny."

She shook her head and even had the audacity to smile. "Oh really?"

"Really."

"So you wanted the plane to crash?"

"Of course not."

"But you have control. You're in charge."

"Not then. That was different."

"Why?"

"Because…because other people were involved. I was a victim of their mistakes."

Her smile grew into a grin. "Uh-huh…just like Patrick Harper is a victim of *your* mistake?"

She was turning everything around.

She moved her chair closer, its legs skittering on the quarry-tile floor. "We all have choices, Anthony. God gives us those—though sometimes I think it would be a lot easier if He'd just take over. The bottom line is that we mess things up when we don't have our focus on the higher good."

Anthony rolled his eyes. "Oh please…"

Her eyes focused on the refrigerator before turning back to him with new fire. "Have you heard the news that the crash was largely due to pilot error?"

He sat up straighter. "When did you hear that?"

"Last night. The pilots didn't have the flaps set correctly. That prevented the necessary lift. In their hurry to take off, they didn't go through the proper checklist."

"That's great news. Now my lawsuit has a focus."

After a moment's hesitation, she shoved her chair away. It teetered but remained standing. "You pathetic man! You don't see anything beyond your own immediate concerns. Don't you understand why I told you about the pilots?"

"Because they're guilty—"

"No! Because their overlooking the common good by being

prideful in thinking they didn't need to follow procedure, or impatient because they didn't want to have further delays, caused the death of ninety-five people and the pain of countless others. Just as your self-focus has probably caused the death of a pianist's career—his dream—and deprived countless others of ever hearing the beauty of his talent." She knelt at his feet, her eyes dark with fervor. "Don't you get it? The more you hold on, the harder it is for God to pry your hands loose. But He's going to try, Anthony. Over and over, He'll try, hoping you'll finally let go of that blasted control and let Him do what He does best."

"And that is?"

"Be God."

"Huh?"

"*You're* not God, Anthony."

He smiled. "I'm not?"

Her eyes changed from the warmth of fervor to the fire of anger in the span of a moment. She got up to leave. "Bye, Doctor."

No more 'Anthony'? "Lissa, I was just kidding."

She paused at the door. "Were you?"

She left him alone with his deity.

George woke up craving a chocolate doughnut—or better yet, multiple chocolate donuts—so he drove to a quick-stop store and picked some up, along with an extra-large coffee. While paying at the counter he spotted the *Probe*. A headline caught his attention: "Crash Survivor Attempts Suicide." He ripped the paper out of its stand.

"You want the paper too, mister?"

He nodded and shoved another dollar toward the clerk. There were two photos: one of Merry with ice in her hair as she was brought onto the shore after the rescue, and another of himself threatening last night's reporter with a crutch. The caption read: An angry George Davanos attacks reporter after being found at the house of fellow survivor, Merry Cavanaugh.

The cretins.

"Hey, mister? Is that picture you?"

George folded the paper in half, grabbed his food, and left.

It's not that the facts were wrong, it was how they were presented. Yes, George and Merry were widower and widow. Yes, she had tried to commit suicide. And yes, they had spent time together, but for the *Probe* to imply they were dating, or even worse, that George was able to find Merry in time because he was *staying* at her house…

He flicked a donut crumb off the paper. He took little comfort in the fact they were not the only survivors of Flight 1382 who were receiving questionable headlines. "Crash Survivor Sued for Malpractice." "Survivor Fired Due to Misconduct." "Survivor Walks Out on Job."

Not a happy camper in the bunch. He wished he could talk to the others, compare notes, maybe even help—

He slammed his palm on the kitchen table. That was it! They needed to help each other. But they couldn't do that strung out across town. They had to meet. Get together.

George nodded as the idea took form. "We'll have a reunion. A get-together. We've never talked. Shouldn't we talk?"

Of course they should. He and Merry had benefited by meeting. He grabbed a phone book, a pad, and pen. Taking the names of the survivors from the articles, he began to gather the numbers.

He was interrupted as an even better idea was added. The pièce de résistance of surprises. The frosting on the cake. The true union to the reunion.

He laughed out loud and called the long distance operator.

Merry looked over the smorgasbord of food in her kitchen. Breakfast could be chocolate cake, Jell-O salad, or lasagna. She peeked under the lids of some Pyrex dishes and spotted a cake that only had one piece missing. Chocolate frosting. *Justin's favorite.*

A surge of sorrow came front and center, displayed like a flashing sign. *Dead. Dead. Dead.*

They're dead.

She turned her back on the guilty cake and fled to the edge of the living room—which was still as neat and tidy and silent as it was two days before when she'd tried to kill—

Die Merry. Die just like them. You deserve to—

With a sudden burst of panic, Merry lunged for the stereo and turned it on full blast to drown out the voice. A country song assaulted her—one of Lou's favorites and one she had moaned and groaned about at his incessant playing.

How appropriate. Music to crack to, break to, die to. But if she was going down, all of this was going down with her.

She rushed to the coffee table and swiped a hand across the top of it. Magazines and a candleholder fell to the carpet. She grabbed the toss pillows from the couch and heaved them against the windows, clattering the blinds, making them a mishmash of closed and open slats.

As the music blared, her chest heaved, and she scanned the room for more potential victims of her anger. Justin's toy chest sat in the corner, mocking her. She fell upon it, flung open its lid, and hurled the toys behind her, not caring where they landed. The sound of a breaking lamp made her laugh hysterically.

No more neatness. No more order. No more everything in its place. No more control or nods or attempts to smile, or deluding myself that everything will be all right.

The built-in wall shelf was next. With the flick of a finger, she tilted the spines of the books, making them teeter and fall to their deaths. A bluebird figurine was heaved over her shoulder. Merry didn't look to see where it landed but was cheered by the sounds of breakage.

The stereo yelled at her, flaunting Lou's song, so she yanked it from its mooring and heaved it toward the television, grunting at the effort. Its electrical cords made it come up short, and it swung back against the shelf two ticks of the clock, until its own weight pulled it out of the wall and into a deathly silence on the floor.

Merry stood, assessing her progress. *Yes. Yes. This is what I deserve.*

But there was more to do…

Her eyes fell upon the entry closet, and she thought of the items inside. She ran to it, tripping over debris on the way. "You think you're safe in there, don't you? But you can't hide from me."

She flung open the door. The closet was stuffed with evidence of her family. Lou's jackets laughed at her; Justin's red snow boots jeered. Gloves waved good-bye to her past life. *Bye-bye, Merry. Don't be fooled. Things will never be the same.* She grabbed a pair of Lou's gloves, the extra-heavy ones he wore to shovel the driveway. She put them on and clapped them together, hoping to quiet their condemning words, the muted *whawp, whawp* ringing in her—

The doorbell rang.

Merry sucked in a breath and froze. She drew her gloved hands to her chest. Her heartbeat made them pulse. She looked out the peephole and saw Polly Frederick, her immediate neighbor to the north. *Maybe if I'm quiet she'll go home.*

Suddenly, she saw Polly's face pressed against the narrow entry window. Their eyes met. Then Polly's eyes moved to the sight of Lou's oversized gloves on Merry's hands. Her gaze migrated to a stray hanger leaning up against a fallen boot on the floor at Merry's feet. "Merry?" she called through the window. "You okay?"

Merry pressed against the window, Lou's gloves like two huge spiders. "Go home, Polly."

Polly's eyes widened. "Let me in. I saw the papers… I want to help."

Papers? What is she talking about? Merry took a step back and clasped her gloved hands together, wishing Lou's strong hands were inside. They would know what to do. Somehow they would make Polly go away. They would make it all go away.

"I know where the extra key is hidden, Mer."

Merry froze. She was beaten. One way or the other, her neighbor was coming in. She shuffled her shoulders and found them incredibly tight. She took a breath and cracked open the door.

Polly tried to look past her. Her eyebrows furrowed. "Merry. How are you?"

How do you think I am? "As well as can be expected." She noticed she was still wearing Lou's gloves and for the first time realized how odd they must look. She tried to hide them behind her back but, by doing so, let go of the doorknob.

Polly was quick. She swung the door open and surveyed the damage. "What in the—?"

"I was cleaning." It sounded more like a question than a statement.

Polly came inside. "Don't give me that." As she closed the door behind herself, she spotted the further destruction in the living room and looked at Merry. "What's going on?"

Merry suddenly saw the mess through fresh eyes. *Did I do all this? What was I thinking? Polly must think I'm crazy.*

Am I crazy?

Polly moved into the mess. She tried to right the broken lamp, but its base was beyond repair. She looked at Merry and repeated the question that had still not been answered. "Merry? What's going on?"

Merry clapped her hands together once, found the muffled sound disturbing, and removed Lou's gloves. She placed them neatly on the back of the couch. "You want to know what's going on? I'm losing my mind." As soon as the words were loose, Merry felt the floodgates open as truth and reality collided. Tears flowed. Her muscles gave out, and her legs crumbled beneath her. Polly was at her side as her knees hit the floor.

Merry sat on the entry floor. Polly wrapped her arms around her. She did not say, "Shh" or the horrid "Everything will be all right." She pulled her close and rocked her, as if Merry were a child. It felt so good...

Finally, Merry sat back and wiped her eyes with her sleeve until Polly dug a tissue from her pocket. "Always prepared," she said. Her smile was wistful.

Merry blew her nose and took a shaky breath. She was relieved to find her mind clear—or at least clearer. "I was wrong, Polly. I had everything and didn't even know it." She opened her arms wide, taking in the room. "I thought I wanted a neat and tidy life. But I don't. And now it's too late."

Merry felt Polly's touch on the back of her shoulders. "What are you going to do now?"

Merry shook her head. She found answers coming to her lips, and yet she wasn't sure if they were based on truth or were merely the *right* words. "Breathe. Sleep. Eat. And try to sort it through."

"Pray?"

Merry looked at her neighbor. She'd forgotten that Polly was a deeply believing woman. And at that moment, Merry knew what she *should* say, what she was expected to say. She should tell Polly that she would pray. But she couldn't. Her head shook back and forth like an empty swing. *If only the swing would stop moving.*

"Do you want to pray with me, Merry?"

That's the last thing I want. Merry scrambled to her feet. "Don't you dare bring God into this! God's the one who did this to me. God's punishing me, and you expect me to pray?"

Polly stood and held out a hand meant to comfort. "Merry, don't say such—"

Merry sidled out of her reach and opened the front door. "You can leave now, Polly. I'm fine. I'm really fine."

"But you're not fine. You need—"

Merry yanked her neighbor toward the door and shoved her through it, nearly making her fall. "I need to be left alone. After all, that's how God wants me, isn't it?"

Polly's face was a mask of shock. "But Merry—"

She shut the door in her face, eating up the subsequent surge of power.

The phone rang. She strode into the kitchen like Napoleon confronting his opposition. "Yes?" she snapped.

"Merry?"

It was George's voice. Another do-gooder trying to help her when she didn't want any help. She wasn't in the mood. "What do you want, George?"

"What's wrong? You sound angry."

"I am angry."

"I'll come over."

"No, you will not come over. You are not my keeper, George." *But he was your keeper. He saved your life.* She forced her voice to soften. "I'm...I'm just going through a bad spell. I'll be fine." *Maybe.*

"It's no trouble coming over."

"I'm *fine.*" She stressed the word a bit too much. "Why did you call?"

"I've decided to arrange a reunion of all the survivors for dinner tomorrow night. My house."

No way.

"Merry? I think it will be good for us. Put some closure on things."

Closure. A funeral word. She scanned the destruction of her home. She'd tried her own form of closure.

"I'll come get you if you want."

Merry sighed. She knew if she didn't go of her own accord, George would come and drag her there. He was a part of her life now. He'd given her back her life. Whether that would turn out to be a good or bad thing, she had yet to determine. But she did owe him. At least this much.

"I'll come." She saw the chocolate cake on the counter. She was surprised that the sight of it did not make her cry. "I'll even bring some dessert. And I have lasagna in the freezer."

"Super. See you at six."

Merry hung up and shook her head. One minute she was crazed and the next calm. Each felt normal in its time. That was scary.

She cut herself a piece of cake and tried not to think about it.

Tina was on her way out the door, heading to her first day on the job, when the phone rang. It was Carla from her Bible-study group.

"Just calling to check on you, Tina. We saw the paper this morning and...is it true? Did you walk out on your teaching job?"

Tina had seen it on the local news channel. "Absolutely."

"How come?"

Tina checked her watch. "How about I come back to Bible study next week and tell you all the details?"

"Are you up to it?"

"You bet."

A moment's hesitation. "You sound different."

"Well, I have been through a crash, quit my job, gotten engaged—"

"Hey! It's about time, but—"

"But what?"

"But it's more than that. You sound genuinely...at peace. I didn't expect that. Not after the news article. I called because I thought you'd be depressed. I thought you might need us."

"I *do* need you. But I *have* found a sense of peace beyond anything I've ever felt."

"Because of David?"

"Because of God."

"Wow. You sound so sure."

"I am sure. I'll see you next week."

Tina hung up, remembering all the times she'd only marginally participated in their early-morning Bible study. Things would be different now. She was not going to be a passive participant in anything anymore.

She grabbed her purse, and the phone rang again. She considered letting the machine take it but wondered if it might be David with a prework love-you call. "Hello?"

"Tina McKutcheon?"

"If this is some reporter, I'm not—"

"No, no…this is George Davanos. I'm another one of the survivors from the crash."

She'd seen a report about him on the news that morning. He was having an affair with the young mother. "How are you doing, George? Some publicity we're getting, huh? I thought things were settling down."

"That's why I'm calling. I think it's time we got together. Had a survivors' reunion. Out of the water this time. Are you game?"

She hadn't been, but she was now. It sounded like a wonderful way to tie things up. "I'm in. When?"

"Tomorrow night for dinner, at six. My house." He gave the address "And, Tina, I've got a surprise for everyone."

"What kind of surprise?"

"Uh-uh, no cheating. See you tomorrow."

Tina couldn't remember the last time she'd been able to concentrate like she did when her new boss, Shelley, showed her around the bookstore. What should have been overwhelming and confusing was clear and felt familiar—as if the information had only been tucked away somewhere, waiting for this moment.

"You're grinning at that book like it's a newborn baby," Shelley said. "Tickle it under the title and maybe it'll coo."

Tina realized she was cradling a book and stroking its cover. "Sorry." She set it back on the shelf and adjusted her crutches.

"No problem. It's a common reaction by bookstore junkies."

Tina smiled. "My secret is out."

"It isn't a secret. Why do you think you were hired?" Shelley glanced around the store, ever watchful for customers needing help. Her eyes stopped wandering, then turned to Tina. "Why don't you see if that man, the one sitting on the couch over there, needs any help. He looks lost."

Tina snuck a look. The man sat with both feet flat on the floor, his arms crossed. "Forget lost. He looks hungry—and not for learning *or* a pizza. He looks like he eats helpful clerks for dinner. Maybe he's in the wrong store?" Tina couldn't imagine a shopper looking more antagonistic.

Shelley gave her a nudge. "Most likely he's a shopper's husband, brought on errands against his will. Most are pretty tame, though he doesn't look quite—"

"Housebroken?"

Shelley laughed. "Battle forward, Tina. I've got your flank."

"How nice of you, sending the wounded into battle." Tina took a deep breath and checked her nerves, feeling foolish for being anxious about asking the simple words, "May I help you?" She approached the couch, put on her most helpful smile, and stopped in the customer's field of vision.

He looked up, glaring. "What? Can't I sit here?"

It took Tina a moment to recover. "That depends. Did you put money in the parking meter?"

"What?"

Okay, so humor won't work. "Are you waiting for your wife?"

"Is that allowed?"

"Only on Tuesdays." She handed him a magazine. "Care to read something while you wait?"

He took a look at the cover, then tossed the magazine on the coffee table where it slid to the floor. "No thanks. I don't get into that God garbage."

Tina felt as if she'd been slapped. She awkwardly picked up the magazine—which was quite a feat with her crutches in the way. The man did not offer help but watched her every move like a child's gauging his parents' reaction to a bad word and waiting for his punishment. *Don't play his game; play yours.*

She looked up and smiled. "Do you like to read?"

"Not this junk."

"Do you like fiction or nonfiction?"

He grinned slyly. "What do you think?"

I think you need all the self-help books you can get. She noted his cowboy boots and his heavy-duty down bomber's jacket. "I take you as a Western fan."

His eyes glimmered with pleasure—a momentary lapse before they reverted to their defensive glare. "I've read a few in my time."

"We've got some good ones. Care to see them?"

He snickered. "You've got Westerns? Christian Westerns?" He laughed. "Don't tell me…Jesus is a cowboy."

"Not exactly." Tina took a step toward the fiction aisles. She was shocked when he got up to follow her. As they walked to the right shelf, Tina wished she knew more specifics about the Western novels, then remembered she knew Someone who did. *Please, Lord. Lead him to the right book.*

With a sweeping gesture, she extended an arm toward the novels. Horses, cowboys, and wide mountain vistas graced the covers. The man's hand hesitated, then apparently overcome by temptation, picked one up. He began reading the back cover.

"Look interesting?"

He didn't look up. "Whatever."

"Then I'll leave you to browse." Tina walked away feeling absurdly triumphant, as if a victory had just been won. No, she hadn't brought a soul to God or spouted one verse or truth. But glancing back at the man, who'd now opened the book to the first page, she knew she'd led him to the edge of something better. If he read one of those books, he'd learn things about God, nestled cozily amid the cattle rustling and the fireside chats he craved. And that was enough. She'd done her job.

She approached the next customer with a spring in her step. Mallory and Grandpa Carpelli would be so proud. God too.

Anthony heard the phone ring but made no move to answer it. He didn't want to talk to a reporter or the hospital or even Lissa.

He had to think. So much had happened in the past twenty-four hours. He'd been disgraced by his own arrogance and challenged by a God he barely knew. Beat down and lifted up. Quite a workout.

He heard the answering machine pick up and listened for the message: "This is George Davanos. I'm one of your fellow survivors. I thought it was time all of us met properly. Come over to my house tomorrow night at six for dinner and a special surprise. Hope to see you there."

George gave his address and the machine clicked off. Anthony had never thought about meeting the other survivors. What good would that do?

What harm could it do?

He'd think about it.

All done. Though it had taken some doing, George had gotten ahold of his surprise guest, had spoken to Merry and Tina about the reunion, and had left a message for Sonja Grafton and Anthony

Thorgood. According to the papers, the latter three were having job troubles. Not a fun thing to come back to after surviving a plane crash. Or had their troubles developed because of the plane crash? Being a survivor was hard work.

The doorbell rang, and though George knew there was a chance it was a reporter, he didn't feel like gathering his crutches to use the peephole. "Enter at your own risk!"

Suzy poked her head in the door. "You always answer the door like that?"

"Don't complain." He noticed she carried a suitcase. A discolored, dented, banged up— "Hey, that's mine. Where did you get it?"

"I just came to check on you and found it on the porch. There's a tag on it from the airlines. They must have had it delivered." Suzy set it on the kitchen table. "It looks like you held up better than your baggage."

"I have a longer warranty."

"Let's see how the contents fared."

She started to open it, and then George remembered… "Don't open—"

Too late. Suzy stared at the jumble of clothes. Irma's clothes. Irma's under things. They were stained and covered with mildew but still recognizable. Suzy looked at her father. "What's this?"

George grabbed a newspaper and hid behind it. "Looks like clothes to me."

"Women's clothes."

George peeked over the top of the paper. "Well, I'll be."

Suzy checked the tag on the handle. "Dad, this is your suitcase. You said as much. But why is it full of women's clothing? Are these Mom's?" She cautiously rummaged through the contents. "And here's Mom's picture. It's damaged but—"

George was out of his chair, grabbing the picture before he realized he'd left his crutches behind. "Give me that!" The glass was broken, and Irma's face was warped and stained. *My favorite picture. Ruined.*

To his horror, he watched as Suzy plucked a prescription bottle from between the soiled clothes.

"Hey, I'll take that—"

She pulled it out of his reach and strained to read the label. But George's hope that it was obliterated was dashed when she said, "Are these sleeping pills? Dad, what's going on?"

George pulled Irma's picture to his chest and returned to his chair. It was time for the truth. "I wasn't going to Phoenix for a vacation."

"That doesn't explain the lack of your clothes or—"

"The suitcase needed to feel full."

"Why?"

"So you wouldn't suspect anything."

Suzy swallowed and fingered the prescription bottle. "Suspect what, Dad?"

George put Irma's picture on the table and looked his daughter full in the eyes. "So you wouldn't suspect I was traveling to Phoenix to kill myself."

Suzy nearly missed the chair. "What? Why?"

George looked at Irma's picture. "I miss her."

"So do I, but…"

"She was my wife."

"She was my mother."

"It's different."

George was glad Suzy didn't try to argue that one. She looked at the floor. "But Phoenix… Why Phoenix?"

George shrugged. "Why not Phoenix? I didn't want to do it here, in the home we shared. I didn't want you to find me."

Suzy sprang from her chair and drilled the prescription into the jumble of her mother's clothes. "But you *were* willing to have me go on without you?"

"It couldn't be helped." *Lame, George, very—*

Suzy began to pace. "How could you even think of doing that

to me? I've already lost Mom, and you didn't think anything about having me lose you too?"

"You're a strong woman."

Suzy stopped pacing, and her finger jutted toward George's face. "That is a totally unacceptable answer."

It was. George knew it.

"You were only thinking of yourself."

"Probably."

"You—" Her eyes lit up with understanding. "That's why your will and insurance papers were out. So I could find them after—" She shook her head. "You thought of details like that, but not about my feelings? My pain?"

George had no defense. How had it seemed so logical at the time? How had it ever seemed like the right thing to do? The only thing? "I don't—"

Suzy started to cry, the grown-up quiver of her chin reminding him of Suzy, his little girl. "How…how could you deprive our child of a grandfather?"

"What?"

Suzy's chin stopped its quiver. "I'm pregnant. Stan and I are going to have a baby."

George sucked in one breath, then had to try again when there still wasn't enough air. "A grandbaby?"

Suzy nodded. "Who needs a grandpa."

George held out a hand and used his daughter's strength to stand. They hugged tightly. "I'm so sorry, Suzy. So sorry."

Suzy pulled back to look her father in the face. "You're not still thinking…?"

"No, no. Not anymore. God saved me for a reason. I just need to find out what…" He put a hand to his mouth.

"What it is. Now you know."

George laughed and kissed his daughter's forehead. "Now I know."

"Grandpa George."

Music to his ears.

George set Irma's battered picture on the bedside table where it belonged. He'd have to dig out a fresh one, but for now, this would do. He sat on the edge of the bed and looked at her.

"We're going to be grandparents, deary. What do you think of that?"

She didn't answer. And she wouldn't. She would never hold a grandchild in her arms or make them cookies or take them to the park.

But he couldn't think of that. He *was* here. He was alive. And he could do all those things—except maybe the cookie part. Yet even though he'd never baked a thing in his life, he could certainly buy them cookies, and popcorn at a movie, and corn dogs at a ball game, and cotton candy at the circus.

"I'll do it up right for both of us, Irma. I'm going to be the best granddaddy. But you're going to have to be patient with me up there. It appears God doesn't want me to join you just yet, and this time I don't plan on hurrying things along." Her faded smile seemed to brighten as if she approved.

And then he knew. It would be all right. Everything would be all right.

Dora Roberts dialed Sonja's number—for the third time. *She has to know I had nothing to do with her job troubles becoming public knowledge. She has to know I kept her confidence. She has to know I'm her fr—*

The answering machine picked up. Again. Dora hesitated. She really wanted to tell her in person, but Sonja obviously wasn't home. Or wasn't answering.

How can I blame her?

The beep sounded. This time, Dora didn't hang up but left the message.

At the moment, it was all she could do.

Or was it?

She sat there with the phone in her hand. The poor survivors had endured so much. And now the world was making a mockery of their ordeal, gnawing at their troubles like piranhas devouring ripe flesh.

And what had she done to help any of them? Listen for a few short minutes? Nod her head and mention God in passing? Their survival, and the means by which it had occurred, was about so much more than merely breathing and moving on. It was about choices and consequences and possibilities.

Choices? No, that wasn't exactly true. Although each of them was facing choices now—in the crash's aftermath—none of the survivors had made a choice to live or die. Only one man had been given that choice. One man.

Dora looked at her computer, which was calling to her from across the room. It was time. It was time to write about the hero.

Sonja unlocked her front door and noticed that someone had stuck a copy of the *Probe* under her mat. She didn't subscribe to that rag. Who would have—?

She flipped it open to the front page and saw the headlines: "Crash Survivor Attempts Suicide." She began reading as she went inside, dropping her carry-on to the floor. She kicked the door shut.

She sat at the kitchen table and read the article. *Poor woman.* Then she noticed another article: "Survivor Fired Due to Misconduct."

Her stomach threatened to do something nasty. *No. This can't be about me. It can't.*

But it was.

Sonja bolted from the chair toward the phone. To think she'd counted Dora Roberts as her friend.

The message light blinked. She had two messages. The first one was from a George Davanos inviting her to a reunion of the survivors. She wasn't sure about that. Getting together to commiserate? But the second message caught her attention. It was from Dora assuring her that she hadn't leaked the story about her dismissal.

Then who had? And who left the paper on her front step, guaranteeing she'd see—

Geraldine.

Sonja tossed the paper in the trash. Phoenix was looking better and better.

Sixteen

Be strong and take heart, all you who hope in the LORD.

PSALM 31:24

D ora hit Ctrl-P, then Enter. Her printer came to life. She looked at her computer screen with a satisfaction she hadn't felt in months. Or years. She'd just completed her essay about the hero. It wasn't full of facts about Henry Smith or even heavy in facts about the crash. It was about all the heroes of the world like Henry—ordinary people who, once put in extreme circumstances, became extraordinary. It was very, very good.

She'd spent the previous evening and the entire day working on it in between her assigned articles for the *Chronicle,* in between stupid stuff about the new bus lines and a threatened construction strike. But even when she was working on other stories, her mind was really on Henry Smith.

But now…she felt a sudden need to share her essay. And not with her boss. It was a long shot that Clyde would ever print it, and she didn't want that reality to squelch the euphoria of the moment. No, she needed the response of a person who would understand. Who cared. Who—

George Davanos. Henry's seatmate.

She grabbed a phone book and wrote down the address.

She pulled the pages from the printer.

George had spent the day cleaning for the reunion. Although he had a cleaning lady who used to come in once every two weeks, he didn't call for her services lest she leak the news that the survivors were meeting. If the media found out afterward, or even during their gathering, so be it. He'd leave it up to each individual to talk or not talk.

Yet he wasn't keeping the media at bay for his comrades, but for their surprise guest. He even sent Suzy to the hotel where Ellen had been staying because he knew that his own presence might draw attention. He understood that an anonymous life was a thing of the past—until the next headline got the spotlight.

Suzy was late. The other guests would be here any minute. George checked the coffeepot: brewed and ready. He had a Caesar salad and bread delivered from a grocery store, and he even resurrected Irma's china from the hutch and polished the sterling forks. Merry said she'd bring a pan of lasagna and a cake. There was a two-liter bottle of Sprite for those noncoffee drinkers, and napkins, sugar, and milk for the coffee—they'd have to make do without cream.

Irma would have been so proud.

He heard a car in the drive and hobbled to the window. A pretty woman got out. He'd seen her before and tried to place—

The reporter! What did she want?

He hurried to the door to head her off and get her gone before the others arrived. He opened the door to find her hand reaching for the bell.

"Mr. Davanos?"

"If you've seen the news today, you'll understand when I say I'm not interested in talking to the press—though that hasn't stopped you from printing lies."

"I haven't printed anything, Mr. Davanos. You told me the name of the hero long before it came out, and I kept your confidence. The *Probe* is your problem. Not me. I'm not one of those…*others.*"

She was telling the truth and he reconsidered. Perhaps he'd

been unfair. He looked down the street. There were no cars.

"May I come in? It's cold out here."

It was stupid having the conversation in an open doorway. "If you must. But I just have a few minutes." Good reporter or no-good reporter, he didn't dare say he was waiting for the other survivors to arrive—or their special guest.

She came in, and he closed the door but did not invite her to sit. "So what is it? Why did you come over here to my home?"

She handed him some papers. "I'd like you to read this."

"What is it?"

"Something I wrote about Henry Smith—about all of you actually."

George read the first line: *No one plans to be a hero.* Not bad. He read the first paragraph and was hooked. He looked up at her. "This is wonderful."

She blushed. "Thank you."

He read more, his eyes rushing over the words like a starving man being fed. His eyes filled with tears. He felt a sob in his throat and looked up. "Wow."

She had tears in her own eyes and nodded. "It's what I feel."

"You're *not* one of them."

She shook her head.

He made an instant decision. "Come sit down." He looked at her name printed on the front page. "Dora Roberts, welcome. Have I got a surprise for you."

Dora listened to George. She couldn't believe her luck. Coming over to his house on the very day, the very hour that the survivors were coming? And as for their surprise? But then she realized it was too awesome to be luck. It was God's doing.

"I feel very honored you're letting me stay."

"No problem," said George, moving to the front window and

pulling the curtain aside. "You've earned it. I want all of them to hear what you've written."

"Hear?"

"I want you to read it to them."

Dora's stomach clenched. Writing was one thing. Performing another. "I'm not sure I can—"

"Of course you can. And they need to hear it. Case closed."

She heard a car.

"They're here." George rushed to the door and opened it ahead of time, just like he'd done with her. A young woman appeared first and kissed him on the cheek. She was followed by the special guest. Dora stood to meet her.

"Welcome," George said.

Ellen Smith smiled and shook his hand. "So nice to meet you, Mr. Davanos." George led them inside.

"Call me George."

"And I'm Ellen."

She looked around the room and spotted Dora. George hurried to make introductions. "Ellen, this is Dora Roberts, a...a friend. Dora, this is Ellen Smith, Henry's wife."

Dora shook the woman's hand, recognizing her from the TV report at the airport. She was a little embarrassed that she'd expected Ellen to be more...unique looking in person. The woman was pleasant in appearance but was not someone you'd even notice twice in a crowd. Shouldn't the wife of a hero glow or something?

George flipped Suzy a look. "What took you so long?"

His daughter shrugged. "Traffic."

The sound of more cars made George jumble his crutches. "Okay, this is it. They're here." He turned to Ellen, then to Dora, then to Ellen again. "Ellen, I need you to—"

"Hide in the other room." Ellen smiled. "I know. Suzy told me."

Suzy showed her the way to the den. Dora joined George at the window. "Do you want me to hide too?"

He shook his head. "No, just her. It's best we get your presence out of the way. To be truthful, I don't want to diminish Ellen's entrance by making her share it."

"Understood."

Two cars had pulled up, and now another. Dora recognized Sonja and Tina. The third woman must be Merry. The three women got out, introduced each other, hugged, and chatted as they made their way to the door. That left one to go. The good doctor. Dora wasn't looking forward to that one. George swung the door wide. "Welcome, lovely ladies."

Merry spoke to the others. "I told you he was a charmer."

He bowed. "You do me justice." He smiled, but Dora noticed him studying Merry's face. She gave him a slight nod, and he seemed to relax. Suzy took her food offerings.

One by one they noticed Dora. Sonja first.

"Dora!" Sonja gave her an awkward hug because of her cast. "What are you doing here?"

"We'll get to that," George said. He initiated the introductions all around and Dora was amazed that the only survivors who seemed to have met were he and Merry. Suzy took their coats and led everyone into the living room.

"We make four," Tina said. "Where's number five? We're missing the doctor, right?"

"Anthony Thorgood," George said. "I never heard back from him, but I'm hoping—"

I'm hoping he skips it. Dora felt bad about the uncharitable thoughts she kept having with regard to the doctor. Weren't they supposed to love the unlovable? From what she'd seen, Dr. Anthony Thorgood certainly fit into that category.

"He may be purposely indisposed," Sonja said. "The headlines… I think he got the worst of it." She gasped, then looked to Merry. "Except you, Merry. The paper said…of course we all know it's not true, but…"

Merry straightened her spine. "But it is true. I did try to kill myself."

Everyone exchanged an awkward look, and Dora was *very* glad she hadn't pressed Merry for an interview.

"Are you okay now?" Tina asked. "I mean, how could you be, losing your family, but…" She put a hand to her forehead. "I'm sorry. I'm bungling this badly."

"No you're not, " Merry said, but Dora noticed her voice was tight. "We've all suffered."

"But you're the only one who lost loved ones and lived to grieve that loss."

The truth of this statement quieted the room; a simple fact that glared in garish neon.

"I guess I am," Merry said. Then suddenly the thought seemed to take root and grow. She looked to George, her eyes suddenly wild. "George, I *am*. All the others who were traveling with their families died. I'm the only one who lived!"

The doorbell rang. They all hesitated, wanting to help Merry yet needing to move on. George gave her hand a squeeze as Suzy opened the door to Anthony. Dora braced herself. He would be no happier to see her than she was to see him.

"I'm here to see George—"

With reluctance, George left Merry and moved to the door. "Come on in, Anthony. Join us."

Dora noticed that Anthony handed his coat to Suzy without a glance, as if George's daughter were a maid ready to serve. *He hasn't changed a bit.* Then the man made the rounds, shaking the hands of the ladies. He hadn't noticed Dora yet, and she hung back, willing to merely observe for a few moments longer.

She was amazed at how he made sure they all knew he was a doctor. *A doctor in trouble if the news is correct.* And Dora became annoyed that he qualified every introduction with the words, "I'm not sure why I came." The only chink in his everything-is-normal act was when he lingered a moment when their eyes met.

Feeling a twinge of guilt, Doctor?

Dora held her breath, waiting for an apology. None came.

"Hey-ya, Doc."

Anthony turned to George. "What's she doing here?" There was repulsion in his voice, and Dora resented it. She didn't like him either, but his reaction was overboard.

Dora took the heat off George. "I came to visit George, and he was kind enough to let me stay."

Anthony turned to Suzy. "Where's my coat? I'm *not* staying."

"What's going on, Dora?" Sonja asked.

"I interviewed him. He was rude and arrogant, so I didn't write the story. He's mad."

"You bet I'm mad. You judged me. You let me pour out my heart, and then you insulted me by—"

Dora laughed. "Heart? Surely you jest? You don't have a heart, Doctor."

As soon as she said it, Dora realized she'd gone too far. *Forgive me, Lord.* She looked at the others. Their faces were drawn and concerned. She was ruining what should have been their reunion. She turned to Anthony. "I'm sorry. I shouldn't have said that." She sat down. "Forgive me. All of you. Please forgive me." She didn't meet Anthony's eyes but looked to George.

He nodded his acceptance and took over. "Well, then. Nothing like a little fireworks to make a gathering interesting. Anthony? Please sit down. We've all come this far…"

Anthony held his ground a moment, then sat as far away from Dora as he could.

George took a deep breath, then stood on the perimeter of the circle. "I am so glad you all came. After seeing the news yesterday, I figured we all could use a little reinforcement, and who better to give it than the other people who have experienced what we've experienced. We are unique. A band of five…" He looked toward the den. "Plus one. As you all remember, there were eight of us in the water. And only because of the one who is not with us are we here today. But in a way, Henry Smith is here, for I have a surprise for all of you."

Suzy opened the door to the den and Ellen appeared.

"Please greet Ellen Smith. Henry's wife."

There was a moment of silence. Dora watched the survivors' faces. It was as if seeing Ellen made them realize that the hero was real. Henry had had a life before the crash; he wasn't a figment of their imaginations, or an angel sent to rescue them. He was a flesh-and-blood man who called this woman his wife.

Tina stood to greet Ellen. "I hated that I couldn't thank Henry, so I'll thank you instead, because your life was sacrificed for us too." Their handshake turned into a hug. "Thank you."

The floodgates of emotion opened and the women swarmed Ellen, crying, embracing, talking at once. Dora noticed Anthony did not join the others. He seemed uncomfortable with the emotional outburst. *Come on, man, buck it up.*

The women returned to their seats, making room for Ellen on the couch. As they sat, unexpectedly—awkwardly—Anthony stood. They looked at him expectantly. His face warred with itself.

"Anthony? Are you all right?" George asked.

He shook his head, and his forehead became a washboard of stress. It was disconcerting—and yet oddly heartening—to see this suave man's armor of strength crack, and yet Dora hoped their little exchange hadn't been the cause of it. "I suppose you read in the paper how I thought I lived because I deserved to live?"

"We know you didn't mean it," Sonja said.

He shot her a look. "I *did* mean it." He ran a hand through his hair. "At the time." He glanced at Dora, then away. He groaned. "I knew I shouldn't have come."

"You have something to say, Anthony. Now's the time," George said.

Dora was amazed at the bevy of emotions that flashed across Anthony's face as if he were trying each one on and quickly discarding it for another. Finally a shroud of sorrow settled in, and he looked to the floor. "I owe one of the survivors an apology, but she's not here."

Tina filled in the blank. "Belinda Miller?"

Anthony nodded. "I took her turn. I'm sorry. I've tried to justify it—and did for a long time—but Lissa, a friend of mine, has helped me see—" he attempted a smile—"the error of my ways?"

Then he turned to Ellen. "And my comments about deserving to live. It's not that I didn't appreciate your husband's sacrifice. I did. I do. But, I had it all wrong. My thinking was skewed. Then this thing at the hospital and the lawsuits…"

Dora was in shock. An apology from Mr. Arrogance? She felt bad.

"Is it true?" George asked. "Did you mess up an operation?"

"Actually I neglected to do an operation that should have been done. The patient was a concert pianist—*was* being the key word."

"Did you mess up because of the aftereffects of the crash?" Sonja asked.

"I'd love to say yes, but the answer is no. I probably would have made the same mistake—or a similar one—eventually. The crash didn't cause my arrogance, but it did test it."

"I can't believe you said that," Sonja said. "I've been going through the same thing. I was arrogant too, cutthroat ambitious. I lost my job because of it."

"Your job? What are you going to do now?" Merry asked her.

Sonja smiled and looked at Dora. "I just got back from Phoenix yesterday. I met the wife of my seatmate, Roscoe Moore, a wonderful man who took keen interest in me while we were waiting to take off. He kept talking about needing to have something *more* in my life." She looked as if she wanted to expand on the thought but wasn't comfortable with it. "Anyway, Mrs. Moore invited me to work with her in Phoenix—with high risk kids who need help getting on the right track."

"You're moving?" Dora asked.

Sonja looked into space, then back. "I haven't really made a decision...but why not? The crash gave me a second chance. I need to start over. Completely. What have I got to lose?" She looked toward Dora and mouthed *thanks*.

Tina raised a hand. "The articles were right about me too. I walked out on my teaching job. On the plane I sat next to a wonderful girl, Mallory Carpelli, a student who helped me realize I was in the wrong profession." She grinned. "But I've already got a new job—in a Christian bookstore, and I love it."

"Henry was my seatmate," George said.

There was a moment of silence.

"You got to know him?" Tina asked.

George nodded. "He was an interesting man." He smiled at Ellen. "And this next bit is something I've been waiting to tell Ellen." He put a hand to his throat and turned to Suzy. "Water, please?" Suzy brought him a glass, and he took a sip.

Dora's stomach tightened. She'd been wanting to learn more about the hero and now...

"What is it, George?" Ellen asked. "Tell me about Henry."

He set the glass down and bowed his head as if saying a quick prayer. He met Ellen's eyes. "Henry was just an ordinary man—I say that with the utmost respect. But there was something going on in his life leading up to the day of the crash. He described it as an anticipation, as if he was supposed to do something but wasn't sure what it was." He looked around the room. "Think about it, people. Henry felt he was supposed to accomplish something."

Merry gasped. "He was supposed to save us?"

"I think so. Henry even had a panic attack on the plane. He wanted off. The stewardess had to calm him down."

Tina put a hand to her mouth. "As if he knew?"

Ellen clutched the front of her blouse. "He knew?"

George raised his hands. "I don't know about that. But he seemed very focused on this purpose he was trying to unravel. He shared with me a Bible verse he read the night before. The part he quoted said, 'This is the way—'"

"'Walk in it,'" Ellen finished. "I know that verse."

"He was searching for 'the way.'"

Anthony shook his head. "Some way."

Sonja pointed a finger at him. "Don't say that. Because of his *way*, we're here."

Tina fingered her lower lip. "I guess this proves that the crash wasn't a surprise to God."

"We are so lucky," Sonja said.

Tina shook her head vehemently. "There's no such thing as luck. God is intimately involved in the details of our lives. He knows every hair on our head, the length of our days, and the plans He has for us. If you believe in God, you can't believe in luck." She looked around the room at each of them. "Don't you agree?"

Anthony adjusted his seat on the couch. "Are you asking if we believe in God?"

A moment's hesitation, then a nod. "Yes I am. Do you?"

Anthony looked to the floor. "I don't know. I didn't. I only believed in myself."

"But now?"

Anthony shook his head, obviously still unsure. Dora felt for him. If he didn't even acknowledge God, then no wonder...

Sonja fingered the armrest of the chair. "I used to feel that way about God. Uncertain. But I believe in Him now. The crash...God got my attention."

"He got everybody's attention," Tina said. She turned to Anthony and Merry. "We've heard about everyone else's seatmate. Who sat in the seat beside you two? And how did they affect you? Anthony? You go first."

He offered a bitter laugh. "I certainly didn't have any influential person next to me. It was Belinda Miller."

"You took the lifeline of your seatmate?" Sonja's tone portrayed this fact as unthinkable.

"Actually, she was a most annoying woman. She hated doctors, and I thought she was way off base."

"But was she?" Dora asked.

He glared at her.

She felt herself blush. "Sorry."

He shrugged. "She was very opinionated and thought she had me figured out."

"How so?" Sonja asked.

Anthony fidgeted in his chair, and Dora had the notion that it wasn't something he did often. Whoever Belinda had been, whatever she said, she obviously had struck a nerve.

"She said I was afraid of taking chances, afraid of losing everything."

"And?"

"What?"

"Is it true?" George asked.

He looked past them into air. "I...I suppose...in a way." He glanced at Dora. "I suppose it's possible I've been so busy holding on to what I had, that I forgot about what I am—a good doctor."

Tina applauded. "Bravo."

Anthony shrugged as if it was nothing, but Dora noticed his blush and felt good for him. At least the guy was trying.

Tina turned to Merry. "You're last. Who was the person in the seat beside you?"

Merry's eyes filled. "They were my husband and little boy."

Tina gasped. "Oh. Of course. I'm so sorry."

Merry sniffed and a tear escaped. She took a moment to collect herself, retrieving a tissue from her purse. "Actually, they weren't supposed to be on the trip. Lou surprised me by showing up. I was heading down to Phoenix to party with a single girlfriend from college." She shook her head. "I thought Teresa had it all when *I* was the one who had everything. And lost everything."

"Not everything," George said.

Merry sighed deeply. "I'm afraid the jury's still out on that."

She and George exchanged a look, and his face flashed with panic. Merry looked away.

Suddenly George's daughter, Suzy, stepped into the circle. "I know I'm the only outsider here, and I find all this fascinating, how your seatmates and the crash have affected your lives and changed you for the better. But there's one person in this room I'm worried about; someone who hasn't figured out his life." She looked to her father.

George took an awkward step toward her. "Hey, Suze, there's no need to go into any of that." He looked worried, as if he was afraid she was going to divulge a family secret.

But then Ellen stood, in a slow smooth movement, as if a puppeteer had raised her out of her seat by pulling a string. "I have something I'd like you to do for *me*, George. For Henry."

He seemed relieved by her diversion. "Anything." He sat down with Suzy beside him.

Her eyes filled with tears, and Dora could see the strength she was tapping into in order to keep them contained. "I miss my Henry with an ache I can't imagine ever lessening, but after talking with all of you, I know his death was not in vain. His death was at the essence of this *way* he'd been searching for, and I thank God he was the kind of man who could walk in it. Henry hadn't told me about the verse, but I'm not surprised God brought it to his attention. Henry had an open heart. It was one of the things I loved about him." She met every set of eyes. "The thing is, Henry could have told God no. Do you realize that? Three times God handed him the lifelines and said, 'Henry? You know what I'd like you to do. Will you do it?' And three times my Henry set himself aside and said yes." She pointed to Sonja, to Merry, to Anthony, and to Tina. "Yes, yes, yes, yes."

They all were crying. Even Anthony's eyes were glistening. But Ellen wasn't finished.

"You know what I want people to understand about my Henry? I want them to realize he was just an ordinary man who was given an extraordinary chance to touch perfection. To touch the face of God. Did he know to what extent that ability was in him beforehand?" She shook her head. "I don't think so. Yet that makes it all the more hopeful for the rest of us. Maybe if we don't have an inkling we can do great things, then there's the chance that we *can* do them. If given the chance, if given the heart, if given the courage to say yes. The key is being ready for that moment. Henry was ready to say yes. Are we?"

"Oh, Ellen, that's beautiful," Merry said.

"It's more than beautiful," Sonja said, "it's something everyone needs to hear."

"Exactly," Ellen said. "Which leads me to my—"

George stood and Dora realized what he was about to do. It was show time. He went to Ellen and put an arm around her shoulder. "Excuse me for interrupting, Ellen. Your words have moved us greatly, but I think now is the perfect time for all of you to hear something that Dora has written about Henry—and the rest of us. That's what brought her over here today. She wanted me to read it. And now I want her to read it to all of you. Dora?"

As George and Ellen sat down, Dora retrieved the pages from her purse and stood at her chair. "I just want to say that all of you have inspired me very much, and—"

George interrupted. "Just read it, Dora."

She nodded and began. "It's called 'Ordinary Heroes.'" She cleared her throat and read. "No one plans to be a hero. It's not on anyone's list of long-term goals, nor on anyone's to-do list for the day. And if asked, most people would say they aren't hero material at all.

"But that's not true. We are all hero material, or rather, we have that God-given spark within us. But as with all life options, being a hero is a choice. God doesn't shove us into it—though He may hurl us into a situation that requires us to choose. As He did with Henry Smith and the crash of Flight 1382."

Dora looked up and was relieved to see that she still had their attention. She returned to her reading. "I never met Henry Smith, nor do I know any of the specifics of his life. At first this bothered me, and I put off writing this essay because I thought it was necessary to know about him, to meet his wife, to talk to his friends. But then I realized that's exactly what is so special about heroes like Henry. There is little about their pre-hero life that hints of their fate—of their opportunity to touch greatness. There is no such thing as hero training. No education prerequisites and no previous experience required. Family background, ethnic origin, age, and gender are irrelevant; heroism is truly equal opportunity employment. You don't even have to be a deeply religious person for God to use you in such a way. But that doesn't mean God isn't involved. He is *very* involved. For He is the One who breathes on that spark within us and fans it into a flame of willing self-sacrifice in a divine slice of time that makes a person stop thinking of himself and begin thinking only of others.

"But perhaps that last statement isn't totally true. For I believe Henry Smith *did* think about his own life as he shivered in the water; I believe his thoughts were consumed with his own life in that last hour. But the difference is that the hero thinks of *giving up* his or her own life, not saving it.

"The survival instinct is strong and can be illustrated in the simple act of putting a protective hand in front of our face when something comes too close. But heroism is born when the survival instinct collides with empathy, when me comes face-to-face with we and the latter is chosen over the former.

"*Former* is an interesting term meaning *bygone* or *old* or *past*. The hero, in his or her choice, makes our normal preoccupation with me, myself, and I fall away into our pasts, into our former nature. The hero shoves such ordinary, understandable considerations aside and thinks in an entirely different way: beyond himself. And the key is that the hero is given the opportunity of saying yes or no.

"Henry Smith said yes. As I watched tapes of the rescue and saw him hand over the lifeline for the first time, my mind accepted his actions as standing on the edge of ordinary. Just being polite. Women and children first. But then, there had to be a moment when he was shivering in that water, his body going numb, his injuries causing pain, that he made a conscious decision to continue his course of action—no matter the cost."

Dora's throat constricted, and she forced a swallow. She took a deep breath to calm her shaking voice. "When Henry saw the helicopter move away from him time after time, he had to realize that by giving up the line, he was choosing death."

The tears came, and Dora let them fall. "And when everyone else was gone, and he saw that helicopter fade into the distance and felt his body shut down, I cannot imagine his loneliness. And yet I have to believe that God gave him comfort in his last moments. Somehow God gave Henry Smith the most intense feeling of satisfaction a person can feel. 'Greater love has no one than this, that he lay down his life for his friends.' For that's the key element of a hero. Love. Though heroes may not know how to show it well in their daily lives, when given the chance by God, they say yes. They *choose* to love.

"And so, Henry Smith, I say thank you for your act of love. And for showing us and challenging us, that maybe we, too, have a hero in us if we only say yes."

Dora lowered the pages. She looked at the faces surrounding her. All were crying now, even Anthony. And then Ellen Smith got out of her chair and came to her, hugged her tightly, and whispered thank you in her ear.

George began the applause. "Bravo!"

Dora shook her head and sat down. She didn't want applause. In fact, what she truly wanted to do was to run into the bathroom and cry.

Sonja came to her side. "When is that going to be in the paper?"

Dora looked down at the pages. "Probably never."

"What do you mean never?"

"My boss will never go for it. Quoting Bible verses is not his thing. Not the *Chronicle's* thing."

"But it has to be printed," Tina said.

Dora shook her head. "It had to be written. I had to write it. I'm just glad all of you could hear it—and approve. That's payment enough."

George handed her a tissue. "Come to think of it, I haven't seen any of your articles about us. You interviewed us, but you didn't write—"

"Oh, I wrote them in here," Dora said, touching her head. "But I couldn't actually write them—not for publication."

"Why not?" Tina asked.

Dora looked at Anthony. "Various reasons. But basically, most of what I would have written was too spiritual for the *Chronicle.*"

"You never did ask us about facts," Sonja said. "Why is that?"

Dora took a deep breath, giving her time to think of an answer. "Probably for the same reason as tonight. None of you has obsessed about why the crash happened. Perhaps the normal journalistic who-what-where questions weren't as important as how the five of you responded to the crash. How it changed your lives." She looked down at the pages. "I shared this with some of you. I was supposed to go on that flight to be with my mother for an operation—an operation that was miraculously canceled. So Flight 1382 changed my life too."

"You were supposed—?" George asked.

Tina waved this subject away. "Hold off just a second. Let's get back to your writing. You're a good writer," she said. "I'd love you to write my story. I'd love—" She stopped in midsentence, her eyes darting around the room as if trying to snap up stray thoughts. "Hey…why *don't* you write about us? Write a book about all of us and our experiences before, during, and after the crash."

"A book?"

Sonja nodded enthusiastically. "Sure. *I* trust you. I gave you all sorts of delicate information about myself that I asked you not to use, and you didn't. And actually, you helped me work through a few things." She looked around the room, gathering support. "What do the rest of you think?"

"I'm all for it," George said. He took Merry's hand. "What about you? It would be a way for Lou and Justin to be honored."

She bit her lip. "I'm not sure." She looked at Dora. "You never interviewed me. Why didn't you interview me?"

Dora couldn't tell if Merry felt hurt or just left out. "I couldn't imagine your grief. I didn't want to intrude."

"But maybe it would have helped. You helped Sonja…"

Dora moved to Merry's side. "I'm sorry. Perhaps I should have asked you and let you make the decision to talk or not talk."

She nodded, then shrugged.

George spoke softly to Merry. "Would you be willing to talk to Dora for a book?"

A breath. In. Out. "I think so. Eventually."

"And I'll talk," Ellen said. "I'd love to have a book honoring Henry's sacrifice."

Everyone was for the book. Except…

All eyes turned to Anthony.

He pinched a piece of lint from his trousers. "Dora. Ms. Roberts. I seem to remember that you said you wouldn't write an article about me because I was an arrogant, egotistical man with a skewed opinion of himself and his position in the world."

George laughed. "You said that?"

Dora covered her face with a hand. "I said that."

"Unfortunately," Anthony said, "her opinion was quite true."

There was a moment of stunned silence, then laughter. "Way to peg it, Anthony!" George said. "I assume this means you'd be open to Dora's book?"

"It's doable."

"And that you no longer hold those character traits?" Tina said. Her smile was sly.

"I'm working on it."

George spread his arms. "I think that's where we all are. Working on it. Learning to live with being one of the living. Learning to say yes."

Ellen stood. "Speaking of saying yes, before I even heard Dora's reading, but now, spurred forward by it…" She took a breath and stood tall in her five-foot-two frame. "I had decided to tell people about Henry's sacrifice and obedience to God—and inspire them toward their own selfless acts by starting a foundation: The Henry Smith Foundation. Its motto will be 'Finding the Hero in All of Us. Providing Lifelines to People in Need.'"

"I like it," Merry said.

"I will be Henry's voice." She turned to George. "And you, George, I want you to speak with me, give your testimony as one of the five."

"But Henry didn't save George," Anthony said. "He was the only one of us your husband didn't save." Anthony received dirty looks from the others. "Well, it's true."

George waved away their looks. "Henry didn't save me from the water, but let me tell you, Henry Smith *did* save me. He saved me from myself." He looked around the room nervously, with a special glance to Suzy at his side, then set his shoulders. "I was heading to Phoenix to kill myself."

A flurry of gasps filled the air.

George waved away their shock. "But in talking with Henry on the plane…even though I didn't admit it at the time, I now know that Henry sold me on life *before* the crash. If we'd ever gotten to Phoenix, I don't believe I would have gone through with it— because of him."

Merry put a hand on his arm. "Just as you've tried to sell me on life."

He looked into her eyes intently. "Tried?"

Her eyes were sad. "I have a ways to go."

Tina raised a hand. "George is the perfect one who should testify with Ellen. It fits."

"Should we be surprised?" Sonja said.

"Then I accept Ellen's offer," George said. He put an arm around Suzy and squeezed her shoulders. "Guess I have another reason for living, don't I? I think this calls for a celebration. Let's eat."

Epilogue

"Never will I leave you; never will I forsake you."
HEBREWS 13:5

George wiped dishes while Ellen washed and Suzy put away. It felt good to have a woman in the kitchen again.

The evening had been a huge success. After eating, George stood alone near the kitchen listening to the stories being exchanged—while Dora took copious notes. Stories of fear, pain, doubt, and utter triumph. He didn't know if these people would stay in touch after Dora's book was finished, but perhaps that didn't matter. What mattered was that their lives *had* touched. For a short period of time these five lives had met in the icy water and had been united by Henry Smith and by the God who had sent him to help—a God whom George would have to get to know better.

Ellen finished the last dish and wiped her hands. "Now that that's done…I have something for you, George." She went into the den, retrieved her purse, and secretly pulled something out. Then she extended a closed hand toward his. He held up his hand to receive the offering, and she dropped a gold watch into his palm.

"What's this?"

"A little present. From Henry."

Then George recognized the waterproof, shatterproof watch with four time zones. It was still working. The last time he'd seen it was on Henry's wrist. "I can't take this."

"I want you to have it. Ever since I came to take Henry home, I've been carrying it around in my purse. But tonight, after what you said, after what you agreed to do…" She closed his fingers around the watch. "It will be a sign of the partnership between us. Between the three of us—the four of us. Let's not forget God."

He smiled. "Nope. Let's not forget God. After all, 'This is the way; walk in it.'"

"Our way and His way."

George pulled Henry's watch to his chest. "Amen to that."

Back home, Merry couldn't bring herself to clean up the mess caused by her tirade. Seeing the destruction of the living room was evidence of the tightrope she walked between craziness and sanity, between wallowing in her grief and moving on.

For a long time, she knew she would be walking through the moments of her life with great care. She knew she could call George if she needed him and, for that matter, any of the others. But she didn't want to need people. She didn't want to be a bother.

The truth was, without her family to take care of, she didn't have anything to do.

The phone rang. It was her mother. "How you doing, baby?"

She hated that question. She despised that question because it forced her to lie. "I'm fine."

"Have you written the thank-you notes yet? Aunt Claudia called and asked me if you had gotten the azalea they'd sent."

Merry glanced toward the kitchen where she remembered seeing a box of thank-you notes handily provided by the funeral home. "I'm working on it."

"Good girl. You always were good about that sort of thing. Would you like help?"

"No!" She toned down her voice. "No, I've got it covered, Mom."

"I know you do, Merry. You're a strong woman."

Funny, I don't feel very strong.

"There are so many people to thank," her mom said. "I wish we could write notes to all the rescuers on the shore, the emergency people, the ones who saved your life. I will never forget the sight of those helicopter men, Floyd and Hugh, pulling you and Justin up, dangling on that lifeline. Those men risked their lives for—"

"Their names were Floyd and Hugh?"

"Sure. Floyd Calbert. And the pilot's name was Hugh Johnson."

Why have I never asked their names before? She shook her head, suddenly appalled at her oversight. "What's wrong with me?"

"What?"

Thoughts assailed her. She needed to get off the phone. "Gotta go, Mom. I have work to do."

"But baby—"

Merry hung up and stared at the phone. At her hand on the phone. At the table that housed the phone. At the living room that held the table...

"I never said thank you."

She rushed into the kitchen and grabbed the box of thank-you notes and a pen. She sat at the kitchen table, flipped off the box's lid, and removed one. She opened it and stared at the blank page for only a moment. *Dear Mr. Calbert. I have been negligent in not contacting you and thanking you for your bravery...*

The words of appreciation flowed. Merry finished one, then immediately started another. And another. And another.

For the first time since the accident, Merry found a reason for going on.

Gratitude.

She'd need another box.

Anthony called Lissa into his office. He'd never been nervous in her presence before, but then he never had to ask her such a question before.

She followed him inside. "Can we do this later, Doctor? Mrs. Greene has a one-thirty, and you know how huffy she gets if we keep her waiting. Plus I know you have an appointment with your lawyer at—" She stopped talking as he closed the door behind them. "Hey? What's going on? Alone in your office. The door closed. People will talk—at least Candy will—"

"Will you be quiet just one minute?" He moved behind his desk and indicated that she should sit in the guest chair.

"Goodness. You certainly have piqued my interest."

"Finally." He picked up a pen, then realized he had no use for it. He put it down. "I've been meaning to thank you for all you've done for me since the crash. Taking me home from the hospital, making me dinner, coming over to my house when the lawsuit hit, talking to me about…stuff."

"Is *stuff* a technical term, Doctor?"

"You know what I mean."

"Maybe." She crossed her legs and leaned closer. "But why don't you make it perfectly clear what stuff we're talking about."

She was insufferable. "God-stuff, okay?"

She smiled. "Gotcha. And you're welcome. But would you care to tell me how things are on that front?"

He grinned. Two could play at this. "On what front?"

She groaned. "The God front."

"Ah." He nodded. "Let's just say that I know I'm not Him. That's a good start, isn't it?"

"Excellent start. But there's so much more."

He nodded. Now came the hard part. "I understand that. And to be honest, I don't know where to start. That's where you come in."

"I'm listening."

His stomach tightened. *This is ridiculous. I'm her boss. I'm her superior.*

But not in this…not in this.

"Would you meet with me, Lissa? Maybe…teach me?"

Her grin was ridiculously happy. "Hallelujah!"

"Hey, don't go overboard."

She headed for the door. "Oh no, Anthony. There's no stopping me now. The floodgates have been opened."

"Oh, brother."

She swung open the door and pointed at him with flourish. "Exactly. You got it, brother Anthony!"

She left singing the chorus from the *Messiah* all the way down the hall. Before he knew what was happening, Anthony found himself humming along.

Anthony's heart was pounding as he dialed the phone. *Can I do this? What if they refuse? What if they think it's just a ploy to make them drop the lawsuit? What if—*

"Millers."

Anthony cleared his throat. "Is this the son of Belinda Miller?"

The voice was suddenly wary. "Yes. Who's this?"

"This is Dr. Anthony Thorgood—please don't hang up, please."

"Talk to my lawyer."

"No, no, this isn't about that. This is about your son. About Ronnie."

A moment of silence. "What about him?"

"Your mother told me about his port-wine stain. I'm a plastic surgeon. I can fix that. Make it disappear."

"We can't afford—"

"I'll do it for free."

Another pause. "Is this your way of making us drop the lawsuit? Because what you did to my mother—"

"Was despicable. I know. And the offer is good whether you sue me or not. I want to do it. I *need* to do it."

"Need?"

This was going to sound contrived. "I'm trying to change my life—for the better. I'm trying to make good use of my second chance."

"My mother didn't get a second chance."

Touché. "I don't know what you want me to say, Mr. Miller. I can't go back. I can't change the past, you know."

The man's voice faltered. "I know."

Anthony felt his own throat tighten. He cleared it. "But I can change your son's future."

The man sniffed, then sighed. "I suppose you can."

"So you'll let me help Ronnie?"

"I'd be a fool not to. And if anyone deserves a second chance on life, it's my boy."

"And I'll do my best to give it to him. I'll arrange for three tickets from Murfreesboro to here. And also a room—a nice room in an upscale hotel. Is that acceptable?"

The man laughed. "Yes, I'd say so."

"Good. How does a week from tomorrow sound?"

"A...only a week?" He laughed again. "That's mighty fine."

"Good, good. Then consider it done."

"Doc?"

"Yes?"

"Maybe you're not such a bad man after all."

"I'm working on it."

Anthony hung up, grinning from ear to ear. How did that "Hallelujah Chorus" go?

"The crutches are a nice touch," David said. "You think they can cover them with white satin or something?"

Tina gave him a look. "My cast will be off long before the wedding. Now pay attention. Picking out a wedding dress is serious business."

"Yes, ma'am."

Tina turned toward the full-length mirror, pulling at the lace around the neck. She wished her mother could be here, but with her father's health and tight finances, this wedding was going to be on Tina and David's tab. And though Tina was willing to cut back on the ceremony and reception, she had her heart set on a lacy white gown, a Cinderella gown changing the cinder girl into a princess. She looked at the price tag. It was last year's style, on sale. On a bookstore clerk's wages, it would be a stretch, but it was doable.

She turned toward David. "Do you like this one best?"

He sighed extravagantly. "You're gorgeous."

"I am?"

She truly hadn't said those two words to elicit another compliment, but the fact that David got out of his chair and came to her side...the fact that he ran the back of his hand across her cheek...the fact that his eyes locked onto hers...

"To me you are the most beautiful woman in the world. God's brought us together forever and always. I love you, you know."

She could only nod. She knew...she knew.

Sonja finished unpacking her clothes. There was a tap on the bedroom door.

"Come in."

Eden Moore came in and looked around. "Quite homey." She picked up a carved wooden box. "Very nice." She looked up. "You all settled then? Ready to get to work?"

"You don't mess around, do you? I've only been in town three hours."

"In which time you've gotten settled into my guest room. What more do you want? Tea and finger sandwiches?"

"Actually, some iced tea would be great."

Eden exited the room and stood in the hallway. "Got some in the fridge. Ice too when the freezer decides to make it. But grab it to go. We need to get to the office. Maria's waiting to see you."

Sonja remembered the girl she'd met during her first visit—the first victim of her advice. "How's she doing?"

Eden put on her last earring. "Fabulous. She's decided to apply to college. She wants to say thanks."

Sonja stopped, clicking her empty suitcase shut. "Really?"

"Really. I told you this is what you're supposed to do."

"But I didn't really—"

"Believe me?" Eden flipped a hand. "Fiddle-dee. There will be no more of that. Come on. We have work to do."

It was music to her ears.

Floyd Calbert and Hugh Johnson made a pass over the river. All was quiet. All was well. But the memories…

As they left the crash site behind, Floyd noticed that Hugh looked back. He knew they shared the same thoughts. "I think of it every time we fly over."

Hugh nodded. "Me too."

"I'm glad we got to go that day—even though it was scary and even though everything didn't work out as we'd hoped."

"Me too."

Floyd thought of the letter in his pocket. "This helps."

"What is it?"

"A note from Merry Cavanaugh thanking me." He suddenly realized that Hugh might feel bad if he hadn't gotten—

Hugh pulled an identical envelope from his chest pocket. "I got one too."

Floyd was relieved. "It helps, doesn't it?"

Hugh patted his pocket. "You bet it does."

Dora sat at her computer. Although she still had tons of research to do on the crash and rescue and still had a myriad of people to interview, she felt the need to get started on her book.

She had no real plan on the direction the book would go. Would it be about the facts of the crash? About the hero? Would it be about the survivors? Or about the people who sat in the seats beside them?

That's it! The perfect title. *The Seat Beside Me.*

But the beginning…how to begin.

And then, with a flick of a thought, Dora knew.

She placed her hands above the keyboard and typed the first line.

I don't want to go…

"God did this so that men would seek him and perhaps reach out for him and find him, though he is not far from each one of us. 'For in him we live and move and have our being.'"

ACTS 17:27–28A

The publisher and author would love to hear your comments about this book. *Please contact us at:*
www.multnomah.net/seatbesideme

Dear Reader,

We live in a time when catastrophes are played out on the news. We are there, seeing it happen, moment by moment. We witness the tragedies and ache with the horror they elicit, but we also grab on to the acts of heroism that stun us with their sacrifice. Watching these events always bring about a time of introspection. *How would I react in such a situation? Is there a hero in the person sitting beside me? Is there a hero in me?*

While traveling I have met many fascinating people who've sat in the seats beside me on airplanes. It's interesting how sometimes we click, and sometimes we barely speak. Why is that? Is it part of God's plan to have us seated next to each other? Wouldn't it be fascinating to find out this answer? To understand that it isn't a coincidence?

The combination of a catastrophe and heroism was the impetus for *The Seat Beside Me*. Place people next to seatmates who affect their lives. Have them crash soon after meeting. And make one of them a hero—though he doesn't even know it.

Little did I know how emotionally draining writing this book would be. The day I wrote the crash and rescue chapters, the day I wrote the death of the hero, and the day I wrote the hero's essay, I ended up a blubbering mess. Putting myself into the heads of each of the characters as they experienced the horrendous tragedy of a crash wiped me out and generated questions I was forced to ask about my own life. I hope these are some of the questions the book has sparked in you:

- Am I ready for eternity? If I die today do I know that I'll go to heaven?
- Am I on the right road for my life, or am I forcing God to do something drastic to get my attention?
- Is there a hero in me? Would I give up my own life for the life of a stranger?

No one knows they're a hero until God gives them the opportunity and they say yes. Heroes are not forced to act; they *choose*. What an exciting yet intimidating fact…to know it's up to us.

A big theme in my life and in my writing is discovering our God-given purpose and then coming to the point of total surrender to Him—in *all* things. To truly *choose* to live our lives God's way. I have come to such a point in stages and find it exhilarating to develop characters who also struggle with this issue in various ways and with varying results. I've discovered that the journey is just as important as the goal. After all, God has a common goal for all of us—to know Him and to serve Him. But the details of how He brings this about and how we react can be fascinating.

I hope you agree.

Many blessings on your journey,

Nancy Moser

BIBLE VERSES FOR *THE SEAT BESIDE ME*

CHAPTER ONE

Hopelessness . . . . .Ecclesiastes 1:14
Direction . . . . .Isaiah 30:19–21

CHAPTER TWO

Hope . . . . .Psalm 62:5–6
Murder . . . . .Exodus 20:13

CHAPTER THREE

Listening . . . . .Proverbs 19:20–21
Riches . . . . .Proverbs 22:1
Rich man . . . . .Luke 18:25
Thoughts . . . . .Philippians 4:8
Surrender . . . . .Isaiah 30:21

CHAPTER FOUR

Death . . . . .Psalm 23:4

CHAPTER FIVE

Courage . . . . .Ezra 10:4
Sacrifice . . . . .John 15:13
Congratulations . . . . .Matthew 25:21

CHAPTER SIX

Death . . . . .Psalm 55:4–6

CHAPTER SEVEN

Vanity . . . . .Philippians 2:3–4

CHAPTER EIGHT

Godliness . . . . .Psalm 12:1

CHAPTER NINE

Deliverance ....Psalm 56:13
Fools ....Proverbs 17:28

CHAPTER TEN

Suffering ....Psalm 119:50

CHAPTER ELEVEN

Redemption ....Psalm 34:22

CHAPTER TWELVE

Strength ....1 Corinthians 1:25
Possibilities ....Luke 18:27

CHAPTER THIRTEEN

Purpose ....Psalm 138:8
Sorrow ....Psalm 55:17
Weakness ....2 Corinthians 12:10
Salvation ....John 14:6

CHAPTER FOURTEEN

Discipline ....Hebrews 12:11
Sorrow ....Revelation 21:4
Rich man parable ....Mark 10:17–23
Wisdom ....James 1:5–6

CHAPTER FIFTEEN

Shame ....1 Corinthians 1:27, 29

CHAPTER SIXTEEN

Hope .... Psalm 31:24
Direction .... Isaiah 30:21
Love .... John 15:13

EPILOGUE

Care .... Hebrews 13:5
Purpose .... Acts 17:27–28a

DISCUSSION QUESTIONS FOR
The Seat Beside Me

1. Have you ever had the opportunity to tell someone about Christ and chickened out? Were there any consequences? Did you get another chance?

2. Have you ever felt like running away from your life? Did you do it? What were the results? Or if you *didn't* run away, how did you find the courage to stay?

3. Have you ever had an instance where God had to do something drastic to get your attention? How did He go about it? How did you respond?

4. Have you ever developed a bond with someone traveling in the seat beside you? How did it affect your life?

5. What is your unique purpose in life? How did you discover it? If you don't know what it is, what are some ways you can discover it?

6. Have you ever been saved from going on a trip or into a situation where a disaster occurred? How did it make you feel? How did it change you?

7. Do you think you would be willing to give your life for a stranger? Do you think anyone truly knows this potential?

"If you have faith as small as a mustard seed, you can say to this mountain, 'Move from here to there,' and it will move."

THE
MUSTARD
SEED

THEY WERE FOUR ORDINARY PEOPLE,
MYSTERIOUSLY SUMMONED TO A SMALL TOWN
WHERE EXTRAORDINARY THINGS ARE ABOUT TO HAPPEN...

THE INVITATION

NANCY MOSER

Julia, Walter, Kathy, and Natalie: four ordinary people with little in common, until each of them receives a small, white invitation from an anonymous sender. It reads: "If you have faith as small as a mustard seed...nothing will be impossible for you. Please come to Haven, Nebraska." At first, they all resist. But amazing circumstances convince them that they should heed the call and go to Haven. In *The Invitation*, Nancy Moser crafts a captivating story of everyday people who come to realize that even a small faith, combined with a heart led by God, can change the world.

ISBN 1-57673-352-1

They never imagined doing God's will would make them targets for evil....

THE QUEST

NANCY MOSER

THEY NEVER IMAGINED DOING GOD'S WILL
WOULD MAKE THEM TARGETS FOR EVIL...

"Nancy weaves a fascinating story showing how God uses ordinary people in extraordinary ways. Get ready for a page-turner!"

—**Karen Kingsbury**
author of *On Every Side*
and
A Moment of Weakness

The Quest, book two in author Nancy Moser's Mustard Seed series, is the continuing story of five ordinary people whose lives are forever changed after they are invited to the supernatural town of Haven, Nebraska. The paths of Natalie, Walter, Kathy, Del, and Julia are once again joined in a quest of faith—and a battle against the forces determined to stop them—as they implement the decisions and direction they received in *The Invitation* and discover the meaning of Matthew 7:7: "Ask and it will be given to you; seek and you will find; knock and the door will be opened to you." When the heat's turned up and the enemy unleashes his greatest opposition, the Havenites learn that it's not enough to know what's right—one must, with God's help, do what's right. No matter what the cost.

ISBN 1-57673-410-2

The Quest

"You're going to what?"

"I'm going to pray." Julie Carson raised one eyebrow. "I assume that is acceptable to you, Benjamin?"

Ben Cranois had to bow to her wish. After all, in just a few minutes, Julia would be accepting the nomination for president of the United States. So, for at least this one moment of her life, she had clout. If Ben wanted to rise from campaign manager to a position within her administration, he knew he had better pick his battles. And this wasn't one of them.

"Ten minutes," she said.

"Maybe, but—"

"I think God deserves ten minutes before I jump into this thing, don't you?"

She didn't wait for his answer. She walked down the hall to find a quiet place in the bowels of the convention center.

"You're impossible," he said.

Julia raised a hand but kept walking. "Glad to know it."

Ben watched her rap on a door, listen, then disappear inside. To pray. Absurd. Though he'd helped her become governor of Minnesota, and though he'd helped her gain the presidential nomination, there were things about Julia's character he would never understand.

He heard footsteps and turned around to see Julia's husband coming toward him.

"You look perplexed, Benjamin." Edward Carson smiled. "Is it possible my wife had something to do with it?"

"As always." He sighed. "Why can't she be a peaceful person like you?"

"Me? Peaceful?"

"You never get riled."

Edward raised a finger. "That's not *entirely* true, but I thank you for the compliment." He looked around. "Actually, I remain peaceful to counter Julia's fire. By the way…where is my towering inferno?"

Ben flicked a hand toward the hall. "Down there. *Praying.*" He looked at his watch. "She's making thousands of people wait."

Edward put a hand on Ben's shoulder. "Surely you know that Julia deals with people only after she's conferred with the Boss?"

Complacency is deadly.
The enemy lurks close by.

"PAGE-TURNING SUSPENSE...SOLID BIBLICAL TRUTH. *THE TEMPTATION*
DESERVES SHELF SPACE WITH SPIRITUAL WARFARE CLASSICS!"
CINDY SWANSON, *WEEKEND MAGAZINE* RADIO SHOW

THE
TEMPTATION
NANCY MOSER

"High drama
and characters
pulsating with
human emotion...
a tremendous
addition to
The Mustard
Seed series."

—James Scott Bell,
author of *Final
Witness* and
Blind Justice

The Temptation continues the saga of Haven, Nebraska, and its visitors
Julia, Kathy, Del, Natalie and Walter as they live out the commitments
they made in *The Quest*. Now successful in their separate pursuits, the
Havenites think all is going well—and therein lies great danger. As
complacency attacks the characters' focus on God, they start believing
their achievements have risen from their own savvy and power. When
Del decides to organize a reunion, the characters face Satan's chaotic
interference and learn the true nature of temptation: inevitable, subtle,
biting, and potentially disastrous. They must recover their courage to
live out their plea to the Lord: "Lead us not into temptation, but
deliver us from evil. . . ."

ISBN 1-57673-734-9